THE
ANGEL
OF
INDIAN
LAKE

Also by Stephen Graham Jones

The Indian Lake Trilogy

My Heart Is a Chainsaw

Don't Fear the Reaper

The Angel of Indian Lake

Novels

The Fast Red Road: A Plainsong

All the Beautiful Sinners

The Bird Is Gone: A Manifesto

Seven Spanish Angels

Demon Theory

The Long Trial of Nolan Dugatti

Ledfeather

It Came from del Rio

Zombie Bake-Off

Growing Up Dead in Texas

The Last Final Girl

The Least of My Scars

Flushboy

The Gospel of Z

Not for Nothing

Floating Boy and the Girl Who Couldn't Fly
(with Paul Tremblay)

Mongrels

The Only Good Indians

The Babysitter Lives

Novellas

Sterling City

Mapping the Interior

Night of the Mannequins

Story Collections

Bleed into Me: A Book of Stories

The Ones That Got Away

Three Miles Past

Zombie Sharks with Metal Teeth

After the People Lights Have Gone Off

States of Grace

*The Faster Redder Road: The Best
UnAmerican Stories of
Stephen Graham Jones*

Comic Books

My Hero

Memorial Ride

Earthdivers

True Believers

THE
ANGEL
OF
INDIAN
LAKE

THE INDIAN LAKE TRILOGY: BOOK THREE

STEPHEN GRAHAM JONES

SAGA PRESS

LONDON SYDNEY **NEW YORK** TORONTO NEW DELHI

SAGA PRESS

AN IMPRINT OF SIMON & SCHUSTER, LLC

1230 AVENUE OF THE AMERICAS, NEW YORK, NEW YORK 10020

First Saga Press hardcover edition March 2024

SAGA PRESS and colophon are trademarks of Simon & Schuster, LLC

Simon & Schuster: Celebrating 100 Years of Publishing in 2024

For information about special discounts for bulk purchases, please contact Simon & Schuster Special Sales at 1-866-506-1949 or business@simonandschuster.com.

The Simon & Schuster Speakers Bureau can bring authors to your live event. For more information or to book an event, contact the Simon & Schuster Speakers Bureau at 1-866-248-3049 or visit our website at www.simonspeakers.com.

Interior design by Erika R. Genova

Manufactured in the United States of America

1   3   5   7   9   10   8   6   4   2

Library of Congress Cataloging-in-Publication Data is available.

ISBN 978-1-6680-1166-9
ISBN 978-1-6680-1168-3 (ebook)

for this kid named Jason.
I would have swam out for you, man.
we all would have.

There's never been a final girl like this.

—CAROL CLOVER

HERE COMES THE
BOOGEYMAN

The Savage History of Proofrock, Idaho opens looking through the two eyeholes of a mask, with some heavy, menacing breathing amping up the menace.

What those eyeholes are fixed on from behind the bushes is a ten-year-old kid. It's nighttime, well after midnight, and the kid's sitting on a barely moving swing at Founders Park. It's where the staging area for Terra Nova used to be, eight years ago.

The kid's head is down so his face is hidden. He could be dead, posed there, his hands wired to the swing's galvanized chains, but then a thin breath comes up white and frosted, and he starts to look up, eyes first.

Before his face comes into focus, *The Savage History of Proofrock, Idaho* cuts to an occluded angle into . . . a shed?

It is. A dark workshop of some sort, like a room you scream through at a haunted house down in Idaho Falls.

No more mask to look through. Just a nervous space between two boards of the wall.

Words sizzle into the bottom of the screen and then flame away: tHe ChAINSAw's bEEN DEAd for YEARs. The irregular capitalization is supposed to make it scarier, like a ransom note.

In this shed, on this grimy workbench, a man in a leather apron is working on this chainsaw. This man's got a bit of size—linebacker shoulders, veins cresting on his forearms. His hands are white and tan, and the camera stays on them, documenting his every ministration on this chainsaw.

It's dark, the angle's bad and unsteady, but that only makes it better, really.

"Is that *Slipknot*?" Paul says about the music thumping in this shed.

Hettie shushes him, says, "He's old, okay?"

He's old and he's taking the top cover off the chainsaw, or trying to. Eventually he figures out to push the chain brake—the cover comes right off. It's enough of a surprise that the cover goes clattering onto the floor, almost loudly enough to cover the squeaky yelp that's much closer to the camera.

Almost loud enough to cover that, but not quite.

Instead of a nightmare face stooping down into frame after this runaway chainsaw cover, there's twelve seconds of listening silence after the song's turned off. The man's hands are still on the workbench, the fingertips to the dirty wood, the palms high and arched away so it's like there's two pale spiders doing that thing spiders do when their cluster of eyes and their leg bristles have told them there's a presence in the room.

And then that grimy leather apron is rushing to this camera, blacking the screen out.

Paul chuckles, draws deep on the joint and holds it, holds it, then leans forward to breathe that smoke into Hettie's mouth like she used to like, when they were fourteen.

"You're going to secondhand kill me," she says with a satisfied cough, holding the videocamera high and wide, out of this.

"Only after I *first*-hand do something else . . ." Paul says back, his hand rasping up the denim of her thigh.

"But did it scare you?" Hettie asks, keeping his hand in check and shaking the camera so Paul's syrupy-thinking self can know what she's talking about: the *documentary*.

She pinches the joint away from him for her own toke, and doesn't cough it out.

Where they're sitting is the doorway alcove of the library on Main Street, right under the book deposit slot. Out past their knees, Proofrock's dead. Someone just needs to bury it.

"Your mom know you snuck Jan out after dark?" Paul asks, squinting against Hettie's exhale.

"She's more worried about who my dad's dating this week in Arizona or Nevada or wherever," Hettie says from the depths of her own syrup bottle. "Janny Boy's a good little actor, though, isn't he? I told him to pretend he was a ghost, just sitting there."

"What'd you do with the snow?" Paul asks, his eyes practically bleeding.

It's nearly halfway through October, now. The snow they always get by Halloween hasn't come yet, but there's been plenty of small ones, trying to add up *into* the real deal.

"I edited it out," Hettie says, sneaking a look up to Paul to see if he'll buy this, but his stoned mind is still assembling her words into a sentence. Hettie shoulders into his chest, says, "We shot it in July, idiot."

"But his breath," Paul manages to cobble together, doing his fingers to slow-motion the puff of white Jan had breathed out that night.

"I didn't give him a cigarette, if that's what you're asking."

"So he's really a ghost?"

"Confectioner's sugar."

"In his *mouth*?" Paul asks.

Hettie shrugs, says, obviously, "He loved it."

"Ghosts and swings and baking goods," Paul says, hauling the camera up to his shoulder, aiming it at Hettie. "Tell us, Herr Director, why do little ghost boys with sweet white mouths like to frequent parks after dark?"

"Because it looks good for my senior project," Hettie says, cupping the lens in her palm, guiding the camera down.

It would be easier to shoot this documentary with her phone, which is much better for low-light situations, but this is *throwback*. Her dad's VHS camera was still in the attic, along with everything else he'd left when he bailed, but Hettie's paying for these blank tapes herself, "to show she's committed," that "this isn't just another passing thing."

What it is is her ticket out of here.

The world will roll out the red carpet for footage like this, from the heart of the murder capital of America. First there was Camp Blood half a century and more ago, then there was the Independence Day Massacre when she was in fourth grade, and then, for junior high, there was Dark Mill South's Reunion Tour. Forty people dead in a town of three thousand is a per capita nightmare, even across a few years.

And that translates to serious bucks.

Now if she can only get this Angel of Indian Lake's tattered white nightgown and J-horror hair and supposedly bare feet on tape tonight, blurry and distant, "ethereal and timeless," then . . . then *every*thing, right? The doors to the future open up for Hettie Jansson, and she walks through with a Joan Jett scowl, squinting from the sea of flashing cameras but not ever wanting them to stop, either.

The problem, though, it's that the Angel isn't reliable, is probably just some practical joke the jocks have kept going all the way since summer. Joke or not, though, she's the missing ingredient for *The Savage History of Proofrock, Idaho*, the piece that sends it into the horror stratosphere. And they've got all night to fit her into a viewfinder, hit record, and hold steady fifty-nine and a half seconds—it's how long that famous Bigfoot recording is, right?

And if the Angel doesn't show tonight, then there's still two more weeks of nights until the rough cut's due. Two more weeks and the rest of the stash Paul liberated from a bright orange Subaru some nocturnal tourists left unlocked for their big skinnydipping expedition.

Sorry, Colorado, Paul keeps saying, every time he's rolling another fatty from the Subaru. The license plates had been white mountains on a green background—the first car you try if you're in a red state, are looking for something to smoke.

Sorry, GPA, Hettie always adds, watching Paul's fingers roll, tighten, twist.

But she's not.

Soon, she's past all that.

"What'd you use for . . . at the beginning?" Paul asks, his hands making binoculars over his eyes.

The mask point-of-view—*slashercam,* Hettie knows to call it, now.

She lets this toke out slow and languorous, imagining herself a movie star from the thirties, and hikes what Paul's asking about up from the front pocket of her jean jacket, where it's been since before the semester started.

"*Shi*-it . . ." Paul says, and holds the little circle of black cardboard up to try to look through. The two eyeholes are sized for an action figure, though, not a full-size burnout.

"Trick of the trade," Hettie says with a shrug, fitting that cardboard circle into the lens so Paul can peer through the eyepiece, see the magic himself.

He stands, feels ahead with his left hand, the right holding the camera to his face.

"Look, look, I'm a killer!" he says. "Somebody do something sexy, so I can stab you!"

Down Main a little ways, a lone light fizzles on, holds itself wavery bright for a few seconds, then dies back down.

That too, Hettie tells herself.

She's going to document it all, she's going to lay Proofrock bare, she's going to show the world this place she grew up in. No, this place she *survived*.

"Push play," she says, pulling Paul back down beside her.

When he can't figure it out—*This is your brain on drugs*—Hettie does it for him.

On the little screen, now, *The Savage History of Proofrock, Idaho* is moving through the cemetery like a balloon let go, a balloon that's lost most of its helium, so it's just riding along about two feet off the ground.

"No, Het, you can't—" Paul says, pushing the camera away.

Hettie tracks up to him but doesn't stop playing the footage.

She knew this was going to be the hard part for him. His aunt was Misty Christy—the most prominent headstone in that scene. Her daughters, Paul's cousins, the little sisters he never had, are the reason Hettie knows he'll never be leaving Proofrock. The whole week leading up to the Fourth back then, Paul had been chasing his little cousins around with all the shark stuff he had—he was a fan, lived for *Jaws*, probably watched it once a week that summer, until he knew all the lines, couldn't stop saying them.

The night-of, he was one of the ten-year-olds with a fin strapped around his ribs, a snorkel chimneying off the back of his head, eyes in scuba goggles, a wide carnivorous smile on his face.

In 2015, there had been no one more excited for the movie on the water than Paul Demming. Hettie still remembers him standing from his parents' stupid raft to sing that Spanish Ladies song, and how it looked like he felt like he was leading that song, that he was part of this adult world now, part of Proofrock, of Indian Lake.

And then, half an hour later, he was trying to drag his aunt up onto shore, and his dad had to pull him off her when he kept trying to breathe into her lungs, even though half her head was gone. Hettie's pretty sure that that's where her love affair with horror started: seeing

Paul at ten years old in the shallows, fighting with his dad, his whole lower face slathered red.

"It's a memorial for all of them," Hettie tells Paul about the cemetery Steadicam, as she calls it, and passes him the joint, has to hold it there for probably ten seconds before he finally rips it from her fingers hard enough that some of the cherry crumbles away, its small light leaving slow orange tracers in the dark.

Paul draws deep, painfully deep, like punishing himself. Like he can erase the past, just be from somewhere else, please. Somewhere normal.

His fingers are shaking now. Hettie creeps her hand over, holds them still.

"I hope you really do get out of here someday," he says to her, snuffling his nose.

"Watch," Hettie says.

The Savage History of Proofrock, Idaho is still playing. She props the camera between them, they resituate to see better, and—

"Fucking Rexall," Paul mutters.

Which is what the words at the bottom of the screen should say. But it already took Hettie all weekend just to get those ransom note letters in place.

Less of that from here on out, thanks.

This isn't technically *due* until January, but if she wants to get it into any of the spring filmfests, she needs to have it wrapped a lot sooner than that.

And? It's counting for the interview portion of senior History, and that *is* due before the semester's over. Without it, no graduation in June. No blasting off into the world beyond Idaho.

On the little screen, Rexall's blurry at the far end of a long hall in the elementary. He's sitting on a mechanic's stool, has his tool bag beside him, is doing something to or with the fire extinguisher cabinet.

"Installing another perv camera?" Paul asks, pulling the screen closer and angling it back and forth like that'll let him see deeper into the frame.

"It's not the girls' locker room," Hettie mumbles. Still, she does have extensive footage—with her *cellphone*—of every square inch of that fire extinguisher cabinet. For whatever that's worth. All she ever found was "R_x" on the fire extinguisher's inspection label.

She's thinking she might should cut Rexall, really. Knowing him, he'll think he's the star, the glue, the beating heart of Proofrock. When really he's just the scum floating on the surface.

Hettie taps the fast-forward button three or four times, bounces past the high school.

"Oh, yeah, gotta have that," Paul says then.

Terra Nova, glittering across the water.

When Hettie was a freshman, Terra Nova was still burned ruins, too thrashed out and spooky to even drink beer in. Now, though, it's coming back to life, construction crews working twenty-four seven again.

She still remembers walking single file from Golding Elementary to see the barge carrying that big bulldozer across Indian Lake. She was the caboose that day, which Ms. Treadaway told her was the most important place in their waddling train of Goslings—it was her job to make sure everybody stayed on the tracks, see?

Hettie was so proud to get to be the caboose.

And it was such bullshit.

But that doesn't change how it felt, watching that barge balance on top of the water. It should have sank, she knows. It should have leaned over far enough to one side or the other to plunk that big yellow tractor down to Drown Town, into Ezekiel's Cold Box.

"Idiots," Paul says about Terra Nova.

It's a sentiment Hettie shares. And most of Proofrock, this time around.

Not that anybody can do anything about it.

"You're not supposed to say that," a small voice says from the darkness, startling Paul enough that he drops the joint, throws an arm across Hettie like protecting her from going through a windshield.

The Angel doesn't speak, though. And this *non*-Angel's a whole lot shorter, anyway.

"*Jan?*" Hettie says, standing, fighting out of the safety of Paul's arm.

Her little brother steps into the weak light coming through the glass door from some glow in the library, the long blond hair that always gets him mistaken for a girl hanging half over his face.

"Guess the ghosts *are* walking tonight . . ." Paul says with appreciation.

Jan's done his own ghost make-up this time. Meaning he probably left a mess in the kitchen—great. Confectioner's sugar everywhere. Just what Mom needs, come morning.

"He must have seen me leaving with this," Hettie says, hefting the camera.

"I want to be in the movie some more," Jan says, his lower lip starting to push out, meaning the waterworks won't be far behind.

Hettie steps out, scoops him up, situates him on her hip. He weighs probably half as much as her, she knows, but she also knows that a woman's hips can hold anything. Especially a little brother.

"What smells funny?" Jan asks.

Paul fans his hands at the smoke danking up the alcove.

"Moths with dirty wings flying into that lightbulb," Hettie says, walking the two of them out onto the grass.

Behind them, Paul's phone buzzes.

"What?" Hettie asks, lasering her eyes to his.

"Waynebo," Paul says with a shrug.

"What, he finally found it?"

"I think it's a butt dial?"

This makes Jan laugh in Hettie's arms. "Butt dial" is his favorite term. Along with anything else to do with butts.

"Can we at least . . . not have my dead aunt's *name* in it?" Paul says then. "I don't want people making fun of it, yeah?"

Hettie notes that he's crushing their roach under the heel of his combat boot. It's against his religion to waste, but he's protecting Jan from their bad influence, Hettie knows.

"But I've already—"

"Reshoot," Paul says. "What's it called? 'Pickups'?"

"Do you know how hard it is to edit actual *videotape*?" Hettie asks. "I have to—"

"I'll help," Paul tells her.

They both know he's lying, that he'll just kick back on her bed and throw a rubber ball against the ceiling the whole time, leaving Hettie to convert the VHS to digital, play it on her laptop, then paste letters or whatever on the screen and record enough stop and start shots of that—because the scan rates don't match up—to add up to a second or three of continuous footage.

"Just to be sure I'm hearing you right," she says, using her mom's point-by-point voice, "you want us to go to the cemetery on Friday the *13th,* at *night*, with—?" Instead of saying the last part, she mimes the joint they were just smoking.

"Maybe we could skinnydip while we're there too?" Paul says.

Hettie looks out over Proofrock, shrugs what the hell.

"Maybe that's where she is, right?" she says about the Angel, looking over in the direction of the cemetery.

"Bet so," Paul says, playing along.

Ten minutes later, via a coasting motorcycle ride Jan's not to ever mention again, under threat of having his *butt* cut off, they're at the cemetery.

"I'm *coming* to *get* you, *Bar*bara . . ." Paul tries, his voice up and down, fake spooky.

"Her name is Hettie!" Jan yells with a thrill, just to be involved.

Paul cocks his bike up on its kickstand and Hettie guides the oversize helmet up off Jan's head. He was sandwiched between them for the ride over.

"Stay here," Hettie says to him, stationing him with Paul, and cues into the blank tape at the end of *The Savage History of Proofrock, Idaho* so she can do her version of Steadicam: her purse strap unlatched, then hooked through the front and back connections on the top of the videocamera. She hangs the camera by her leg a little ahead of her, hits record, and is walking through the graves again—so many, since 2015—this time avoiding Misty Christy's headstone, even though this scene's going to lose some of its oomph now, from being censored.

Still, it's Paul, right? Paul who she actually trusts with Jan. Paul who she's broken up with probably a dozen times since junior high. But they always find each other again, don't they? When you're a reject in Proofrock, have undercuts and piercings and intricate plans for full sleeves, you can't stay away from the one other person drawing on their arm with a ballpoint pen.

If only she could take him with her when she leaves.

But don't think about that now. *You're a filmmaker*, she reminds herself. You're documenting, you're documenting. And, never mind that the smart kids in horror movies avoid graveyards at night.

This is for school, though. And it's not like they're drinking beer on the actual headstones, it's not like they're sparking up—they're being respectful, observing the rules . . . It'll be fine, Hettie tells herself.

Until she looks up from her feet and the camera that's so hard to keep from spinning, sees the grave over by the fence.

It's where the county buries those who don't have anyone to bury them.

And, "grave" isn't the right word. Not anymore. More like "hole." More like the crater left after an eruption. Either somebody dug this dead person up, or that dead person clawed through the dirt themselves, and walked away.

"What the what?" Hettie says, pulling the camera up to her shoulder to document the living *hell* out of this.

Through the viewfinder she can read the name: GREYSON BRUST.

"Who?" she mutters, trying to dredge up anyone in school with a last name *Brust*, but is interrupted by snow crunching behind her. She turns fast and scared, is already falling away, one arm out to block whatever's coming.

It's Paul. He's got Jan on his hip.

"What?" he says, holding Jan halfway behind himself.

Maybe Hettie *won't* leave him?

Maybe she'll just stick it out here in Proofrock like her mom, and forget about who she used to want to be, where she wanted to go. How she was going to have the world wrapped around her finger. When you've got someone's whole hand to hold, *that* can be all that matters, right? That can be enough.

"Look," she says, stepping to the side.

Paul edges up to the open grave.

"Who's he?" Paul says about this "Greyson Brust," and then reaches for the lens, points the camera to the light snow to her left, his right.

Tracks.

Hettie lowers the camera, her face slack.

"I don't—I don't—" she stutters.

"I'm the map, I'm the map!" Jan says, bouncing in Paul's arms.

It's from Hettie's old *Dora the Explorer* DVDs. He's addicted to them.

And he's right.

If they follow these tracks, then they get to the, to the—to the what? The dam, the way the tracks are headed?

Except: why is Paul just staring at the tracks like they don't make sense?

His phone buzzes and he rearranges Jan, reads the text.

"Don't fucking believe it," Paul says, holding the phone face out like this proves it. "He found it."

What Waynebo—Wayne Sellars—has been on the trail of all summer is what some out-of-state hunters are supposed to have stumbled on in the woods, when they were lost themselves: half a white Bronco. Maybe three-quarters of one, if it held together enough for its long roll down from the highway. Because they were traditional hunters, though, just stickbows and compasses, even had fringe on their canteens, they hadn't been able to direct anybody back to wherever they were. Everybody knew that was shorthand for the two having been hunting where they weren't supposed to be—bows without wheels are quiet—but that didn't make the Bronco any easier to find.

The Bronco's pretty much the last mystery left in Proofrock, though: after Dark Mill South brought his special brand of violence to town, a trucker had reported a Ford buried nose-first into a snowbank on the high side of the highway—the temporary grave of the previous sheriff and his deputy. Because there had been so many dead in Proofrock to deal with, though, Highway Patrol had just cordoned the Bronco off, set some rookie up to guard it, and then not got Lonnie to drag it out for a week.

It turned out not to be the whole truck, but just its ass end. Evidently it had been hit broadside by Dark Mill South's stolen snowplow, at *speed*, and then had just slid sideways in front of that big blade until it calved off in either direction. The Bronco's tailgate and rear bumper landed upright in the snow on the high side of the road, and the rest of the truck? That was the thing: *Where?* Directly across from that tailgate and bumper made sense, but the thing is, wrecks don't *have* to make sense. On the down side of the highway, the Indian Lake side, the country was rugged and rough, deep as hell, and not even a little bit forgiving. And it doesn't give up its dead until it wants to.

Which, according to Waynebo, must be tonight.

He'd spent the first week of summer gridding Fremont County

up on his computer, somehow plugging that into a hand-held GPS he had, and ever since then he'd been working those imaginary lines back and forth on his horse, insisting the Bronco had no choice but to show up. And, now that it maybe had, he was going to be the one to collect the twenty-five-hundred-dollar reward Seth Mullins, the deputy's husband, had somehow pulled together, for whoever found his wife's body.

Well, Waynebo was going to collect that twenty-five hundred *and* the ten grand Lana Singleton had added on, because, as she said in the announcement in the *Standard*, Proofrock needs to *heal*, doesn't it?

"He wants you to bring your camera," Paul says, lowering his phone. It won't stop buzzing with Waynebo's celebration.

"He doesn't have his phone?"

"He says this should be in your movie."

"But the footprints," Hettie says, about the tracks in the snow.

"About those . . ." Paul says, kind of like he . . . regrets saying it?

"What do you mean?" Hettie asks, stepping in to see.

Paul waits for it to make sense to her. There are footprints like there should be—even in snow this light, you can't avoid them—but it's just the front part of some dress shoes? Then Hettie sees it, has to gasp a little: to either side of the footprints, the fingers leaving clear ridges, there's *hand*prints as well.

"Like this," Paul says, and slings Jan onto his back like a cape, Jan squealing with delight.

Paul leans forward beside the tracks, and he's right: his hands are wider than his feet, and only the front parts of his combat boots are leaving prints in the snow.

"I don't underst—this doesn't make sense," Hettie says. "The Angel, she . . . she *walks*, she's upright."

"*Angel?*" Jan asks, excited.

"She doesn't wear shoes either, does she?" Paul says.

"Meaning?" Hettie asks.

"Meaning we're in a cemetery at night on Friday the 13th," Paul says, popping up easily with Jan on his back. "I'm not just super sure things are supposed to make sense. Why come out here to dig some-one up. Why leave on all fours."

"Maybe they fell down," Hettie tries, trying to squint it true.

"Maybe," Paul says, but he's not buying that.

"And where are the tracks coming *in*?" Hettie asks, trying to make sense of the snow they've trampled.

"More important," Paul leads off, shifting Jan around to his side, "would you rather follow these tracks and film some sick graverobber, or, would you rather . . . you know. Solve the biggest mystery in town?"

"It's videotape, not film," Hettie mumbles, kind of bouncing on her feet, not sure which way to go.

"These tracks'll still be here tomorrow . . ." Paul says with a shrug.

In his arms, Jan does the same shrug.

It's so damn cute.

"But we call it in?" Hettie says, slinging the camera around her neck like the purse it isn't.

"We can be *he*-roes," Paul sings, and leads them back to the motorcycle, going through what he knows of the rest of the song, which isn't much.

Half an hour later, three on the bike again, they're picking their way down the rut-road that eventually tiptoes under the dam, crossing Indian Creek at the big clearing and going back where the hunters go. Hettie wants to get a shot from there, of the dam looming over them. Maybe she can even superimpose a *Jaws* poster over all that concrete? It might be perfect—the image that sends *Savage History* viral, into the stratosphere.

Just that lone swimmer, and the shark coming up from the depths for her.

Jan's helmet bounces up for the fiftieth time, taps her in the chin.

She's the one holding Paul's phone now, directing them to the pin Waynebo dropped, that he insists is so top secret that this message is probably going to self-destruct—sorry, Paul's phone. As soon as they stop, she keeps telling herself, she's hauling her own phone out, to call the grave robbing in.

But they're going so fast. It's like this night's a slip 'n slide. She took one tentative step out onto it and now she can't stop, is just going faster and faster. Weren't they looking for the Angel? How'd that turn into a tour through the graveyard, and now a stab out into the timber to see a dead body or two?

This is Proofrock in October, though, she knows.

Once the clock strikes midnight, anything can happen.

Two hundred yards up, Waynebo's paint horse is standing in the road, its reins hanging down by its feet.

Paul slows, his feet to the ground to keep them from falling over.

"Just up here," Hettie says, and Paul takes them into the tall grass dusted with snow, to keep from spooking Waynebo's horse. Under Hettie's chin, Jan's helmet pivots slowly. He's watching that horse with wonder. There's something about horses at night, isn't there?

Hettie'll have to come back, get this on tape too.

This documentary is going to be longer than the twenty minutes she promised Teach. Much longer.

Proofrock just keeps opening up and opening up, doesn't it? And then she decides that, no, she won't superimpose *Jaws* on the dry face of the dam, she'll get those elevator doors from *The Shining* up there, with blood crashing through, to paint the valley red—just how *Savage History* already opens up. Which is to say, all she'll have to do is project *Savage History* up there. It'll be perfect.

"There," Paul says, because he's the only one not looking back at the horse.

It's the front part of the Bronco, lodged in a thick tangle of fall-downs, their root pans making a sort of cradle around the wreck, the better to hide it. And, really, Hettie can tell, this is where the wreck rolled down *to*, and recently, judging by how the pine needles it jarred loose are on *top* of the crust of snow.

Paul stops, waits for Hettie to lift Jan down before rocking the bike onto its kickstand. The way he does it, there's something fifties about it, like he should be rolling the cuffs of his jeans and combing his hair back until it's a perfect ducktail.

No, Hettie isn't leaving Proofrock, she knows. And she guesses she's always known, goddamnit.

Home is where your heart is, though, isn't it?

And her heart's parking the bike, right now. And setting her little brother up on it, and telling him to wait here, to not get down no matter what, okay?

Jan nods his little-kid nod, his eager-to-please nod.

"Promise?" Hettie says to him, and he nods faster, is thrilled just to be tagging along for this grand nighttime adventure.

"I can't believe this . . ." Paul says, about the Bronco actually finally *being* somewhere.

"Are they still in it?" Hettie says, stepping around, leading with her camera, not sure if she wants to see actual dead people or not.

Paul has his phone's flashlight on, winking on a piece of red reflector somehow embedded in the trunk of a tree. He steps forward gingerly, and Hettie sees that the passenger side of the Bronco isn't just crushed, it's *flattened*.

"Shit," Paul diagnoses.

Hettie nods slowly, has to agree.

"It was probably caught upslope for the last four years," Paul mansplains, looking up there. "The trees holding it finally got cold enough to snap, and—"

"It rolled the rest of the way down," Hettie finishes. Then, "But are they still . . . ?"

Paul shines his silvery light into the cab, and, just like in *Jaws*, there's a rotted head bobbing up into the brightness.

Hettie and Paul both fall back, holding onto each other.

The camera dislodges into the grass and snow, some button jarring the tiny heads into furious motion. When no zombies lumber up from the wreck to eat their brains, Paul laughs an embarrassed, nervous laugh. Hettie knows she should as well, because it's so stupid it's funny, except—

She's seen these movies.

That might just be a cat in a closet, but there's probably a penis-headed alien bug unfolding from the backseat, its mouth already slavering.

"*What?*" Paul says, holding his hand up, fingers spread away from each other.

With his phone, he lights them all up.

Blood.

He spins around on his ass and hands, drops his phone, has to get it back from the snow, and—and . . .

It's Waynebo.

"No," Hettie says, or hears herself saying, not even aware of having pushed back from all this already.

Waynebo's been ripped open. His blood looks so red, so fake.

Hettie crabs farther back, her arms and movement stiff, no scream erupting—she knows not to put that bullseye on her back.

Any more than it probably already is.

"Paul, Paul, Paul," she gulps out, still trying to buttslide away, which turns out to be into the missing door of the Bronco.

A rotted skeleton arm falls down on her shoulder and what's left of the truck settles down with a sudden *whoompf*, nearly crushing her.

She flinches away, surges almost all the way up, her feet already running, never mind if the rest of her's ready.

"Paul, Paul! We need to—!"

She stops a step or three away because: *Paul?*

Hettie desperately pans around to every quadrant. Except you can't watch all of them at once. Your back's always to one of them.

She spins, spins again, stumbles, is about to cry, can feel it welling up in her throat, in her chest, in her soul.

"*Paauuullllll!*" she calls out all around, who cares about bulls-eyes now.

She shakes her head no, that she doesn't want to make the documentary anymore, that she'll stop, she'll throw it away, she'll do something *normal* for her senior project.

The woods don't answer.

She hugs herself, still looking left and right and behind her.

"Paul?" she says, quieter.

She falls to her knees, shaking her head no, no, please, and fast-crawls ahead to the videocamera, its light blinking record-red, now.

Hettie claws it to her to use like a hammer, to swing at whatever's coming, and inadvertently hits play, then drops the camera when she turns around fast, sure something was just behind her.

On the small screen of her videocamera in the snow and yellow grass, the documentary is playing back, now.

It's past the cemetery, is to . . . the Pier.

It's a wide shot from the side, and's far away but that's just to make it feel like she's spying, like she's not supposed to be seeing this.

Really, though, she knows the sheriff.

He was the one getting that chainsaw going, to Slipknot—his choice.

It was setup for this: to the end of the Pier, now, Sheriff Tompkins fires that chainsaw up, its blue smoke gouting up into the night sky in a way that would make David Lynch sigh with contentment, a way that would make Martin Scorsese have to wipe a single tear away.

Sheriff Tompkins revs that chainsaw once, twice, then takes a knee like he's going to saw through the planks of the new Pier, and now Hettie's over his shoulder for this dirty-loud work.

He's not chewing those fast teeth into the Pier, though. He's chainsawing the town canoe in half, the blunt leading end of the blade frothing the lake water, the pale, gummy fibers of the hull writhing and flailing.

It's supposed to mean Proofrock's slasher days are over.

The chainsaw chugs through the green fiberglass and finally the canoe falls into two pieces, both of them *Titanic*'ing down into the murky depths, and then it's a wide shot again: Sheriff Tompkins holding that chainsaw up and shaking it at the gods.

Just as Hettie wrote it.

In the viewfinder of her camera, though, nothing's scripted. Or, it was all scripted long before she was born. Hettie's on her knees, she's spinning around again, she's sneaking a look to her camera like to pick it up again, but then the rabbit in her senses she's . . . not alone?

She clamps her hand over her own mouth, holds her breath, muffling what would have been her scream.

Slowly, so as not to draw attention, she turns, and whatever she sees just out of frame makes her fall away and then rush to the side, which is right into the camera.

A flurry of motion later, her face slams down right in front of the lens, comes up caked with snow. The blood from her nose and mouth is bright against that whiteness, is either stringing away from her or trying to hold her together, and she's still reaching ahead, like the camera's heavy enough that, if she can just grab it, it can become her weapon, her savior, her way out of this, whatever it is.

But she only manages to jostle it the littlest bit.

Her face is still filling that viewfinder slightly off-center, and her hand is reaching around to the controls, to push record, so she can say something.

"Mom," she whispers right into the camera, her voice shaky, and then she's ripped to the side like Chrissie in *Jaws*, some snow flecking up onto the lens, distorting the left side of the frame.

Moving from bubble to bubble through it is . . . it's more upright than a dog or bear, is nightgown-pale, black and loose at top, like a headful of hair.

So much hair.

A woman.

The Angel of Indian Lake.

She's ethereal and wrong, dead except for the walking-around part, and when the thing perched on Hettie steps off of her—snapping from bubble to bubble on the camera lens, it's a man on all fours, a pale man in the tatters of a suit—when this thing that's also dead approaches her, its head dipping obsequiously over and over, as if it knows it's in the presence of its god, it's also . . . dragging something?

Something large and squirming, held between its teeth like an offering.

Which it lays at the Angel's feet.

After a moment of what feels like consideration, the Angel lowers herself to this offering, then looks sharply up at the thing that delivered it to her.

A flurry of motion later, the thing's head is rolling across the lens, past the bubbles to the clear part, where a pause would show a staticky human face, mouth ringed with blood, eyes hollow, hair still perfectly in place from whatever glue or spray the embalmer used.

And then it's gone. As is the Angel.

All that's left in the camera eye is the top of the tall grass and the pale crust of the snow and the trees and then, forty or fifty feet out, centered just like Hettie would have done if she were operating this camera, the motorcycle.

There's no little boy up on the seat.

The Savage History of Proofrock, Idaho isn't over, no.

It's just getting started.

SCARY MOVIE

This isn't Freddy's high school hallway, this isn't Freddy's high school hallway.

If it were, Tina would be twenty feet ahead in her foggy plastic bodybag, being dragged around the corner on a smear of her own blood.

Instead—again, but it always feels like the first time—*I'm* the one in that bodybag.

I'm helpless on my back, there's no air in here, my feet are travois handles to pull me with, and the lockers and doorways and educational posters and homecoming banners to either side are blurry, are in a Henderson High I'm not part of anymore.

Not since Freddy got his claws into me.

I want to scream but know that if I open my mouth, what's coming out is a sheep's dying bleat. I clap my scream in with my palm, try to clamp my throat shut, tamp the panic down, but my elbow scraping on the plastic wall of this bodybag rasps louder than it should, and—

He looks back.

His face is scarred and cratered, and there's a glint of humor in his eyes like he's getting away with something here, a glint that spreads to his lips, one side of his twisted mouth sharpening into a grin right before his head Pez-dispensers back because his neck's been chopped open, and what comes up from that bloody stump is the grimy hand of a little dead girl fighting her way back into the world, and—

And it doesn't have to be this way, according to Sharona.

She's my twice-a-month therapist, courtesy of her champion and main benefactor, Letha Mondragon.

It's only a movie, it's only a movie, Sharona's taught me to repeat in my head.

To fight my way through panic attacks, I'm supposed to think of my life as playing on a drive-in screen. Not that I've ever been to a drive-in. But evidently, late in their evolution, there would be six or eight or ten drive-in screens all in this big-ass Stonehenge circle, each with their own parking lot. If you didn't like what was playing on one screen, you could take your popcorn, cruise over for the next movie, and the next, until you found one that worked for you, that helped you through this night instead of trapping you in it.

"You're the *consumer* here," Sharona told me so, so earnestly our first session. "And what you're paying with is anxiety and dread and panic, see?"

The first part of me being the one carrying the popcorn, it's supposed to be buying into this being all a movie, all a movie. Like that was ever enough to keep the horror in *The Last House on the Left* from touching you where it counts.

Sharona doesn't know horror, though. Just feelings, regrets, strategies, and how to see through my own rationalizations and paranoia, my bad history and worse family shit.

I say *quid pro quo* to her a lot, but I don't think she ever really gets it like I mean it.

The way she explains what I'm feeling in moments like this—"feeling" being clinical-speak for "consumed by"—is that my anxiety is a straitjacket constricting me: at first it feels like a hug, like something I should nestle into, but then . . . then it doesn't know when to stop, does it, Jade?

StraitJacket of course being a 1964 proto slasher, post-*Psycho* but very much providing a model for *Psycho II* nearly twenty years later. Thank you, Robert Bloch.

Sharona has it wrong about straitjackets, though. In a straitjacket, you can breathe. I know this from experience. You don't open your wrist out on the lake and then get trusted with your own fingernails and teeth, I mean.

Where you *can't* breathe, though?

In a bodybag.

When Proofrock and all what I've done and *not* done and should have done if I were smarter and better and faster and louder are collapsing in on me and there's no air at all, then a knife finger materializes blurry and real through the foggy plastic cocooning me, it materializes and then it loops through a delicate metal tab, to zip me right in.

Sorry, Sharona.

One bullshit tool you've given me to work that zipper down from the backside is to write letters to someone I respect or care for, who could and would offer me a helping hand, to clamber up out of this.

Which is just a reminder that everyone I love is dead, thanks.

Sheriff Hardy. Mr. Holmes. Shooting Glasses.

I don't know if my mom's in that group or not.

I know my dad isn't.

Pamela Voorhees, she's who I should write to, isn't she? Or maybe Ellen Ripley. Put her in a dark hallway like this one in my head and she would lock and load, call her nerves a bitch, and tell them to get away from her.

I'm no Ripley.

Instead of locking and loading, what I do for about the thousandth time since the semester started is stumble on these stupid heels and lurch to the left, ramming my shoulder into a locker.

Just when you thought it was safe to walk like an adult.

Clear the beaches, mayor, Jade's coming through again.

God.

Letha's right about me: I'm always hiding in the video store, wearing all my movies like armor. Never mind that Proofrock's video store's been closed for three years now, is pretty much a memorial for all the kids who got skinned in there, are probably still haunting it.

That's just playing on one screen, though.

Keep moving, Jade, keep moving.

On one of the other screens, though, are the two sleepless nights the weekend of the thirteenth, when Proofrock was in a panic over Jan Jansson going missing. But then word came in that his dad, who had split, had also rented a red Mustang convertible the day before. One fast enough to drive back from Nevada or whatever state he was hiding in, one alluring enough for his only son to want to take a ride in. So all the flyers were peeled off the windows of the bank, of Dot's, of the drugstore, and a certain ex-con was finally able to sleep again.

They'll find him, everybody is assuring themselves. He's just with his dad, having an adventure—top down, hair in the wind, not a single drive-through window being missed.

Either that or he's a kid-shaped bargaining chip in an escalating divorce.

There's no blades looming, though, that's the important thing. There's no shadows lurking, no heavy breathing, no drunk shapes suddenly standing in the doorway at two o'clock in the stupid-ass morning.

I right myself from the locker I've crashed into—I think it was Lee Scanlon's, once upon a time—blink my eyes fast like trying to get the lights to come back up in this hallway, but . . . okay, seriously now: Where in the living hell *is* everybody?

It's Monday, not Friday, meaning no pep rally for football. Nobody pulled the fire alarm. It's not senior skip day, and Banner hasn't instituted some curfew to keep everyone safe—there's no reason to. Ghostface isn't out there slicing and dicing. Cinnamon Baker doesn't live here anymore. There's no once-in-a-century blizzard spooling up: been there, done that, we're good for ninety-six more years, thanks.

A shooter drill, maybe? We are eight thousand feet up the mountain, meaning even the guns have guns, but . . . no.

There's a lot wrong with Proofrock, but not that, anyway.

So far.

Could it be that seventh period just started? Is that what emptied the halls out? All the students dove into their classrooms and fought for seats because they really-really wanted to learn?

Dream on, slasher girl.

A fluorescent tube of light flickers in the ceiling a body length ahead, then sputters out again. It's not for lack of money—Letha's bankrolling the whole district, could put her name above the front doors if she wanted.

"Excuse me?" I say up to the light, holding my books to my chest.

The light buzzes back on, holds steady.

"*Fuckin A . . .*" I mutter to it, and keep moving, my clacking footsteps sounding all around me, and, passing a fire extinguisher I become one hundred percent certain that Rexall's just caught me on candid camera "engaging in profanity on school grounds," is going to turn it in to Principal Harrison, just moved up from Golding Elementary.

He's already not fond of my full-sleeve tats. My hair's okay in principle, I think—long now, to my waist, and silky as everliving shit—but it's not all black, either.

C'mon.

And I don't wear my spider bites or my bull ring or my eyebrow stud to school anymore. Though there may be a piercing or two that are none of a principal's business.

Sharona says I'm still trying to armor up, can't I see that?

I tell her back that she just likes the way I was before, which is sort of a line from *Return of the Living Dead III*, featuring the queen of all piercing junkies—she's no slouch with the eyeliner, either.

Well, okay, maybe I don't say it exactly like that. But I think the hell out of it.

What I also don't say out loud: that you just slipped, My Sharona. That bit about armoring up is pure Letha, which means the two of you talk about me and my progress, which . . . isn't exactly the key to get me to be forthcoming?

What I *did* say out loud in reply to that armor line, though? Sort of on accident, sort of not?

"Jealous much?"

Where Sharona went after her high school beauty queen days, after she won the big Blonder Than Thou contest? That adult daycare called college. Where I went, *twice*? That finishing school for criminals called the clink, the slam, the stir. That old greybar hotel waiting at the end of every road my kind slouches down.

If you don't armor up in there, Sharona, you never get out.

But, like you, I've also geared up with books, thanks. They all had to be paperback, because hardcovers can brain a girl, or get sharpened to a one-use point, but they finally added up enough to get me a degree. It's correspondence, sure, but it was enough for Letha to strong-arm the school district she now *owns* into . . . this.

It's strictly trial basis, nobody expects it to actually last, but . . . I'm trying?

And the school's not actually dim, I can see that now. That's just my idiot eyes, dialing the hallway down to a tunnel. The kind with a nightmare boiler room way down at the end, rushing up all around me with the first blink.

I'm still in Tina's bodybag, I mean.

In spite of the three cigarettes I just trainsmoked back by woodshop, lighting the next off the last, praying against all hope that the nicotine would open my capillaries up enough to keep this clench from happening in my chest, in my head.

Things do not happen, I say inside. *Things are* made *to happen.*

This from John F. Kennedy, in a book I had to read twice to get it to stick enough for the test.

What JFK's saying is that I'm doing this to myself. I didn't walk into another panic attack. It wasn't lying in wait for me. No, I made it happen, by allowing the bad thoughts to spool up, loop me into their spin cycle of death, my hand stabbing up like on the VHS cover of *Mortuary*. Once your thinking starts swirling around that chrome grate of the shower drain, good luck stopping it without cutting yourself.

Which is another thing I don't do anymore. Or, can't start doing again, anyway.

I can still slice into this bodybag, though.

Not with a razor, but with something almost as sharp: pharmaceuticals. After checking to be sure I'm alone, I peel two warm tablets up from the elastic waistband of the boy shorts under my long black poodle skirt, crush them between the pads of my thumb and index finger, and snort them deep into my head fast, before I can think about what I'm doing.

My theory on mood stabilizers and beta blockers and the rest of the usual suspects I've cycled through is that it's stupid they have to go all the way down to the stomach only to slowly percolate back up to the brain. So I do it more direct, save them some travel time, get more bang for my buck.

And, I can take four at once and still be mostly myself, as far as anybody knows, but I already took one on my cigarette break, so.

As for what they're supposed to dial back, make less unmanageable? Oh, I don't know. A yachtful of one-percenters who were also parents, and I think sort of actually maybe wanted to be good members of the community, in spite of their rich asses? A lakeful of people I've known since before I could walk, none of whose insides I ever expected to have to see, and swim through? A video store of kids who didn't *ask* to be skinned for Christmas? My mom, standing up to the scarfaced predator about to attack me, even though it was hopeless, and years too late? Mr. Holmes, sinking under the surface of the water, his fingers finally slipping from mine in a way I know I'll never forget? Sheriff Hardy, and the way he looked back at me and nodded once before stepping into the water with his daughter?

And so many more, among and between.

I like to think that each particle of every tablet I take is just enough to cover up the memory of one of those dead people, at least for an afternoon.

Meaning they swim back up at night, yeah. Surprise.

But that's hours later.

This is now.

With the cold heat of these last two tablets sizzling through my mucous membranes, I have to reach out for the wall on the right side to keep steady until the post-nasal drip starts like the slowest pendulum, swinging back and forth so steadily that, if I let it, if I just exercise a little mental discipline, it can even me out, it can quiet the splashing, the screams, it can let me step between these gusts of blowing snow, into a little pocket of safety.

I push off the wall with my fingertips and it's like standing in a canoe, not a hallway, and I know I can spill over into the deep dark water at any moment, but—this in Principal Harrison's judgmental tone—I'm already late enough as-is, don't have time to wallow in my feelings.

So I don't.

Sharona would never understand, but the way I finally step ahead, out of this tattered bodybag, is that I age Freddy ahead fourteen years, until he's the snarky prof at the front of that grand classroom in *Urban Legend*, teaching about the babysitter and the man upstairs, about Pop Rocks and soda.

He's completely in control up there, isn't he?

He is.

So am I, so am I.

At least until I hear footsteps running up behind me.

In Nancy's nightmare of a daydream, the admonishment she receives is that there's no running in the hallway.

But there is, isn't there?

I turn, am suddenly in a different hallway—one from 1996: a Ghostface is coming fast down the hall, slaloming from side to side with pitch-perfect goofiness, doing boogedy-boogedy hands left and right.

At first I retract into myself, clutching my books tight. It's the day before Halloween, and even if Halloween's functionally illegal in Proofrock, still, the rules have to sort of be off, don't they?

But you used to walk these halls too, Jade, imagining them Slaughter High.

And these footsteps coming at you, they aren't from 1996.

This Ghostface wasn't even born, then.

When he makes to blast past me all anonymous, I step forward, make a fast fist around the long tail of this pull-on mask. I know how these masks work, I mean. It's like a nun's wimple. Just, for slasher church.

This would-be Ghostface's head whips back, his arms even more Muppet now, but when he falls to his knees, starts sliding and leaning back, that Munch of a pale face finally comes off with a harsh snap, the mask wrapping once around my wrist and then just hanging there.

"*Dwight*," I say down to this junior on his knees.

He probably thinks it's a Dewey reference, but I'm really calling him Brad Pitt from *Cutting Class*. Because that's what he's doing.

"Um, Trent, ma'am," he stammers, trying to peel out of the glittery Father Death robe he's now tangled in.

Like I don't who he is: Trent Morrison, of the Morrisons who came here with Tobias Golding and Glen Henderson, to pan Indian Creek. This great-great-whatever-grandson of miners has made it through two massacres to get this far in his academic career. And that's after his grandparents made it through the Fire of '64 *and* Camp Blood. After his parents knew better than to ever get into a car with my dad, because he was bound to go cartwheeling off the road sooner or later, trashing his face forevermore.

"And what is this?" I ask, about the mask.

"It's—it's *Halloween*," he says, whines really, and I look away like casting around for a reason not to punt him to Harrison's office.

What I see down the long hallway in my head is a punk girl with a sour expression and a goth heart, dull orange hair so dry it crunches, and a gloved hand curled around the plastic knife fingers she's wishing real, so she can slice through all these stupid years, carve her way to whatever's next. She's glaring at me, is a hurt animal under the porch, is going to snap at whoever tries to come close. Here in a few minutes, her shirt's going to get her sent home from school, and she's going to come back, try to Carrie blood down onto the big dance. Some days, instead of going to class, she's going to ruin her eyeliner crying in the band closet, and I just want to take her hand, lead her up from that, tell her there's more, there's more, just wait, just hold on—*this* is next, if you can make it through.

"Get the fuck out of here, Trent," I say, and when you're a teacher deploying profanity on school grounds, you don't have to repeat yourself.

On the way gone, Trent jogs backwards, says, "You're coming, right?"

"*Go*," I tell him, pointing ahead of both of us, and he scampers off, only looking back once.

The spike of adrenaline he jolted up my spine has, by my reckoning, canceled out at least one of the circular white fingerholds I have on the day.

Knowing I shouldn't, I work another dose up from my waistband, pinch it to dust, slam it into the dark cavern behind my eyes. Somewhere in there, the Pamela Voorhees head at the end of the second installment opens her eyes like she was originally meant to, and all the candles Jason's arranged around her flicker alive.

Yes. Yes yes yes.

Jade Daniels, reporting for duty.

I stand outside the classroom with my back to the wall for maybe twenty seconds, my books clutched to my chest like a shield, my lips moving around the shape of words, to be sure I can still make that connection, that I'm not going to slur and drool and try to grin it off as fallout from having faced down two killers, and come out on my feet.

Not that my feet are exactly whole, mind. Not all the little piggies made it through the frostbite. Not all of my face either, if we're being technical. Three of the fingers on my right hand won't curl into a fist, even, and still show toothmarks. But they don't get cold, so I guess I shouldn't complain.

At least my jaw's still connected, right? Unlike certain people I know. Some of whom I visit on and off, at the cemetery. One of whom I have coffee with once a week—our standing date. Which is still, what, Saturday, if she's back by then?

Maybe I can text her for emergency coffee, though.

We can sit at our usual table at Dot's, under the huge, mounted bear the hunters went out for so long ago, for killing Deacon Samuels over in front of Camp Blood—what they're calling "Deacon Point" now.

Except some unnamed crusader keeps sneaking over there in the small hours, pulling that sign up just for the joy of slinging it out into the lake.

The first few were metal, just sunk, but lately they've been wooden, so they float back in.

I'm stalling, though. One thing Sharona's taught me that's actually good is how to identify my own bullshit: the little defense mechanisms I kicked up once upon an adolescence, to get through the day.

"You're not seventeen anymore," she tells me very supportively, very therapeutically.

Some sessions, I even sort of believe her.

At least until I try to wrap the fingers of my right hand around a pencil. Until, applying the old eyeliner in the morning, I want to just keep going, keep going, darker and darker, daring Harrison to have a reason to send me home, not renew my contract.

I should tell him about one of his predecessors, paddling along the Pier in an invisible canoe like the best joke ever. And how that dead principal's son was gutted under our big neon Indian, last time around.

No, not last time "around"—last time *ever*.

Jaws might have gotten a stack of sequels, but one was enough for Proofrock.

And all I'm doing, I know, is trying to step back down into that bodybag, zip it up over *myself*.

I've got to be better.

Inside, whiling away the days, the years, doing my time, I could mull and dwell in my cell or the yard all I wanted—sad Jade, Jade the victim.

This is the world, though. Out here, you have to participate. People have expectations—there's duties, there's responsibilities. Anyway, I tell myself, you've been doing this since August already, right? After nearly nine weeks, I can just flick autopilot on, coast through the next fifty minutes.

Except I owe them better than that.

Two of their own have been absent-without-excuse for two weeks—two weeks and one day, counting today. Any other town, when two kids go missing, then they probably ran off together, are seeing how far they can get.

In Proofrock, if somebody's late by ten minutes, then you're casing the shadows, the windows, the doorways, because this might mean it's all starting up again.

Except it can't be. I won't let it.

In spite of the murmuring in the hall, in the lounge, at Dot's, and who cares what actual *day* they went missing, it's just a day, doesn't mean anything, Hettie and Paul have to have gone after Jan, Hettie's little brother, right? They got word of the dad cruising the hug-n-go lane, and were gone so fast their pencils were still standing up on their desks. Or? Or they took advantage of that weekend's panic to run away to Boise like they were always saying, or to Seattle, to Los Angeles, to Salt Lake City, to Denver. When you're seventeen in Proofrock, the glittering lights of the big cities call to you, don't they?

And my feelings aren't hurt that she didn't tell me.

The last thing you need on the way out is for your older model to hold onto you and hug and hug, and slip fifty dollars into your pocket.

You're supposed to ride away broke on that sputtering motorcycle, wearing your boyfriend's jacket. *Broke*, not broken, which is how you end up if you stay here too long. Case in point: my sessions with Sharona. "Continuity of counseling" is part of my parole, meaning, I guess, that the powers that be think I'm about to become Tommy Jarvis at the end of *The Final Chapter*, and go all Mandy Lane and Cinnamon Baker on the student body.

What they don't know is that I'm really Nancy from *Dream Warriors*.

I made it through, and now I'm back, and in fucking *heels*, thank you.

In the lake eight years ago, yeah, I saw all the names and dates of Idaho's history spill out into the water. But I found them in the prison library, and I ate those pages like Francis Dolarhyde, and now all those names and dates are in me, sir.

I inherited your old tests and quizzes, too, can you feel that from up in the sky? Can you even hear me over the buzz of your ultralight's little engine? All your notes are still in your precise handwriting, even, with little ticks and additions from you updating them through the years. It's not like history changes, right? No, all of it went down just like you told us it did. Some afternoons I even lean back against the desk after the day's quiz and look into the distant past and tell class about all the sparks that used to populate the darkness across the valley, which were either dreamers trying to dig their future up from the mountain or killers trying to hide their kill*ees*. Some days I even lower my voice to "campfire" and tell them about the nameless boy left behind by his family when the lake was rising, and how an old tradition around here is making paper boats for him to play with, and sailing them out into the day's brightness. I tell them about the Shoshone coming in on their painted ponies to behold this new lake on their old land, and how they just watched and watched, and how that was like a metaphor in action, right? And when we have enough time, I even tell them again about the giant sturgeon or catfish supposedly down there in Drown Town, its eyes glassy and knowing, and how a raft of young pirates in the sixties saw it cruising through the shallows one magic afternoon, and their hearts grew three sizes in their chests that day, and none of them could ever move away from Proofrock after that, because once you've felt the magic of a place, then that place, it's got you.

And, yeah, I let them write extra-credit papers for me, when they need to.

It's sort of a promise I've made, sir.

My lips might be numb from the drugs now, my fingers might be trembling with panic, but I'll read those papers however deep into the night they need me to. And if I hold these books tight enough, then you can't even see my nerves, can you?

Just—breathe in deep, hold it, hold it, and . . . release.

Again.

You're already late enough, can't stall any longer, girl.

I pivot on my heel, come about in the open doorway with my lips firm, eyes properly grim, and I walk into seventh-period history like annoyed with whatever held me up, made me late.

Just like the old days, I still smell like smoke.

But I'm going to quit. That's another promise.

I clap my books down onto the desk and case the room, finally nod, and, like every time, I sneak a look out the window as well, for Michael Myers standing there by his stolen station wagon, waiting for me.

But I make myself be here again, in this classroom.

Only here, not 1978.

Dear Mr. Holmes, I say inside, in secret. *I'm not the misfit slouching in the back of your classroom anymore.*

Now I'm at the front.

In my day, a presentation in history—in any class—was you up by the teacher's desk monotoning your way through your stack of index cards, one hundred percent certain that everyone can hear the tremor in your voice, and how you're probably about to cry.

Now how it works is the students have slideshows and videos stashed online. Because I was warned not to let them log in on my computer—their fingers are a blur, can do so much with just a few keystrokes—most of them bring their own laptops, or tablets, or phones. I'm waiting for the day when one of them uses their watch to connect to the projector.

Anyway, another thing that's different nowadays is that, used to, the blinds didn't get drawn, the lights didn't get lowered—no reason to. So you couldn't hide, were just stranded up there in everyone's bored headlights, knowing full well that your course grade depends on your performance, but also, in the moment anyway, completely willing to cash your whole transcript in if this can just please be over.

Which is to say, you think it's so, so important, that your whole life and social standing and reputation and future happiness depend on not messing this up too badly.

Really, though?

It's a blip, it's nothing.

You can get jeered at, sure, you can fumble a fact, get your slides in the wrong order, but most of the class, they're not really even listening, are going through their own index cards in their head, running through it just like they did for their mom or dad at breakfast.

All of which I explained to class last week.

"Did *you* practice like that, over breakfast?" Ellie Jennings asked in her usual timid way, though, kind of messing things up.

Her question was so earnest, too, so honest, so innocent. It was the perfect opportunity for me to bond with everyone. This was where I could have shown them I had been just like them, once upon a troubled Proofrock coming-of-age.

Just, most of them know my history: breakfast in the Daniels household wasn't nearly so *Leave It to Beaver*. More like "Leave it to the Reject," which usually meant scrapping together a bologna sandwich, flipping my dad off through the wall, flipping my mom off from across town, then trudging to school, my finger in the air the whole way, to save myself the effort of lifting my hand again and again.

Such is high school.

"Practice is important," I answered Ellie, which wasn't an answer at all. Then, very solemnly, like we were still all in this together, I asked for volunteers for our first day of presentations—"Just anyone who wants to get it over with?"

In my other classes, this is usually a who's-gonna-be-the-first-penguin-off-the-ice-floe kind of thing, but that's just because Christy Christy isn't in any of those classes.

Her hand shot up immediately, and the way she was squirming in her seat, I sort of thought she might be about to pee.

What she was raising her hand for was today, seventh period.

After taking attendance and passing back quizzes and peeling up the Post-it notes stuck to Hettie and Paul's seats—"Casey" and "Steve" respectively, fourth time in two weeks—we finally dial the lights down, JT lowers the blinds for us, and Christy sashays up to the front of the classroom, plugs into the hub that feeds the projector, turns around to all of us and blinks twice like clearing her mind for this.

Standing against the six inches of wall between the two windows, the painted brick so cool and stable, I nod for her to go ahead, go ahead, and . . . another good thing about this murky darkness we're all stranded in?

Teach's pupils aren't on display.

My head's still working, mostly, good enough for seventh period, but my face has that kind of numbness that means I maybe took a bit too much again.

When I filled that sterile cup for the mandatory drug test Letha assured the board I would pass with flying colors—that color being "yellow," I guess?—I made sure to bring my clutch of prescriptions in, since they were likely going to ring some certain bells in the lab.

But?

When you're trauma girl, when you're just out of lockup, trying to find your feet in a world without guards, where you're sort of nervous in open spaces now, then people expect it's going to take a pharmacopeia to level you out, get you through the day.

I passed, I'm saying.

There *was* a conference with the new Doc Wilson, about saturation and long-term impacts and mixing this and that, what the liver can and can't tolerate, how the kidneys do and don't work, but that was just for my own good, didn't have any real bearing on the results Letha proudly passed on to the board.

And, I should say, this—me up here teaching, being the new and completely fake Mr. Holmes—it's more Letha's redemption arc for me than anything I ever had planned. When I processed out with my manila envelope and my nothing-check, my dim plan was to maybe hire on to wash coffee cups and saucers at Dot's, knowing full well that the only things I really had waiting were my old custodian coveralls and a to-do list written in Rexall's cramped hand, where he doesn't dot the *i*'s but never fails to center-dot any two *o*'s that wind up beside each other.

I was going to be that janitor working a mop in *Scream*, waiting for Principal Himbry to surprise me.

Well, in my dreams, I was.

Really?

I was going to be Dorian, the *Die Hard 2* janitor from *Disturbing Behavior*, who's himself not exactly undisturbed.

Dorian didn't have my prescriptions, though. They're the spoonful of sugar that lets Christy Christy's presentation go down.

The "history" she's chosen is, technically, town history: Glen Henderson kills Tobias Golding with a pickaxe, which he then coats in gold and drops in the creek. The gold is melted down from his wife's jewelry, which was a small fortune. Well, a huge one, back then.

Fast-forward to the creek getting dammed into the lake, and that golden pickaxe is forever buried in silt and washing machines and Christmas trees.

Unless it isn't?

Christy Christy's theory leans on rumor instead of fact, which you would probably wince about, Mr. Holmes, but it's not like I can call her out on it. She testified against me in my trial, I mean. But maybe that's why her presentation is so polished, right? A failing grade could be construed as me coming for her, her then having to defend herself, re-hurl certain accusations concerning her mom, and . . . better to be civil, right?

When Harrison was arguing against me at the big school board meeting, that was one of his main points: I'd done my time, but had I ever really been *cleared*? What if my father's corpse bobs up some fine day, and he has a waterproof camera around his neck, happened to document me swinging that machete at him?

Okay, he didn't say that, that's me.

But still: what if, right?

Letha's comeback to this was that I'd never been convicted of a *moral* crime—really, I'd only been sent up on a technicality, for destruction of state property. Which had really been in *service* of Proofrock.

Not exactly what I was thinking in the moment, but sure.

And, while I can maybe never be trusted with a notary public seal or hold office, I can be trusted with twenty-five students at a time. Provisionally. Until I mess up.

The school board's sort of holding their breath, yeah.

Me too.

So? So I don't call Christy Christy out on leaning on rumor instead of fact.

As for that rumor, it's that *Mrs.* Glen Henderson knew where her husband had deposited that golden pickaxe, and, wanting her jewelry back, since tickets to the world aren't free, she stepped out into the waters of that creek one night, felt around until she came up with the guilty thing.

What did she do with it then, though—"*That's* the question," Christy Christy ends with.

Her emphasis is supposed to be a mic-drop if not an actual conclusion, and her still-raised eyebrows are probably supposed to be what makes her case.

I lead class in polite applause, write "F" in my notebook, then bubble the two horizontal lines into a "P," for *pass*, and let that letter get pregnant, its belly pooching out into a reluctant "B," for—you guessed it—*blackmail*.

But so be it.

Like I told them, it's only one presentation in a whole high school career of them. Just a blip.

Next up is supposed to be Hettie, according to my list, showing a clip from her documentary, but Marisa Scanlon is the one plugging in. Lee's littlest sister.

"Thank you, Marisa," I say.

I should have already dealt with their two absent classmates and our presentation order, I mean.

Absent, not "missing."

"I've got the sequel, don't I?" Marisa says, and the good thing about your face being numb is that you can wear it like a mask.

"Go, go," I tell her, ushering her on.

Where Christy's slides were all cameos of Glen Henderson and Tobias Golding and Mrs. Henderson, daguerreotypes and tintypes of Henderson-Golding before it became Drown Town, Marisa's first slide has been scavenged from . . . Banner's dad's social media? Yep, looks like. MySpace, maybe? The dinosaur age of the internet. It's Mr. Tompkins from twenty or thirty years ago, posed behind the mighty rack of a bull elk he's brought down—one for the record books. That and his walrus stache both, good grief.

In the photo, Banner's dad is beaming. His rifle has been laid across the forks of the top tines, which seems more than a bit gamey, gun worship being not so cool anymore. But nobody calls it out, so I let it slide—calling attention would only make it worse, probably?

Tell yourself that, Jade. Give yourself every out you can.

"The year was 1995," Marisa recites, like sad for the elk. "The year OJ Simpson was found not guilty. Rwanda's still reeling from genocide. *Toy Story* premieres. Michael Jordan comes back to basketball. But that's all down the mountain. Up here, as Rocky here could tell you, rifle season was extended eight days, because the snow came late."

"*Yeah*," some male student in the darkness says.

Nobody shushes him.

"Go on," I tell Marisa.

"Wasn't Rocky the *squirrel*?" JT asks, though.

Aside from being a whiz with the miniblinds, he's also the pop-cult fiend of the senior class—maybe studying the seventies and eighties is where he learned how to work those impossible strings, even.

Marisa's eyes dart left and right.

"This elk was a *fighter*, though, right, Marisa?" I prompt, getting my dukes up like a boxer. "Aren't most trophies like that, hard to get?"

"That's . . . why they're trophies," Marisa manages.

"And let's let her continue without interruption?" I say.

It's not a question.

JT slumps lower in his seat and crosses his arms, stares intently at the screen.

I'm not unsympathetic. In my day, if someone at the front of the classroom had put Michael Myers at Crystal Lake, then no force in the world could have shut me up.

You don't walk into my house and tell me what's what.

JT's either, I think.

But we've got one more presentation after this, too.

"Marisa," I say, giving her the room again.

"Okay, okay," she says, warming back up, swallowing loud somehow. "We all know Rocky, this *fighting elk*, was donated to Henderson High when Sheriff Tompkins' dad's new house in Pend Oreille didn't have room for the mount, right? Right."

No, I say inside, to Marisa. *Please, no.*

"And, we all know what happened in 2019," Marisa says anyway, rolling Jensen Jones's senior photo up.

I'm the only one in the room who actually saw Jensen Jones speared on the brow tines of this massive, disinterested elk. But it's town legend, now. You no longer have to have been there to have seen it.

And no, Marisa doesn't know to put Linnea Quigley up as Jensen-surrogate, from when she got speared on an elk rack in *Silent Night, Deadly Night*.

"1984, Alex," I want to say in my head, to center myself, not fall howling back to that forever afternoon in the snow, except the weird thing about seventh-period history is that there's an Alex in the second row.

Marisa actually does that tracing-the-cross thing across her chest and face, about Jensen. I'm guessing she knows it from mob movies.

"Marisa, I don't think—" I start, but she's already clicking past Jensen Jones's senior photo.

"You said this could be, like, a *photographic* essay, right?" she asks.

On-screen now is the wall where that bull elk used to hang. I walk by it probably twenty times a day, five days a week. On the same nail the elk used to be, there's now a long plaque of the names of all the students the world still thinks Dark Mill South killed—that Cinnamon Baker's really responsible for. There used to be a short bookshelf under the plaque, but stuffed animals and roses and beer bottles and condoms and resin-stained alligator clips kept showing up, so Rexall was told to cart it off, please and thank you.

"Did I say that?" I ask kind of generally, my voice ramping up like I hate, so I won't sound so confrontational, which Letha's warned me about.

"'Pictures can do all the work of words,'" Alex of all people quotes back at me without turning his head, and, yeah, I do have a dim memory of having said something along those lines. Just, I was talking about the opening of *Halloween*, which isn't exactly about talking—twenty-four words across four minutes, four of which are "Michael."

I kind of doubt Marisa Scanlon's slideshow is going to be up to John Carpenter standards, though.

"They can, they can," I say about words over pictures, knowing full well that for the next few days, I can now expect nothing but "video essays"—so much easier to drag and drop images than to write a sentence.

Next year I'll do it better, I promise, Mr. Holmes.

I won't say whatever the class wants to hear, I'll tell them what they *need* to hear.

"Go," I tell Marisa again, flicking my eyes to the door, for the chance that Harrison's stationed there, for another impromptu observation.

Marisa clicks on, taking us with her.

After the plaque, it's a snapshot of the *Proofrock Standard*, an article I'd missed. The headline is "School Vandalism Goes Unpunished."

I don't need to read the blurry print to know what the article's about, though: Jensen's dad breaking into the school, wrenching Banner's dad's trophy elk off the wall, and walking right down Main with it, throwing it off the Pier, into the lake, as you do with things that have killed your son.

Marisa's slideshow transitions into a series of grainy snapshots then, each slow-dissolving into the next.

That elk head, bobbing in the water by Devil's Creek.

Some tines just breaking the surface, framing Camp Blood.

Close on a marble eye, somehow reflecting Terra Nova.

"What does it see out there, do you think?" Marisa reverently intones.

"Photoshop . . ." JT grumbles.

He's not wrong.

Still?

That head *is* still out there, always showing up when you least expect. Supposedly a bear drowned, even, trying to swim out to it for an easy meal.

"It's got a foam core," Alex informs us all. "Foam doesn't sink."

"Neither do ghosts," someone says back.

"Why didn't you haul it in if you were so close?" JT asks. "Sheriff could give it back to his dad."

"It's nobody's elk," Marisa says back, ready to fight.

"Not even Jensen's?" a deep voice from the back of the room says.

"Okay, okay," I say. "Thank you, Marisa. Very informative. Next?"

"But—" Marisa says, and clicks one slide deeper.

It's a re-do of the "tines breaking the surface of Indian Lake" shot, just, at an angle, like Marisa had lost the handle on the camera or phone for a moment.

"Why's it so blurry?" Jen asks, not in a mean way.

"In *Night of the Living Dead*, Romero used cheesecloth over the lens to make the closing credits look like documentary footage," JT declares, like dropping the most boring fact bomb on all of us and not even slowing to see the explosion.

"Well, I'm sure Marisa—" I start, trying to keep Marisa from crying like she's done before, but then: "It's her!" Alex says, standing, his desk rising with him.

"Oh, shit," someone else adds on.

"What?" I ask, stepping forward.

"There, right there," Ellie says, stepping up to the screen to touch her finger to a V between two of this elk's briny tines.

"The Angel," someone intones.

I close my eyes, open them back to be sure this is really happening.

Lately there's been word of "the Angel of Indian Lake" moving along the shore, picking through the trees like looking for a lost earring. Or, in light of Christy Christy's presentation, Mrs. Henderson, not looking for an earring, but a golden pickaxe head.

It's just wishful thinking, though.

"Photoshop . . ." JT says again. "Shouldn't she have a shadow?"

"No, I don't even—I didn't see her until—" Marisa says, tears welling in her eyes.

"Believe it if you want," JT says to the rest of us.

I step closer, to see better, and JT's right. Something about this Angel is wrong, like Marisa or her big sister copied this from some La Llorona page online, smudged it into the background of this elk bobbing in the lake.

"Thank you, Marisa," I say, ending this. "Next?"

That deep voice from the back of the room says, "Me, ma'am."

This is followed by a gulp or two of silence, in case there's more coming. Class is nervous—understandably. Nobody's sure about Lemmy Singleton yet. Including me. Like, that *ma'am* he always uses for me: mockery or respect?

Lemmy Singleton is a question mark wrapped in a sphinx, in a very dark room.

But he's also a student in my seventh-period history.

I flourish my arm like rolling the red carpet out, giving him the floor, which is maybe a bit showier than absolutely necessary, but four tablets in ten minutes doesn't exactly do anything great to your inhibitions.

Lemmy stands, stands, and then stands some more.

Last time I saw him before the semester started was . . . my graduation? He was a kid then, barely ten, and after the massacre, Lana Singleton spirited him the hell out of this charnel house.

But he's back, and's probably six-five at least, and just as shaggy and biker as his namesake. I've seen him lurking in the parking lot after school, just leaned back on a fender, a cigarette loose in his fingers, and when he's wearing that curl-brimmed black cowboy hat with the dull pewter conches on the hatband—I know Lewellyn and Lana just named him what they named him because they'd been listening to "Ace of Spades" for their first kiss or something, but Lemmy, he's leaned into it, he owns it. Motörhead would be proud.

As for why he's back, word is he got kicked out of every high-dollar school Lana enrolled him in, so he finally made a deal with her: if he could come back here, finish where he'd sort of started, then he *would* finish.

Lana Singleton bought the spindly house way up Conifer that Donna Pangborne had built. Or, she got it anyway. With the Terra Novans, maybe they just give each other stuff like houses, I don't know.

The house is just for the physical address the school needs, though. Her and Lemmy don't *live* there. There's a yacht on the lake again, I mean. A 235-footer, if talk at Dot's is accurate, which is like overkill's big brother. But money's gonna do what money's gonna do. This time it's not moored, or anchored, or whatever you do to keep something that big in place. It's all over the lake, is working back and forth from shore to shore like a spider, crafting a web.

It and Rocky both.

I wonder what Hardy and Melanie think about it, out there above them like a bloated zeppelin. But I don't wonder too much, because it always lands me at the bench by the lake, smoking another thousand cigarettes.

I'm the one who keeps that bench clean now, yeah.

Who'd have ever thought.

"Jen?" I say, when Lemmy's just snarling at the connection hub.

She's our unofficial tech support.

She scuttles in under Lemmy's broad shoulders, isn't at all intimidated by his looming presence—Clarice Starling in that sausage party elevator.

"Good?" I ask her.

She's already backing away.

"Thanks," Lemmy says, even his quiet voice booming, which I try to convince myself must be a terrible burden to carry.

Who he reminds me of even more than his namesake? Rob Zombie's Michael Myers. All Lemmy'll have to do to give Teach a heart attack is wear a paper-plate mask to class tomorrow, for Halloween.

I wouldn't put it past him, really. I don't think the things he thinks are funny are what other people generally find amusing, which may be the cause of his multiple expulsions.

But—yes: his presentation flickers alive on the screen pulled down over the chalkboard. Unlike Christy Christy and Marisa Scanlon, this isn't a slideshow. It's a recording. A video.

"Drone . . ." Benji or Alex calls out, identifying it.

Just because Lemmy's got that outlaw mustache doesn't mean he doesn't have his mother's credit card. His footage is so high-res I don't doubt that it's military, somehow.

"The lake," I hear myself say.

Jen's the only one who hears me. She sneaks a polite look over, then flicks her eyes back to the front of the classroom.

Of *course* it's the lake. There some other giant body of water around here, for Lemmy to fly one of his drones over?

Most of the students maintain a sort of patter while their visual aid is on-screen.

Not Lemmy.

He's turned around, his hands clasping each other in front, just watching with the rest of us, and the way his drone's rocketing across Indian Lake, I can almost hear your ultralight buzzing, Mr. Holmes.

But I'm always hearing it, I guess.

"Here," he finally says, right before it happens: the image flickers into another mode—thermal imaging.

Predator eyes. Wolfen eyes.

The surface of the lake is cool, featureless, but . . . of course he's going to Terra Nova.

Goddamnit.

"Lemmy?" I say.

He looks over to me like the bother I am, then back to the screen.

Well then.

I guess we're doing this, aren't we?

When the drone crosses the threshold of the dock over there—it's the same one Tiara Mondragon died on—the playback slows down. Which I think means Lemmy was shooting at some impossibly fast speed or rate, high enough that he can slow it down here, to pump the drama up.

It's not just me feeling it either. Jen, the closest student to me, is sitting higher up in her desk as well, now.

Because the lead house, what used to be Letha's, doesn't quite have brick on it yet, Lemmy's drone can see right through it, to the construction workers in there doing their thing.

My heart jumps a bit, seeing these grunts hammering trim, hanging drywall, plumbing bathtubs.

"Lemmy, what's the educational value of this?" I ask, and cringe to hear it.

I am the girl who wrote all her papers on slashers, I mean.

But still.

He looks over enough that I can see his grin, but he doesn't say anything.

His drone banks high over Terra Nova, taking all the new houses in, and the playback switches to normal, no more heat-vision stuff, the speed accelerating all at once, which makes a body or two out there in the dimness of the classroom lean forward on accident.

Lemmy chuckles.

In the distance on the left, looking back to Proofrock, there's the new island everybody hates, that you would have found a way to sink, Mr. Holmes, but Lemmy . . . isn't going there?

He's skimming the water again, is slamming faster and faster to . . . to *himself*, standing on the spine of the dam, tablet in-hand as joystick, that trademark smirk on his face.

The drone is going to hit him, is going to hit him, knock him off the back of the dam, until—at the last moment, timing it perfectly, Lemmy steps to the side like a bullfighter, all his weight on one wore-down boot heel.

The drone plunges off that sudden concrete cliff and a few people in class gasp, which makes some others laugh. Two clap.

"Shh, shh," I tell them, because I'm stupidly thinking Lemmy needs concentration to keep this mad dive from flaming out.

The drone spirals down and down, down some more, to the big clearing around the creek, then jars left from that, following the over-grown rut-road.

"Lemmy, we only have—" I try, but then stumble a step ahead myself when the playback slams into torturous slow motion again, like the moment's straining to burst through, explode.

What's on-screen now, in high enough resolution that we can nearly smell it, is a paint horse. It's flicking its tail, looking up at the drone with ancient eyes. Its saddle has rolled around to under its belly, and there's frost on its haunches, and coating its long eyelashes.

"Oh, we should—" I say, like I'm the only one seeing this animal in need.

The drone's at about head-height now. Normal-person head-height.

"Wait . . ." Lemmy grumbles, leaning to the side a bit as if still directing the drone.

Around the horse, not close enough to scare the horse . . .

D, F, I'm telling myself inside. Lana Singleton's going to have to come in, talk to me about this. History? Where's the history, here? And, Mr. Holmes? I'm not giving Lana any slack, any special treatment.

But then Christy Christy, who's understandably sensitive to this kind of stuff, stands from her desk, her thermos and laptop shaking onto the floor.

"*No!*" she gets out through her hands.

It's Rex Allen's white Bronco, after all this time.

In the snow in front of it, and up on the root of a fallen-down tree, is Hettie Jansson, her head at a very wrong angle, blood all around her, even on her blocky camera in the snow beside her, and—

I step back into the blinds, my own hands steepled over my mouth, light splashing in all around me.

Is her *jaw* gone?

"Lemmy, Lemmy, did you—?" I start to say, but now Paul Demming is on-screen, speared through the neck on the root pan of a giant tree.

Paul who asked to sit by the window because he was claustrophobic. Hettie who always smelled like smoke, and wore her eyeliner so goddamn thick.

And off to the side, another dead kid, his insides very much on the outside. I don't recognize him at first, then: "Wayne Sellars," Ellie Jennings says, for us all.

"Lemmy, Lemmy—" I'm saying, pleading, and then . . . I'm the last one in the room to cue in that we have a visitor.

Standing in the doorway, squinting in this darkness, is Principal Harrison, in one of his five suits.

"Ms. Daniels?" he's saying, maybe for the second time.

"We've got to call—we need to—" I'm sputtering, but he hasn't clocked what's on-screen yet, is already doing his stepping-aside thing, to present—

Banner.

His eyes flick to me then back down the hall he's standing in. Like he's watching his six, and his ten, his two—the whole clock.

My heart drops in my chest.

I shake my head no to him, just the slightest, almost imperceptible movement, but for people who have been through the fire together, it's enough.

In return, Banner shrugs one shoulder maybe a sixteenth of an inch.

Lately he's taken to wearing the stiff brown cowboy hat that goes with that uniform shirt that hasn't been updated since 1962. He's holding the hat by the brim now, out of what feels like respect for these, um, hallowed halls of learning.

"No," I say to him, my eyes instantly hot. "This isn't—it can't be . . ."

"Um," he says, kind of hooking his head for me to follow him, so we can do this in a less public forum. Because, I'm sure he's thinking, it's not just someone we know this time, but probably even someone within hearing.

It can't be, though.

I try to picture Jen cranking Hettie's head around until it clicks over. JT, slinging Paul hard enough to impale on that dull root. Lemmy standing up on the dam before or after, and flicking a butt down the dry side, turning away while it's still falling.

"Do you like scary movies?" someone behind me says, not with a voice-changer but with that same kind of murderous chuckle that promises the game's only beginning, here.

"No, we're not done, we still have—" I say, trying to peer through the darkness for the clock on the wall, because if I have to be in here doing this, if I can just make it last and last, then . . . then I don't have to face what Banner's here for.

Whatever's starting again.

What Lemmy's drone already found.

"I've got it, Ms. Daniels," Harrison says, and when he makes to step to the front of the classroom, Lemmy doesn't step aside for him.

"*Hey*," Banner says to Lemmy, like a warning. A reminder of who's the high school senior, who's the sheriff.

Lemmy doesn't care about the law, though. He does look around to me, though.

I nod that this is okay, this is fine, this is . . . this is Proofrock, don't you know? Didn't your mom hide you in the diving-gear closet on the first version of the yacht, and then tag Rex Allen with a speargun when he opened the door, because anybody who wanted her precious boy, they were going to have to come through all five-foot-two of her?

You don't measure moms in height, though. You measure them in ferocity.

Lemmy steps to the side, lets Harrison take my class from me.

Walking across to the door, I look back to class like saying goodbye to them, like apologizing to them, like snapping one last picture of them that can be worth all the words, and the light from the projector sears this image of Hettie and Paul into my retinas.

I bring my hand up to shield my eyes and—

I'm still holding those two Post-it notes I peeled up from Hettie and Paul's chairs.

"What?" Banner says, the fingers of his right hand opening for the pistol he thinks he might need, because Jade, the girl always crying slasher, is alerting on some threat.

I shake my head no, nothing, and crumple the Post-its, trail them into the brown trashcan.

One says *Casey*, one says *Steve*.

Casey who was gutted and hung from her childhood swing, Steve who was tied to a chair in his letterman jacket and gutted just the same.

"Now where were we?" Harrison asks class, behind me.

Proofrock, I tell him, Mr. Holmes.

Proofrock, the day before Halloween.

When the monsters come out to play.

BAKER SOLUTIONS

Report of Investigation
22 July 2023
#01c22

re: Preliminary Observations, Regarding Vandalism to Deacon Point

As requested, Jennifer Elaine "Jade" Daniels's daily activities during the weeks of the vandalism in question:

A. Ms. Daniels meets irregularly with Letha Mondragon-Tompkins of Mondragon Enterprises. These meetings take place either at Dot's Coffee on Main Street, at the home of Letha Mondragon-Tompkins and Sheriff Banner Tompkins, or on the porch of Ms. Daniels's home. Two times (30 June and 16 July), Ms. Daniels has served as childcare provider for Mr. and Mrs. Tompkins. Preceding each of these babysitting engagements, Ms. Daniels turns around almost in sight of the Tompkins property, where she hides a machete under the leaf litter. She then returns to it from the Tompkins porch, (seemingly) to assure herself it's hidden well enough. Her reasons for electing to bring a gardening tool with her to a childcare obligation are unknown. The machete still has its factory edge, with the blade beveled to 35°—optimum for chopping, not slicing. *Note: a hacksaw was used for the vandalism of Deacon Point, not a machete.*

B. Once a week, Ms. Daniels participates in court-mandated therapy sessions with Dr. Sharona Watts, formerly of Jackson Hole, Wyoming. These sessions have been taking place in and around Founders Park in Proofrock, which, at this elevation, is sustainable for Summer. Fall and Winter weather conditions will surely force them to seek different locales for these sessions, however. Of note is that both Ms. Daniels and Dr. Watts have agreed to wear "Ghostface" masks (not robes) for these sessions, so as to promote "honest talk."

C. Twice to three times a week, Ms. Daniels visits the local cemetery. This is where the bulk of her cigarettes are smoked (American Spirit Originals). The headstone she grinds her cigarettes out on belongs to Grady "Bear" Holmes (74m-199). Though en route to that grave, Ms. Daniels often lets her fingertips slide across the tops of various other headstones. Presently, listening devices will be placed proximate to the Holmes headstone.

D. The end of each day often (only one [1] day missed over the three [3] week observation period) finds Ms. Daniels at the lakeside memorial bench for "Melanie Hardy, 1981–1993." Here she smokes more cigarettes. Unlike at the cemetery, however, she never leaves her butts in the gravel around the bench. Rather, she assiduously collects them in her hand, and instead of depositing them in the trashcan by the Pier, she walks them back to her home for disposal. Thus far she's said nothing in therapy sessions nor in digital/cellular communications about this practice, so presumedly it's a private ritual or superstition. *Note: local resident Jocelyn Cates similarly uses the memorial bench, sometimes requiring wordless coordination between her and Ms. Daniels.*

E. Ms. Daniels only visited Henderson High School once, on 4 July. She gained access through a window propped open for ventilation by the school's custodian, Regini "Rexall" Bridger. It took Ms. Daniels two attempts to gain entrance, as she was showing evidence of an emotional or psychological breakdown, which was affecting her focus and coordination. As the whole town was quiet for that holiday, everyone adhering to the directive to stay inside, "no fireworks, no boats" (communication from the Office of the Sheriff, 934-11i), Ms. Daniels's activities inside the high school were assessed indirectly, via an illicit video feed and its archived recordings discovered 27 April 2023 (see 12f in its entirety). On the recording, Ms. Daniels is in the women's room in the east wing, by the boys' gym. She's brought a pry bar with her, which she uses to deface a portion of the tiled wall above the mirror. Her efforts are incomplete, however, as her continuing emotional or psychological breakdown keeps leaving her collapsed onto the floor. She finally ceases her vandalism altogether to better indulge her breakdown, electing to lean against the trashcan and drag the claw of the pry bar up and down the thigh of her jeans, destructively, perhaps with suicidal intent (suicide accounts for 14% of all deaths of recent prisoners, per https://www .ncbi.nlm.nih.gov/pmc/articles/PMC4520329/). Ms. Daniels is through the denim and to the skin beneath when the door of this restroom opens. It's Letha Mondragon-Tompkins. She rushes to Ms. Daniels and embraces her, pushing their foreheads together. When this embrace is complete, Mrs. Mondragon-Tompkins stands holding the pry bar at port arms, as if judging its weight and effectiveness. Being both taller and stronger, and not suffering from an emotional or psychological breakdown, she's able to complete this destruction of school property Ms. Daniels had started. On their way out, Ms. Daniels stops, removes what appears on the recording to be a pen or pencil from her back pocket, and places it above the mirror, for no reason she's ever divulged in therapy or in any of her online or cellular/digital communications. Regardless, this wanton vandalism of school property is in keeping with a pattern of criminal behavior, including her efforts to resist the naming of Deacon Point.

BATTERIES NOT INCLUDED

"**Y**ou pulled me out of class just to see how I'm *doing?*" I say to Banner in front of the school. Right before pushing him back onto his sheriffy ass.

A dad in a gold Honda in the hug-n-go lane stands from his car and looks at us across his roof, a powdery white donut chocked in his mouth, his cellphone already recording what looks to be an "incident," which translates to *will get a lot of likes online.*

Like I'm not already on there enough.

I step over Banner, right onto the crown of his cowboy hat, and hold my middle finger across to this dad until he looks around like for help, then finally gulps his donut in like a snake swallowing an egg and folds himself back behind his steering wheel, pushes the button to roll his window up even though there's a sign asking waiting parents not to idle their cars.

I guess maybe teachers aren't supposed to flip parents off, either. If so, they should have said it in the faculty handbook. In big letters. In the chapter specifically for me.

"Jade, you can't just—" Banner says, clambering to his feet, and he could be talking about intimidating people in the hug-n-go lane, or this could be about assaulting law enforcement. When you're me, the shit kind of just accumulates.

I whip Banner's precious cowboy hat up from the stiff grass, punch the crown back out and fling it across to him, daring him to ask me for an apology.

"It's all . . ." he whines, working the flat brim around to inspect this damage.

"It's an Indian hat now," I tell him, and am already storming back to the front doors, to save my class from Harrison's pedagogy.

I feel like you for a moment, I mean, Mr. Holmes.

I don't have your wore-out loafers and brown slacks, your short-sleeved dress shirts and ties even I could tell were from a decade or two ago, but just like you, this girl will raise some serious hell before she lets anybody else tell her students what Idaho state history is, and isn't.

Except Banner's got hold of my arm.

I go to push him again but he's stronger than I am.

"Don't make me cuff you," he says through a forced, "public face" grin.

"Oh, you wanna try?" I say, pushing my inner wrists together right in front of his face.

"Jade, I—"

"*This* is my job now," I say, flinging a hand back to the school. "I'm not the girl who cried slasher anymore, can't you and Proofrock and the whole world get that through your head? It's not my job to—to . . . Hettie. Paul. I've already done it twice, haven't I? Isn't that e-fucking-*nough*?"

"That's not a word," Banner mumbles, ducking into the cowboy hat and moving it around to seat it right, which gets his head tilted down to exactly that Marlboro Man angle for what would be a knee-weakening instant, if there were someone here with knees that went weak like that.

"You're such an ass," I tell him, smiling to match him, for all the cameras in the hug-n-go lane. All the white-mouthed dads chewing their donuts and slurping their coffee and enjoying the show.

"I'm not really going to cuff you."

"It looks good on you, I mean," I say, knocking the underside of that wide brim with the back of my hand. "But don't wear it home. Not unless you want a little brother or sister for Adie."

"Are you ever *not* changing gears?" Banner says, working his hat down again, and sneaking a glance to the wall of windows in the school.

Lemmy's standing there watching us.

Meaning? Meaning maybe Harrison isn't as in charge in there as he wants to be.

Good.

"When's she back?" I ask, hooking my head for Banner to follow me away from all these eyes.

"We're talking about Leeth, now?"

"Here," I say, pinching his uniform sleeve to pull him through a tall hedge with me, to my second-best smoking cubby.

"She gets back tomorrow," he says about Letha. "That's why——"

"Did it work?" I ask.

Banner toes the grass with a cowboy boot, says, "It worked last time too, didn't it?"

One of the attachment points for Letha's new and mostly plastic jaw came slightly unmoored around a mouthful of organic baby carrots three days ago, so: airlift to Salt Lake, activate the top surgeons in the world.

"You ever watch *Joy Ride*?" I ask, sitting on my upturned trashcan and sparking up.

"To shift gears again," Banner narrates.

"2001, first of a trilogy," I tell him any-the-hell-way. "The big bad in there likes to rip people's jaws off to . . . you know. It's what he does. But none of them are as tough as Letha. That's what I'm saying."

"That she could have survived that movie?"

"The whole trilogy, with both hands tied behind her back."

"She won't even take the pain pills anymore."

"Good. I—inside, I knew a lot of those cottonheads. It was . . . it's ugly. Not good."

"But she cries from it."

He probably doesn't know it, but he rubs his jaw when he says that.

I nod, ash, squint.

"I'm not going out there with you," I tell him, pointing south with my cigarette, in the general direction of the dam, then waving the smoke away with my other hand. "I mean, I'm sorry for Hettie, I'm sorry for Paul, but it's not my—it's not my responsibility anymore, see? Every time I get involved, it's a one-way ticket to the big house."

"Paul *Demming*?" Banner asks. "Hettie *Jansson*?"

"Yeah, didn't you see the—in there?"

Lemmy's drone footage.

"I wanted to be the one to tell you," Banner says, a slowness to his delivery like he's reading from a memorized script. "Rex Allen finally turned up. And Francie."

"Yeah, obviously," I tell him right back. "But they've been dead for four years already? Aren't the freshly dead maybe just a teensy bit more important?"

"There's—" Banner starts, but doesn't know where he's going. He squints, rubs his chin with the web of his thumb and middle finger like that friction will get the right gears turning. "You're going to have to explain this to me, Jade. Please. Just make sense. I'm begging, here."

"You make sense first. Why *are* you here, Sheriff?"

"Because Rex Allen and Francie—"

"Yeah, the woods finally spit the Bronco up, great. Now how do you *know* about that? It's not exactly on a patrol route, I don't think. Is it?"

"This isn't public knowledge," Banner whispers, eyes darting around Dewey-style.

"And I'm not the public," I inform him. "You pulled *me* out of class? I didn't come down to your office for this."

"Photo in email," Banner mumbles. "Anonymous source. With coordinates. Like, longitude, minutes—"

"It's not a photo," I tell him. "It's a still from some drone footage?"

He processes this, staring into a point right beside my left shoulder, then says, "You have a drone?"

"I don't even know your email address, Banner. Have I *ever* emailed you?"

"I just didn't want you hearing about Rex Allen and Francie from . . . from anyone else," he says, talking through his fingers, all the friction against his chin not starting much of anything up in his head.

"I don't care about the former sheriff and his dead deputy," I have to say. "I mean, big tragedy, it sucks, but we all knew they weren't coming back. Hettie and Paul, though—"

"Is this about Jan, the little brother?" Banner asks. "Did Hettie take him with when her and Paul ran away? If you know something, if Hettie told you something, then—"

"He's with the dad. *Isn't* he? What do you know that I don't?"

"Not a lot, evidently."

"Then let me tell you, Sheriff. Jan Jansson wasn't out there."

"Out *where*, Jade?"

"Out *there*," I say, tilting my frustrated head dam-ward. "With Rexall and Francie?"

"Rexall?"

"Rex *Allen*. Wishful thinking, sorry."

Banner palms his phone, swipes into his email, presents the

guilty still: the wrecked Bronco, the dim form of Francie there through the windshield, the shadows too dark to show behind the steering wheel. Burned into the bottom of the image like a subtitle are those degrees and minutes in yellow LED-looking letters, that starved-down font where the tibia is so much skinnier than the knee joint.

"You went out there?" I ask.

"It's not Photoshop," Banner tells me, repocketing his phone.

"So you saw Hettie and Paul, then?"

"I don't . . . Paul Demming and Hettie Jansson ran away, Jade. Even Mrs. Jansson says it, that they'd been planning it since summer. You know about the divorce, the custody bullshit, all that drama. And as for Witte Jansson—what the *hell*?"

I slash my eyes over to whatever's stopped him midsentence, and he's leaning over to see into the hedge better, his right elbow high because that hand's cupping the butt of the pistol at his hip.

"Oh, yeah," I have to sort of confess. "Michael, this is Banner Tompkins, former football star, current sheriff. Banner, allow me to present . . . Michael Myers."

I'm talking to the cheapie white mask I've stuffed back into the branches, so you can only see it from a very certain angle. Because, in the 1978 *Halloween*, that's the only place Michael could have hidden when Annie jogged up to "catch" him after Laurie saw him lurking on the sidewalk ahead of them. I mean, okay, he could have scrambled and ran behind the house? But, is he ever undignified enough to run anywhere *else* in those ninety-one minutes?

Nope.

Meaning: he must have slid into that tall hedge, then just stood there *so*, so close to Laurie. Close enough to have reached out, hovered his hand over the shape of her shoulder.

Maybe this is my *best* hidey-hole for smoking, really.

"You're still a weirdo, you know that, don't you?" Banner says.

"I do keep coming back to this town, yeah," I say back, but with a sort of grin and shrug, then a long delicious inhale.

I hold it, hold it, my eyes watering with nicotine.

"So what is this about Paul Demming and Hettie Jansson?" Banner finally asks, eyes squinted in that way that makes me want to squint mine with him.

"I don't—I just saw that footage," I tell him. "Something happened to them out there."

"*By* Rex Allen and Francie."

"But they're not out there now, that's what you're saying? What about Waynebo's horse? Paul's motorcycle?"

Banner shakes his head no, but it's slower, now.

"Wonder if Wayne Sellars is in class today?" I say, sneaking a look back to the school.

Banner shrugs, says, "Why Wayne?"

"He was with them too."

"In this . . . *footage?*" Banner clarifies.

"Lemmy's drone," I mutter, not interested in this part. "I think he just found them randomly, flying around. You know how drone-crazy he is."

"*Them* being Rex Allen and Francie."

"And Hettie and Paul and Waynebo. But not Jan."

"Sounds like I need to have a discussion with Lemmy Singleton."

"He's not exactly a talker."

"You volunteering to be his counsel, Ms. Daniels?"

"Yeah, I was in long enough to become a history teacher *and* a jailhouse lawyer."

"But you vouch for him?"

"I don't even vouch for myself."

"'It can be anybody,' yeah," Banner drolls. "Believe me, that's gospel to Leeth."

"Any trust you give will be used against you," I sort of recite. From my own personal creed.

"How long has Lemmy had this footage?" Banner asks.

"He presented today," I say. "I guess . . . I don't know? Does it matter?"

"If he found it a week ago and's just now showing it, yeah, that matters."

"It wasn't due until today."

Which is about as weak out loud as it was in my head. Sorry, Lemmy.

"So you were only here to tell me about Sheriff Allen and his deputy," I say, ticking all this off out loud. "Because you thought it might be a shock for me to hear it in the teachers' lounge. But someone's removed the three actually *fresh* bodies. And their motorcycles and horses."

"*Alleged* fresh bodies," Banner tags on.

"I bet there's knobby tire tracks out there," I say. "Hoof prints?"

Banner doesn't answer.

"You just drove over everything, didn't you?" I ask, already knowing the answer. "Listen, Hettie's jaw is . . . it's—you know. And Paul's got this tree root through his neck. And Waynebo's all—"

I mime my torso, tearing open.

"Just like a movie," Banner says.

"And now you're here, all—all *Jade, quick, hurry, if we time this just right, we can get our necks on the chopping block! C'mon, it'll be great this time! There's no way we survive!*"

"Which would be an admission that I can't handle it myself, if there were even anything to handle," Banner adds. "Thanks for the vote of confidence."

"You think I voted for you?"

"Ex-cons can't vote."

"Thanks for the remind."

"I'm not here because of whatever Lemmy faked for his presentation," Banner says, flinging the backs of his hands at the school. "And I don't know anything about horses and motorcycles."

"So it never happened," I tell him.

"No body, no crime," Banner says, hearing it a moment after he says it and sucking air in, pressing his lips together about it. "Sorry," he says.

"No, no, you're right," I say, never mind that he accidentally brought my father's corpse up from the lake as much as it's ever *been* up. "And, even if Hettie and Paul and Waynebo *were* out there? Guess what? This still isn't my thing anymore."

"Never thought I'd hear you of all people say that."

"Yeah, well." I hold my nearly bitten-through fingers out as exhibit one. For exhibit two, I direct him down to my work heels, where I'm already waggling the seven toes I have left in my nude knee-highs.

"You're darker than that, aren't you?" Banner says about my feet, his hand opening like his fingers want to touch, in spite of his head telling them not to.

"Who's shifting gears now?"

"Just, they don't match your—"

The rest of me, my skin, the Blackfeetness I got from my dad.

"They're white girl feet now, yeah. Move along, Sheriff. Move along. I'll buy the dark-girl ones when they're back in stock."

"Guess they don't exactly fly off the shelves around here," Banner admits.

"Wrong altitude, wrong decade," I say in agreement, blowing smoke again, this time into the bushes, like sharing my cigarette with Michael. "So you're not here to drag me out to the dam, make me look at dead bodies. Then why am I not in there talking about the Oregon Trail?"

"That's what Lemmy was presenting on?"

"Why are you here, Banner?"

"Adie," he says, catching my eyes for just long enough to tell me this is serious.

I come up from the bucket all at once, am right in his face.

"*Where is she?*" I demand.

Of all the promises I've made, the one I can't ever break, no matter what, is to protect that little girl, to go to the wall for her every time, no thinking involved.

"Whoah, whoah, she's fine, godmother," Banner says, backing off, into the hedge. It doesn't give, would never admit anybody, no matter how bad they needed to hide, no matter which mechanic's coveralls they've got on.

"Then what?" I insist.

"You might want to sit back down for this."

"And you might want to kiss my brown ass, Sheriff."

Banner rolls his lips in, rubs his scruffy chin with the pads of the fingers of his right hand, knows better than to push me.

Moving slow so this won't be in any way aggressive, he takes the cigarette from my fingers. I watch this happening the same way a scientist who just gave a monkey its first cup of Jell-O might peer into a smelly cage.

"Wouldn't your ass be, you know," he says, very delicately, "*white*, if you're wearing those?"

He tilts his head down to my feet, is talking about my knee-highs, which I guess he thinks are full-on hose. Like I'd ever stoop that low? Harrison can boss me around up to the hem of this stupid skirt, but no further than that.

"Okay, then you can kiss my *white*-girl ass," I tell him. "Might take some aiming, though. You know how we watch what we eat, mostly do yoga."

Banner chuckles and, holding my eyes, inserts the butt of my cigarette into his mouth and inhales all at once, like having to do it before the rest of him can clock just what it is he's trying.

Immediately, he's coughing and coughing, his hands on his knees, kickstands to prop his body up. After a few more coughs that come, I think, from his soul, a thin line of puke strings down and down, barely touches the ground. Of what was going to be my favorite smoking cubby.

"Well, that was pretty," I tell him.

"Thought it would—*help*," he says, dry heaving again.

I guide the cigarette away from him, hold it high and draw deep on it, that cold heat swirling in my chest, so black and wonderful.

"Must be something really bad," I say down to Banner.

He nods, snorts, coughs once more into his hand, then says, "Adie's with . . . she's at the office."

"Bring your daughter to work day?"

"Keep your daughter safe day," Banner says. "But Jo Ellen and Bub have to be doing deputy stuff, you know, not—"

"Not babysitter stuff."

Banner nods, kind of squinches his face up, the obvious question right there in his pleading, scared-to-say-it eyes.

"You want me to be in The Babysitter Murders," I say, doing the narrating myself, now. "That's the original name for *Halloween*, sort of."

"You never stop, do you?"

"Or *When a Stranger Calls*, right? The call's coming from inside the house, know that one? 1979, year after *Halloween*. But the short film it was based on came even before—"

"I don't care, Jade."

It seriouses us down a smidge.

"So you want me to babysit, and you know I'll say yes," I tell him. "But it couldn't have waited twenty minutes?"

He looks to a honk from the hug-n-go lane, but here in what used to be the best smoking cubby in the world, all we can see are leaves and branches. And Michael Myers.

"It's just—" he says, wiping his mouth with the back of his hand and then studying it like unsure what to do with a loose runnel of vomit. "Bub and Jo Ellen, I need them to be . . ."

Instead of finishing, he looks up.

I follow his lead.

"Hold your cigarette over there," he says, directing my hand away. The smoke above us stays. I close my eyes to taste it.

"Woodsmoke," I identify, my word balloon dripping with icy dread. "Oh, no. No no no. Don't tell me the fucking *forest* is on fire again?"

The last time Caribou-Targhee burned, or tried to, I had to smash into the dam's control booth to raise the lake. The time it burned in the sixties—we haven't gotten to that unit yet in class.

But maybe we should have.

"Campers or Boy Scouts?" I ask.

"Seth Mullins," Banner says right back.

"The *game warden*?"

Banner nods. "He's . . . not taking it well. About Francie."

Since December 2019, when his wife went down the mountain with Rex Allen to find Dark Mill South, Seth Mullins has been walking the trees all along the highway, looking for that white Bronco. So far, he's found my dad's high school Grand Prix on the drive up to the dam, he's found a sixteen-foot camper from the seventies that must have been the definition of "off the grid" back when, he's found two poacher camps, one of which used to be an outfitters camp, and—so he says—he even stumbled on Remar Lundy's ancient old cabin halfway up the mountain.

But no dead wife.

"So he's not taking it well," I say, obviously.

"We had to radio the rangers so they could patch us over to him," Banner says. "They said he's been living in one of those fire towers, swimming in the lake every day, living like Jeremiah Johnson or something. The tower's what he set fire to while I was talking to him on the radio. He told me he was doing it, that he was, like, watching his hands do it."

"Burning down the place you're supposed to report a fire from," I say. "I like it."

"Not if the forest goes up."

"It's a love letter to Francie."

"It's hate mail to her being dead."

"Think he stayed in it?"

Banner shrugs. "I saw him a few weeks ago. His beard is . . . it's a grief beard, I think. And his hair's all pandemicky, you know."

"Beards can catch fire, can't they?" I say, thinking out loud. "He could get all scarred up."

"This isn't a movie, Jade."

"If you go down in the woods today, you're in for a big surprise," I recite, then, when Banner's looking over, waiting: "*Rituals*, 1977. Also called *Deliverance 2*. Hell if it's not a movie."

"You're still doing this?"

"Dude in that has a beard. And's kind of on a rampage."

"Does Letha know it, this movie?"

"More important, does she know about Hettie and Paul yet?"

"And Wayne Sellars," Banner's sure to work in, his tone dismissing all three of these supposedly dead bodies. "And, you still haven't told me how you know about Terry."

"'Terry'?"

"Wayne Sellars' horse."

"Never heard of a horse with a name like that."

"Short for Terrance," Banner says. "So you're saying there's more to that drone footage?"

"You sound like him."

"'Him'?"

"Your predecessor."

"Rex Allen?"

"Hardy. He asked me the same thing once. 'How did I know about what happened to that Dutch boy and his girlfriend?'"

"The one Letha found at my party, in high school?"

Like that, I'm back there again, the bonfire trying to die down.

Letha in the shallows with a corpse she thinks she can breathe back to life.

It's sort of where everything starts.

"There was a *girlfriend*?" Banner asks. "Thought only a guy ever turned up?"

"Ezekiel's Cold Box," I say, using my lips to point out to the lake.

What I don't add: that blond girl's down there with my dad, now. And Stacey Graves, if that big pale hand that wrapped around her ankle was really Ezekiel's.

I'm sorry, I say to the Dutch Girl and to Stacey Graves. *I hope he's a lot deader than either of you*. Really, though? My dad in the lake, all he'd be doing is scrounging for beer bottles that have been dropped down there, for if they have just half a drink left in them.

And he'd be more interested in someone Stacey Graves's age than that Dutch girl's, I guess.

"What are you doing?" Banner asks.

Just closing my eyes against the world, I don't say.

I don't know if I'm telling Sharona any of this, either.

Probably not.

I've been talking to counselors and therapists since I was seventeen, I mean. One thing I've learned is not to tell them anything that makes them tap their pens against their lower lips and say "interesting," with all this open space opening up after, for us to "discuss" and "work through."

Can't I just seal stuff in a barrel, roll it into the cellar, and forget about it? Please? Talking about it all just keeps it alive and happening, when "dead and buried" is what it should be.

That being a zombie movie from 1981, Alex.

Which makes my *student* "Alex" turn around in his desk in the classroom in my mind, damnit.

Trebek, then. *Dead & Buried* is a zombie movie from 1981, "Trebek." Said with that early James Bond lilt.

"No, I don't want the forest to burn," I monotone to Banner, like that's what he was asking—like I had my eyes closed so I could pray the fire away, I don't know. Stupider shit's surely happened.

"Jo Ellen and Bub are on it," Banner says, hitching his pants up like he's in a Western. "They'll find him too. Seth, I mean."

"Not if he doesn't want to be found, they won't."

"He can't stay out there forever."

I shrug, say, "Ginger Baker did?"

Not *forever*, but she did live for four weeks out there, once upon a post-massacre. If a junior-high city girl can live that long on berries and dew and whatever, then how long can someone last who actually *knows* the woods, the animals, the seasons?

Next time we see Seth Mullins, he might look like Dewey from the second-to-last *Scream*: grey, grizzled, a sort of wince to his step.

Letha sends me a lot of catch-up movies, yes. I try to work them in between the loop I have the 1999 *Mummy* on—a loop I wish I even halfway understood.

"They really made a second *Deliverance*?" Banner asks then. "But didn't that squeal-like-a-pig guy die?"

"It's not really a follow-up," I tell him, watching the smoke wisp across the sky. "Kind of like . . . you know how Romero's *Dawn of the Dead* was released in Italy as *Zombi*, without the *e*? Then Fulci's *Nightmare Island* was retitled *Zombi 2*—still no *e*—to cash in?"

"Why do the Italians hate the letter *e*? Oh, oh, wait. It's not in their name, is it? I get it now."

"This is great, talking to you. We should do it all the time."

"You started it."

"Yeah, well, I'm ending it."

To prove it, I crush my cigarette out on the sole of my high heel. Well, "mid-heel," I guess, but high to me, anyway.

Banner watches, waits for me to be done.

"You haven't said no," he says. "About Adie."

"This is because Hettie's little brother went missing, isn't it?" I say. "One kid disappears, so the rest of them might too? Including yours?"

"I—"

"No, it's good thinking," I tell him, taking his shoulder in my hand. "You're a good dad, Banner Tompkins."

To my surprise, this makes him blink fast.

He fumbles for his chrome shades, slides them on so no feelings accidentally escape.

"Still a man, so, ninety percent an idiot," I add, taking my hand back like I might have caught something. "But you're a good dad to her. Letha chose well."

"Sorry for . . . class," Banner says, cranking his head around again for a longer honk out there in the hug-n-go lane.

"I'll walk away from anything for Adie, you know that. Even this job."

"It's not just—"

"And while we're talking slashers," I say, resisting the urge to fire up another cigarette.

"We're talking slashers?"

"Two kids dead in the woods?"

"Three the way you tell it, but sure."

"And now we already have a Leonard Murch," I say, tilting my head up to the smoke—the forest, about to be burning.

"That dude from . . . *The Munsters*?"

"You're thinking of Lurch. From *The Addams Family*? Leonard *Murch* is the red herring for *Prom Night*. The Jamie Lee Curtis one."

"Like that first zombie in *Night of the Living Dead*?"

"Forget it. I'm just saying we have a red herring already."

"'Already' . . . you mean *Seth Mullins*?"

"Harry Warden wore a miner's outfit. Seth Mullins has a game warden uniform, might as well be the ranger in, well, *The Ranger*."

"But—"

"He's pissed off, he lives in the woods . . . shit. I couldn't have designed him better, I don't think."

"But it's not him," Banner says.

"That's what I'm saying. He's a red herring."

Banner pulls a pained expression, looks away.

"What do you know?" I say. "There's more here, isn't there?"

"If you'd ever slow down and let me say it."

I flourish my hand out, giving him the floor, but right when he opens his mouth, another car out there honks.

"It always like this?" he asks about the hug-n-go lane.

"There's a fire across the lake," I tell him. "Parents want to pick their kids up and hit the road, get the last hotel room before it's gone. But you were telling me something?"

"The reason it's not Seth Mullins," Banner says, like he's playing this for drama, "is that . . . do you know Sally, um—" He grubs the notebook from his chest pocket up, flips it open, reads, "Chalumbert. Sally Chalumbert."

"She used to live here, what?"

It's a stab in the dark. The name doesn't mean anything.

Banner shakes his head no, lowers the notebook, his cop instincts pulling him to all the honking just forty yards away.

It really is getting sort of excessive.

"Um, she, Sally Chalumbert," Banner leads off. "She was that Shoshone woman up in Elk Bend who—"

"Put Dark Mill South down the first time," I finish, my face going cold.

Banner gives a terse nod.

"And?" I add.

"She broke out of her, um, facility."

"Which was in Idaho?"

"A tourist reported a woman with crazy hair stowed away behind the cab of a semi headed up the mountain."

"Shit."

"Yeah, shit."

"A real live escaped mental patient."

"Can you really say it like that anymore?"

"It's the sub-genre we're in," I explain. "Slashers come in two basic flavors, revenge and mad-dog. That second kind, it's usually an escaped mental patient. *Slumber Party Massacre, Stage Fright*, even him"—Michael, watching us from the wall of hedge. "And here I am, right?"

"Here *you* are?"

"I've done time in a facility like hers, haven't I? And I'm about to be a babysitter, on top of that? Shit, can you draw any redder of an X on me?"

"Listen, I just wanted to see if you can help with Adie until Leeth's back, but if you think she's coming for you, this Sally Chalumbert, then—"

"Why does this keep happening?" I ask. Just generally. Philosophically.

"It's the lake, I think," Banner says, parting the hedges a little with his hand, like to set eyes on the water. "It's . . . I don't know. I don't think it should have been a lake? Like, it should still be a creek, maybe."

"Maybe it's that golden pickaxe down there," I mumble.

Banner flicks his eyes back to me about this, but I don't explain Christy Christy's presentation.

"Just, I need to send Bub and Jo Ellen over there to help with Seth Mullins," he says.

". . . and the fire keeps all the authorities occupied," I fill in. "And it's almost Halloween, and there's two—*three* kids dead, and our hero isn't even here."

"Letha?"

I nod.

"What about you?" Banner asks, weakly.

I shake my head no, wrong, not me.

"I'm a teacher now, remember?" I say. Then, quieter, "And the Cassandra, too, I guess."

"*She* used to live here?"

"A Cassandra's someone doomed to know the truth but nobody believes her. I'm like the sidekick, the Randy. Good for a little comedy breather, some out-loud exposition, but ultimately not a real factor."

"That's not what Leeth tells me."

"She wouldn't," I say. "She's good like that. Most final girls are."

"It was you who killed Dark Mill South."

"Yeah, well. He wasn't even the real killer."

"And Stacey Graves."

"Remind me why I'm your babysitter? Because I like to drown little girls?"

"Letha says if . . . if anything ever happens to her, that—"

"Don't," I interrupt. "Even saying it is bad luck."

"She says you'd be a good . . . that you'd take care of Adie. You'd help."

Now it's me who's batting my eyelashes too fast.

I'm seeing myself hanging laundry on the line in May, a little girl hugged tight to my knee because snowflakes are falling right here in *summer*.

But, "No, never," I say. "I will watch her, though, at least until Letha—"

This time I'm interrupted. By rending metal, shattering plastic.

A long, plaintive scream, the kind that makes the moment syrupy and slow.

Moving through it tenth of a second by tenth of a second, I register that Banner's already got his pistol up by his face, his precious cowboy hat hanging in the open air behind his head, surely going to fall but not falling yet, just hanging there.

In the time between that hat starting its tumbling descent to the ground and the crown actually touching the dirt I've packed down from standing here so many times, my stupid head slaloms me through all the boats and bodies Stacey Graves left in the lake, slams me to a stop in the snow on Main Street, Dark Mill South standing over me, except when I look past him, it's not my mom standing up from that snowmobile back there, it's Hettie and Paul and Waynebo dead in the woods, and I swear my heart can't take any more of this, I can't do this again, please.

I told Banner I'd done my duty, served my tour, that that five o'clock whistle's already blown for me, that I can come blinking up from the slasher mines and leave all its pickaxes and masks behind me.

Truth is, though, it never should have been me.

In our second session, Sharona said something about imposter syndrome—me not thinking I was worthy, me certain everyone was going to see that I just got lucky, that I wasn't really final girl material—but then she reeled that back in when it clicked for her that she was just reinforcing my "fantasy" version of events, which is supposed to be my elaborate defense mechanism: how my head makes sense of all the trauma.

Maybe, I don't know.

Either way, I wasn't lying to Banner when I told him I can't do this again. Imposter or not, I don't have the nerves for it anymore. When that woman out there screamed, I mean? At first I thought it was me.

"C'mon!" Banner hisses, that pistol still up by his face, his eyes ready for anything.

I shake my head no but he's got my wrist, is fording the hedge, and bringing me along.

The smoke from Seth Mullins's fire is thicker out here.

Banner hooks me behind him, is aiming everywhere at once.

The woman screaming is on her knees beside what must be her SUV, and this isn't a fear-scream, I can tell. It's a birth-scream. The kind that wells up in you whether you want it to or not, when you've been dragged from a place you thought was safe into a much, much worse place.

I understand.

Two cars ahead of her in line, the truck that just rear-ended the gold Honda is trying to extract its front bumper from the Honda's crunched-in trunk. The truck's rear tires are boiling white smoke up and up, like they're spinning in bleach. When the smell rolls over to us, I have to cover my nose with the back of my wrist, which unmoors me from Banner.

Floating in the moment now, I have to wonder if this is all a hallucination. Have all my fears and paranoias balled up inside me with the four tablets swirling through my bloodstream to play my own personal horror movie in my head?

Except I only like one kind of horror movie.

When the truck finally breaks free, it flings the Accord up over the curb, sends it skating across the cold grass.

It comes to a stop maybe twenty feet in front of Banner. Twenty feet and eight or ten more inches from me, because I'm slightly behind him.

Shaking my head no, I step around Banner to be sure I'm seeing the last thing I want to be seeing: the dad behind the wheel, he doesn't have a head anymore. His neck stump is still gouting blood. His hairy-fingered hands, just like Pamela Voorhees's, are grasping at his throat, like to stop this from happening, except . . . one of his stupid white donuts, it's around his thumb.

Which is just a nothing-detail I'm trying to make mean something, so I don't have to take in the whole, I know, Sharona. I know I know I *know*.

"We've got to—" I start, not saying the rest of it: *get to Adie*.

Just thinking her name alerts me to a motion in my peripheral vision, way over to the left, right at the corner of my left eye, already wriggling away.

At first I think it's Adie scuttling under the fence Harrison put up to keep students from walking the deer path. But kids in Proofrock have been coming to class that way for decades. Before first bell, that chain-link was split into a flap, like on a tipi in a coffee table book about Indians.

And Bub and Jo Ellen are deputies, not babysitters, but still, if their sheriff tells them to keep his daughter at the station, then that's where she is.

Not here.

But—I'm processing what I just sort of saw, trying to cobble it into something real—if that was actually a kid scuttling under the fence, did he or she or they have a full head of hair?

I open my mouth to outscream that mother by her SUV, to fill Pleasant Valley with my voice, my terror, loud enough that it washes over the dam, flows down into Idaho, but then clap my hand over my mouth. Not to stop the sound bubbling up, but to clamp my jaw in place.

Because I remember.

But . . . she can come ashore, onto *land*?

This doesn't have to be Stacey Graves, though.

It doesn't, it doesn't. It isn't. It can't be.

"Ch-Ch-*Chucky*," I manage to get out instead, about the small form, because an evil doll from a movie is something I can process, deal with it, understand.

"What, *who*?" Banner says, swinging his pistol every direction.

You can't see everything at once, though. That's one of the rules. That's what's so wonderful, and so terrible.

Another rule is that only one person sees the killer at a time.

This way it's not real enough to call the big guns in. This way it can just be one girl's fears, making her see things.

Trying to be calm and not draw attention, I step back against the hedge, to fade from view, but, feeling behind me for the entry point, I think I feel Michael take my hand.

BAKER SOLUTIONS

Report of Investigation
2 August 2023
#01c26
re: Incidents of Vandalism

Jennifer Elaine "Jade" Daniels is solely responsible for the re-occurring vandalism at the location hereafter referred to as Deacon Point, the pronounced spit of land in front of the former Camp Winnemucca on Indian Lake just outside the township of Proofrock in Fremont County, Idaho. See 18a-17 through 18a-34 for photographic confirmation on 18 June 2023, and 11 July 2023; the 11 July series, the "hacksaw shots," confirm her identity the clearest, as she had to saw on the newly planted sign's post for eight minutes and fifty-seven seconds. As our continuing search uncovers more evidence, it will be included in subsequent reports, along with other material(s) apposite this vandalism.

Means of ingress:

Undetermined, though the only two possibilities, save delivery from the sky, are approach by land or approach by water. As the trail camera activates upon motion within its maximum sensing radius of forty feet, the attached photographs solely document Ms. Daniels's presence and activities, not her means of delivery or egress. However, as is evident in 18a-22 and 18a-26, where Ms. Daniels's blouse [sic] and jeans are dry, then it's safe to assume she didn't swim.

In addition, in the three (3) months since her release from South Idaho Correctional Institution ("SICI"), Ms. Daniels has never been observed participating in any variety of cardiovascular training save the irregular walks necessitated by her never having acquired a state driver's license. When her smoking habit is taken into consideration (average of one-third of a pack per day), then the chances of her having either the conditioning or the lung capacity to navigate the lake's waters at night are low (average summer temperature, 52°F/11°C). In addition, there are no indications swimming was ever part of Ms. Daniels's lifestyle, either for sport or for leisure, to say nothing of the psychological and/or emotional trauma her therapy sessions [see subsequent reports] establish she associates with the lake, and lake activities generally.

Which of course leaves either delivery by water craft or an overland approach. If her multiple approaches to Deacon Point have been by land, then she's either crossing the dam at night, presumably without a flashlight, or she's taking what Proofrock locals call "the long way." This manner of ingress entails following the unmaintained hunting/logging road south of the dam, across Indian Creek, and then walking along the high bluff behind Deacon Point to the periphery of the Terra Nova subdivision, which shares a shore with Deacon Point. As such an elliptical approach would take no less than two and a half hours, provided no motor vehicles were used for the early portion of the journey, it's unlikely it would be Ms. Daniels's first choice. Efforts are in-process to ascertain Ms. Daniels's whereabouts for the three hours leading up to the vandalism on the nights of 18 June 2023, and 11 July 2023.

If Ms. Daniels's approaches to Deacon Point have been by water, then presumably she has an accomplice. Otherwise her skiff or boat would have been dragged up onto the spit for her return, and thus been present in the background of the photographs. However, in-situ tests have demonstrated that there exist blind spots proximate to Deacon Point but outside the trail camera's sensing radius that could, with foreknowledge, be used to "hide" a water craft.

As for the form of water craft Ms. Daniels must be using to cross from Proofrock to Deacon Point, the options are numerous, Proofrock being a lake community. The so-called "town canoe" was, until recently, a viable option, as are the many kayaks stored against sheds and garages. Just as viable are the various skiffs and jon boats moored to docks or in wet garages along the bank of Indian Lake, many of which are outfitted with trolling motors. Presumably, any Jet Skis or other recreational water craft would be too loud for a clandestine approach, and the local sheriff claims the airboat his department was gifted by a former sheriff (1996 Air Ranger) is currently awaiting a new throttle assembly.

As for the ultralight Ms. Daniels is purported to be assembling in her backyard, and the remote chance that her approaches have been by air, we can confirm that this ultralight is neither complete nor airworthy. See 002-a17 for a list of the items she's purchased to incorporate into this project, which suggest airworthiness is not the goal. Rather, this "ultralight" [sic] would appear to be a trophy or an art installation [see 002-b01–b02]. Note the purchase of three wheels/tires intended for wheelbarrows, and the abundance of 3/4" brass unions. As Ms. Daniels would presumably have to gain enough elevation to parachute in to Deacon Point and then build a new ultralight after the one she abandoned crashed into Caribou-Targhee National Forest, this is the least likely of her methods of approach.

Of note regarding Ms. Daniels's means of approach to Deacon Point is that, in 18a-30, Ms. Daniels is barefoot, suggesting that her approaches haven't been overland. See 45y-22 for a cast of that bare foot, which could indicate Ms. Daniels "borrowed" a paddleboard for these nocturnal vandalism excursions.

As for the aforementioned hacksaw Ms. Daniels used to fell the "Deacon Point" sign (which sign she then disposed of in the lake), she attempted to hide it under the floorboards of one of the cabins. The hacksaw currently under those floorboards is the same model and color as the one she used, and has been outfitted with the same wear patterns. The blade is still functional.

NIGHT CREW

Adie's standing with her hand to the cold glass of Banner's office window. She's this small little thing touching her palm to the vast darkness out there, and all I want to do is stack cinderblocks around her, to keep her safe.

Build a tower around a girl like that, though, and it's not anybody on a white horse who shows up to spirit her away. It's a dragon.

And, this being Proofrock, that dragon probably has a machete.

Not that whoever left that head in the hug-n-go lane needed a blade at all. But watching Adie be her cute little self stops that neck stump from pumping blood through my vision over and over.

Well, it slows it down to a burble, anyway.

"Mommy?" she says about the red and white plane swooping down from the sky to skim the surface of the lake, some hatch or scoop in its belly opening up to drink a few hundred more gallons of water in, to rain down on the fire. It's flicking condensation off your beer into the raging bonfire, but I guess you do what you can.

"No, baby, that's not her plane," I say to Adie, my voice so pleasant and neutral.

I'm standing right beside her, can see our reflections in the glass, but there's a much larger form standing right there with us too, maybe a little more see-through—Sheriff Hardy. My senior year of high school, we stood here just the same, watching Mr. Holmes sputter and glide back across from Terra Nova, a wing of his ultralight shot through with a nail gun.

"But Mommy'll be here soon," I add for Adie, and hitch her up onto my hip.

I don't think it's a lie?

Unless air traffic's shut down. She's Letha Mondragon, though, and her baby's here, and her man's here, and this is her town, her home. She'll buy a set of car keys from the first person she sees, setting them up for life, and she'll look up the mountain like Sarah Connor staring the future down, and then she'll put her foot all the way in it, kill that car getting up to us.

It's not a lie, Adie. Mommy really will be here.

Assuming there's still a *here* to come back to.

Past the lake, a mile or ten into the national forest, is the fire.

For the moment it's just an orange glow and roiling smoke, and ash sifting in to coat everything pale, making Proofrock feel like a ghost town, like an in-process Pompeii, layer by sooty layer.

I can still see the taillights through the grey haze, though. Everybody who can, they're getting the hell out of Proofrock, never mind that we've always been guaranteed a big dump of snow by Halloween. A lot can burn down overnight, though.

"Daddy?" Adie says next, about the large form on Melanie's bench, watching this fire.

"No, honey," I say, and twirl Adie away before she can ask who it is, then.

Rexall.

He's got his afterwork do-rag tied around his head, the two tails of the bandanna drooping down over his face like handlebar eyebrows, and there's a boombox propped onto the bench beside him. I can't hear it from Banner's office, but it's his nineties rap music, I know. He used to play it in the gym when he was waxing the floor and thought it was just him in the building.

Thing is? After the settlement he got from Letha, for how she peppered him with bird shot, he doesn't even need to stay in Proofrock anymore, I don't think. Still? He's head custodian for Golding Elementary and Henderson High the same as ever, never misses a day.

Far as I know, he didn't buy a truck or anything with his windfall, not even a bigger boombox, just socked that quarter-mil away, toasted the world with his first beer of the night, and settled back into his ratty chair.

But he has spent one chunk of his change, I guess. According to Banner, Rexall's been granted the necessary permits for running a submersible drone through Indian Lake—a little remote-control sub with a camera for an eye.

He's looking for his best friend, I know.

My dad.

Last time Rexall left that submersible in its wagon by the side of his house to dry out, I hear somebody ripped all its guts out.

Some people, right?

I've also been into the ceiling of the faculty restroom, and am working my way through all the restrooms and locker rooms of the high school. I leave the little pinhole cameras on the wordless mat in front of Rexall's door, trailing their eye-stalk cables, their glass lenses stomped useless. It's up for debate whether I've saved Proofrock twice already or nearly killed it two times, but this is my real legacy.

And, yes, Banner already knocked on Rexall's door in an official capacity when Navene Jansson came in about Jan being gone. When a little kid's gone missing in Proofrock, you maybe go speak to the local Chester the Molester, just because you can't leave any stone unturned, even when you don't really want to see what's under that stone.

Rexall sat on the porch while Banner searched his house from the top shelves of the closets to the bottom of the lowest drawers, and Rexall even left his just-cracked-open beer inside, so no picky law enforcement officers could haul him in for public intoxication.

There were no kids in hidden rooms, no secret computers, no medieval dungeons, no serial-killer tackboards. And Banner says he knocked on every wall, then used an app on his phone to listen for even the slightest breath, the lightest finger tapping, the most quiet scrape of a shoe, the most rabbitty heartbeat.

"So you haven't seen him?" I imagine Banner asking on the way out, dipping his head to work that cowboy hat back on.

" 'Him'?" I hear Rexall asking back playfully, which is pretty much a confession: what interest would he ever have in a *boy*?

Next year Adie's in kindergarten at Golding Elementary.

Its ceiling tiles are very much on my to-do list.

"Do you want to draw some more?" I ask Adie with as much perk as I can, settling down on the couch beside her.

She shakes her head no.

"Juice?" I ask.

No.

"Mommy," she says in that quiet way that means she can start crying at any moment, here.

There's no way she can know that a dad had his head ripped off in the hug-n-go lane a few hours ago, but I'm pretty sure she can tell that this afternoon and evening haven't been business as usual, either. And there's probably some strain to Banner's and my voices. And our eyes are probably saying everything our mouths aren't. Kids aren't stupid, I mean. When you're small and can't fight yet, you learn how to watch the world around you for the slightest deviation, right?

There's deviations to go around, right now. Most nights, there's not red and white planes skipping across the surface of the lake. Most nights, it's not Adie and Aunt Jade locked in Daddy's office while he talks to the state detectives at what used to be Meg's desk, what I'll probably never be able to call Tiff's desk.

Things change, though, I have to remind myself. People move on, retire, pass the ring of keys down to the next generation.

And I shouldn't be so hard on Tiff, I know. Banner used to be an idiot too, didn't he? If Tiffany Koenig is going to be locked into the same kind of stupid she was in high school, then that means I'm stuck just the same, right?

The me from back then never gets trusted with this perfect little girl, though. The me from back then isn't at the sheriff's office at all. The holding cells, sure, been there, done that.

I'm different now. Tiff can be as well.

But not Proofrock. The massacre at Camp Blood might have been nearly sixty years ago, but it never really stopped. Where else do you lose your head just for going to pick your kid up from school?

According to the few witnesses not already jumping the curb out of the hug-n-go lane, they maybe saw a grimy little kid walking up between the cars? If they did, it was cute. A little gamey, maybe, letting a second-grader go from a mom's car to an aunt's all on their own, but this is small-town America, where it takes a village: everybody would watch out for this kid. Nobody would run them over.

But then that kid used their cute little arms and their cute little legs to climb up into the open-again window of that gold Honda.

A moment later—*rrriüpp!*—thick red blood splashed onto the glass. A breath or two after that, Carl Duchamp's head tumbled out the window, rolled under the car beside his so immediately and soundlessly that those close enough to see weren't even sure what they had or hadn't seen. A basketball? His box of powdered donuts? Did he actually just toss his bag from Dot's out *here*, right in front of the school?

With the few who saw this doing a doubletake to be sure they'd seen what they thought they'd seen, the kid had more than enough time to scramble out the other door, or the same window, nobody could say. It had taken Banner and the other parents a good five minutes to even work the nerve up to approach the Honda, sure a little badger of a human was going to snarl out, rip *their* heads off.

Yours truly was standing well away, of course. Step in the wrong mess, you can track it home.

Which doesn't mean I didn't stand at the two sets of double doors, guide Sadie Duchamp back in when she was rushing out with the rest of the school to see what all the fuss was about. It was a close thing, though. Until Banner dug Carl Duchamp's wallet up from his khakis, he was just a dude with a camera phone, trying to be internet-famous. But now he was a dad, too. Of Sadie, who both could and couldn't understand why all her classmates could go out, see what the fuss was all about, but not her.

"*What is it?*" she kept saying to me.

I didn't have the heart, just delivered her to the assistant principal's office, told the front desk she wasn't to leave until her mom got her, and anybody who let her slip past, out to the hug-n-go lane? They were answering to me, clear?

Crystal.

I could have walked home after that, too, but Banner was waiting for me, making eyes that said he needed the kind of private words a ride around Proofrock could provide.

"Is it her?" he asked, looking over from behind the steering wheel so I'd be sure to know who he meant.

"Can't be," I mumbled back to Banner, trying to find the button to get my window down. Mostly because the backseat of his truck could hide any number of Chuckies.

I wasn't lying that it wasn't her, but all the same, Christine Gillette's old jumprope song was already cycling through my head:

Stacey Stacey Stacey Graves
Born to put you in your grave

You see her in the dark of night
And once you do you're lost from sight
Look for water, look for blood
Look for footprints in the mud
You never see her walk on grass
Don't slow down, she'll get your ass

It's the "Look for footprints in the mud" part I can't stop thinking about in Banner's office, now.

Does it mean Stacey Graves *can* walk on land? Didn't Cinnamon tell me that her and Ginger found a bare footprint on shore, once? I've seen Stacey Graves up close and way personal, though, and that kid I saw scampering under the chain-link was shaggy and dirty and feral like a cat, sure, but I don't think it was her.

At the same time, though, in 2019 the lake gave Melanie Hardy back, didn't it? And she wasn't the same, either. It took a dad to recognize her.

What's worse to someone like me, who knows horror's big on anniversaries, is that Stacey Graves was eight years old when those boys threw her out onto the lake and she figured out what she was, ran away across the top of the water to find her dead mom, cling to her.

Eight years ago, I held Stacey Graves under that same water until her small little body bucked and then went still in my arms.

Was that just a reset, though? Has she grown up again over the last eight years, made of different stuff this time? More lakey stuff? Did she spend enough time in Ezekiel's waterlogged church down in Drown Town that she remembered who she was, what she does? Is she this Angel of Indian Lake the kids keep insisting isn't just wishful thinking?

I haven't asked this out loud to Banner yet. Because if I don't say it, if I don't make it real, then it can't be. That's the rules.

And, Banner has his own big question, anyway: "Why him?"

Why Carl Duchamp.

It's a good question. One a slasher expert like I claim to be maybe should have already been asking.

Except I'm the babysitter now.

The one who just left her charge on the couch, because little kids shouldn't be studying the manila folder Banner left right there on the desk calendar.

It's photos of what Lemmy already projected up onto the wall, footage that had been catastrophically deleted *off* his phone by the time Banner asked for it, because, Lemmy said, he was maxed out on memory.

And, being seventeen, his phone is his main computer: no back-ups. The drone feeds what it sees to the phone, and the phone holds onto it until . . . until it doesn't.

"Tiff's been busy," I mutter about the photos, leafing through them.

The shots are high-res enough that it's like I'm right there.

First is Rex Allen. His tin star is still there on the tatters of his shirt—that's why Banner's star is shiny and new: the one he was supposed to have had passed down was lost. I make myself study our former sheriff for a ten count, like penance.

Next is Francie. Her jaw is hanging by one hinge like she's still chewing the piece of gum she always had, and her left hand's been crushed up against her chest, showing her now-loose wedding ring.

I don't know if it's better to get that to Seth Mullins or better to slide it into a drawer, not force it on him.

Like he's not going to be in lockup anyway, for starting a forest fire.

Not that I think he has big plans to survive the next few days. If I lost somebody like that, maybe I set my house on fire too, and then just sit there, satisfied that what's outside me finally matches what's inside.

What does it feel like to be loved like that? I ask Francie.

I caught her mid-chew, though—no answer.

And, why am I even punishing myself with this? There's probably a coffee table book around here I could flip through instead, about birds, or flowers, or the scenic wonders of America. Or even a pamphlet about, I don't know, a new and improved way to read the Miranda rights.

Sharona would have an explanation for me making myself study these, I bet. Letha too. *You feel like the former sheriff and his best deputy are your fault. If you never show back up in Proofrock, then maybe the killings never start up again?*

Hettie and Paul and Waynebo aren't on me, though, are they? They can't be. And they're probably not even dead, were just holding their breath until the sound of Lemmy's drone whined away, because high schoolers love to prank the older set.

"Two people . . ." I say aloud about them all the same, wheels turning. Two *verifiable* people, I mean. It is how slashers like to open: a Barry and Claudette going down, a Casey and Steve deader than dead. A sheriff and his deputy turning up minus their heartbeats.

"Two," Adie confirms from the couch, not looking up from her sketch pad, which I guess she pulled over to herself as consolation prize.

"One *two*," I singsong back cheerily, like we're just practicing our counting, here.

Adie presses her lips together in pride and goes back to her drawing.

The way I'm going to know this isn't a horror movie I'm in? When I look at what she's drawn here in a couple minutes, it's not going to be anything scary, that I have to try to write-off as a kid's random, doesn't-mean-anything imagination.

C'mon, Adie, c'mon. Just something normal. A non-scary house. An alive dog. Your mom on her exercise bike. A birthday cake.

Well, one without eight candles, please. And also with *candle*-candles, not fingers reaching up through the cake, their tips burning.

I keep flipping through the photographs of Rex Allen and Francie and the Bronco, studying the snow for knobby tire tracks, for hoof prints—for anything to prove that Lemmy's footage wasn't faked.

Nothing's jumping out.

Rex Allen and Francie died on impact up on the highway, obviously. What's left of Rex Allen's leathery face has been shattered into clumps of gravel, and Francie's left arm shouldn't ever have been at that angle.

Wonder who gets the reward money for them now? Lemmy? What's a few thousand dollars even matter to a Terra Nova kid?

Lana Singleton'll probably donate it to some general Proofrock fund—there's got to be a town kitty, doesn't there, Mr. Holmes? Like your extra-credit one? Anyway, Lana doing that, it's how you buy the good will of a community. Which is what you need when you've built an artificial island out in the middle of what used to be an unbroken lake—sort of the spitting image of that island up-front in *The Shining*, which I'm pretty sure is Blackfeet. It's maybe a weird thing to feel pride about, but the front of *The Shining*, that's the closest I've ever been to the homeland in my blood.

I watch it over and over, I mean. And then again, just swooping past and coming back, swooping past and coming back.

As for that island up in Montana, I don't know what it's called, either now or back before the trappers and the church and Teddy Roosevelt, but I bet it's not "Treasure Island" like we have here, now.

Technically, since it's on floats, our Treasure Island counts as a barge, as a dock that floated away, needs to get tugboated back to shore. Barges don't look like little islands ten yards across both ways, though. Barges don't have enough soil mounded on them to grow grass and wildflowers and one transplanted tree—like a kidnapped, imprisoned tree is supposed to make everything all right.

According to the press release, Treasure Island is just a staging area, a matter of convenience: when the scientific equipment that gets carried out there periodically has mapped Drown Town thoroughly enough for it to be rebuilt stone by stone and board by board, then the island gets disappeared, or parked for the school to use for field trips.

What it's working towards right now, though—so says the press release—is the razing of the "hazard" Camp Blood is and the subsequent rebuilding of Henderson-Golding in its place, letting that idle land over there become a tourist trap. Just, no mannequins. The real sell, of course, is the hiring preferences for the actors pretending it's 1880 from nine to five every workday: all local, all Proofrock, from kids to grandparents poached from the nursing home.

You're probably turning over so much in your grave, Mr. Holmes, that that fancy equipment on the island is picking up the seismic activity.

If everybody in town paddles or walks over to Camp Blood every morning for another day of entertaining tourists? Then yeah, they've got steady work, they don't hate the Terra Nova Consortium so much, there's a new economy in the valley. But, once again, Proofrock is just the junky place on the way to another fabricated wonderland. We're the workers' barracks, I mean. And Terra Nova is to us as the "company" is to the coalminers in the history books—pretty soon we're being paid with store credit, and we're locked in a cycle that just keeps eating us through the generations, until we're drones, zombies, not even alive enough to remember we're *not* from 1880.

I'm sorry, Mr. Holmes.

I've tried and tried to stop Pleasant Valley from becoming what it's trying to become, what the Terra Nova Consortium's trying to turn it into as payback for what we did to the Founders, but, like you, I'm just a pissed-off history teacher, right?

Well, one with a sheet, with a history herself, I guess.

But, if you want to know why that fancy equipment on Treasure Island gets locked up after each night now, it might be because, for a while, whatever was left behind was getting, you know, *tossed into the water*.

Indian Lake's a mysterious place.

Weird stuff's always happening.

I haven't had as much luck keeping Terra Nova from building up again, though.

This time the houses are even more palatial and grand, and now there's a helicopter pad over there, and this summer some of the New Founders—that's what I call them—even came in to cut some ribbons, break some ground, and then strip down, swim the lake with these foam briefcases tied to them, like they were just going to work.

Talk about idiotic.

I was there with the rest of the townies, though, and all the media trying to shoulder past us for a more iconic shot.

I want to say these New Founders did this big swim for the spectacle, but what it really was was a bunch of tycoons peeing on what they were claiming, so the world would know it was theirs—so *we* would know that the boys were back in town, and this time they weren't going anywhere.

All because Deacon Samuels got lost once upon a summer, stumbled onto our idyllic postcard of a mountain town with a golf bag in the backseat of his Porsche, and had that Christopher Columbus feeling, like he was just discovering something. Something that could be all his.

If I'd have known, I'd have found that goddamn golden pickaxe myself and taken it out to the highway, churned up the asphalt so he would have had to have taken a different route.

Coulda woulda shoulda, I know.

There's time-travel in *The Final Girls*, though, isn't there? And that *Happy Death Day* that I missed the first time around? And *Detention*? *Totally Killer*?

I used to pray to Craven and Carpenter to send one of their savage angels down to straighten things out for me. Now I know how indiscriminate those spirits of vengeance can be. Now I know that "justice" to them is much more broad, that it pretty much includes anyone within their slashing range, and anyone between them and their prey.

I'm sorry, Proofrock.

I say it over and over to Sharona, and at the cemetery, but I don't even know if you can hear, Mr. Holmes, or if you're just tapping your pencil's eraser on this new stack of quizzes, waiting for me to stop standing by your desk, waiting for me to please stop going on and on about slasher-this and slasher-that, my words falling all over each other, my eyes hot, my hands balled into fists because this matters so, so much.

Really, sir?

I think I just wanted somebody to listen to me.

There, I said it.

Happy, Sharona?

In my head at least, I'm honest. It's when I open my mouth that things get complicated.

"Two," Adie says again, like still proud to know it.

"Two," I say, confirming that she should be proud.

Never mind that we're counting bodies, here.

Back to punishing myself with the manila folder.

After Rex Allen and Francie, there's all the close-up shots, usually with a wooden ruler for scale. The license plate and VIN of the Bronco, who knows why—probably to prove something beyond a doubt, to match up to some records, I don't know. Rex Allen's seatbelt, still clicked into place. Francie's hanging jaw, and what face leather it's hanging by. The police radio. The odometer, that ruler right there with it. Some oil or black paint spattered onto the snow, with . . . an icy white footprint in it? A bare foot.

I work that one out, check to be sure Adie isn't watching, and study it.

It's not brutal-cold yet, but still, who goes without boots in October, at eight thousand feet?

There's a ruler by this shot, too. This foot is nearly ten inches long.
Which means about nothing to me.

I start to shuffle this shot back in, but then can't let it go.

"Fuck it," I say, and pull Banner's top drawer out.

There's a wooden ruler there that's probably been there since Don
Chambers's day. But inches don't change.

I work my foot from the prison of its high heel, lower the ruler to
the seat of the chair, and line my foot up alongside it.

Just short of ten inches. And I'm an 8.5 in most shoes.

Does this mean this footprint's from a woman?

"Who?" I say, coming back to the front of the report.

"Who," Adie the little owl repeats, not looking up from her art.

I look past her to the window.

The fire is a long orange worm crawling across the top of the
trees.

This could be it for us, couldn't it? It was a good run, but it's
time for the land to reset, shake us off. Glen Henderson and Tobias
Golding never should have come here looking for ore. The dam never
should have been poured. Indian Creek should never have been made
to pool up, drown the valley.

My dad never should have looked across a bonfire at my mom,
and then led her by the hand into one of the cabins over at Camp
Blood, to conceive an angry little girl who had already used a life's
worth of eyeliner by the time she was seventeen.

But Sharona says I shouldn't let myself think this kind of shit.

What's done is done, and thinking about how things could have
been just leads to feeling that the way it is isn't the way it has to be. There
is no "better way," she insists in her soft, comforting, supportive way.

It's what you say when you grew up like she did.

"Must be nice," I say to her, flashing my eyes across to Adie, because I don't want her repeating my tone, catching my bitterness.

She's into whatever she's drawing.

I start to close the manila folder back, leave it right where it was so I can pretend not to know any of this, just go back to being a history teacher, but . . . I haven't gone through the whole stack of photos yet, I don't guess. My punishment's not over. And, stupid as it is, it's like I owe the last few photos? Like if I leave them unlooked-at, then I'm playing favorites. I'll be leaving a few of them out in the cold.

Being a girl who's been left out in that cold and nearly died from it, I peel up the footprint-one, fully expecting the *next* footprint.

It's body number three.

I suck a sharp breath in.

This body's been dead even longer than Rex Allen and Francie, you can tell from how drawn-in and decayed it is.

Still, that blackness with the white footprint from the other photo? It's from this . . . this corpse, isn't it? Not the footprint, the blackness, which I guess must be blood . . . or embalming fluid gone bad?

Say it, Jade: *zombie.*

I slam the folder shut, shove it away from me.

Meaning, of course, I have to surge forward to catch it, keep it from sailing off onto the floor, exposing Adie to these skeleton faces, these burst-open chests, these decapitated zombies.

I just catch the folder.

Adie doesn't bat an eye. Aunt Jade's just freaking out again, no big.

I stand like this was all intentional, straighten the folder against the top of the desk, and lay it gingerly onto the pile over to the right side of the calendar, away from the couch.

Which is when I see what's written on this other folder that was *the* folder until Lemmy's anonymous email came in.

The label on this folder's tab has been printed—Tiff runs a tight ship—has these all-caps blocky letters.

"Friday the 13th."

I swallow hard, the sound loud in my ears.

What has Banner been keeping from me? I guess I can sort

of understand him not divulging that somebody's dragged a dead body out under the dam and then wrenched its head off—this is Proofrock—but . . . something happens on this holiest of holy days, and I'm not the first call? Does the crew in *Final Destination* not go to Tony Todd the undertaker when they need to know more about death? I may not be *in* the slasher game anymore, but the last round didn't shake all the facts from my head, either.

But no. It's good he didn't call me about this.

It just would have pulled me in.

It was two weeks ago, though? Seventeen days, then? Does that mean that . . . if Banner had told me about this "Friday the 13th" folder, then Hettie and Paul and Waynebo don't get slaughtered?

I hate being me.

Especially because I know I'm opening this folder as well.

Adie's humming and drawing now, which means she's not going to be skipping over here anytime soon, to tippy-toe over my shoulder.

I settle into the office chair again—*creeeeeak*—pull the "Friday the 13th" folder over like it's just another adult thing I have to do, like taxes and bills.

Is the top form going to be from the parents of someone named "Annie," claiming she came out here to Crystal Lake to be a cook, but hasn't checked in yet? Is Crazy Ralph in here, calling the doom down from on high? Did Banner leave this out specifically for me, as bait? Is there a single hair Scotch-taped to it, ready to give me away?

Do I care?

I cough for cover, peel the folder open fast like pulling a bandaid.

It's the cemetery.

I'm usually there twice a week, but it's been midterms the last couple weeks—sorry, Mr. Holmes.

"What the hell?" I have to say out loud, then.

"What the hell?" Adie parrots, just replaying the sounds, not really registering them.

It's a grave, dug up.

I flip through, and the bulk of the crime-scene shots are all close-ups of the sides of this new hole.

The sticky notes stuck to the photographs are in Tiff's handwriting—I remember it from cheating off her in Geography, and English, and . . . the rest of them, sure, okay. She might be a pure idiot, but she's pretty damn smart, too.

Not shovel blades, she's saying to Banner with the Post-its, junior detective that she is.

Meaning . . . a backhoe? Isn't that what they mostly use to dig new graves?

But not over here by the fence, where the headstones are all shoulder to shoulder, would break off if a big tractor tire so much as brushed them.

You don't dig a hole like this with your hands, though.

Do you?

And, I'm no state detective like Banner's got on the horn down the hall, but it's no great leap to connect that corpse out by the dam to this empty grave. That doesn't explain *why* someone would do this, but the *who* is more important than the *why*, at least for now.

What I need to do is spread all these photos out side by side, to get a sense of who's where, and then I can—

"No," I say, standing fast away from the next shot in the stack, that I was going to put up at the top corner of the desk like a puzzle piece, waiting to finds its place.

Banner's chair bounces back into the wall from my sudden movement, shakes the wall of historic Proofrock stuff—Glen Henderson and Tobias Golding, giant trout, dead wolves taller than the person holding them up, muskrats on some old-timey clothesline in front of the drugstore.

Adie looks up, her pencil paused. The frames behind me swing on their nails but nothing falls, nothing shatters.

Except everything I thought I knew.

"Spider," I lie.

Adie draws her feet up onto the couch beside her, checks the ground, looks back once more to me, then recommences her Very Important Artwork.

My heart beating in my throat, I make myself look back down to the photo again.

It's a close-up of the headstone over this empty grave.

GREYSON BRUST.

It's a good name.

I stand there tapping my toe until Tiff registers my presence and ups her chin to Banner, about who's standing beside him.

Adie's on my hip and she's got my earbuds in, my phone clutched to her chest.

It's never too early to get into Fugazi.

More important, I don't want her hearing Aunt Jade's mouthful of cuss words.

"What the *fuck*?" I say to Banner, just mouthing the profanity, but sharpening it with my eyes.

To show what I mean, I slap the "Friday the 13th" folder down on Tiff's desk.

Tiff licks her lips, then purses them tight.

The tension between her and me, it's part leftovers from high school, her being at the party, me always just watching it, but, too, it was her recording of what happened in the water eight years ago that snatched the next four years of my life away, and pretty much derailed things for me. This summer she pulled me aside once when Banner and Letha were leading me down to his office, said how she never meant anything, how she *had* to turn that footage over, that she never knew—

"*Had* to?" I asked back, looking her square in the face until she looked away.

And that's where we've left it.

All the same, it's not like I *didn't* swing that machete into my dad's neck. Just, I didn't know it was him.

Not that that would have changed anything.

That's what I tell myself, anyway.

In your head, and your secret heart, it's easy to be tough.

"You're going through my desk now?" Banner says, about the folder.

"Cut the shit," I say, shifting Adie to my other hip.

Tiff steps forward, her arms out, hands open like gimme. Banner nods about this so I pass Adie across, and Tiff's already making baby sounds right into Adie's face like she's not already a big girl, isn't ever going to have monsters of her own to put down.

"See if you can resist putting her on Instagram?" I say, blinking twice so she can catch what I'm slinging.

Tiff very intentionally doesn't make eye contact, just spins a step away, twirling Adie.

Coming back to Banner, I linger for a moment on the front door, to be sure the next thing isn't already standing there waiting for us, chest heaving with impatience from all our blood still being on the inside.

"Greyson Brust," I say about the folder.

"There's bigger shit today than grave robbing," Banner says, stepping over to the water cooler. He pulls a pointy-bottomed cup down, holds it up to me. I shake my head no and he fills it, slams it. It's just a stall, of course. He's looking down into that paper cone's belly for an explanation.

"It's *related*," I say, though. "Or are your cop instincts telling you a body dug up from a grave and dragged out by the former sheriff's dead body is nothing?"

"It's something, yeah," Banner says, clocking the front door as well, which makes me pause, reconsider.

But then I get it: seeing the previous sheriff dead probably unsettles current sheriffs.

"What?" I ask, sit-leaning against Tiff's desk enough to jostle her calendar over, ruin all her beautiful order.

"I don't *know* what," Banner says, crossing his arms, that paper cup crumpled in his left hand like a tough guy. "What I do know is that the fresh murder at the high school is more important than . . . than whatever all that out there is."

"But you could have brought this to me two weeks ago," I tell him about the "Friday the 13th" folder.

Banner shrugs, mutters, "Letha wouldn't let me."

"Excuse me, *Sheriff*?"

"She told me you were out, finished, done," Banner says, with a touch more force. "That it wasn't fair of me to pull you back in."

"You're saying *she* knew?"

"Now you're pissed at both of us."

"I'm pissed at the world," I tell him, pushing up and pacing, so I can open and close my hands in frustration.

I get some water myself, which I guess is supposed to be some sort of small victory, I don't know. It tastes like bandaids, like it's the melted ice at the bottom of a cooler. It does feel good to crumple that paper cup, though. I deposit it in the trash and Banner arcs his high, banks it off the wall, swish.

He holds his hands up like reluctantly accepting the crowd's applause for what's, to him, just this everyday thing.

He's still pretty hatable, I mean.

"So, the state dicks?" I ask.

"Don't think they like to be called that," Banner says with a half-way grin. "But they—they say it happens."

" 'It'?"

"That with Proofrock's notoriety, we shouldn't be surprised about a little grave robbing. They've seen it before. People want artifacts."

"I mean what do they say about—"

"The parents' lane, yeah. They're sending someone up."

"ETA?"

Banner curls his lips like he was hoping I wouldn't ask this.

"They say it—that it doesn't fit with the pattern or style of—"

"Of Dark Mill South? Of Stacey Graves? No shit."

"Don't think they know about Stacey."

"Just me, yeah."

Banner shrugs, adds, "They say that daylight killings—"

"Of course this doesn't conform," I plead. "That doesn't mean *ignore* it."

"They say it's probably an isolated incident."

"'Probably.'"

"Believe me, I said that," Banner says. "Why do you think it took so long?"

"And?"

"Like I said—they're sending someone up."

"*Seriously?*"

"Seriously. What do you mean?"

"It's just . . . the cops, the teachers, the parents, they—they never believe it when the kids say somebody's killing them in their sleep, whatever."

"We're the kids in this?"

I shrug, hadn't really thought it through.

But, "When?" I ask.

Banner mumbles something I'm not supposed to catch, what with him rubbing his nose with the side of his hand and averting his eyes and generally just trying to slink in place.

"Excuse me?" I ask, stepping in to hear better, in case he can't gear up from a mumble.

Just ever so slightly, Banner shrugs, says, "Soon as they can spare someone."

"And tomorrow's a holiday," I say, the obviousness dripping from my tone.

"Not for us," Banner says.

He's talking about the big ban on Halloween in Proofrock. Not a literal ban, just, jack-o-lanterns and haunted yard decorations are considered to be in poor taste in a town where there's been blood in the streets, and on the wall, and . . . well, all over the place, pretty much. Isn't there some thirsty old Western movie like that, with the whole town painted red? I remember slouching across the living room once freshman year, seeing all that red, and wanting to stop. Except stopping would mean I'd be watching a movie with my dad, and there were certain lines I'd promised myself never to cross.

"So they won't get to us until they've had their candy," I say. "Meaning they don't show up here until Wednesday at the absolute earliest, if all the stars line up in our favor. So really they just want to help with the clean-up, right? That what you scheduled, Sheriff? Someone to write the report?"

Banner's watching the front door again.

"There won't be any clean-up," he says. "I already canceled the— you know."

"Lana's bad-idea movie," I fill in.

Yes. The anniversary screening that was supposed to heal us all, like watching *The Legend of Boggy Creek* would be healthy for a community still reeling from a massacre on the lake.

"Thank you for that," I tell him. "It would have given poor taste a bad name. But . . . *Wednesday?*"

"That's not even forty-eight hours away," Banner says. "And everybody's already leaving. What can happen?"

"You know what can happen," I say, kind of needlessly.

We both end up watching Tiff and Adie. Tiff has her at the copy machine now, is letting her push the green button, probably just for the sound, so Adie won't pick up what her dad and me are arguing about.

"Then it's up to us again," I finally have to say out loud, just to be sure he gets it.

"No," Banner says. "It's up to *me*, Jade. Letha'll kick my ass from here to Sunday if—"

"I'll handle your wife."

"But you're out," Banner says back, squinting like trying to really see me.

"Not saying I'm going out there with a machete," I say. "Just . . . I can help from in here, can't I? Like—Carl Whoever. You asked it already."

"'Why Carl Duchamp,' yeah."

"Well?"

Banner walks around to the other side of the tall counter, running his fingertips along its top, which has been smoothed down by a thousand elbows.

"I could have gotten Big Daddy the other day, you know?" he says.

"Big who?"

"My dad's elk," Banner says with a shrug.

"Rocky," I say.

"What? No—Big Daddy. That's what my dad always—"

"Doesn't matter."

"He was floating right by the Pier."

"Why didn't you?"

Banner is just watching Adie and Tiff some more. Like trying to hold onto what's good? It's an impulse I understand, for sure. Adie has her hand on the scanner now, Tiff shielding her five-year-old eyes with her hand like she should be doing, at least with Aunt Jade standing right here in the same room.

"I think I—that I didn't know," Banner says. "I was afraid if I pulled it up, it might have . . . you're going to think this is stupid."

"You are the one saying it."

"The way it was sitting in the water, it was like—it was like it had a body now?"

"A body?"

"And I didn't know what kind of body it might have."

"It's the head of a *dead elk*," I tell him, coming over to the tall counter so my voice won't make it to the copy machine. "It's Styrofoam or something on the inside now, isn't it?"

"I was always scared of it, growing up," Banner says.

"This doesn't matter," I say. "Sadie's dad?"

"Carl Duchamp," Banner fills in. "Second-generation Proofrocker. Think he was in your mom's class, maybe?"

"Can't exactly ask her about him, but thanks for that remind."

"I asked my mom," Banner says. "There's nothing special, with him. Good dude, more or less. Minds his own business. No bad history, no bodies on his backtrail."

"He must have done something," I tell him. "He was the only one who got his . . ." I go on, amending on the fly because little pitchers have big ears, "who suffered what he suffered. Him specifically, not anybody else."

Banner shrugs the same shrug he used to shrug when you'd call on him, Mr. Holmes. The one that meant he knew that no matter if his answer on this oral pop-quiz was right or just amazingly off-base, there was no way he wasn't playing in the big game on Friday.

Just, the stakes are considerably higher than football, now.

"Maybe he was the only one with his window rolled down?" Banner tries, tracking Tiff and Adie going hand in hand down the hall, either to his office or the ladies' room.

Thank you, Tiff.

"Was he?" I ask.

"A lot of them left, didn't give statements," Banner says. "But, your turn. You saw something. I mean, right before you freaked out."

Right before I nearly jumped out of my skin when the pinky of my left hand touched a branch on the bush I was backing into, and I thought Michael was about to hug me into the darkness.

"Probably just some kid with a healthy survival instinct," I say. But Banner knows me too well, is just staring at me, waiting for the rest. For the truth. I peel my lips back from my teeth, spin around, jam my fingers through my hair. "It wasn't her," I finally say. Again.

"Because you don't want it to be?"

"Think I need your bullshit, Sheriff?"

"No, you've got plenty already."

"Present company included."

"You just don't want to say it."

"Say what?"

"That it's Stacey Graves."

"Because it's *not*," I say, and look around to be sure we have the room. "I told your wife already—Ezekiel took her down with him."

"The dead preacher at the bottom of the lake took her?" Banner clarifies, so I can hear myself.

"I saw his hand," I mumble.

"I'm sure you saw something."

"So you believe a little dead girl can walk on the water, but you don't buy that Ezekiel can still be down there singing with his evil choir?"

"They weren't evil, were they?" Banner says. "Just . . . Christian, right?"

"'Evil' and 'Christian' are interchangeable to Indians," I tell him, daring him to clarify *that*.

"Oh yeah," Banner says. "Letha said you converted, in prison."

"She said that, 'converted'?"

Banner backpedals, hands up, says, "No, no, she—she said you found yourself, I think?"

"Found myself in a *cell*, yeah. But this isn't just a tan, you know? I've always been Blackfeet, *Sheriff*."

"Same as your dad."

"Not at all like my dad."

"We're off . . . Carl Duchamp."

"What about Hettie and Paul and Wayne Sellars?"

"Lemmy's trying to recover that file."

"Sellars hasn't been in class," I say. "I checked the front office."

"Nobody reported him missing."

"That doesn't mean he isn't," I say. "It just means his dad's a trucker, is never home."

"His mom?"

"2015," I say in that low way we all use in Proofrock, that means she died in the water, with *Jaws* playing overhead.

"What did you see, Jade?"

"I think I liked you better when you didn't think like a cop."

"Which is your way of saying 'good question, officer of the law.'"

I rock my head back, study the ceiling, trying to wish myself into some different set of circumstances.

"It was a little kid," I finally say. "All dirty, like."

"Dirty?" Banner asks, considering this out loud. "So . . . Jan, maybe? He didn't go with Hettie? He . . . he ran away, has been living in the trees, what?"

"I don't know, okay? Yeah, I guess the kid I saw was the same size as Jan Jansson. And they both have long hair. But, talking hair . . . what about Amy Brockmeir?"

"I don't—"

"Camp Blood, 1964," I recite. "Sheriff Hardy saw her, or saw Stacey, really, and Don Chambers convinced him he'd seen Amy."

"Oh, oh, the Lundy girl, yeah," Banner says. "Remar Lundy's niece, daughter, something?"

"Doesn't matter anymore," I say. "She ate the blanket she was supposed to be sleeping in, died in her institution."

"And Greyson Brust died in his bed at the nursing home."

"Somebody dug him up," I insist. "He didn't just claw out of that grave, go walking around."

"Because the dead always stay dead around here."

"When does your pretty wife get back?"

"Now who's dodging?"

I close my eyes, make myself breathe in, breathe out.

"So we've got four verified bodies so far," I say, my eyes still closed. Until I open them, to check the door again for shapes. "Three have been dead a long time, one's fresh, new, headless, and then there's three that are just, technically, missing—four if you count Jan."

"And the world's on fire, and it's almost Halloween," Banner adds.

"And the real cops aren't coming until it's all over."

"Hey," Banner says about that.

"You know what I mean. But it doesn't matter. Police are useless in these situations."

"Still right here . . ."

"Your job's to keep that one"—Adie—"safe."

"According to you and Letha," Banner says. "According to this"—his *badge*—"my responsibilities sort of cover the whole valley, and everyone in it."

"And I have to make sure *you* don't die," I mutter, mostly to myself.

"Other way around?" Banner tries.

I shrug, let him believe this.

"But—" he starts, except Tiff's suddenly swishing in, her eyes bouncing from me to Banner.

"You don't have to ask," I tell her. "You can hit the head whenever you need to, Tiff, you know that, right?"

She grins an apologetic grin, is going up and down on her toes, about to burst with whatever she's got, here.

"What?" Banner asks, clocking the front door once more.

Tiff holds her phone up, face out.

We both peer in.

"Instagram?" I say, not believing she would really be showing *me* this.

Tiff scrolls or taps or enlarges, shows it to us again.

"Henderson Hawks alumni," Banner identifies.

"Here," Tiff says, and opens something else for us.

Banner takes the phone, and I take it from him.

"What the hell?" I say.

It's a photo of, of all things, a *chainsaw*.

The comments all under it are some version of "8pm?"

I case the walls for a clock, finally land on it.

Eight o'clock on the dot.

"What's happening?" I say.

"Tiff?" Banner chimes in.

Tiff chucks her chin at the front door in a way that drifts all of us over there.

"Stay here . . ." Banner says, leaving me in the doorway, stepping down onto the crunchy grass and what snow there is.

My eyes aren't adjusted yet, but I can see dots of light on the Pier, and . . . out on the lake? My first thought is how the oldsters from the Pleasant Valley Assisted Living like to come down once a year to sail those paper boats out across the lake, for that kid who drowned in the rising water.

These are real boats, though. And canoes. And kayaks.

"What the hell?" I say.

"No!" Tiff yips then, ramming back into me.

It's someone striding out of the darkness, a chainsaw held low.

It's Jocelyn Cates.

Her lips are firm, her eyes hard.

Her husband died in the water in 2015, and her son was suffocated with a dry-cleaning bag in 2019.

And now she's got a chainsaw.

"Joss, Joss," Banner says, skipping out toward her, away from Tiff and me.

When his hand touches Jocelyn's shoulder, though, she shrugs him off, doesn't even think about stopping.

"Let her go, let her go!" Tiff says from behind me.

Banner looks back to us.

"'Let her go'?" I repeat.

Banner does. He comes back to us. To Tiff's phone.

"They're all, um, deputized now?" Tiff says, shrugging so we can know this wasn't her idea. "By Walt."

Walter Mason, the chief of the volunteer fire department.

"Deputized?" Banner says.

"To stop that," Tiff says, opening her hand to present the fire to us, like we might not know about it.

"With *chainsaws*?" Banner asks.

"TNC put up some cash," Tiff says. "They, I don't know—if all the trees around Terra Nova are cut down, then maybe the houses won't burn down this time?"

"The Terra Nova Consortium?" I ask. "You mean Lana Singleton?"

Tiff shrugs.

"But it's the national forest!" I say. "They don't own that!" I look to Tiff, to Banner, then add, "Do they?"

"Will it work?" Banner mumbles, kind of impressed, it seems.

"How much?" I ask Tiff.

"Three thousand for chainsaws, fifteen hundred for axes," she answers.

"Shit," I say, shaking my head. "This is that scene in *Jaws*, isn't it? Where all the stupid fishermen are going out to catch the big killer fish?"

"They don't want it to burn again," Tiff says, like convincing me of this plan.

"And what about the houses right *here*?" I ask, flinging my hand at Proofrock.

"Somebody's going to get hurt," Banner says.

"Think?" I say, my high school self rising for a moment.

"I should—" Banner says, making to go and be official and sheriffy.

"We've got her," I say about Adie. But then I look around, say to Tiff, "Don't we?"

"She's in the office," Tiff says, watching Banner stride into the darkness. "He didn't even bring his jacket."

"You're his secretary, not his wife," I remind her.

"And you're the babysitter?" Tiff says right back.

I have to shake my head, impressed. It's either that or tackle her, fight right here in front of the sheriff's office.

"We should—" I say, pushing the door open behind us.

Tiff watches the darkness and the fire like interrogating it, then ducks under my arm to do her job.

I stand there a moment longer. Long enough to hear a chainsaw fire up out on the water.

This should go great, yeah.

Tiff stops at her desk. I'm beelining the office.

Adie's drawing again. Still.

I ease in, trying not to wear my nerves on the outside, even though my fingers just—again—grubbed in my waistband for another pill.

I learned early on to only carry so many on my person, though. Because you can forget how deep into them you are, only figure it out when you're Samara at the bottom of a pharmaceutical well, looking up to a distant ring of light.

"Can I see?" I ask.

Adie tilts her pad up on her knees, shakes her head no, not yet.

I step to the side so she can know I'm not peeking, and it's right when another local with a chainsaw is walking past the window, her eyes practically dollar signs, her mouth the grimmest slash.

Banner's going to have his hands full, isn't he?

Next, farther out, walking on the street, is someone I don't know. Someone carrying an axe.

I didn't even think there were this many people *left* in town.

But maybe some of them were already on the highway when their phones chimed about this.

It's raining money back there. All you have to do is stand there, catch it.

I guess I get it. But still.

I step closer to the window, trying to see the crowd moving to the Pier, but the boats and canoes people are turtled under make it hard to see faces.

And—and . . .

I draw a breath in sharp and cold.

One of those faces is looking right back at me.

It's a woman with long crazy hair, black and tangled.

She's in a pale nightgown, is barefoot, and isn't moving with the chainsaw crowd. Rather, everyone's flowing around her, their eyes across the lake.

"Maureen Prescott," I mumble.

Sidney's mom from the third *Scream*.

Except, I remind myself, this is real life.

Meaning: Sally Chalumbert, former final girl, current escaped mental patient.

I step neatly over to Banner's desk, punch the button on his phone for Tiff's desk. The button still says MEG in Hardy's cramped scrawl.

"Um, Jade?" Tiff says into her receiver.

"You've got Adie," I tell her, and punch off before she can object.

When I step around the desk, though, Adie's standing there, holding her pad out to me.

"Oh, thank you," I tell her, and take a knee to appreciate this like she wants.

It's . . . the shore of the lake? A little inlet, a cove. Just like the mouth of Devil's Creek, but without Proofrock behind it? Just a tree shaped like the number four, which is probably a mess-up Adie did, but she kept going anyway? Meaning this is somewhere across the lake, that she saw when Banner was touring her and Letha around on one of his days off. Well: it's either some other cove around the lake, or it's a *made-up* cove.

Standing in the water is either a little girl or a not-to-scale woman. My heart drops.

"Who is this?" I ask, trying to keep my voice so, so neutral.

"It's me!" Adie says, and after a beat to reset my head, let my heart start beating again, I hug her to my side, close my eyes tight.

"Thank you, thank you, it's beautiful," I tell her. Then, "Tiffany's coming to, to . . . you can show this to *her*!"

If Adie clocks my forced cheer, she doesn't show it.

She tears the drawing out, holds it over to me.

"You sure?" I ask, already pinching the two sides together but not folding it, quite.

"It's for you!" she says.

I hug her again, for longer, then stand, say, "Aunt Jade has to—the bathroom."

I nod my head like Adie might not understand what I mean, here.

The phone's ringing in the front office, and then it cuts off mid-ring, meaning Tiff's not coming back here yet.

Good.

I stand, smooth Adie's mess of hair down, and walk away while I still can, distinctly aware of her little shuffling footsteps trailing behind me, then veering off for the front office.

Meaning I'm not leaving that way. Guess I really am going to the bathroom.

And, no lie, crossing the hallway to the ladies' feels like stepping off a cliff, into the void. *In* the bathroom, I lean over the sink, clutching both sides.

"Don't do this," I tell my reflection.

Before my reflection can say anything back, though, I spin away, run a crease down the middle of Adie's drawing, then fold it into quarters to stuff into my rear pocket. Except I'm still wearing this stupid skirt.

I look around the bathroom for some nook or cranny to hide this drawing, but then have to imagine Adie finding it, and thinking I threw her present away, or forgot it. She's still short, though. Meaning she won't look on top of a ceiling tile.

"Screw it," I say, standing on the lip of the sink to nudge a tile up enough to slide Adie's drawing up and in. When the sink starts to creak and crack, letting go of the wall, I grab onto the ceiling, push with my feet, don't need some stupid plumbing emergency right now, thanks.

Gingerly, using the top of the stall, I lower myself back to the floor, and take this neatly averted disaster to mean that all disasters will be averted tonight just the same. Nobody will get crushed by a falling tree over in Terra Nova. No chainsaws will kick back into anybody's face. And this isn't another slasher cycle starting.

This and other unlikely things, courtesy of Jade Daniels.

Tiff's heels *tap-tap* across the front office, probably to scoop Adie up. Thank you, Tiff. I do sort of hate you, but . . . I don't know. I'm also jealous, I guess? Of how well you walk in adult shoes. So easy, so natural. And that you never mind holding Adie while you work.

It almost makes up for the rest of it.

Almost.

I step out of my heels, am a good two inches shorter.

And then I flinch hard when there's a knock on the door.

It's Tiff, probably with Adie on her hip, which I'm suddenly *not* appreciating quite as much.

"Just a minute!" I call out, trying to keep my heart in my chest.

And then—I hate it hate it hate it—I'm pulling myself up into the rusted-open window, dropping my shoes ahead of me before flopping out into the scratchy bushes and crusty snow.

Do you like scary movies, Mr. Holmes?

I used to. Until I had to try to live through them.

Report of Investigation
2 August 2023
#04a49, supplementary
re: Overview / Confession of Vandalism

Isolated individuals like Jennifer Elaine "Jade" Daniels engage in vandalism for a variety of reasons. In juveniles, negative feelings of subordination and boredom can lead to outbursts of destruction in hopes of alleviating or ameliorating those negative feelings. Unless Ms. Daniels's emotional maturation has been interrupted by the various traumas she's been involved in, then, at twenty-four (24), she should be well past that dynamic (for more on this "Arrested Psychological Development" and the "scar model of psychopathology," see "Mental Order During Adolescence," *Clinical Psychological Science* 8.3, Ormel *et al.*). While Ms. Daniels has been twice diagnosed with PTSD, such trauma doesn't directly correlate to vandalism. Indirectly, however, PTSD can lead to social isolation, which is often punctuated with outbursts of various types, including but not limited to willful destruction of property. In "Social Isolation, Loneliness, and Violence Exposure in Urban Adults" [*Health Affairs* 38.10], Tung *et al.* argue that "the highest loneliness was found among people who were exposed to <u>community violence</u> and screened positive for <u>post-traumatic stress disorder</u>" (our emphasis).

Being unmarried, an only child with no children, and taking into consideration that both her parents are deceased and that she isn't in contact with any remote relations or "elders" (see C.1 below), and allowing that her internet activity no longer includes the discussion boards she claims to once have used as a social network of sorts [2a for the recording of session with Dr. Watts / 2a-tr for the transcription], Ms. Daniels is keenly vulnerable to this type of social isolation, even up to and including her attempts to seek support and "socialization" from unconventional sources (below, one such "unconventional source"). Though friendly with former classmates and fellow "survivors" Letha Mondragon-Tompkins and Sheriff Banner Tompkins, Ms. Daniels is nevertheless isolated from them. Indeed, aside from her documented criminal outings [see 18a-17 through 18a-34, as well as her "outing" of 28 April 2023 (report in-progress)], the bulk of Ms. Daniels's evenings are spent in the confines of her childhood home (980ft^2). In addition to her documented PTSD, other possible reasons for this self-imposed isolation are:

A.   <u>Ms. Daniels has yet to adjust from life as an inmate</u>. As often happens with the recently released, one cell can be traded for another. See 10p-04 through 10p-18 for a selection of Ms. Daniels's shopping receipts, which establish that she prefers to eat with plasticware instead of conventional flatware. In her second session with Dr. Sharona Watts [*ibid*. 2a . . .], Ms. Daniels explains her reason for this as "metal doesn't taste right in my mouth anymore?" [her interrogative]. In total, Ms. Daniels has spent the last seven of her twenty-four years as an inmate (eight [8] if pre-trial incarceration is included), the result being that she acclimatized to that regimented existence to such an extent that adjusting to un-institutionalized life with limited social support is proving difficult, resulting in a withdrawal from society, save her documented outbursts of vandalism.

B.   <u>Rejection by local community</u>. After the events of 2015 (the "Independence Day Massacre"), Ms. Daniels was a prime suspect. Though cleared of any legal culpability, many in Proofrock feel Ms. Daniels escaped on a technicality. As for the killings of 2019 for which Ms. Daniels was never a suspect, she was nevertheless indicted in the court of public opinion (see B.1, as well as the limited selection of articles, columns, blogs, posts,

and videos collected in folder 4t). In sum, the asper-
sions are that, had Ms. Daniels not elected to return
to Proofrock and Pleasant Valley, then serial killer Dark
Mill South wouldn't have followed her to town. Though
Proofrock establishments do business with Ms. Daniels, observations confirm that these interactions are
purely of a transactional nature, with no added pleas-
antries. Whether this is a result of Ms. Daniels's violent history; of her piercings, tattoos [see C.1], and hair
coloring(s); or of her suicide attempts (March 13th,
2015 and July 3rd, 2023) is beyond the scope of this
report.

> 1. *A search of "Jade Daniels" + "Proofrock"*
> *returns, as of the date of this report, some*
> *4,878,498 results. Many champion her as a "fi-*
> *nal girl" [for definition, see 743d], while others*
> *revile her as the instigator and/or perpetrator*
> *of the two cycles of violence she claims to have*
> *single-handedly stopped. In addition, in the wake*
> *of her high school writings on the horror genre*
> *[see 1A in its entirety] being posted in various*
> *online forums, Ms. Daniels has become a figure*
> *of cult status.*

C. Non-mainstream ethnicity. Since the death of her father, Ms. Daniels is now the lone Native American resident of Proofrock. As such, any sense of community
she could draw support from is inherently limited, as
no one around her can empathize with her culturally,
nor can they participate in ritual or ceremony with her.
Additionally, Ms. Daniels, being of Blackfeet extraction,
lives in the territory of her tribe's traditional enemies

the Shoshone and Bannock. In a sense, she's not only living behind enemy lines, but she also grew up behind those same lines, which perhaps explains her behavior and outbursts (including multiple acts of vandalism, establishing a trajectory of such behavior) while a student of Henderson High School.

> 2. *Though not technically an "elder" in the Native American tribal structure, as she's only three years older than Ms. Daniels, fellow inmate Isabel Yazzie (Navajo/Pueblo; b.1995; manslaughter) nevertheless, according to SICI's records, "mentored" Ms. Daniels in traditional life patterns [see 3c-12 for SICI's photographic documentation of the "tribal feather" Ms. Yazzie tattooed onto the back of Ms. Daniels's left arm].*

D. The disappearance of longtime Sheriff Angus Hardy, one of Ms. Daniels's foremost adversaries during her adolescence, and one of her last social tethers to the community. According to Ms. Daniels's own admission, after the threat of Dark Mill South had been neutralized in December 2019, Ms. Daniels and Sheriff Hardy walked out onto the ice of the frozen Indian Lake together, for reasons she refuses to divulge, and only Ms. Daniels returned. Of import here is her statement to Dr. Watts that "when the three [*sic*] of them reached that place that never freezes, I learned something about myself—what I could *do* (her emphasis) [2a / 2a-tr]." Witnesses [see 1d for the trial transcript] confirm that Ms. Daniels was also present at the death of Henderson High School history teacher Mr. Grady "Bear" Holmes, with whom she had also had an adversarial relationship [see directory 3g, where many of the infractions are signed "GH"]. According to notations on Mr. Holmes's grade book [322c], he was the sole impediment to Ms. Daniels receiving her high school diploma by the conventional route.

E. Activism. On 9 April 2023, Ms. Daniels chained herself to Cabin 5 of Deacon Point. This was the beginning of her efforts to "preserve this historical site." However, 9 April 2023 being a holiday (Easter Sunday), no work crews or media were on-hand to witness or document this protest. Three (3) weeks later (1 May 2023), Ms. Daniels emerged as a vocal member of the Terra Vetus Society [sic] (current membership, insofar as any records or statements that exist, is limited to Ms. Daniels and Ms. Mondragon-Tompkins). Primary on their (signed) list of requests, which Ms. Daniels nailed to the unused front door of the courthouse [2f-16], was the renaming of Indian Lake, that name being, she claims, pejorative. The suggested replacement name is "Glen Lake," in keeping with the state's original intentions concurrent with the damming of "Indian Creek." However, in light of Ms. Daniels's recurrent vandalism on Deacon Point and Temporary Research Islet H-G (local designation: "Treasure Island"), it's feasible that her participation in this renaming effort is an attempt on her part to appeal to "sacred" history, Deacon Point being, in local lore, where the Native Americans for whom Indian Lake is named supposedly appeared after the damming of Indian Creek (as well, Deacon Point contains the condemned remains of the former Camp Winnemucca).

F. <u>Emotional/Psychological state</u>. In addition to the aforementioned PTSD, observation suggests that Ms. Dan-
iels also engages compulsive behaviors. One domestic
illustration of this is that, after sending an email, Ms.
Daniels immediately opens up her sent mail folder
and rereads the missive she just sent, and then sends
no more messages for up to two hours, during which
she paces from room to room of her house, muttering to herself. For a more public—and thus socially
isolating—illustration, when alone and approaching
the front doors of the high school, Ms. Daniels has to
"generate momentum" or "gather a head of steam" to
finally, after up to three failed attempts, push through
the rightmost (south) set of doors, suggesting a superstition of unknown origin [for video recording, see
55e]. And then there's her suite of medications [see
81a–113d for a complete list of her prescriptions, the
schedule of refills, and the cluster of contraindica-
tions]: *clonazepam* to deal with panic attacks; *ateno-
lol* for social anxiety; *desipramine* for depression and
the aforementioned PTSD; and she's currently, under
the auspices of Dr. Sharona Watts, cycling through the
SSRI and SNRI family. In addition to this compulsive
behavior regarding sent messages, Ms. Daniels also
sends emails to dead addresses:

To: grholmes@fvsd.edu
From: demonchild_69@yahoo.com
Date: 04 July 2023 11:39:14 -0800
Subject: Hi
Message-Id: 982573188
MIME-version: 1.0
Content-type: multipart/alternative; boundary="==_
MIME-Boundary-1_==
Content-Length: 8,434

Mr. Holmes--

the lake doesn't want me.

first time it was hardy who came out to be the big hero and save the little girl from hreself. this time it was lana singlton. in her YACHT! it's calld the english rose which is probably some duchess in a mystery book from 1916, I don't know, you probably read it as a kid, ha.

anyway lana got letha out there in the airboat which I didn't even know Banner had the keys to and you can guesss what it was like for a while. or you don't have to do you? you got pulled out of the water once too ecaxtly the same. also by angus insert-nickname-sheriff hardy I guess. huh.

but I'm not even sure for certain that I was trying to do what they said I was trying to do. okay sure, maybe I did have too much in my system and the breathing wasn't so great and perfect so what. and okay so maybe I was in the town canoe again, which I can understand would make certain people think certain things.

and you maybe would't guess it but you probly would. I was thinking about final girls again sir, or still and always, you know me. specifically it was something you and I both having history degrees know very well. that being that the victors write the books of how it all went down. but if this is so, then it should be final girls writing the slasher stories down, don't you think?

I was thinking this because in a weak moment of mine where Dot didn't have a spot for me and I couldnt ask a certain non-family friend for a mop and broom and gum scraper and litter stick, I was thinking I should have a fake name to write the book of indian lake with to make some steady money. or maybe I should just go with my real name jenny daniels. that way my mom when she hears about it will know it's me. but anyway as I'm sure you can guess if you were guessing, then protecting camp blood from having to live under a new and wrong name doesn't exactly pay the bills, surprise.

it pays the bills in my heart though.

i think you'd be proud, I mean. I think if you were still here, you'd be right there with me, sir.

anyway so letha last night as you can imagine hugged me so hard on the big deck of the english rose which is like if a cadillac were a luxury liner actually that it wasn't exactly helping my breathing. but I guess it sort of was too. she thought I was having an ashtma attack but it was my chest and lungs hitching up and down like an idiot, like a broken uesless thing, like somebody who floated out there to take all her pills at once and just see what happens. and those pills are still in my fingertips for this, all sorries about that, it's making me spell like a high schooler I'd probably give a D. unless she was really really trying, I mean. unless she was crying while she was writing it, because of who she was writing to.

if it worked out there on the lake before superwomen Lana and Letha paired up to fight the crime that's me, I was going to finally get to tell you what our former sheriff told me the last time I was ever going to see him, which is the day I found something BIG out about myself, which is that I can when pressed enough do things I never would have in a 100 years thought I could do.

but maybe hardy already told you himself. he looked at me while I was doing it, I mean, and he nodded once like Of Course.

you and him are probably smoking all the heavenly cigs up there aren't you?

goddamn you, sir.

I miss you I miss you I miss you so much.

to prove it sort of, you probably remember how all the facts and dates and people and places about Proofrock and Idaho in general that you knew from personal experience and your own memories of childhood leaked out in the lake that night whose anniversary is tomorrow again?

with letha hugging me and lana watching and her mountain of a son standing at the railing of the english rose watching this strang woman shiver and sob, I started trying to get all those dates and facts back by saying them out loud in a single long line, into letha's neck and shoulder.

after a bit of it she held me out at arm length which is kind of forever far because she's an amazon from wonder woman land and she looked at me right in the eye like checking was I still there and she asked me jade, jade what is this? what are you doing here?

I shook my head no that it was nothing, because it wasn't anything, it was definitely nothing, just me, but sitting in the front seat of the airboat with her for the ride back to town she whispered to me that she would BUY that fucking coffee shop if I wsnted to work there. but I sh9ok my head no that it was alrite, that that's dorthy's place since forever, it wouldn't be fair, and letha being letha she held me closer to keep the wind from me even though my clothes wern't even wet and she said to me then that I really must have listened in your history classes to still know all those people and places and dates, and then proofrock gets blurry for me in the distance sir, because no one has ever said anything that nice to me ever before, connecting me to you outloud, like that.

after banner skidded us up onto shore in that showoffy way that I guess comes with the badge or something and letha was holding my hand so I could step down, like I was this delivate thing, not someone who had ran into a hell tunnel of dead elk with her 1nce upon a senior year, banner looked back to the canoe he had toed back to the pier and letha said to him about that What? but he just shook his head no, nothing, but it was a lie I could tell.

riding back to their place in banner's tall monster truck, me sitting by the door but with the lock on that ford sucked down in the door because you never know, or with me maybe banner did, letha said that she kept all these spoken memos on her phone for adie, for if mommy wasn't going to be around anymore, and I clutched my hand onto letha's wrist to please get her to stop talking like this please, but she went on, already had it all scripted out in her head to say. she said she wanted me to be the holder of those memos now. what I am I chopped cheese? banner said, but he was joking, and I think it's chopped liver anyway, but I can completely get not wanting to force that smell into anyone's head when they're all unsuspecting and don't have their fortitude up.

letha touched the top of his leg with her left hand but kept her eyes on me, and I looked away sort of into my own reflection in the side window of the truck, and proofrock was sliding past, it was a carousel spinning all around me, and I'd ben riding this ride sicne I could remember already, but know what? I'd never had anybody to ride it WITH, sir.

I nodded once that that that was good, that was fine, that was okay, IK'd hold those memos for adie, and I know this was just a way letha was using to keep me from doing anything stupid again, because now I have a RESPONSIBILITY, and this is probably a trick sharona told her to do, but if it works and it's good and it keeps me among the living and breathing then who cares, right?

inside over the years, yazzie who's another letha, just the imprisoned varity, she told me about how in bow and arrow days there would be certain people who would be bundle holders or pipe holders, and how these bundles and pipes were only trusted with very certain people, because they carried and meant everything to the tribe, and were important for their prolong-ment, like.

I think I'm that now, sir?

because of everything you taught me, that I'll never let go of. because of those memos letha's going to send. because my mom threw her purse at a giant she could never kill one day when it was colder than it had ever been, and she screamed at him just likke Pamela Voorhees would have, sir, and if I die in a canoe by my own hand or palmful then she'll have done that for nothing.

which, that would be a pretty good song, If I Die In A Canoe. especially if one ADRIENNE KING sings it in a whisper voice where she's right up against the mic so you can hear her lips touching it sometimes.

anyway, from the way banner was looking at that canoe, I kind of doubt that I get any more lasting chances with it. but we'll always have that song that doesn't exist I guess.

see you tomorrow, sir. I'll stand there by your place in the ground and I'll hold my hand out with my eyes closed and you'll spiral a lit cigarette down from the sky for me, and so long as I don't look, then you're up there buzzing around.

not me, Mr. Holmes.

I'm still living it out right here.

for now.

—JaDe

HOUSE OF EVIL

"Ms. Daniels?"

I hand-over-hand up from the depths of sleep, which I'd warned myself not to fall into. Nod off in a slasher movie, wake with your throat soaking a red bib onto the front of your shirt. Or, if not the blade, then what I probably deserve for falling asleep out in the open is a lone ember dipping and bobbing all the way across the lake, beautiful and magical and Disney as fuck until it lands in the oh-so-flammable material of this teaching skirt, at which point I'm sitting in a throne of flame here on this boat.

Inside, about two years in, a woman from A Block found some way to light herself up in the yard. We're not supposed to have accelerants, but, since cigarettes dial our nerves down to less jangly, there's contraband lighters to go around. What are we going to burn? Our world was concrete and steel.

This woman must have faked like the worst nicotine junkie ever, and for months if not years—long enough to stockpile enough lighters to drip little drops of lighter fluid all over her like suntan lotion. Or? Maybe under her clothes she'd mummy'd herself in toilet paper, and just held the cherry of her cigarette to a few strategic tatters, then stood there with her arms out to the side like a superhero, her flames coming on.

She didn't swoop out of the yard when the flames engulfed her, though. What she got was tackled with blankets, rolled hard back and forth. She died in the infirmary three weeks later.

It's the only time I've smelled human flesh searing like that. So of course that day at chow it was rubbery Grade D pork chops for lunch—no bones, of course, because who wants to get shiv'd with a ground-sharp piece of pig. I mean, who wants to get shiv'd at all.

I didn't eat my meat that whole week, and the pudding was suspect as hell too, scorched on top into a skin of baked blood.

I think the burning woman's name was Mel, maybe? But in death she became the Phoenix Lady. She was sort of our hero. I've always wondered how religions get started, but now I have a better handle on it, I think. Take some subjugated group of people and give them something to hook their hope claws into. Something that can, in the retelling, just get better and better. Then by the time it's climbed high enough, you can't let go anymore, because the fall's too scary, so you go all in on that it really happened this way, and only this way.

What I'm saying is that after about six months, the story had been pared down and built back up into the Phoenix Lady giving the guards the finger with both hands even as the flames were sizzling big globs of her flesh down onto the concrete of the sun-bleached basketball court. After a year, the story became that when the guards tackled her with the blankets, they'd only gotten the physical body—her flame-self, the part that was really her, it kept that same magical form, and it lifted into the sky, looked down on us all, and nodded in its beatific, long-view way that we would be all right.

Phoenix Lady might have just been pulling the old eject lever, checking out on her own terms, but I'm pretty sure that a lot of us inside kept on living because we saw her escape—we knew now there was an end, that there was a way out. That if we just held on a few more months, then the board would consider our petition, weigh our souls, and nod that smallest of all nods, that means the best of all things.

The parole board, I mean.

Not the school board from summer, which is my first thought when I hear this voice above me with its low and gentle "Ms. Daniels? *Jennifer?*"

Where I'm sleeping is Hardy's old airboat, which Banner's been tinkering on for a month or two, now. It's tied to his dad's stubby old dock, which he was always so meticulous and paranoid about. Was somebody going to wear golf shoes on it, poke evil little holes through his sealant? Were one of us kids going to try to carve their sordid initials into a post? Was a bird going to have the gall to actually *shit* on it?

And, I should stop calling it Banner's dad's dock, I know.

It's probably the first place Adie's going to jump into the lake from. But she has to have already done that, Jade, c'mon. Just because you were locked up doesn't mean the world stopped turning.

"W-*what?*" I say, jerking away from this hand touching my left shoulder so lightly. No, not "hand"—cup, mug.

Someone's waking me by nudging coffee against me.

I guess there's worst ways to come to.

Blinking against the brightness—it's just *after* dawn, sleepyhead—I can make out a blurry-tall silhouette with me on this gently bobbing boat. And then I get why I thought the voice was from this summer's endless trials with the school board.

"Principal Harrison?" I say, my voice creaky.

He holds that mug in front of me until I take it.

It's a real ceramic mug, not a paper to-go one from Dot's. He got a coffee pot on a daisy-chain of extension cords, what?

"I didn't want any students to . . . to see you like this," he mumbles, giving me my privacy by turning his back, looking across the lake.

Last night, the fire was an orange glow. In the daylight, it's smoke billowing up and up.

As for why I'm in Hardy's old airboat wrapped in a scratchy

blanket, part of it's that I wanted to feel safe, so I fell back into arms I trusted, that I knew would wrap me up, but the other part's that by the time I got down to the Pier last night to tackle Sally Chalumbert—to reason with her, really, to ask her what she was doing, to explain to her that it was over, that Dark Mill South had been buried back in Minnesota—all the husbands and wives and sons and daughters who had been left behind by their chainsaw-toting whoevers were just standing vigil, waiting for their loved ones to come back with smudged faces and a clutch of cash in their blackened fists.

The American dream, right?

What it meant for me, though, was too many eyes, too many witnesses. And Sally Chalumbert, our Angel, wasn't there anymore anyway.

Walking across to Banner's, away from the completely maddening crowds—hadn't everybody *left*?—the branches scratching my cheeks and arms, I realized that the last time I'd taken this path, I'd been skulking on Letha. I'd been crashing Banner's bonfire party.

This little bit of the shore scooped out under his and Letha's back porch, it's where the Dutch Boy turned up, half his face ripped away. But if I start going down that memory lane—*he died here, she bought it there*—then trying to move through Proofrock will be wading through syrup, won't it?

No, Jade. It'll be wading through hardly congealed blood.

Be realistic. Don't try to dress it up, tone it down.

"See me like *what*?" I ask Harrison, looking down at myself, because, I don't know, maybe I'm suddenly wearing blue mechanic's coveralls, maybe I'm spattered in blood, maybe I'm wearing some lingerie I don't even own.

It's still just yesterday's teaching clothes—skirt and drab-ass blouse. And even if they're somehow offensive or riding higher than acceptable to a principal, I'm cocooned in this scratchy blanket.

But then I get it: bare feet.

That's it, isn't it?

I look up to Harrison in slow wonder.

Once in the teachers' lounge the first week of classes, I was kicked back on the napping couch—that's what I was informed it was called—my comparably high heels tucked in beside the couch's apron very neatly, not just kicked off over the arm, to fall wherever.

But Harrison, washing his lunch bowl out at the sink, had cleared his throat in that way bosses have, that straighten-your-back way, that I-need-the-floor-for-something-very-important way.

Chin Treadaway, who I'd only ever known as an elementary teacher, had made hot eyes at my feet, *about* my feet, and it took me a moment or two to put together what she was trying to get across: Harrison was weird about bare feet? Seriously? And he moved to a *lake* town?

But, on the napping couch that day, when I finally made the connection Chin wanted me to make, I looked down to my feet to see if I had tiny skulls painted on my black toenails or what—more like Ghostfaces, thanks—and kind of wiggled my toes in greeting to myself, and . . .

Oh.

It wasn't that Harrison didn't like having to be confronted with bare feet. What I have now is worse than bare feet, though, isn't it? I have feet missing some toes.

He was grossed out about my amputations. Well, two amputations. The pinky just sort of cracked off all on its own, like it had had enough. Peace, *out*. The stumps of it and the other two, anyway, the hospital had to clip the rest of the dead skin off then sew the tops and bottoms, so that what's left of my toes looks like Smiley's smile.

Which is why I wear these stupid knee-highs from 1962, now—of my two pairs of teaching heels, only one is closed-toe. When you want your contract renewed, want to make a career out of this, maybe even a *life*, then you . . . well, I was gonna say "toe the line."

You "cover up the abomination you are" is the better way to say it, I guess. It's the kind of thing that really makes you feel great about yourself, getting dressed for work.

I wave my remaining toes over the side of the boat, slide them across the top of the water, wishing so hard I could dunk my foot, get that cool wetness for a proper wake-up, but . . . I've got to pull on the tiresome hose that were probably old-lady even when my mom was coming up.

Shoes next. They feel like hard little prisons.

I stand in them, a bit unsteady, and Harrison feels the airboat rock.

"No class today?" I ask.

"Canceled," he says, tilting his mug up to slurp some off the top.

Not because it's Halloween, but because the spooky props in the hug-n-go-lane aren't just props—the high school is a crime scene for the moment, at least until Banner clears it. And Banner's across the lake, can't clear anything.

I take a drink off the top of my coffee, say—even *meaning* it— "Thank you. This is just what I needed."

"Dorothy's bringing donuts, she says," Harrison tells me, looking back to be sure I'm decent.

Hardly, dude.

At the school board meetings, he was the one enumerating the many reasons forcing him to let me teach history to his students wouldn't be in their, or anyone's, best interest.

You don't come at Letha Mondragon, though.

Her dad might have been a dick and a killer—something we avoid talking about at all costs, thank you—but he knew how to impose his will on the world, that's for sure. He never walked out of a board room not having gotten the best of everyone in there. Letha inherited that from him. She's not a bully, always does it with kindness, where it doesn't even feel like she's being persuasive, or flexing her fortune, but she gets what she wants.

This coffee *is* good, though. I'll cover my grinning toe stumps for it, sure.

Nothing to do about the freezer-burned craters on my face,

though, Mr. Harrison. Or these three stiff fingers, nearly bitten through by a dead girl. Or this black-as-midnight heart, sputtering exhaust up through my nostrils.

"Here it comes again," he says, obviously, like I could miss that heavy thrumming.

It's the big red and white plane, swooping in for another load of water. A pretty magical damn thing to see, first thing in the morning.

"I hear they're about to transition to fire suppressant instead of water," Harrison says, exactly like a former science teacher might.

"What are you, um . . . ?" I try to say, but the words keep slipping away. *What are you doing over here at Banner's? Why haven't you left town with all the other sane people? Where the hell's your coffee pot, dude?*

"Captain goes down with the ship?" he turns around to say with a small grin and raised eyebrows, so I know he doesn't really plan on standing in Henderson High while it burns to the ground. "But what are *you* doing here, Ms. Daniels?"

Fucking bosses. They always know exactly the worst question to ask, don't they?

"I'm the babysitter," I tell him.

Mr. Harrison takes a drink and skates his eyes around our general vicinity for my charge.

"Me and Tiffany Koenig are tag-teaming it," I add, sucking some more go-juice down.

I can feel it opening my brain up like a flower blooming in time-lapse.

"Shifts, I see," Harrison says. "And you're sleeping here because . . ."

"Ever see a movie called *The Sentinel?*" I ask, stepping in beside him, like whoever's closest to the fire across the lake is watching it the best. "There's this, like . . . it's a gate to hell, I think?" I chuck my chin at Caribou-Targhee to show what I'm meaning, here. *The Sentinel* isn't anything like a slasher, but it does have a jumpscare that the slasher shelf can only dream of. "If you stand there and watch the evil, keep it in check, like, then it can't come across."

"So you're that, um, *sentinel*," Harrison says, index finger a metronome against the side of his mug.

"Believe it or not," I say, "I don't actually want Proofrock to burn. At least not this way."

He catches my eye, nods to me that he likes this, that this is the proper attitude for one of his teachers to have.

"Whatever happened to that other history teacher?" I ask. "The—"

"Mrs. Dixon," Harrison fills in.

"Before her."

Most of my quizzes are cribbed across from yours, Mr. Holmes, but Dixon's were in the file cabinet as well. They're not better, but I don't think the kids' parents still have versions of them in their parents' old boxes in the garage.

"Oh, you must mean Claude," Harrison says.

"Armitage, right?"

It's a last name from one of the movies Letha caught me up on.

"Greener fields, I suppose?" Harrison says. "Less . . . snowy?"

By which he means less "dangerous," I can hear.

None of Armitage's stuff was in the file cabinet, though.

Probably for the best. It all would have been slasher stuff, I bet. Or drafts of the book Banner says Armitage was pulling together, about the Proofrock killings—all of them. A very long book, yes. Maybe multiple volumes. With an open ending, and bloody fingerprints.

"There he is," Harrison says, holding his mug out as pointer finger.

I peer ahead to see what he means, at first thinking he can make out some distant shape on Treasure Island—some chainsaw wielder stranded, the canoe they tried to paddle across popping a leak. Leatherface marooned, waving that family saw above his head with Muppet arms, his dried-leather face somehow still managing to register "panic" and "sadness" and "loneliness."

But Harrison's meaning closer in than that.

"Oh," I say, and immediately cast around for Christy Christy, setting her tripod up to document.

It's brown woody tines poking up through the surface of the lake.

Banner's dad's trophy elk, making the rounds.

If I was a swimmer, if the lake would even take me, I could paddle out there right now, haul it in, hang it back in Banner and Letha's living room like it used to be.

It wouldn't bring us back to before Stacey Graves, though. Before Dark Mill South.

Before whatever this is.

"The kids say that, at night, it clambers up onto shore, clops down Main Street," Harrison says about the elk. "It looks in the windows with one marble eye, and if you see it watching you like that, then you have seven days."

"A hundred years ago, it was Ezekiel," I throw in. "And after him, or before him, I don't know, it was . . . there was this woman who was supposedly murdered, and hidden across the valley somewhere."

"Josie Seck, yes," Harrison says.

I flash my eyes over to him about this.

"Mother of the supposed Lake Witch Stacey Graves?" Harrison says playfully, batting his eyelids after it almost coquettishly. "Shouldn't the high school history teacher be up on all the local legends?"

"Married to Letch Graves," I say back, rising to this. "*Murdered* by Letch Graves at the behest of Ezekiel, the fire and brimstone preacher they found naked and gibbering in this woods in . . . was it 1879?"

"'Gibbering'?" Harrison asks.

"When you're evil, you gibber."

"Maybe all preachers were evil back then."

"'Back then'?"

Harrison chuckles about this, takes his last drink. He slings the dregs out into the lake.

"Caffeinated trout, great," I say, but swirl my last half-drink around to get all the grounds going and add them in with his.

"I talked to Mrs. Jansson about Hettie," he says then, gearing us down.

"You didn't tell her about Lemmy's video?"

"Video?"

"Never mind, sorry," I say too late, because of course Lemmy would have unplugged his phone from the projector before Harrison cued into the dead bodies pasted up there.

Harrison shakes his head no to this, says, "Mr. Singleton was a student in Greta Earling's homeroom when I was at Golding. Never had to come to my office once."

I try to picture a kindergartner sitting in the unforgiving chairs outside the principal's office at the elementary. Their feet not even touching the institutional carpet.

"I never had to go to the office either," I say, kind of quiet. "I mean, in elementary."

"Before my time," Harrison says, pressing his lips together, meaning there's a lot he's not saying, here.

"Really, what are you doing here?" I have to ask.

"We need people to help go door to door," Harrison says. "There's a lot of holdouts who won't leave, even though—"

He nods across the lake to the fire.

"You need my help," I say, getting it. This is his way of asking without asking.

"Community service goes a long way to engendering good will among . . . the *community*," he finally lands on, though I know what he means is "the school board."

"So you were coming by to check if Letha and her daughter had left."

"The sheriff is otherwise occupied."

"Letha's in Salt Lake City," I tell him.

"Well then—*good*."

"And Adie's with Tiff."

"At the sheriff's office, yes."

And I'm, for once, not in the middle of everything, I don't say out loud, just realizing it. Whatever's going on . . . I *wasn't* out in the woods with Hettie and Paul and Waynebo, if they were even really there. I wasn't the one to stumble onto the Bronco. And I only got to the hug-n-go lane *after* a dad had his head wrenched off. And, right now, I just slept the night through, didn't I? I'm not over in the chainsaw woods with Banner and the rest. The fire isn't licking at the ends of my hair, curling it up, making it char and stink.

Used to, I wanted nothing more than to be in the bloody center of the swirling madness, because . . . because I wanted to touch the grail, I guess. I wanted to brush my fingers across the rough plastic of a certain hockey mask, I wanted to hear the *schtiing!* of an escapee from a mental institution sliding a chef's knife from a wooden block.

I've seen a Casey strung up from a tree by her guts, though. I've been in that cell Rod died in.

No thank you, Mr. Craven, Mr. Carpenter, Mr. Cunningham. I'm fine being on the outside for once.

Slashers are strictly a spectator sport for me, now. History teachers don't wade through an acre of gore to get to the chalkboard. We're mousy and academic. Not the final girl kind of mousy and academic, but the nervous, timid kind. The kind that's not a shell a princess-warrior can unfold from, flashing her killer eyes left and right, but the kind of shell that's a pretty okay place to hide, ride this out.

"So?" Harrison asks, taking a knee to wash his mug in the lake.

He reaches back for mine, to wash it as well, and I hand it across gingerly, because this is monumental: it's not the principal who does the dishes for the teacher, it's the other way around.

But this isn't the teachers' lounge.

"Yes, I can help," I tell him, and he even holds a hand back for me, to guide me up from the airboat onto the shaky dock.

"I already did Pine," Harrison says, and looks to the south, kind of calling dibs on Cedar and Aspen and the rest, that direction.

Leaving Third to yours truly.

There's less houses down this way, but it's also where the trailers are, and the houses that people hammer random rooms onto over the summer. And then I get even more what's going on, here: Harrison needs me to knock on *those* doors because, to him, these are "my people."

Inside every sort-of compliment is a burrowing insult, yeah.

Surprise.

What Harrison probably doesn't know about asking me to work Third, though, is that my mom used to live down that way. And that I haven't been down there for . . . I honestly don't know how long. Used to, maybe sophomore year, I would slouch that direction, hiding from all headlights, all porch lights, all smokers and maker-outers, and I'd watch the windows of my mom's trailer, try to imagine her in there cooking dinner, watching gameshows, flipping through photo albums from before everything went bad for us.

Though, for her to find a time before everything went bad, she probably would have had to dial back to the pre-Tab days. So . . . junior high? But me, a sophomore, thinking of her in junior high, I had to wonder if she and I would have been friends or not. If I could have saved her from paddling over to Camp Blood one Friday night. If I could have pulled her back to that canoe instead of letting her be led into one of the cabins by the boy who could become my dad, and then, later, become something else, something worse.

I don't know how many cigarettes I smoked, watching the lights in her trailer glow on and die down, taking my heart with them. When I get the lung cancer I have coming for me, I'll look back to the me from then, I know.

And I won't even regret it.

Harrison salutes me away, pivots on the heel of his loafer, and, the handles of both our empty mugs hooked in his fingers, he slopes over to the less bad part of town—his own kind.

Me, I guess I'm where I belong.

The first place is a ramshackle house. I don't even know whose.

I knock on the door, knock some more, no response.

"Hello!" I call out, trying to make it not come off aggressive, but when you're me, it's hard to keep the edge out of your voice.

There's wisps of smoke coming up from the sort-of chimney, so somebody's here, but . . . screw it.

"There's a fire . . ." I say at volume, like just covering myself so I'll feel less guilty later, and then it's the next house—also empty, but the boarded-up kind—and the next, which is Rexall's.

Yeah.

I walk on the other side of the road from it, just to be less in its sphere of influence.

That submersible drone is still taken apart on the workbench beside his place, though. And the box it must have come in is there as well, like he was maybe looking for re-assembly instructions.

"Good luck," I mutter to him, trying to move my lips, for in case he's got the curtains parted, has a bead on me.

Rexall has a tarp stretched across the workbench, slanted down so it doesn't become an overhead swimming pool—he's not a complete idiot—but . . . the drone's a submarine, isn't it? What's it care about water?

Not my business.

I'm almost past his place when he lumbers out in his robe, a bottle of beer in his left hand, the breakfast of the kind of champion he probably thinks he is.

"Your hair!" he bellows across to me, lifting something to his mouth to crunch into.

I touch my hair to, I don't know, check if it's on fire or something. When it isn't, I flip him off with both hands, walk sideways so he can't miss this.

He chuckles, it looks like, takes a long draw on his can to wash down whatever he bit off, and nods good morning to me as well.

When my dad rolled his Grand Prix after getting my mom pregnant with me, he was alone, which is one of the big regrets of my life. Rexall could have slung up from that passenger window, saved all the girls of Proofrock so much violation.

When he brings his right hand up to his mouth for another bite, I see what he's eating for breakfast: a monster carrot.

It makes me suck air in through my teeth.

Has he been keeping that carrot by the door for weeks, just waiting for me to walk past, so he could torture me? What he's saying with it, about my hair, is that used to when I'd try to dye it, it would come up pukey orange half the time. Meaning? Meaning Rexall's been part of my life since I was an idiot kid. And he wants to be sure I know it.

"Pass," I say, just loud enough for myself, and bring my fingers back down, stuff my hands into my pockets, except I'm not wearing a jacket, and this stupid skirt doesn't *have* pockets.

I hunch my shoulders all the same, shuffle and scrape away. Score one for him, I know. He got exactly what he wanted from that interaction.

I look up into the sky for the ember I need, floating down to the roof of his house. It's just skeins of swirling smoke, tangling together into a constant dim greyness. None of that snow we always get for Halloween. Yet.

Just keep eating your insult-carrots, Rexall.

Choke on them, please.

The next lot over is where the trailers get going. I step up onto the soggy porch, knock politely, not loud and insistent like a cop, fine grey ash calving off every tiny ledge of the door so I have to step back or get it in my stupid shoes. The knock is kind of soggy, too. Not because the door's wet, but because it's been stapled together at some point?

It pulls in all at once, more of that ash coughing out, so I have to shield my face.

"Jade?" some guy says through it.

When the air clears enough, it's a skinny twenty-two-year-old in boxers and a sleeveless t-shirt. My first thought is he's a student from one of my classes, that I shouldn't be seeing him in his underwear. But then I remember him from when I knew him, for all of about four minutes.

"*Jace?*" I say, my eyes so hot.

He steps forward and hugs me hard. I pat him back, give myself over to this.

"Jace Rodriguez," he says, stepping back into his doorway, presenting himself in all his current unpresentableness.

"You're not leaving," I say, obviously.

He steps to the side, presents the seriously old man sinking into his easy chair, a clear tube snaking up from an oxygen bottle to his nose. He's not quite the grandpa from *Texas Chain Saw Massacre*, but he could stunt-double for him.

"Oh," I say, and don't ask why this grandpa's not up the hill in the nursing home. Inside, Yazzie told me about how many generations of her family lived in her house when she was a kid, and, maybe I'm a bad Indian, but I didn't even know that was possible.

Jace is like her, though. Instead of wheeling his grandpa through the double doors of Pleasant Valley Assisted Living, using it like a storage facility, he's letting his grandpa ride these last few years out here, with family.

"You do know about the fire?" I say, stepping aside to present the sky to him. Like he can't smell it, can't see it.

"We're good," Jace says.

"And—"

I swallow, breathe in through my nose.

"What?" Jace asks quietly, stepping forward to let the screen door shut gently behind him. It won't actually stop our voices from making it in to his grandpa, but the idea of having a barrier between us and him somehow makes this feel more private.

"It's—" I start, not sure how to say it all.

And? Most other people, I don't even try to get it said right. But I haven't huddled behind a video rental store's shelf in the dark while a killer stalked the aisles with most other people. Jace and me, we've seen his classmates skinned and pegged to the wall, laid out on the floor.

We're also maybe the only two people who know that it wasn't Dark Mill South who killed them, but a batch of poison cupcakes. Or, who knows, maybe Jace imagines Dark Mill South in an apron, his hair tied back, pouring just enough batter into each cup in that muffin tin, I don't know.

"*Is he back?*" Jace asks quietly, casting his eyes all around because he can already read my face, I guess.

"Not him," I say.

"Who?"

I hold my hand down to about my waist, like measuring the height of a kid.

Jace cocks his head, doesn't get it.

"I don't know either," I tell him. "Just . . . be careful?"

"Is this the thing that happened at school?"

I nod a reluctant nod.

"I heard it was the game warden this time," Jace says, sort of squinting his whole face.

"Him too," I have to admit.

"'Too'?"

"There's also—" I wince, squint, don't want to have to say it: "This woman, a victim of . . . of *him*, Dark Mill South. She's in town too."

"What the hell is going on, Jade?"

"The usual," I have to say. "People are dying. The real cops aren't coming. There's—"

I hold my open hand to the fire: the thing giving these killings cover to keep happening.

"What's wrong with this place?" Jace asks. "Why does this keep happening?"

"Hundred-plus years ago, a husband killed his wife, abandoned his little girl, and I think that, like, polluted the lake?"

"Do not eat fish from these waters," Jace recites.

I wasn't here for this, but I've seen the photograph that was on the covers of all the magazines. It's July 2015, after the massacre, when a sign shows up on shore right by the Pier, warning people not to eat fish from these waters. The unsaid part of it was "because a piece of your relative or best friend might be in that fish's belly."

"Letch Graves," I mumble. "I think he started it all. One bad act, it—it sort of infected this place?"

"History, history . . ." Jace says, like putting pieces together in his head. Then, "Oh yeah, right. You're the new Defense Against the Dark Arts teacher, I forgot."

"The what?"

"Harry Potter?"

I nod, know *of* him, sure. His books were on the library shelves, inside, but didn't really circulate. Yazzie said it was because it made all the moms locked up with us sad, thinking about their kids reading this kind of stuff. I did see a few minutes of the movie version for one of them this summer, though, at four in the sleepless morning, after another groggy play of Brendan Fraser versus Old Egypt. The bad guy in Harry Potter was pretty much Dr. Phibes, who was pretty much the Phantom of the Opera, and on and back to Dr. Frankenstein, it never stops. These kind of guys have been with us forever.

It doesn't exactly leave me hopeful for humanity.

"So you're gonna . . . ?" I say about him and his grandpa, riding it out.

"I tell you a secret?" Jace asks.

I shrug sure.

"I kind of actually like *The Price Is Right*," he says. It's what his grandpa's watching right now. It's the old host, the one who's all about keeping all dogs from ever having any more dogs, I guess because he had a bad experience with dogs or something.

"You're spinning the Big Wheel here, that's what you're saying?" I say, getting it.

"Think we're gonna win this time, yeah," Jace says with a mischievous grin.

"You've got power?" I have to ask, to be sure I'm not imagining this.

"Generator," he says with a shrug.

"And you have no pants . . ." I droll out like I have to, finally.

Jace looks down, contracts from a standing position, kind of eeks his mouth out, his eyes popping wide.

"I'm sorry," I tell him, more serious now. "For . . . all this."

"You just live here," Jace says, still covering himself. "Same as the rest of us."

It feels better than six months of talking to Sharona.

Because I don't trust my voice not to break, my eyes not to spill over, I lift a hand to him in farewell and back off the porch, don't look back.

"You just live here," I repeat, a little ways down Third.

If only I could believe that.

Like to prove it, the next place is my mom's trailer. Like that, I'm thirteen again, watching the windows through a scrim of my own smoke. Until a drone rises up from the roof like some great malignant bug, hovers in place, and then tilts over, coming for me like the end of the world.

I take an involuntary step back, splat on my ass, my hand up to ward this off.

"Don't worry," a deep male voice booms behind me.

It's Lemmy Singleton.

I spin around to kick with my heels if I need to. Not because it's him specifically, but because it's someone who wasn't supposed to be there.

Lemmy's just standing there, was lurking in the trees, evidently. Which is a great thing to do when folks are turning up dead.

"Lemmy?" I say.

"Teach," he says back, watching the drone land ever-so-gently at his feet. He says about it, "Guess one got away. Sometimes they have their own mind. But if I get within about fifty yards, they reconnect, wake up."

"'They'?" I have to ask.

He smirks, still guiding the drone.

I stand awkwardly, in clunky stages, and wonder again what it must be like to move like a gazelle who knows martial arts—like Letha. Some of us are born to clamber, though. And then stare down whoever just didn't have the tact to look away, let us rise in our stupid way.

"What are you doing here?" I ask.

"Just told you," Lemmy says, squatting to inspect his runaway drone, which I guess is part of the fleet or swarm or whatever that he tried to fly for the Fourth, before he had full control of them.

"I mean—" I say. "What about the *fire?*"

"Lake's safe enough."

I hadn't considered that. One of the benefits of yacht life, I guess.

"You know Sheriff wants to talk to you about that?" I tell him.

Lemmy shrugs, isn't concerned.

"Anything else?" he asks, when I obviously have something.

"Who put those *Scream* Post-its on Hettie and Paul's chairs?" I ambush.

Lemmy grins and looks down.

"You?"

"I don't even like that movie."

"You don't like *Scream*? How can someone not like *Scream*?"

"Ever notice how those movies always focus on the . . . the norms?"

The clean-cut kids, the non-Goths, all the many opposites of John Bender and his bologna-throwing ilk.

Or maybe that's a ham sandwich, I don't know.

"Focusing on the jocks and princesses makes it scarier for the parents," I explain, ever the teacher. "They've done everything right, have their kids in the right classes, the right clothes, have given them all the right chances. But it still doesn't mean they get the right to live. That's terrifying. Playing by the rules is supposed to be the key to survival."

"So . . . so my mom doesn't care about me, then? Because I look like this?"

"Try *The Craft*," I say. "Or—do you know *Disturbing Behavior*? And there's those bikers in . . . in the third *Friday the 13th*?"

"That all die?"

"What about the bikers in *Dawn of the Dead*?"

"You think I'm a biker?"

"I mean, that was . . . Motörhead's main fan base?"

"Who's Motörhead?" Lemmy asks, holding my eyes in his long enough that I sort of lose my mental footing. But then he can't help it, has to grin under his heavy metal mustache.

I push him in the shoulder, and it really only pushes me away.

"You never finished your presentation," I tell him.

"The big finish . . ." he says, standing with the drone like it's his puppy.

"But let's let everybody else go first," I say, watching my mom's former trailer. "Listen, I've got to—"

He looks to the trailer as well.

"There?" he asks, sort of incredulous, I think.

"What do you mean?"

"Just—Holy Crow . . . I don't know. You shouldn't be there alone."

"Phil?"

"What?"

"His name, Phil. My mom's ex–common-law husband, and general degenerate?"

"Your mom was with Holy Crow?"

"Are we even speaking the same language, here?"

"He's your *dad?*"

"No, my dad's——"

I hook my chin out to the lake, obviously.

"Oh yeah," Lemmy says, chastened. "But, Holy Crow——"

"Phil Lambert."

"He's bad news."

"News flash, news flash."

"I mean . . . he's dealing now, I *hear*. So he might not take kindly to unannounced visitors?"

"*Dealing?* There's drug traffic in Pleasant Valley?"

Lemmy shrugs like he doesn't really know, has no reason to know, what's he even doing here, is this . . . what? *Idaho?*

Yeah.

So my mom's common-law widower is Proofrock's connection. Great. Just what this town needs.

My guess is that what he used for stake money was the settlement from my mom's death—her boss was hiking her home from work, hadn't clocked her out on the timesheet yet, so, technically, she bought it in service of the dollar store.

Worst epitaph ever.

Phil's take was twenty-five thousand, I hear. None of it to me, probably because I never asked after it. Is twenty-five thousand enough to start a drug empire, though?

Maybe at eight thousand feet, I guess. In a town of three thousand. Never mind that the last dealer I knew of in town was Rexall— it's how he got his name.

But it sounds like Phil's on top of the name-game himself, already.

It doesn't matter, I tell myself. All that does is that I for sure never knock on Phil's door for a baggie. Because, knowing him, he'd probably gift it to me, and he's one person I don't want to be indebted to.

"Come with, then?" I say to Lemmy, nodding ahead, to the trailer.

Lemmy looks over there, and I can see the wheels turning in his head: if Phil answers, says something along the lines of *Hey, Lem,* then . . . that'll mean a certain little something, won't it? And in front of a teacher?

"I don't care," I say, though. "You said it's not safe? That he might shoot through the door, just on principle?"

"Principal . . ." Lemmy says, and steps over, scrolls some video back on his phone.

It's Harrison, walking the other way from me a few minutes ago. Still swinging those two coffee mugs, not a real care in the world.

What if it's him? I have to ask.

Who even is he, really?

Like I have to, I flash on the first time seeing Principal Himbry in *Scream*, and how, for a moment, it was definitely him chewing through the senior class. But I guess *The Faculty* would cover that soon enough.

I can't start thinking like that, though. I'm not in the middle of it all this time, I'm way out here at the edge, just doing clean-up. I'm strictly support, at best the survivor from last round, who the current victim pool comes to for advice. I was always meant to be Randy, a Cassandra, a Clear, never the Sidney, never the Laurie, the Nancy. And, I might worship at the shrine of Ripley, sure, but nobody gets to be her.

Stokely, maybe? I could be Stokely, I think. She lives, I mean. I'm sort of into that, these days. I used to imagine myself as Gavin from *Disturbing Behavior*, with his grand and eloquent breakdown of all the castes and cliques of high school, but things don't exactly go great for him, proving that insight isn't armor.

"Just thirty seconds," I say to Lemmy.

He stares at Phil's trailer for probably *twenty* seconds, then finally nods once, like answering some call of duty.

Walking up, navigating the washing machines and derelict Toyotas, Lemmy lofts the drone ahead of us. It sinks nearly to the top of the tall grass, digging for air, then rises on its furious little blades, hangs above us.

"Just in case," he says.

There's no porch, so the doorknob is well above my head.

I knock on the bottom of the door, step to the side. Lemmy too.

When there's no answer, he steps in, knocks higher, and harder.

"Holy Crow!" he booms out, pretty much shaking the trailer on its rotted-out tires.

We listen for footsteps on the hollow floor.

Nothing.

"He used to be just Phil," I say through my gritted teeth.

"He's Indian, isn't he?" Lemmy says back, with all due delicacy. "I mean, Native American?"

I don't dignify this, just knock again, hard enough to hurt my knuckles.

"He took his stash and left?" I say, turning to face the lake, clock the fire.

Lemmy doesn't follow, though. He's . . . looking at his phone?

"What?" I say.

He tilts the phone so I can see what the drone at the window is seeing: Phil's living room.

"That's probably not jelly, is it," I say, the defeat pretty palpable in my voice, I have to think.

There's blood splashed across the white curtains behind the couch.

"We should call Banner," I say, palming my phone. "The sheriff, we should call the sheriff."

My phone's dead, though: no charging ports on an airboat that just came out of retirement.

Lemmy swipes away from the drone-cam, hands his phone to me, keypad already popped up. I do the area code like you have to now, and the first three numbers we all share, and then . . .

"Seriously?" Lemmy asks, about this mental failing on display.

"I just touch his name," I say, sort of with a guilty gulp. "I never—"

"Nobody knows numbers anymore," Lemmy says with full-on disdain, like *he's* the adult, here.

"He probably doesn't have service over there anyway," I say, tilting my head to Terra Nova—the fire.

Lemmy shrugs not like he's doubting me, but like he's aware of the uselessness of either of us being right, here. Kid's older than his years.

"C'mon," he says, and doesn't wait, is taking his long steps to the north end of the trailer. "Here," he says, and uses his boot to slide a section of the trailer's skirt to the side. Instead of being bolted on, it's somehow hanging on rollers, like the screen in front of a sliding glass door.

"What the hell?" I have to ask.

"He says drug dealers and Indians, they always have an escape route."

"We do?"

"You don't?"

Lemmy shines his phone's flashlight in.

"No critters," he says, and looks back like to let me go first. Which I almost have to smile about. He gets it, shrugs again—his main gesture, but I guess, at his size, it tracks, since he can't go around scaring the breakable mortals—and works his way into that square of darkness.

I shake my head no, that I'm not doing this, I'm not this stupid. But he's my student, I'm his teacher, right, Mr. Holmes? Weren't you there for me that day Letha confronted me about my dad?

The least I can do is follow.

It's easier for me because I'm half Lemmy's size, but it's harder for me because, ducking through and under, I almost catch the scent of rotting elk, and feel the walls shrinking in on me, to suffocate, to drown, to fill my mouth and nose and ears and eyes with wriggling maggots.

I yelp and irrationally stand up all at once, conking my head on the underside of Phil's floor. His and my mom's bedroom, probably—it's how trailer homes are laid out.

"Teach?" Lemmy calls back, shining his phone back at me, lighting my shame up.

There's fine dust sifting down all around me, and a runnel of what

I hope's blood snaking down my face, between my tear duct and my nose, making it look like I'm crying red, probably.

"Shit," I say, holding my head.

And, if it's not blood? Then the toilet up there flooded, and I hit the floor hard enough for some of it to seep through.

Blood, blood, please be blood, I say inside, probably for the first time ever.

Lemmy pops an actual bandanna up from his pocket, just like the real Lemmy probably carried, and holds it across to me.

"Not used?" I ask, which I know is sort of rude.

"Not allergy season anymore," Lemmy says with a grin, and turns around, can tell, I think, that I don't exactly want attention right now.

I dab at the wetness, can't confirm it's blood without tasting, but can't quite bring myself to apply cloth to tongue to see. The way my scalp's stinging, though, I have to imagine I've got some brain pushing through.

"Duct tape," I mutter, crawling.

It's what the campers in *Decampitated* use to reattach that guy's head. It's what Carl Duchamp could have used, in the hug-n-go lane.

Hilarious, Jade. Way to deflect.

"Here," Lemmy says, a few feet ahead.

He's banging the side of his fist against the floor. On his next hit, the escape hatch he knew was there flaps open, *Evil Dead*-style.

"Holy Crow!" he calls up ahead of himself, because poking your head up through a drug dealer's floor's probably a good way to catch a shotgun blast to the face.

Nothing. Still.

"Yeah, not jelly," I say, mostly to myself, about what's splashed on the walls.

Lemmy stands up, places his hands to either side, and pulls his legs through as neatly as a gymnast.

The whole trailer shifts with his new weight.

I worm into the pale square of light, look up at Phil and my mom's water-stained ceiling.

There's some blood splashed up there too.

I shake my head no, don't want to have to see this, but when Lemmy lowers his great hand for me, I let him lift me up like I don't weigh anything. Which—the Lethas of the world probably don't know this, and, nothing against her, she was born the way she was born, but when a guy can make you feel like you're light, like your weight's not going to break him?

It's a first for me.

But then I remember Dark Mill South palming Jace's head, lifting him up and up from in front of the video store counter, and I have to suck air to make it go away.

Sharona tells me it's a function of evolution, our inability to forget trauma. She says that crows, when they gather around one of their own dead in the street, they're not there to mourn like people say, they're there to document and investigate and sear this into their memory, so it never happens to any of them.

In the same way, people who barely made it through this or that, they're constantly replaying it in their head. It's a survival strategy, one only meant to keep us safe.

Never mind the cost of never being able to move forward, *away* from that bad scene.

I shake my head to try again to put it behind me, and blink in the comparative darkness of Phil and my mom's living room. So this is where she spent all those years after walking away from our house one morning, not even taking any clothes, or pots and pans. Or daughters.

I'd like to go back to thinking about Dark Mill South, please.

I settle for focusing on the couch with what looks to be scratchy fabric, the coffee table that's an old cable spool, the TV stand that's two tires stacked on top of each other. Looking around, I have to admit that this is pretty much how I'd decorate, if Letha hadn't had my house ready for me, every piece of furniture new, every wall painted, all the carpet smelling like wet plastic.

"Holy Crow?" Lemmy tries again.

"Phil?" I ask, my voice not nearly so big.

"Hold on," Lemmy says, doing something on his phone that takes all his concentration. After about twenty seconds of it, his drone pops up through the hatch in the floor, nearly giving me a heart attack. He really is a lot better with these things than he was on the Fourth.

"It's like *Star Wars*," I mumble, about this drone surfacing.

"*Empire*," Lemmy mumbles back, bumping the drone into the ceiling. He corrects, directs it away from us, to the kitchen.

Meanwhile, I'm studying this splash of blood on the curtains, the ceiling.

And then I'm studying the foggy bag of what's got to be cocaine on the cable spool.

It's burst, is everywhere.

Does twenty-five thousand buy a kilo? Is that even what this is? All I know about cocaine is from cop shows. Does heroin look different, or the same? Baby formula? Laxative? Is this just that powdery cooking sugar, for some afternoon cupcakes?

"Doesn't matter," I say to myself, and turn not to the kitchen, which the drone has covered, but the other way. Because bad things never come from the direction you're looking. Or, if I'm being *honest*, Sharona, maybe it's because my mom might come walking up like nothing ever happened, sure.

"Yep," Lemmy says behind me.

It's not a good *yep*.

Instead of turning around, giving my back to the hallway, I step backwards, past Lemmy.

"What?" I say.

He holds the phone out. On-screen, Phil's on the kitchen floor in a pool of blood. No head.

"It came here too, then," I say.

"'It'?" Lemmy asks.

"Whatever did—at school yesterday?"

Lemmy nods, gets it, doesn't need me to say it.

"But where is it?" I have to ask. "His head?"

Lemmy directs the drone back to us, grabs it by the edge like a Frisbee, and walks into the kitchen ahead of me, like ready to take the brunt of whatever's waiting.

"There," he says, covering his nose with the back of his hand.

Phil's head is in the oven, looking out. His cocaine or heroin or baby formula or powdered sugar is dusted over his face, I guess like he was slammed into it.

"Holy Crow," I say.

Lemmy chuckles in his chest, which . . . shouldn't he be in some sort of shock, from seeing his first dead body? And of course now I'm wondering how he knew to drive his drone into the kitchen, not the hallway, and what he was doing standing across the road, and why he isn't on his mom's yacht, and what the chances are of one person's drone finding two murder scenes.

"Let me see your phone again," I say.

I don't know Banner's number, but I've had the sheriff's office number in my fingertips for nearly ten years, now.

Tiff answers.

"I need to talk to him," I say.

"Jade?" Tiff says, switching ears it sounds like.

"Aunt Jade!" Adie says nearly as loud as Tiff, meaning the reason Tiff's shifting the phone is that she's carrying Adie around. Probably not exactly in her job description, but in small towns, you wear a lot of hats.

At least her and Banner never dated in high school, though. It would make it extra-special weird, for her to be the one hiking his daughter around now.

"Just his cell," I say to Tiff. Then, even though it hurts, "*Please.*"

She reads it off and I repeat it out loud for Lemmy to keep in his head.

"You good?" I ask Tiff when she's done.

"You mean have I had any state-mandated breaks for the last two days?" she asks back, forcing an overtaxed grin, I'd guess. "Or are you asking if there's any food up here a five-year-old can eat?"

"I know, I know," I tell her.

"I usually have holidays off," Tiff says.

"There's usually not fires and dead people," I say back.

"Yeah, yeah. There anything else, or can I—?"

I can hear the other lines ringing. Probably people reporting the fire, knowing Proofrock. And, according to Banner, probably a third of the calls still ask for Rex Allen or Hardy. It's the town's way of reminding him he's not either of them, and suggesting that maybe he only got that big badge because of his wife.

I don't envy him.

But? Nobody said it would be easy. You don't take on a law enforcement job in a town with a history like Proofrock's and expect to just fish your days away.

"Go, go, answer them," I tell Tiff about all the calls, and hand the phone back to Lemmy.

Before saying anything, he enters those digits he's been mumbling, holds the ringing phone out to me. Four rings later, it dumps to Banner's stupid voicemail, where he low-whispers like Batman, saying he's the hero the city needs at a time like this.

"There still not signal over there?" I ask Lemmy. "What, is this 2015?"

"I was ten in 2015," Lemmy says. "Leave a message?"

"Answer your phone!" I say to Banner's voicemail.

Lemmy thumbs the connection away then makes another call, turns away.

Still, I hear "Mom," and "Pier."

He nods to himself, looks around the living room again.

"My mom," he says, both of us pretending I didn't hear him.

"Good," I tell him. "You shouldn't be out and about right now."

"Neither should you?"

"Yeah, well. Not exactly my first rodeo."

"That what this is?"

"Clowns, death, living life eight seconds at a time . . ."

Lemmy appreciates that, says, "Well, she's coming to get us out of it, anyway."

"*What?*"

"In the yacht."

"Because?"

"Because if we can't call the sheriff, we can *go* to him."

"How do you know he's over there?"

"Chainsaw brigade," Lemmy says with a shrug. "And we sort of saw him riding across in the county boat . . ."

"I *slept* in the county boat."

"The bass boat one."

I nod, could have guessed that. Though, how did Bub and Jo Ellen get across, then, to help with the Seth Mullins situation? Does Proofrock have a *fleet* of police boats, now?

Not your concern, history teacher. You're just the one getting the good intel to the proper authorities. Adie's safe, Letha's not even in town, so . . . yes, you can ride first-class across the lake, use that big foghorn to call Banner to shore, and trail a Dixie cup on a string down to him, speak into your end about what-all's falling apart in town.

He'll need to reel Bub and Jo Ellen back in, call in some volunteers probably—*Halloween 4*, anyone?—and . . . with three "ostensibly" dead in the woods, one *for sure* dead at the high school, and one righteously dead in his trailer, surely that's enough to get the state detectives to send in the National Guard or something? Or, even better, the slasher response team like in *Jason Goes to Hell*.

This isn't the movies, though, I have to remind myself.

A lot.

You were always trying to get me to buy into that one, Mr. Holmes, but I always had Sidney and Billy in my head, picking their genre.

"I got time to change clothes?" I ask Lemmy.

He looks into his phone, slides around, and holds the screen out to me: the blip labeled "Mom" is already almost to the Pier.

"Thought the yacht wasn't supposed to come in that close?" I say.

I'm softening it some because it's his home, but, there's no "thought" about it: Banner explicitly told Lana Singleton that the yacht's keel stabs deep enough into the lake that it could run aground, as gradual as the slope is on this side of the valley. Never mind that a yacht a lot like this one came in to blast its horn when Letha graduated, and was close enough we probably could have caught some shade from it.

"That truck's not there anymore," Lemmy mumbles, meaning the snowplow Banner scraped the old Pier off with, trying to run over Dark Mill South. Though? He could be talking about Cross Bull Joe's old tow truck from the black and white days, that sunk out there just the same, off the original Pier.

Doesn't matter, Jade.

This Pier should be safe from the yacht. I wasn't there for the rebuilding, but word is the pylons are set even deeper and more solid than before, so any truck that tries Banner's stunt again is going to stand up on its nose.

Which I'll believe when I see.

And I don't have clue one how anybody dredged that snowplow up from the water. The only way I can imagine is . . . a crane on shore, maybe? A couple of those skeletonized cargo copters? Or a lot of workers with underwater torches, to cut it into manageable sections for winches?

I'm never here for clean-up, am I? Only for when everything's falling apart.

Harrison's right: if I'm going to be part of this town again, if Proofrock's going to accept me instead of just tolerate me because of Letha, then . . . then I need to pull my weight, do my part.

I should have been leading the charge for this chainsaw brigade, I guess? Except taking money from the Terra Nova Consortium would be a thing I wouldn't get over anytime soon. Even if I spent it all on cigarettes, or a statue of you, Mr. Holmes.

Wouldn't you like that, to be thirteen feet tall and bronze, right there in front of the high school? Every football game, you'd probably get dressed up. And everyone walking by would probably touch your foot for luck or something, until the top of your loafer wore out. And some loyal former student would probably ladder all the way up to your hand once a month or so, to paint the end of your cigarette flaky red.

Or, maybe I'm your statue, right? I'm the part of you that's persisting, that's passing history on and down, never letting it die.

But it sounds like Harrison knows that history as well. At least the Leech and Stacey Graves thing. And . . . what was her name? "Josie" something? *Seck*, yeah. As in, gimme a *sec*, I'll be right there. But back before there were ticking clock hands on every wall, I kind of doubt that was a saying.

Where does a name like that come from? She was Shoshone or something, I guess, but . . . so was Cross Bull Joe, except his name makes sense.

You'd know, Mr. Holmes. Probably "Seck" is a French breakdown of whatever her real name was in Shoshone.

And? Why does it even matter, right? I'm not wondering where Sally Chalumbert's last name comes from, am I? Always Dwelling on the Wrong Shit, a memoir by JD Daniels. And yes, the "D" in that is for Daniels. Deal with it.

"Okay, okay," I say to Lemmy, about the yacht almost already being here.

I'm not moving toward the front door, though, but the . . . kitchen?

I step neatly over Phil, careful as I can be of the blood, and am opening each cabinet, cataloging it. If I know Phil's type, then after my mom was gone, he didn't rearrange. Meaning this organization, it's all her.

The coffee mugs are on the lowest shelf by the sink, and above them are the taller glasses, like you start low in the morning, can rise higher throughout the day. The pans are all on their side in a wire rack, also from smallest to largest. Judging by the TV dinner trays perched on every flat surface in here, I'm guessing Phil doesn't really use these pans much.

I reach in, run my fingers along their edges, making the metal sing just slightly, but enough. No, my mom probably didn't keep human heads in the oven, but she did stencil her personality over how she stacked glasses, and pans.

Squint as I do, though, I can't dial back far enough to recall how she organized the kitchen at home.

And, did she learn it from her mom, or an aunt? A grandma?

I know so little about her childhood. Getting her to talk about herself usually only made her eyes unfocus, like she was trying to look all the way back to then too, but she kept finding nothing.

I wonder if, after the yacht delivers me back to this side of the lake, I don't go into my kitchen, pull everything out onto the counters, then put it all back from littlest to biggest?

Not that I'm telling you about that, Sharona.

It would be some big, revealing deal to you, I know. Which means it would make me feel like a specimen under a microscope. Like you're going to change my name, whip up some article about "Sad Patient 1428."

"1428" being for you, Mr. Craven.

Signed, DemonChild_69.

When I finally step into the front doorway of Phil's trailer, I'm holding on tight to the sides, because I don't want to tilt out, spill over.

Lemmy's waiting for me. It's improper probably, but he takes my waist in his massive hands and lowers me slowly, like I'm a balloon he's tugging down from the sky. Meaning, I'm sure, that he's probably behind all this somehow, right? Them's the rules, slasher girl: once you find yourself kindly disposed towards someone, which takes them out of consideration for doing all the bad deeds, then . . . *surprise!*

But I'm still thinking it might be Harrison, running around on his knees going *Scree! Scree! Scree!* with a kitchen knife.

Never mind that I know, and saw with my own two eyes, that it's definitely and one hundred percent Sally Chalumbert, come looking for her old sparring partner but willing to climb up into the ring with whoever she runs into in the meanwhile.

Where's she from, even? "Elk Bend" or something? Maybe this means that, when she dies, it needs to be by the antler points of Banner's dad's old trophy, like that dad in *Sick*?

Doesn't matter, Jade. Not your job anymore.

I do wish like hell I could change out of this bullshit skirt, though, and lose these useless heels. Kid-me is turning over in her grave, seeing what she's become. Meanwhile, Adult-me's traipsing and stumbling behind her giant of a student, cutting back across Devil's Creek to get to the Pier faster.

"You should have let me change," I tell Lemmy between ragged breaths—I'm not exactly the cardio goddess of Pleasant Valley. What I am is a girl carrying her heels, a girl who walked through her stupid knee-highs she doesn't know how long ago.

And no, Princi*pal* Harrison, I didn't save anybody on Third from the fire. Which won't matter if the flames don't come this far. If they do, though? Maybe we're all born with a bucket for holding regret that's only so big, so that the next big avalanche into it has to splash some out the other side.

I'd take that.

"Listen, maybe I can just swing over to my—" I start to say to Lemmy, angling for a breather in my own living room just a few streets away, but I'm saying this right as we're stepping out of the trees, and the yacht's right there gianter than life.

I stop, my hands to my knees.

"You know each of your steps are two of mine, don't you?" I ask Lemmy.

"But my legs and feet weigh more," Lemmy says back, and, if I could actually breathe, I might be able to poke holes in this. Instead, I just suck air.

"Remember the *Umiak*?" I ask Lemmy when I can, for just a little bit more stall.

"Boat's a boat," Lemmy says back, and steps out onto the Pier without looking back.

I shake my head, exasperated, and follow.

The rope ladder slings out above us and I flinch and cover, sure this is *The Birds 2: Pterodactyl!*, but then the rope and plastic ladder unfurls against the side of this impossibly tall, slick hull.

"What?" Lemmy says, truly concerned, I think.

"When you have long hair, birds make you nervous," I inform him.

"Birds?"

"Things coming from the sky?" I explain, flinging my hand to the ladder.

He shrugs about this, then grandly steps aside so I can go up first. In a *skirt*.

"Serious?" I ask.

"Mom kicks my ass if I'm not a gentleman," he says, wowing his eyebrows and his shoulders both.

"Good enough," I tell him, and wrap the extra fabric of my skirt in my hand and hold it to the side, pulling the rest tight around my legs. With mincing, hardly climbing steps, I hand-over-hand it up and up—again, it's so damn *tall*, like scaling a building that just thrust up from the lake.

Lemmy practically vaults up after me, kind of grins a no-big-deal grin about how easy it is for him, and how ancient I must be to have made such a chore of it, like I'm just on a day pass from the nursing home, here.

"Well then," I say, looking around for attack dogs, for security in black suits, for bear traps fashioned after *Jaws* jaws.

It's just us, as far as I can tell. And this top deck, at least to my very untrained eye, is a spitting image of the deck on the other yacht. The one that, the last time I was there, had dead Founders draped all over it, and blood squelching underfoot, a trophy wife sailing down from the top deck, her legs pedaling the air.

If I understand correctly, that murder yacht's sunk now, very much on purpose, or it's in a boat junkyard, at least—I don't know exactly what "scuttle" means. It sounds like how a crab walks, but nautical stuff is way beyond my tax bracket.

Lana Singleton walks up out of what I officially consider nowhere, her lips pressed together. She's wearing faded jeans and old sneakers, and the denim button-up draped over her five-foot-nothing frame is speckled with paint, her hair in a messy bun at the crown of her head. I mean, at that part of her skull—she's maybe a queen of Terra Nova, sure, but her regalia is her bank account, her social standing, this yacht. And, I should be more generous, I know, less suspicious, but still, I can't help but wonder if she threw this all on when Lemmy said he was bringing me along, and then only remembered to mess her hair up at the last moment, coming up whatever hidden stairs berthed her up top.

She's carrying a fancy paper bag that looks to be from a designer store in Hollywood, or Dubai.

"Lem says you need a change," she says, passing the bag to me, her arm straight out because she doesn't want to crowd me, doesn't want to freak me out.

"Thanks?" I say to her.

"Had to guess on your . . . size," Lana says, blinking a touch faster.

"Where can I—?" I ask.

She tilts her head over to the open door behind us, says, "We'll be at the prow?"

"The Leo and Kate place," Lemmy adds, which sails right past me. But: *front*. I get that much.

I take my bag up the ramp and through the doorway, and inside this cabin or room or whatever it is, it's probably five degrees warmer. It's not bitter cold outside, just the usual October chill, but it's better in here. And, this isn't a cabin, it's a kind of a, I don't know: lobby or main place? No steering wheels to fight a big storm with, just a lot of couches and chairs, a bar back in the corner, a big central table, and— oh: this is the party room, isn't it? All these tall round tables to stand at with a drink, and then one low, two-person table that's not like the rest. It's been dragged here, it looks like. For Lana and Lemmy to have dinner together each night. Someone's even left a laptop there, I guess because they had to eat alone.

But, there's blinds down over all the windows, special for my privacy, probably, and more than likely done with a remote control Lana has on her person somewhere. No, with her *phone*, stupid.

I stumble a bit to the side when the yacht moves, but find my feet soon enough. The laptop slides a bit as well so I rush over, secure it, don't need to get blamed for destroying even *more* property. It does surprise me that Lana would leave me in a room with a computer like this, but I'm sure I don't have the right whorls and arches to get into it.

My fingers find the buttons on the side of this skirt and I suck in to make it easier, and while my hands are busy, my eyes settle on that big central table that's probably mounded with lobster and caviar on the weekends.

I immediately forget that I'm supposed to be undressing.

"Seriously?" I say out loud.

It's a scale model of Henderson-Golding.

I drift over, not even breathing.

Growing up, how many times did I imagine how it must be, down in Drown Town? Not just for class projects, but because it was the first and constant place I could never go, never see. There were the blurry photographs on all the walls around Proofrock—at the walls of Dot's, the bank, the drugstore, the main office at school—but they . . . they weren't like this.

What this is is the product of all the scans gathered by Treasure Island, floating in place directly over Ezekiel's church.

You'd like it, Mr. Holmes. It's a diorama like we all used to make, except it's been 3-D-printed and then painted—oh, of course: Lana's smock.

She's hands-on, then.

The paperweight for the photographs she's been using as color-guide is a hard rubber shark about ten inches long, which I want to float above the buildings, doing the *duh-dunn* music myself while the tiny miners scatter and scream.

But I shouldn't touch any of this.

Also, I should hate it, of course.

Seeing Drown Town in miniature is a magical and impossible thing, but this model isn't just to gift for the nursing home lobby, to be the touchable version of the senior citizens' grandparents' stories. It's a blueprint for the amusement park that's going to replace Camp Blood.

Like scraping those cabins out of the valley will also magically remove from memory everything that happened there?

Bullshit.

Or, if tearing the buildings down is how you wipe blood from the collective memory, then that means Proofrock's next, doesn't it? Right down to the paving stones.

Maybe I should push all this off the table, say it just slid when the propellors kicked on. Except, of course, it's never slid off before. And it's some spun version of plastic anyway, so it wouldn't shatter. All leaving it on the floor would do is make me look ungrateful and petty, confirming everything Lana Singleton probably already thinks about me.

But, I have to slow down to remind myself, I also didn't think much of the Founders, did I? Theo Mondragon proved me right, even if Letha still won't consider it, but the rest of them, including Lana Singleton's dead husband Lewellyn . . . I don't know. Sure, they were filthy rich, probably filthy in all the usual ways besides, capitalism doesn't exactly keep your hands clean, but they maybe weren't that bad, all things considered? Well, either that or they never got a chance to show their true colors. But *benefit of the doubt, benefit of the doubt,* Sharona's always telling me. *Don't expect the worst of people.*

Maybe Lana Singleton isn't rebuilding Henderson-Golding on top of Camp Blood out of vindictiveness, but . . . she honestly thinks she's doing good for the valley? Like that movie she wanted to show? Or maybe her dead husband's family took over all the banks he used to run and left her out in the cold, so she's having to tap into every revenue stream she can?

Though plunking a shiny new yacht down into the lake when Donna Pangborne's monster of a house is empty and probably available doesn't exactly scream frugality, does it?

No, it's got to be some flavor of revenge, even the "killing us with kindness" kind. Lana Singleton wants to shellac over the quaintness Deacon Samuels saw once upon a Sunday drive, proving to him that this place is just as chintzy and grubby as the rest of America.

Arguing with a dead dude is something I guess I can understand.

Understanding is one thing, though. Approving of what she's doing, that's a whole other thing. Sure, this is the place that killed your husband. But if you're looking to lay blame, then who was it chipping into the rock over on the national park side of the lake in the first place, and waking up a certain little dead girl?

Which . . . this lodges in my head, won't go down: has rebuilding Terra Nova woken something *else* up? Is that what's happening?

If the Terra Nova Consortium had just been students in your class, Mr. Holmes, they'd know that over on the other side of the lake, that's where all the bodies are buried. And if any of them knew horror, they'd know you let the dead rest.

When you're the kind of rich they are, though, you probably think none of that applies to you.

In spite of what happened last time.

"Idiots," I mumble, stepping out of my skirt, my phone hand to the tabletop the model's on, because not everybody's a ballerina with perfect balance. And because, if the yacht lurches through a swell, then who knows, maybe I get thrown onto this Disneyfied Drown Town, shatter it like it's made from Legos.

No such luck. I don't think Indian Lake ever gets rough enough to actually jostle a boat this big. Stay for the winter, though, Lana. We'll see what the crush of ice does to this hull.

"You don't turn the other cheek much, do you?" Sharona said to me, our first session.

I didn't explain to her that, in the yard, inside, if you don't come back with fists and kicks and teeth when somebody just brushes your shoulder, then you're getting walked over for the rest of your bid. I also didn't explain to her that some men take not coming back hard as invitation. And that some of those men are fathers.

No, Sharona doesn't know everything about yours truly.

Unless Letha's told her, sheesh.

But no, Letha wouldn't do that. What's mine is mine. What's the poem you made us memorize freshman year, Mr. Holmes? About eating your own heart not because it tastes good, but because it's bitter, and it's yours and yours alone?

I used to know the hell out of that one, sir. Not the words, but how they felt. I never knew somebody from so long ago could be so metal.

But . . . am I talking about me or about Lana Singleton, right? I mean, first, you don't name your son "Lemmy" without being at least somewhat metal, but, second, coming back to the place that killed your husband and trashed your future and holding it in your hand hard enough to squeeze it into another shape, that's Black Sabbath War-Pigging it up at the drive-in's playground while *Black Sunday* flickers on-screen, every car out there either Christine or that big Lincoln from *The Car*, with a certain Peterbilt idling hungrily in the back row—no, two Peterbilts: *Duel* and *Joy Ride*—Dimebag Darrell painted in above it all like the saint he is.

Maybe Lana Singleton's *not* one to tangle with, never mind that she looks like someone who knits or crochets when the pressures of the day are crowding in on her. If Jason keeps coming back because someone cut his mom's head off, then what of a wife whose husband had his head scooped clean?

In slashers, it's the righteous who get the bodycount.

But this isn't a slasher yet, I remind myself. It's just a lot of dead and missing people. In a town known for slashers. And, even if it is a slasher, then it's not about me.

I wish Letha were here to talk this through.

Letha, are you getting my mental texts? Hurry, girl. We need you.

But, I guess if Lana hadn't come back to Proofrock, then Lemmy's never in my class, either. And I think he's actually decent and interesting, isn't spoiled like a kid from Terra Nova should be. Not that that cleanses this scorched-earth stuff his mom's doing.

I would ask Sharona about Lana Singleton, but therapists evidently have this strict policy about theorizing on the motivations of people not in therapy with them. Which I only know from asking her why Harrison has it in for me.

And? I can't stay in this grand dining room forever, I don't guess.

I slide into the clothes from the bag, and, the bag might be fancy, but it's just long black sweat pants with no elastic cuff at the bottom, thank you, and a tan t-shirt with sleeves long enough to have thumbholes, the fabric so thin Lana could probably sunburn through it, and, silkscreened on front—of course: that hockey-mask guy from Teenage Mutant Ninja Turtles. No way is this Lana's, then. It'd even be out there for me in my prime. Turtles? C'mon. Whose could it be, then?

It's about two X's too small for Lemmy, and the material's too expensive for anyone doing the work on the boat.

Solve the mysteries you can solve, Sharona tells me. It's good advice.

And, these clothes are new anyway, still have the tag on them, so it's not really anybody's yet.

Whatever.

My black bra shows through the thin tan, my tats are right there just the same, but that's for other people to deal with. If you don't like it, don't look. That's straight from Yazzie.

I bite the tags off, place them neatly on Drown Town's main street, and nod to myself that I can do this, that I only have to go out there on deck for maybe three more minutes—ten, counting calling Banner in, then riding back like . . . sorry, Mr. Holmes? Like George Washington crossing that famous river, which I didn't even learn from correspondence class, but from that moveable poster you used to have on the wall by the chalkboard. That maybe wound up in, um, compromising positions a time or two, by completely unknown parties.

Girl's gotta do what a girl's gotta do.

I push through the heavy, completely silent doors, walk out in my bare feet, stumble almost immediately on a pair of soccer sandals. Not the G-string kind that wedge up between your toes, but the slide kind that wrap around the front of your feet. They're too big, flap against my heel, slap against the deck, but I don't have to balance to stand in them so: score one for the good guys.

"Everything fit?" Lana asks without turning around, because she—I'm guessing by design—heard me coming.

She's at the railing with Lemmy, who looks back to me and nods hey, like I've been gone on some world-weary adventure, not just changing clothes.

"Thanks," I tell her, holding my arms out to present myself in this gimme outfit that suddenly, out in the cold sunlight, feels a lot like pajamas.

"Here, let me—" Lana says, and before I can stop her she's dabbing at my hairline on the left side with some sort of medicated wipe. I flinch back, but then remember: I hit my head on the sharp underside of Phil's trailer, didn't I?

"I can—" I try, but Lana's in mom-mode. I'm surprised she's not licking this wipe to get it more wet.

"Just a scratch," she says, when through the crusted trail of blood enough.

"Who am I?" I ask, faking amnesia.

Lana hits me lightly on the shoulder with the wipe then stuffs it in the hip pocket of her high-waisted jeans.

"Lemmy was just showing me what the two of you found over in the . . . on Third Street?" she says then.

What did she just keep from slipping out, there? "On the *poor* side of town?"

"I need to tell the sheriff," I say, coming up to the rail and holding onto it, the brushed aluminum pipe so thick my fingers don't come all the way around.

The lake looks so much smaller from this height. Like I'm dreaming. A flying dream. I mean: *another* flying dream.

I'm up there with you some nights, Mr. Holmes.

Oh, the cigarettes we smoke.

The air kind of hurts the scratch on my head, but at least it won't get infected, now.

"Hey, food," Lemmy says.

We all turn and, sure enough, some staff are swirling a table and chairs down, and others are trailing in with covered plates and a patio heater with wheelie-wheels at the back.

"I get cold at this elevation," Lana curtly explains, offering me a chair.

The heat is nice, especially in a shirt you could blow smoke rings through.

Lemmy doesn't sit, but scoops a pile of buffalo wings onto a plate, drifts back to the railing.

"He's afraid these chairs will break," Lana says, leaning across a few degrees like trying to say this where Lemmy won't have to hear.

The chairs are plastic, but not the kind of plastic I'm used to. This plastic feels more substantial than wood.

I flinch when a heavy guitar comes through some speakers I can't see, but this is everyday for Lana.

"You're not connected!" she calls over to Lemmy.

He looks down to his phone, touches the earbud in his right ear, and the Bluetooth figures out what it's supposed to be doing.

"Kids, right?" Lana says.

I take a bowl when she nods that that's what I'm supposed to do, and then scoop some of the pasta in, garnishing it with two of the three remaining buffalo wings, which I plan on counting as dessert, after forcing myself to swallow whatever these noodles are.

"Fork?" I say, not sure what's the polite way to ask.

Lana already has hers—fancy, shiny, heavy looking, initialed ER— but, instead of passing me another one like that, she discreetly slides me flatware wrapped in a cloth napkin, just like in a restaurant, their tops dull and . . . *un*initialed?

"Thanks?" I say, and dump the fork and spoon and knife out, expecting to have to wince from the rude clatter, but . . .

Plastic? Still silvery, but definitely not metal, like Lana's. I heft the fork to be sure.

"Hm," I say, sort of on accident.

"I don't want you to be . . . uncomfortable," Lana says, patting the top of my fork-holding hand with the undersides of the fingers of her right hand, like telling me everything's hunky-dory.

"Thank you," I tell her, and dig in, not sure exactly what's just happened. But? If there'd been plastic and metal silverware, yeah, plastic's what I pick. But I'm not sure I like her knowing this about me, because then I have to wonder what *else* she knows. And how.

The noodles have some sort of fragrant oil on them that I don't think I've ever had.

"I'm glad you're here," Lana says, dabbing her lips as if she could ever have food smeared on her mouth. "It won't take us very long to get to the other side, and I know you have . . . pressing business. But I—I feel that there may be unresolved tensions? Between you and the Consortium, I mean."

I give up on the weirdly slick noodles, bite into a wing, managing to pull all the skin off in a single bite, getting zero meat.

"You could say there's a history there," I tell her, picking through about twenty verbal landmines to get to that.

"I just want you to . . . to know," Lana says, touching the top of my hand again. "That was before. We—we made mistakes. But that's why I'm here now, isn't it? What do the Boy Scouts say? 'Leave it better than you found it'? That's all I want to do with my year here."

"Year?" I ask around a bite.

The noodles are good for taking the sting out of the wings, anyway.

Lana waves her hand in front of her face and crinkles her nose, says, "Lem, Lem! Over *there*, please?"

She's talking about the cigarette he's fired up, that she can somehow distinguish from the smoke of the fire. But, she's a mom, isn't she? This is a thing mothers can do, Letha tells me. She can distinguish Adie's play-sounds from her hurt-sounds from across the house, knows sleep breathing from fake-sleep breathing, and on and on, down to nuances I'd never even thought to suspect.

Lemmy chuckles good-naturedly about being called out for his cigarette, makes his way down the rail at his own pace, like he was going there anyway.

"Yes, a year," Lana goes on. "Lem's senior year? He's loving your class, by the way. I'm so glad we didn't listen to . . . well, I'm glad he enrolled. He's really taken a shine to you, considers you a mentor of sorts."

"He's got a good head for facts," I say, managing to tear all the skin off *another* wing. What I don't say is that Lemmy will also, if Teach is getting that kind of trembly other smokers can clock, leave a single cigarette on the corner of my desk on the way out of class.

Maybe some teachers like shiny red apples, I don't know. This one, she runs on nicotine.

"But you can't tear Camp . . . Camp *Winnemucca* down," I say, falling into Lana's speech pattern and immediately hating myself for it.

"It's so unsafe, though," Lana says, catching my eyes for just a moment. "And . . . and all those *kids*."

"Crane Howarth, Anthea Walker, Jackson Stoakes, and Melanie Trigo," I recite, finally tearing into the wonderful necessary meat of this wing.

"Excuse me?" Lana asks, her fork of two whole noodles still hovering over her plate, because she's evidently one of those women who don't actually eat, just go through the motions.

"The kids who died in the sixties," I say. "I'm the history teacher, remember?"

"It was only four?" Lana asks, then purses her lips like she could have phrased that better.

I get it, though: four isn't much, when compared to everyone who died on the first Terra Nova yacht. And it's nothing compared to the next night. Or 2019.

It *is* more than the construction grunts Theo Mondragon killed and hid, though.

I hiss air through my teeth.

"What, dear?" Lana asks.

"Bit my tongue," I mumble.

"You?"

I have to smile about this instead of answering—she's saying that

I'm not the kind to bite anything back. More importantly, I think this is the first authentic thing Lana's said, here. It's the first time I'm sort of seeing the real her. And? I don't hate her, even though I need to hate her. But this is the way the devil does it, isn't it?

"I appreciate the food, the clothes," I say, pushing my plate away a few inches. "But if you're trying to get me to take my name off that petition—"

"I signed it too," Lana says, discreetly. "I don't know how Deb Haaland missed this renaming when she was . . . renaming the rest of them last year."

I stare at the railing and the trees beyond, knowing full well I'm supposed to play along, supply some examples, except . . . Deb *who?*

If it's not Idaho, then I didn't study up on it. Sorry, Mr. Holmes.

"Ho!" Lemmy calls out.

We both look up to him—one of us gratefully, one with annoyance—and he directs us to . . . to Terra Nova.

"Not that big a lake, is it?" Lana says, standing and draping her napkin off the edge of the table, which is maybe a rich-person thing, I don't know.

I ball mine up, leave it on my plate by the two bones with too much meat left on them. But, growing up, I saw Rexall crack bones like this open too many times, to suck the marrow out, paint his teeth with it, then lean into me making gross sucking-mouth sounds—*Lecter* sounds, I would figure out later—some of those wet black flecks flying out to stick to my face.

I should probably be vegetarian, I guess.

Maybe next week. And when there's no buffalo wings in play.

"Thanks for the ride," I say, and stand into the chill outside of this heater. Is the temperature lower over here in Terra Nova, the way it's supposed to be when there's a ghost around? Or, we are docked where we are: *ghosts*, nature's air-conditioner.

"See you in a few," Lemmy says to his mom, opening a pass-through in the railing so we can ladder down to the dock.

"Wrong, wrong?" Lana says, stepping in to block him out with her 115 pounds, give that swung-open railing to me and me alone.

"Mo-*om*," Lemmy whines.

"There's people dying out there?" Lana says right back to him, eyebrows way, way up. Just like her tone.

"She's right," I tell Lemmy. "I can't be responsible for you."

"I can handle myself."

"I just—listen to your mom?"

Lana nods thanks to me and I step through, give my weight to the third rung down and swing more than I want, so that my first instinct is to panic and cling.

But not in front of them.

"Keep the clothes!" Lana calls down.

Oh yeah.

Thanks for the sweat pants, Terra Nova. They make up for all of it. Everything's forgotten now. Just keep this land over here, you're all paid up.

Idiots.

I make it down to the dock, wave up that all's well, and can almost feel Tiara Mondragon sailing down from the top deck of the old yacht, to splat right where I'm standing, her fixed-open eyes staring back at the yacht like that cover for *Dead Calm*. Which I guess she was, right about then. And still.

"It's nothing, you're being stupid," I tell myself, hands balled into fists, and robot-walk up the dock, fully aware I'm on display here—that Lana Singleton's got her small hands on that brushed aluminum railing up there at the top of this *Ghost Ship*, her lips prim, her eyes flat and dead now that she doesn't have to put a kind face on.

Doll's eyes, Quint said, once.

That about sums it up.

But don't look behind, only look ahead, Sharona's always telling me. I do, my steps taking about two and a half of these plasticky planks in at a time, the floats down there bobbing with my weight, sending small ripples out, like announcing me.

Good, fine. Yeah, I'm back, bitches. My hair's different, I'm older, less eyeliner, and this isn't exactly the outfit I would have picked, but I'm still that same pissed-off girl, her hands balled into fists.

Which is how you talk when you're sort of scared, I know. And when you're not actually saying it out loud, either.

Breathe in, Sharona says. *Now breathe out. Good, good.*

Terra Nova's spread out before me like a brochure.

The rule the first time it was going up was that none of Caribou-Targhee's trees were going to have to die to accommodate these houses. What this guarantee meant was that the Founders had to build where it was rocky and unaccommodating—where they could accidentally punch down into a cave, wake certain horrors up.

You'd never know it now.

The house that was going to be Letha's has got to be complete. Just look at it in all its splendor. It's kind of the flagship of this gateless gated community, *three* stories tall this time, with private balconies and so many monstrous windows to watch the sunrise.

Behind it are the other nine homes, each just as grand.

There's driveways now too, which is weird, since this is a lake-access-only kind of place. But? If Lana scrapes Camp Blood away, plants her version of Henderson-Golding down where it was, then the tourists will need to get *to* that day of activities, won't they? Hammering horse shoes, churning milk, panning for ore, hitting the saloon. There'll probably even be some Angus Scrimm lookalike to play Ezekiel, lead congregation after congregation in sanitized hymns.

What won't be there is Letch Graves killing his wife however he did—*Josie Seck*, that's her name—stuffing her body into some crevice or cranny over here, and then stepping back from the rising waters with everyone else, all of them leaving his eight-year-old daughter to live like a cat underfoot in the new town of Proofrock, eating whatever scraps she can find, sleeping under wagons, in horse stalls, under porches, her big eyes always watching, watching.

If I were younger, and had no standards whatsoever, no human decency, I could play Stacey Graves in that re-enactment, I think. Wouldn't take any study at all.

I step off the dock, down onto the terra firma of Terra Nova. Each time, it feels like I've discovered the monster's lair at last. Just, instead of lava and caves and pools of murky water, there's houses and gazebos and a little gravel path, construction equipment scattered among it all but no workers.

"New World," my big brown ass.

I should hold my lighter to the carpet of each house, leave Terra Nova smoking behind me. Instead, I turn to the yacht still behind me, make my hand into a fist up by my head, and pull it down once, twice, three times, asking them to blow their air horn, please.

Lana just stands there. Might as well be a mannequin.

Did she never learn how to make truckers honk, out on the highway?

I pivot slow on the heel of my new sandal, and the next step is into the sound radius of all the chainsaws. They're buzzing, grinding, growling. This is how a forest dies.

I sneak a look over to where the bank of port-a-johns, as Hardy called them, used to be—where the grass was green and salty, drawing the elk in from the safety of the trees—but there's a well there now, with the waist-high circular stone wall, bucket hanging over it, a cute little roof, the whole deal.

Wait till they're asleep, I say to Samara in my head, skating my eyes away. Because saying her name might conjure her, though, I drift over to that well, sneak a look in, down. It isn't even as deep as it is tall, is just for show. Hilarious.

I move toward the delicate sound of chainsaws, which is where Banner has to be, and for a moment their tearing sound falls into step with the yacht's big diesel engine, propelloring it away, Lana's good deed for the day done. Having no ride suddenly, I cast around for all the canoes and kayaks the chainsaw brigade took across, but . . .

Where are they?

Weird.

I clock the sun for how much time I have, and it's not much. Nightfall's always closer than you think, this high up the mountain. Well, this deep into my chosen genre. But I'm hiding in the video store again—hiding in my own head. Time to be the messenger you said you were going to be, slasher girl. Just . . . walking through Terra Nova again, after all my promises never to again, it's like I'm trying to run up Nancy's oatmeal and pancake batter stairs—each step is goopier than the last.

I haven't even looked up these New Founders' names this time. Since they showed up to swim the lake, I don't think they've even come back, really—well, two of them *can't*: one went *Berserker* in a board meeting, strangled some sad sack, and the other drove his cute little sports car into a bridge abutment.

None of which is helping me zero in on Banner, to ring the alarm.

I go to my phone to text Lemmy about honking that big horn, never mind that I don't have my students' cell numbers, but—

"Shit," I say, turning back to the retreating boat again.

My cell. I must have set it down when I was changing? I mean, it's dead, sure, but that doesn't mean I don't still want it.

It doesn't matter, it doesn't matter, I tell myself. And, this isn't the slasher genre, dealing with the problem of cellphones. It's just me, being an idiot.

I go well around the flagship house, walk purposefully between the two sort of to the side behind it, and . . . and I'm following the same path Theo Mondragon did, when he was playing *Nail Gun Massacre* with Shooting Glasses and Cowboy Boots and Mismatched Gloves.

I turn sharply to the left, to go an even *less* direct way back to the forest, just to get my heart beating more like a normal heart. I'm out of pills, I mean, don't have anything to tamp a panic attack down with. Breathing exercises and being in the moment aren't going to cut it, Sharona. But, from the bottom of my chainsaw heart, *thanks*.

And then I see it.

At first I think it's a little black bear, drunk on berries or sick from smoke, just propped up against the back of what was going to be the Baker house, its legs splayed out in front of it.

The reason I knee-jerk "bear" is the khaki-colored uniform. Fremont County sheriff's department officers wear brown on brown, top to bottom.

And this officer, it's not Jo Ellen—he's male—meaning . . .

Banner?

I open my mouth to scream, but right when I do the yacht's foghorn bellows long and loud, deep and far, shaking the forest down to its roots and scaring me down to my knees, making it feel like that massive sound came from me.

And it sort of did, I think.

"Please, please," I say, and scramble up, am running to the Baker house, running as hard as I can.

BAKER SOLUTIONS

Report of Investigation
12 August 2023
#25a11
re: Intentions to Vandalize

As part of processing back into society, inmates of Idaho Falls Community Reentry Center (IF-CRC), in order to become "graduates," have to submit multiple drafts of an autobiographical document intended to supply a stable foundation for their post-institutional lives. The document is edited and/or annotated by an assigned counselor, and then, as part of the ritual of completion or, as IF-CRC would have it, "graduation," they read the final version of this document aloud to the group, promoting both transparency and accountability. IF-CRC's promotional material positions this process as a form of narrative therapy, that being an iterative method of retelling a "life" such that trauma's impact can be properly absorbed and more positive aspects can become characterizing traits. IF-CRC's rate of recidivism is 39% over the first year, compared to an average of 44% for institutions of similar classification. Jennifer Elaine "Jade" Daniels's willful destruction of property, when that's specifically what she was incarcerated for twice before, will perhaps bump IF-CRC's rate of recidivism closer to the institutional average.

Bill of Mental Health
by Jade Daniels

I was conceived in Cabin 6 of Camp Winnemucca in my Idaho hometown of Proofrock, a.k.a. The Town That Dreaded Sundown, but by the time my high school dad led my high school mom through the door of that cabin,

Camp Winnemucca was known commonly as "Camp Blood". So maybe with that you can understand where I'm coming from. Literally. Biologically. And what I promise always to defend, even to my own detriment no matter what. This is also super key in why I leave the kind of footprints I've been leaving, that are red and dripping. Being conceived by beered up high schoolers on the site of a massacre where one little girl Amy was taken to be a second little girl Stacey, and that first little girl was institutionalized like I am now, I'm guessing that's not exactly the secret recipe to be an honor student. But where that first little girl ate her blanket and suffocated herself to escape this life of suffering and unfair accusation, I prefer graduating like this and living to fight another day, thank you. I haven't fought tooth and nail twice in my hometown to die all the way down the mountain.

So then after being born, lo and behold in junior high when I needed it the most I found A Bay of Blood in a 55 gallon plastic blue barrel to the right of the glass door of a gas station probably three miles from where we are now. My life at that precise moment went one way and not the other. If you want to know more about that movie and what it can do for you, I'm down the hall from the canteen, can tell you about the ways of our lord and savior Mario Bava.

And I say that Cabin 6 is where I start, but I'm supposed to be being strictly factual here, meaning I have to go back even before that. One thing I figured out in my first year of high school that confirmed many important things, was that my dad was 18 when I was born in 1998, which is H20, that being the 20 year slashiversary of Halloween. 1998 is the return of Jamie Lee Curtis a.k.a. Laurie Strode, and 1978 twenty years before that is the introduction of this final girl of final girls. "Do as I say!" Laurie told the children she was watching, and you can't see me in John Carpenter's angle on that dark living room of her babysitting gig, but I'm standing right over there behind the curtains where Tommy Doyle was hiding before, and, Laurie, I do, I do as you say, I do like you taught us. I fight and I fight and I refuse to die no matter what, and it ends me up in places like this over and over, but that's better than being stuffed open eyed in a cabinet or posed on a bed with a headstone. But the food is probably about the same for both instances.

Anyway, so my dad's 18 when he leads my mom into Cabin 6, and maybe she thought this was the start of her love story, but I'm sorry about that, Mom. Your new husband's about to wreck his car and Freddy his face up and wake up an even worse version of who he already was. But being 18 in 1998 means he was born in 1980, and I didn't even have to look up the next part because I can't ever forget it, and I didn't tell anybody this before, not even my old teacher, so get ready, but my dad's birthday was you guessed it, May the 9th, 1980. This is the summer of Jason. This is the exact date in history when Sean Cunningham gave us Friday the 13th, which was originally, you guessed it again, called A Long Night at Camp Blood, a name that can be no accident, since it's the name Camp Winnemucca earned, from being what it is.

We're having a moment of silence here.

Little bit longer.

Thanks.

So what I'm saying is that my dad was born the same day as Jason Voorhees was born into movie theaters, and I was born the year Halloween turned 20, in a place that might as well be Crystal Lake, and then Mario Bava reached up from a blue bucket with a spooky Vincent Price hand and led me into the rest of my life, providing me with the tools and means to live when I should be dying, and if I'm being honest like Clara says I have to be here, where "honest" means "not hiding behind trivia," and you have to trust her because her name's sort of from Final Destination, which is what this I'm reading now is supposed to aim me at like an arrow, then when I was 11, right before that gas station down the road, my dad took my hand too, to Drag Me to Hell Sam Raimi style, which is a 2009 movie from that same year. Also that year Friday the 13th came back in the form of a remake, because boogeyman never die, are always coming back, but also from that year is Orphan, which I guess I am now, and <u>Triangle</u>, about a woman doomed to keep repeating the same thing, and finally <u>The Loved Ones</u>, which is what all of you are to me. Really.

Thank you for listening to me all the time even after lights out, and I wish I was saying "see you later" here but Clara with her Clear eyes says that what I have to say is actually "goodbye", because my past doesn't foretell my future. I might have been born in blood, I might have been dragged to and through hell, but what Clara tells me is that when you're going through hell, KEEP GOING, GIRL. So this right now right here it's a moment or two after all those boogeyman, after all those bodies, all the screaming. You can see the light over the hills because it's <u>Just Before Dawn</u>, which was written in <u>Halloween</u>'s year, filmed in <u>Friday the 13th</u>'s, and released into the world the next year, which isn't a <u>Deadly Blessing</u> but a <u>Bloody Birthday</u>, so <u>Happy Birthday to Me</u> it says. But look up over <u>The Burning</u> of those candles in <u>The Funhouse</u> just for a moment. Gale Weathers is staring right into her new camera man's camera, she doesn't care how beat up she looks after this <u>Hell Night</u>, what she looks like is a SURVIVOR, one with <u>Friends</u> now, and what she's telling the world is that the <u>Dark Night of the Scarecrow</u> is over. Right behind her the sun is rising.

It's a new day, I mean.

For me too.

Wish me luck,

JaDe

NIGHTMARE AT SHADOW WOODS

Yes, yeah, of course I run for all I'm worth for thirty yards, to the house this khaki shirt and brown cowboy hat are slumped against.

Thing is, it's *forty* yards if I want to actually get there.

But I can't. I don't want to. I stop and pace back and forth, trying to get my breathing under control, trying to get my face to not be so hot, telling myself that if I just scrunch my hands in my hair and pull it a little bit harder, then none of this has to be real.

My sandals are . . . I don't know, I don't care. Somewhere behind me. And they're not mine anyway, and I hate them.

And I hate this.

Shit shit *shit*!

But?

As long as I don't walk up to this house, to this body that hasn't stirred even a little from me calling out to it, pleading with it, even on my knees to beg beg beg, then it doesn't have to be Banner. Those are the rules. Because? Because if it is Banner there, then—then I've let Adie's daddy die, I've let Letha's husband get killed, I've let Proof-rock's sheriff get taken from us right when we need him the most.

And, yes, Sharona, I know in all the ways I need to know that I can't take responsibility for things that aren't actually in my control, and that that's sort of the root of a lot of my bullshit.

But fuck that noise.

You've never tried to survive something like this. Twice.

Please please *please* don't be Banner?

You remember him from seventh period, don't you, sir? Do you remember all the stupid papers he wrote? It was when you were mak-ing us read our early drafts out loud to the class. Lots of mining facts copied and pasted in from internet searches, lots of nouns with as many adjectives stuffed in front of them as they would take, to make the wordcount, and . . . Banner Tompkins, always finding a way to make his assignments be about football, football, football.

Back then, that's what his future was.

His life was going to be stadium lights and airplanes, locker rooms and cheerleaders. But then the Lake Witch Slayings rose up over Proofrock, and in its cool musty shadow, the whole town's screams sifting back down into the water one mournful voice at a time, Banner Tompkins fell in love.

I understand, I think.

I've smoked hundreds of cigarettes behind the bank. I've stared out across the glittering water and let the twentieth century fall away to either side. I've stepped out into the new snow of my street and been the first to stomp through it, and looked back at my drag marks and nodded that that's me, that's me, and I'm here.

I never would have guessed it, but I'm starting to think I'm a Hen-derson Hawk the same as Banner, sir. For better or for worse. Rah rah.

And if he can just *not* be dead against the side of this house, I'll . . . I don't know: I'll get a Hawk tattoo, say? Would that do it?

No?

Okay, okay, then . . . how about I won't provoke Harrison anymore? And what if I stop always buying one suspicious thing I don't actually need when I'm at the drugstore? It's only to razz whoever's working the register, I mean. It's not that I need more duct tape, or zip ties, or rat poison, it's that, juvenile as I know I still am, I like to imagine the kid checking me out relaying these purchases to whoever they talk to after work. Relaying them in a lowered voice. A watch-out voice.

Yeah, that: I can stop harassing people in Proofrock, no problem.

But part of the deal, I can feel, is that I walk over to this house, this body, before a steady ten count.

By the fifth step, I can feel the muscles in my forearms and my thighs clutching my bones. By the seventh step, the air hissing out from between my teeth is all I can hear. By the ninth step, there's tears running down my cheeks, for this idiot I used to only wish the worst on.

"Ban?" I say, dropping to my knees, easing the brim of this wide hat up and only looking with the very corner of my right eye, so I can take that look back if I need to.

It's not Banner, Mr. Holmes.

I sag lower, my whole body the top part of a question mark, my arms limp, my face slack.

It's not Banner, but it is someone. In a deputy's shirt, and hat.

"Bub?" I say.

I've never talked to him directly, but he's been standing a few feet back from Banner and me a time or two. Can't say I know his story, just that he's from Ammon. I'd assumed Banner had hired him specifically so he wouldn't have connections to town, but he corrected me: there had been exactly one application for the empty slot on the force. Probably because of the short life expectancy of law enforcement around these parts.

"Sorry, dude," I say, lifting that brown cowboy hat the rest of the way off.

I did hear that, even though Bub's last name isn't "Rodgers," there's still some hazy relation to Clate Rodgers, but that doesn't mean he deserved whatever this is. You can't control who you're related to.

And, now that I've taken his hat off, there's sort of a knot or pro-tuberance in his forehead? The skin isn't split, though. Maybe it's just a knot he's carried all his life, since dinging himself on the handlebar of a snowmobile one winter? Or a knobby fat deposit, like wiener dogs get? That why he wanted to be a deputy over here in Proofrock—so he could always keep this hat snugged down?

Without the brim of his hat keeping him propped up against the house, too, Bub starts to sort of collapse to the left. Instinctually, I hug him to me, and my right hand cups the back of his head carefully, like I can hurt him if I'm too rough, and . . .

"Head Cheese?" I say into his ear.

Once upon a hot Texas summer, that was the working title for *The Texas Chain Saw Massacre.* And it's what's mushing between my fingers now, and clumping down the back of my hand into Bub's collar, and there's some sort of ruptured sac involved with this, like what I always imagined afterbirth might feel like. Just, what's being born here, it's a warm brain.

I let Bub continue his slump, gentle him down to the ground. His muscles, with the blood drained out of them, sort of creak, try to stick, like c'mon, c'mon, what's wrong with the position we were in, we were just getting comfortable?

In a perfect world, this would be my first time feeling this distinct dryness inside a dead body.

Proofrock isn't that perfect world. Neither is Terra Nova.

I work my way kind of behind him enough to see—

His skull has a new back door, one that's more or less square, and punched in, gaping open, with an odd glittering at the edges, like . . . it was a prom queen's pointy shoe that kicked him? What, there some "Sweetheart of Caribou-Targhee" pageant nobody told me about?

Then I hear one level under that, to what my brain's whispering just loud enough for me to hear: not the Sweetheart of the National Forest, but . . . the Angel of Indian Lake.

I stand fast, case all of Terra Nova I can, waiting for a shadow to break, rush me.

It's what I deserve, for going so long without looking up.

Either I'm alone save the buzz of chainsaws, or I was slow enough that any shadows had a chance to hide, wait for my next moment of inattention.

"Hey, hey!" I yell, to try to get some chainsawer back in the trees to come help, but I'm not a foghorn on a giant yacht, and all the money-hungry Proofrockers carving through two-hundred-year-old trunks probably have ear protection on anyway.

I take a step their direction, hoping to wave one down, get them all over here, and I admit, part of it's that I want them to see that I didn't *do* this, but then I stop, realize I'm doing exactly what I accused Banner and his team of doing: walking over evidence.

I hold my hands out for balance, to keep from taking another step, and try my best to figure out which tracks lead to Bub's boots, so I can see which way he might have come from.

Which is when it hits me: with the back of his head crashed in, it's not very likely that he staggered in from the treeline. No, this happened to him right *here*, didn't it?

By reluctant degrees, I crank *my* head over, my neck popping in the process, Billy-style.

There's blood on the pale wall, level with my eyes.

Enough that it's dripped down.

Meaning whoever did this, they were standing nearly exactly where I'm standing now, in this churn of snow that I'm not Indian enough to read anything from except for a half-smoked cigarette. The last smoke of a dead man. And me without my matches.

But I can't be jonesing right now. Not if I want to keep living. If I want to keep my insides on the inside, then I need to process this scene. Who- or whatever did this to Bub, I mean, they might be hunkered down right around the corner, snickering about the hatch they're about to kick open in the base of *my* skull.

No thank you.

I backpedal, trying to step in my own footprints, and my feet are cold as hell, sure, but I'm Idaho born and bred—it's going to take more than cold feet for me to complain.

I back up to as open a space as I can manage, then start to loop around for the chainsaw brigade, my eyes on the trees the whole time. Meaning, of course, that anyone in a high window of the house behind me can just stand there, have plenty of time to pivot away when I turn that direction.

The reason horror movies punish crews that split up? It's because it's put them in exactly this position, where they can't watch their backs, leaving them vulnerable to being rushed the moment they turn around.

Or, the moment after that.

Or the next one.

My fingers find my waistband, grub for my dampeners, but I *still* haven't been home to reload. Meaning I have an hour, maybe two, until my fingers start to tremble, twitching around for the ghost of a tablet, that wonderful feel of an oblong little pill.

It's best I don't have anything to crush and snort, though. This is no time to be checking out.

And, what was that about splitting up?

"Shit," I say out loud, and turn to the dock—to the yacht, the bow coming around like this big boat's lifted its chin, is pivoting out of the rest of this conversation.

"Come back!" I lean forward to scream to Lana and Lemmy, and then am running for them in my bare feet. Because the planks on the dock are plastic, they don't splinter my feet, but my feet are wet enough from the snow patches I crashed through that, when I get to the end of the dock, I'm a cartoon character trying to stop.

I have to turn around, lay myself out on my frontside and claw my fingers into whatever rounded-off cracks will take them. It's my chin clunking on ridge after ridge that finally stops me, my bare feet hanging out over the water, one of them *on* it, I think.

I roll around, stand as fast as I can on the dock, and scream again for the *English Rose* to stop.

The blood from my bit tongue spatters out onto my chin from it, and I know there's no way they're going to see me, much less hear me, but . . . maybe a drone will pop up, randomly? Luckily? Except of course that's not the kind of luck I have. When I clamber up to make myself bigger, I can see Lana at the rail, I think, small and already distant, just a silhouette pretty much, and she's done with the plastic chairs now, is sitting in some kind of *throne* or another, her messy bun undone so her hair's this blowing haze all around her, and . . . that feels about right. She's up there, and I'm down here, just this small little nobody against the vastness of wild Idaho, smoke billowing over me, flames licking over the tops of the farback trees.

And, okay, yeah, I am from Idaho, but my feet *do* want to be somewhere warmer, and fast. This sort of sucks. I shake my head from side to side, hiss pissed-off air out through my teeth, and use both hands to flip the yacht off, since that's pretty much what it's already doing to me.

"But not you, Lemmy," I mutter behind this super effective display.

Teachers aren't supposed to make crude gestures to students.

I turn my back on the lake, to reconsider Terra Nova, but before I can, a flurry of motion on the shore to my right pulls my eyes that direction. This is right below Sheep's Head Meadow, and . . . not again.

It's an elk, a young spike. He's tilting his two antlers down at the water like trying to intimidate it away, so he can cross.

If only.

I stand as tall as I can, wave my arms to him, and he cranks his big head up, fixes me in his eyes. When I'm no threat, he rakes his antlers down into the shallows again. Just, this time, he hooks something enough that it rises to the surface for a moment before sliding back under.

What the hell?

Now I want to see what this elk is starting a fight with, but I also really really need to find Banner.

"What the hell, what the hell . . ." I say to myself, my hands opening and closing by my thighs. What finally makes the decision for me, is that, from where I am, that house Bub died against is pretty much the last house on the left, which I know to take for a warning.

I'm acting like it's either investigate whatever that elk's found or walk through Terra Nova, but I could also take that slope behind Camp Blood, walk that chalky white bluff one more time. Just, I'm not super sure I have the nerve anymore to tightrope the dam, and, given any kind of choice, I also don't choose to skulk down the poacher road across the creek under the dam. That's where Hettie and Paul and Wayne Sellars died. Sure, I might stumble on a motorcycle stashed in the bushes, or a horse might amble up to me, blowing steam every third step, but . . . stay where the people are, slasher girl. You know who doesn't get beheaded? It's the ones who don't put their neck under the machete.

Anyway, who- or whatever did that to Hettie and Paul and Waynebo, maybe it's territorial, right? Jason is, about Crystal Lake. Freddy seems to be, about Elm Street. Michael doesn't care about Haddonfield so much, but the territory he claims for his own, it's Halloween night, isn't it?

This Angel might be staking out the parts of Pleasant Valley where there's no light shining. Where there's no eyes watching.

And I can't let myself forget about Greyson Brust. Whoever dug him up, was dragging him that way, they weren't just having fun, they were taking him somewhere. Meaning there's a lair back in the trees over there—a den, a hut, a shack, a murder shed, a haunted outhouse, something. And, in a slasher, it doesn't matter how big the forest is, you can plunge into it at any point and you're ending up at that same cabin in the woods, aren't you, Ash?

So, no going around the lake that way. And no going around the *other* way, because that's miles to go before I sleep, which is about thirty thousand steps with my head cranking around after each one, to be sure an axe isn't sailing for my face.

And, anyway, I didn't let myself get ferried across just to hoof it back, did I?

I'm here to be the bearer of bad news, and then retire to my living room, click that deadbolt over, crush some tablets into my head, and wait this out.

But first, on the way to *be* that bearer of bad but essential news, this young dude of an elk, and whatever's he's trying to tell me about.

"Go, go," I tell myself, thinning my lips with resolve. Well, with fake resolve, but you take what you can muster.

I stiffleg it down the dock and hook it left, staying as close to the water as I can without actually touching it with my bare feet, telling myself the whole way that, really, this is just twenty yards out of the way. Thirty at most. It's practically safe, is almost still Terra Nova.

The spike bolts once he registers that I'm coming his way, and then, maybe three or four seconds away, he plunges into the lake, is churning steadily across, looking, every few bobs, like two narwhals in a stop-motion Christmas show, swimming in perfect tandem.

I stop where he tore the frozen ground up with his hooves.

"Shit," I have to say out loud.

I couldn't see it from where I was, but the reason he didn't have the nerve to go in here, start his big swim, it's that . . . there's people bobbing in the shallows?

My knee-jerk first thought is that this is the chainsaw brigade, drowned when some rogue wave from the yacht capsized all their little boats, but . . . no. There's no bright-colored clothes, for one. No chainsaw chaps, no slickers, no motorcycle boots with bright buckles.

What the hell?

And, no, I definitely do not step out there with them. Among them.

I do grab a branch, though, hook the closest one, drag her in.

When I turn her over, at first I can't really process what I'm seeing. The hollow eyes, the drawn cheeks. And then I connect it to an image already in my head: Victorian death photos. What did you call them, Mr. Holmes? "Memento Mori"? This woman's the spitting image of that, except . . . she's in a half shirt, with a string bikini underneath?

This isn't someone with a chainsaw in their hand and dollar signs in their eyes. This is someone from years ago who got lost in a skiing accident.

They all are.

The lake is . . . returning its dead, after all these years?

What?

I count seven of them, and then get suddenly frantic, have to reach my branch out to the others, pull them close enough to confirm they aren't the blond skinny-dipper from the Netherlands who's been missing for eight years, now.

What pulling each of them in shows me, too, is that these corpses have that same roughly square hole slammed into and through them. For some it was the chest, others the face, but . . . what kills people who are already dead?

I back off, nodding like this actually makes sense, and, past the mud that spike tore up, there's soggy boot prints. And bare footprints.

I'm pretty sure the boot prints match that dead guy with the long beard this stick tangled in so well. And the bare footprints are about my size, probably go with half-shirt girl.

"No," I say, shaking my head no like that can make me right, can mean that I'm not seeing what I'm seeing. Because what it *looks* like is that these people were walking up out of the lake, at least until some-one killed each of them again, pushed them back into the water.

That doesn't make any kind of sense. This isn't *Shock Waves*, after all. Indian Lake holds a lot of things, but I'm pretty sure evil Nazis aren't one of them.

And, even if they were? What put them down again? *Who* put them down again?

No, this has to be . . . something else. I must be reading the sign wrong. The footprints, they're just—yeah, yeah: the chainsaw brigade slid their boats up here, meaning they walked up here, leaving work boot tracks, and, because some of them got their boots wet stepping down from a rocking canoe, one or two of them was barefoot. And then, starting to pull the boats up onto shore, someone noticed the dead bobbing all around and pushed back.

All the boats? They float off. All this damage done to the corpses? Walter Mason used his fire chief swagger to wade out, push his Halligan down through each of them, to show everyone they were really and for sure dead.

It's a bullshit version of events, I know. But without it, I fall back on my ass here, hug my knees, and never go find Banner. Sometimes lies are the only thing that can keep you moving forward. Lies and the most wishful thinking.

I'm full of both.

"Banner!" I yell into the trees.

The chainsaws drown me out.

Screw it, then. I kick back along the shore, still not daring the timber's smoky darkness. A few steps away I clock my six, because I do *not* need one of these corpses sitting up in the shallows, cranking its dead eyes over to me. Instead of giving any of them the chance, I walk backwards almost to the dock, watching them the whole way.

"Stay," I tell them all, like they're trained zombies, and finally turn around, face the last house on the left. And the rest of them.

My feet are officially freezing now, too. I might be Idaho born and bred, but the toes I've got left, they're a lot more tropical, I'm thinking. I'm not the only one caught in a death-spiral of past trauma, I mean. None of these piggies want to go to market, thanks.

There's something I can do about that, though.

Apologizing the whole time, my ears dialed up like a mouse out in the open, I work Bub's cowboy boots off his dead and—no insult, Bub—pretty rank feet. One of the socks comes with so I take the other one as well.

The boots aren't quite small enough for me, and have heels as high as my teaching shoes, and one of them smells like pee, but they're better than going open-toed and stumpy into the woods. And the socks, never mind that they're off a dead dude, they're one hell of a lot warmer than nothing.

I stand, clamp that brown cowboy hat on. It sort of matches my TMNT shirt.

"I hereby deputize you," I say to myself, and case Terra Nova again, now taking into account the brim hiding the sky from me.

And, because I'm not Laurie with that knife, I take Bub's belt and holster as well, his big pistol snugged down into that shaped leather, and like that, I'm dressed up in a cowboy costume.

It really is starting to feel like Halloween.

Six steps through the tall grass of Terra Nova, moving into the fall radius of probably ten trees at once, angling around wide so as stay out in the open as long as I can, my shin thunks into . . . a pipe?

No: it's one of those basketball goals on wheels. The workers must have smuggled it across piece by piece for lunch hour, for break, but since helicopters do land here, they have to settle this tall thing down when they're not playing, to keep it from catching a rotor.

Shooting Glasses would have liked to have lined a free throw up here, wouldn't he have? And Cowboy Boots. Mismatched Gloves.

Sorry, guys.

You just stumbled into this, just wanted a day's work in the pure mountain air, maybe a beer on the slow chug back across the lake.

It never could have worked between Shooting Glasses and me, though. Okay, "Grade," but I never called you that, man. Reason it never would have worked? It's not that I had to go be an inmate twice, it's that . . . we could actually *talk*, couldn't we?

From what I understand about relationships, they're all about cold shoulders and that kind of glare that lingers after the other one's left the room. Without that kind of festering resentment, I give us six weeks at the outside.

Said the cynical girl.

No: said the girl burned by life again and again.

Sharona's right about the impulse to wrap ourselves in our trauma because some protection's better than none, but I think she has this idea that, if you say and think just the right things—and don't forget your *breathing*, Jade—then that trauma you're wrapped up in can be a chrysalis. When you're healed and ready, transformed and different and better, you tear it open and walk out onto the runway of life, staring every person down who still remembers the old you and then executing a neat flip turn at the end of that stage and stalking away, into the future.

I wish.

It's more like you try and try to maintain forward motion, but Pinhead's got his hooks in you, and each step is agony. You can step forward, out of it, sure, but what you leave behind is your skin. Now even just the air hurts your raw muscle, the striations of fat. And I guess you don't have eyelids either, which can't be super ideal.

But I'm probably just saying that because I've seen a kid skinned down enough that he couldn't blink, because he didn't have anything to blink *with*. And also because if I can be in the past, then I don't have to be here, in Terra Nova, about to step into the big bad woods, where the people who don't have chainsaws have axes. It's one place I've successfully avoided for nearly twenty-five years. But I need to tell Banner to get his ass back to Proofrock, batten down the hatches.

"Do it already," I tell myself, and step over that basketball goal, then across three or five or ten fallen-down trees that I'm pretty sure can still burn even *if* they've been cut down, and—

It's another Bub.

Just, not in county brown.

This is . . . it's Walter Mason, our volunteer fire chief.

He's been slammed into a still-upright tree. By that same thing that left a square hole in his back, right through his spine. A hole shaped like a xenomorph's pharyngeal jaw.

My impulse is to sit down right here, count on my fingers and toes how many bodies there are so far, but you're missing some toes, aren't you, slasher girl?

I'm not sure I have enough.

Ahead of me, Chin Treadaway, who told me about Harrison's amputatee-aversion, is going Chainsaw Sally on a monstrous tree. Sawdust is flying out, the tree's probably groaning with pain, and I shake my head no, please. But I know what teachers make, and what that does and doesn't cover—I don't begrudge her the fistful of dollars she's reaching for.

Just . . . not like this?

Her whole body is shuddering with the effort, and I have the dim notion that you don't cut a tree down with a single horizontal cut, do you? Don't you angle in from all sides like a beaver, until there's only a toothpick left? If you don't, then that spinning blade can—

"*Chin!*" I scream.

She's wearing ski goggles and earmuffs, though. Her teeth are bared with effort, her right foot's planted on the trunk like her pushing on this trunk is all this tree needs to finally come down, and she's deep enough into the wood now that her little engine's coughing black smoke.

Something's got to give.

"Chin, Chin, Chin!" I scream some more, running for her now, forgetting to watch either way, but I'm too slow, I'm not loud enough.

Again.

The chainsaw catches, kicks back hard like chainsaws like to do, and that whirring blade whirs right into Chin's neck on the left side, spewing blood and meat in a roostertail that mists down over me.

I fall back trying to wave this away, trying to get Bub's big pistol out like grossness and bad luck are things I can shoot away, and then my heel catches a root and I'm on my ass again, the pistol flying out behind me.

It's right in time for me to miss the axe slinging for my head.

It plants in the tree I'm up against, and I'm already rolling away, am already running in my head, except my stupid feet in these huge boots have much slower ideas.

Above me, Jocelyn Cates rips that axe from the tree, splinters raining down over me.

Her chest is rising and falling, one of her shirt sleeves is torn away, and there's red blood and black grease spattered across her face.

"*Jocelyn!*" I scream as loud as I can, holding my hand up, completely expecting it to split down the middle, and for that axe to keep on going down my forearm, pushing my ulna and radius apart until the wishbone at my elbow.

Jocelyn hauls the axe back, steps forward, but then doesn't swing. Is just glaring down at me, breathing great breaths in through her nose.

"You're not him," she says.

"'Him'?" I say, still scrambling back.

Jocelyn steps in over me like to protect me now, her axe in two hands, one high, one low. She's watching all the dark places at once, and I can see now that Letha Mondragon isn't the only final girl in Pleasant Valley.

Jocelyn Cates is a survivor through and through, and the hungry look in her eyes, the sneer curling her mouth—all she wants is more, please. All she wants is to drive a blade into the horror that took her husband, her son.

I'm glad to have her standing over me.

"Jocelyn, Mrs. Cates," I say, pulling myself up and being sure to keep both hands in view, because killing rages don't always distinguish between friend and foe.

"Stay here," Jocelyn says, and, before I can even hold onto her shirt tail, she's striding away, into this instead of back to the shore— the sensible thing to do.

I'm alone again.

Bub's dead behind me, Walter Mason's dead behind me, Chin

Treadaway's dead four feet from me, and the pistol I need to stay alive's in the leaf litter somewhere.

How the fuck does this keep happening?

I step around the tree Jocelyn planted her axe in—didn't she have a *chainsaw* the last time I saw her?—try to track her retreating form, which is when I see . . .

It can't be.

This is just something the kids were making up, not something they were actually *seeing*.

Walking directly at me, maybe sixty feet away, draped in darkness, it's the Angel of Indian Lake again, her once-white gown dingy, her hair long and black and stringy, her eyes hollow, cheeks drawn, gaze unwavering, but definitely locked on me.

"Sally," I say.

The first person to put Dark Mill South down.

Compared to him, I'm nothing.

Backing up but not looking away from her for even an instant, I rationalize on the fly, trying to explain her away.

It's *not* Sally, it's *not* Sally.

Then who, history teacher?

Stacey Graves, all grown up? Maybe she wriggled her ankle free of Ezekiel's big hand on the way down to that soggy church, maybe she wriggled free but then drowned, drifted to the bottom, and the lake did its Jason thing to her, or some Tina up here raised her on accident.

But there's also Amy Brockmeir from the sixties, isn't there? Never mind how dead she is. "Dead" doesn't seem to matter that much anymore, around here. Was her little body delivered back here after she killed herself in that institution she shouldn't have been in? Delivered to Remar Lundy, wouldn't it have been? Rexall's great-great-whatever, but I've always pictured Rexall as a sort of updated clone of him.

That could have been her wriggling through the fence by the high school, I mean.

And, those two mountain-man hunters did claim to have stumbled onto Remar Lundy's famously lost cabin not long ago, didn't they? Are *they* the ones who started all this, by waking her up? And? If it is her, then her revenge mission is so righteous and pure and just that I don't know if Letha and Jocelyn together could even stop her. She *should* have gotten to grow up, have a life, not been falsely accused of being Stacey Graves.

And I realize what I'm doing here, Sharona, don't worry.

I'm Xeno's Paradox'ing my way out of this bad moment I'm mired in. Xeno's Paradox is that to cross a span of distance, you first have to go half that distance, and half that distance, and half *that* distance, meaning . . . you never actually cross that distance, right? Because it keeps halving. In the same way, if I throw up enough explanations between me and this Angel of Indian Lake, then she can't climb over them all, and she never gets to me.

Except that's just the way I want it to work. How it *is* is that she's already ten paces closer to me. Now twelve, shit.

She's going to strangle me with her hair, I know. She's going to point her fingers into a blade and punch the back of my skull in, or reach through my back in that movie-way, where I have to look down at my beating heart in her clenched fist.

Shit. Please no.

And? If it *is* Sally Chalumbert, then maybe I'm who she's really after, right? I mean, the final girl and the slasher locked in their violent dance, there's a certain affection there, isn't there? Is she pissed at me for taking Dark Mill South away from her?

"I'm sorry!" I yell ahead to her.

She just keeps on coming.

It makes sense now why the chainsaw brigade's scattered, doesn't it? Why Chin was left behind to finish the work? It's because she couldn't hear the warnings. But Jocelyn Cates did, only, she didn't have it in her to run away, she only knows to fight tooth and nail, because justice doesn't extract itself, you've got to pull it bloody and pulsing from the chest of whoever wronged you.

Everybody else ran for trees, though. Better the fire than this Angel's kiss.

My index finger and thumb on my right hand twitch, trying to conjure a desperate cigarette up from the forest floor. I should be snapping for the pistol, I know, except . . . a pistol against a slasher? The only things guns do is prove to everyone that bullets don't work, that this is truly hopeless.

Like I don't already know that.

No cigarette rises to my twitching hand, of course. Doesn't matter. I'll smoke my lungs crispy black when I get back across the lake.

When, not "if."

I shake my head no to Sally Chalumbert, not this day, and take one step ahead, because I'd rather die from the front than the back, I'd rather be Billy Sole in *Predator* than all the other de-spined victims, which is when—

The ground trembles under my feet.

I look down to it in wonder.

What the hell?

Is the heat from the fire doing something to all the caves and caverns networked underground on this side of the valley? Is lava about to geyser up? We're not all that far from the thermal funhouse of Yellowstone, after all.

I lower to fingertips and the toes of my oversize cowboy boots, snug my hat down low to hide the whites of my eyes.

Growing up, when my dad was regaling five-year-old me with grand hunting exploits, he'd get so into it he'd start re-enacting them in the living room, before his liquid dinner. A key part was him dropping down to exactly the position I'm in now. It always felt like he knew ancient things I could only wonder at, smile about. His fingers were listening through the ground, I mean.

Mine are too. What they're feeling is . . . thunder?

It makes me suck a gasp of air in. I stand away from it, and right on cue, pine needles start to waft down from whatever's happening.

Through them all, this Angel is still coming for me.

It's not a good day to die. It's a pretty crappy day to die. Let me start it over, do it different—I'll watch *Psycho* and *Halloween* and *Scream* back to back like the trilogy they want to be, strung together with "Loomis," and then and only then will I go down to the cellar to see what that sound might have been.

No, I'll go share one last smoke with you, Mr. Holmes. And then I'll spark up on Melanie's bench as well. And I'll play Letha's death-memos again, especially the one she made when she was about to die about seventy-five yards from where I'm about to get it.

The chainsaws are still whining just out of sight, some axe is plunking steadily into the side of a tree, pine needles are still sifting down, the whole world is shaking and losing focus, and—

What?

This isn't how smoke works, is it?

It's a wall of shadow, billowing in a time-lapse speed along the forest floor.

No, not shadow, and not smoke. It's . . . dust?

Before I can be sure, a symmetrical tree branch punctures the front membrane of this coming cloud and rips up and up, birthing—

A *monstrous* bull elk. One of the giant ones that have never seen us two-leggeds. One of the ones that the other elk don't look in the eye, but talk about later in whispers: the size of his rack, the cows in his harem, the hoof prints he leaves so deep you can trip from them. How the tips of his antlers are mossy, from dragging through the clouds day in, day out. How his bugles make the firmament tremble, how his snorts drive worms up from the loam.

The fire's bigger than him, though, is driving him and his out of their ancient places, their hides charred and singed, their eyes wild, nostrils wide to suck more and more of this good air in.

It's not sweet and Bambi, either—it's not the dad leading the baby away, because we all know that's not how dads really are. This is the dad of all these elk running for his life, and the rest of them scrambling after him not because they trust him, but because his selfishness has always worked for him, hasn't it? You don't grow a rack like that year after year by running *at* the danger, you get that kind of magnificent headgear by *surviving*.

They thunder in behind this Angel of Indian Lake and look for a slice of an instant like her attendants, her wild retinue, but then the dirt and smoke and flying leaf litter and falling tree trash all hide her for the moment, and my heart embiggens three sizes just like that book my mom used to read me, and it stays like that, because maybe that big bull is about to crash past with a dangerous woman speared on his antlers.

Wrong.

The bull elk crashes past at car-speed, his woody rack naked, tucked back like these dudes do when they're racing through the trees.

I gulp, only have time to look halfway around before—

The rest of the herd.

It's like nothing I've ever felt, or seen. It's a wall of muscle and hoof, a surging wave of knees and haunches coming down all around me. I bring my right hand up like I can possibly hope to stop these thousands and thousands of pounds of stampeding elk.

But there's grace, too, out here where nobody can call it out.

The elk course around me like I'm a rock they're folding themselves around, and when one big cow hasn't gotten the memo, is definitely and for sure going to pound me to slurry with her hungry hooves, all I can do is chirp my terror out and fall back even farther.

At the last moment, though, our eyes lock, we see the panic in each of our souls, and then she—there's no other word for it—*launches*, and I'm looking up at her pale, beautiful, stretched-out belly, one of her tucked-under leading hooves coming close enough to my eggshell forehead that it tips Bub's cowboy hat back and off, and if this amazing and perfect queen of the forest ever lands, then I don't know it.

Like that, it's over.

I roll over on my belly, breathing hard, and see the herd surging through the giant summer homes of Terra Nova, churning up what landscaping's been done so far.

When the bull runs right into the water by the dock, the rest of the herd follows, and I stand, my hands in fists by my legs, to give this herd the strength it needs to swim across. It worked for Bambi once upon a forest fire, didn't it? They rode that waterfall down, deer-paddled across. Maybe these elk will come up wet and blowing on the other side of the lake as well, and crash through Proofrock, clamber across the highway, and keep going, on into Wyoming and Colorado, and whatever's left of this dream America calls the West.

Inside, Yazzie had a poem memorized, would say it in the sag between other shit, when she wanted her head to be in a better place, a not-there place. I never could get it right like she could, but the title was long, a poem itself, something about "Upon Reading That Three Buffalo Escaped Their Train Car in Sometown, New Mexico, and Went Running Down Main Street Tearing Up This and That and Whatever." All the poem said under that was "Run on, brothers."

That's what I say to these elk, now.

I lift my hand palm out like trying to hold onto the memory of them, and, it's stupid I know, but it somehow feels Indian. But then I realize that's the final gesture at the end of one of my dad's stupid Westerns.

Everything's fucking corrupt, isn't it?

I breathe in, breathe out again, snatch the hat up. I hold it by the brim, slap it against my thigh and then look down to my chest, because I know what comes next: Sally Chalumbert driving something in through my back, my insides splashing out.

If she put Dark Mill South down, knocked all his teeth out, and cut his hand off, then . . . an unathletic town girl?

Sally won't even have to break stride, for me.

Still: Billy Sole, right? I'll never forget him. And he would face the monster at least, wouldn't be caught looking away. Following his lead, I clamp the hat on, twist it to get it seated right, and turn around to face this bad music, which—

Why am I thinking *music*, of all things?

Oh, yeah: when I was clawing for purchase on the dock, sliding along those plastic planks. I wasn't exactly processing extraneous shit then, but . . . something?

What, Jade?

Doesn't matter.

I let my eyes settle on where I expect Sally Chalumbert to be, and know full well that, as dead and scary as Samara was, Sally's going to be more Sadako, from the original, except . . .

"What?" I have to say.

Where is she?

"Um, hey?" I say all around.

She's not to either side, and she's not behind me.

I flinch all at once, then, and cringe down, sure that her not being in my eyeline can only mean she's above me, about to drift down, her arms spread wide, her hair floating all around her.

Nope.

What the everliving hell.

When I bring my eyes back down, though, there is a shadowy figure running from tree to tree. It's stupidly comforting—at least *someone* knows the genre. We're playing Casey and Ghostface, here, or, in *Fear Street* terms, Heather and Ryan.

I step in front of a tree so as to not give my silhouette away. We're only barely out of Terra Nova, here, and the chainsaws and axes have done enough fire mitigation that there's all this open space behind me.

And then, "Oh, shit," I say.

It really *is* Ghostface?

Definitely a flowy, tattered black cloak, and that's no human face in that hood, and there's a Santa-satchel slung over its shoulder, straight out of *Audition*.

"Um," I say in my head, and my heart.

I've fantasized on exactly this so many times. Now that I've got feet on the ground in that specific dream, though—careful what you wish for.

"Hey!" I say ahead to this Ghostface, right when it's slashing from tree to tree, and it actually stops in place, is holding its bag with both hands and peering up to give me my first glimpse of its face when—

A gun blasts.

The tree this Ghostface was running to shudders, and bark dust poofs out from it.

Ghostface stands to its full height, and it's not got a knife like I guess I was expecting. What it's unlimbering from its belt is Walter Mason's Halligan! I remember it from when he came to talk to our fourth-grade social studies class and let us hold this axe–hammer–pry bar one at a time, standing over each of us as we did so we didn't drop it on our ten-year-old toes.

Probably would have saved me some frostbite.

A *second* gun blast comes, and Ghostface is thrown back, and I realize what I should have realized a bullet or so ago: I'm right in the line of fire.

I drop like *I've* been shot, am on knees and fingertips and chin and belly now, watching through the scrub.

Ghostface struggles up, climbing the Halligan, trying to hold its Santa bag together—evidently that's what got hit, mostly—then, instead of looking deeper in the trees, where the shots were coming from, it looks right back at me.

It's not a Father Death face. It's a pale gas mask. For the smoke. The kind with two canisters or snouts or whatever, pointing either way down from the bottom. And this poncho, it's some dark green XL job, for rain.

"Fucking A . . ." I say to myself.

Sally Chalumbert, stampeding elk, chainsaws and axes and gun-fire, not to mention *actual* fire, and now one of us in make-do Harry Warden get-up? And I thought my side of the lake was bad. How did junior-high Ginger Baker make it through one night over here, even? Much less four whole weeks.

Respect.

"Hey!" I say to Ghostface, and it clocks me for a moment, then dismisses the threat I'm not, runs at an angle that'll take it above Terra Nova, to the chalky bluff behind Camp Blood.

Banner rushes into the space Ghostface just was.

His face is smeared black, his sheriff shirt is trash, his hat's gone, and his pistol is out. He holds it up by his head while he reloads, I guess so he can bring it down and pull that trigger fast if he needs to.

When I stand, hands up—they're my palest part, are the only white flags I have—he brings that pistol to bear on me, his feet going into the stance I guess you know if you're a cop, like the recoil from the gun, this sound, this act, is something he's going to need bracing for.

"It's me! It's me!" I call across.

He cocks the barrel up, spits to the side, then looks to be . . . inhaling through his nose? Smelling the air?

When I walk in, picking my path quietly for some reason—is there something *else* to wake up over here?—he says, about my hat, "Thought you were Jo Ellen."

"Who was that?" I ask about Ghostface.

"More like who *is* that," Banner says back.

"Oh," I kind of say then, getting what Banner was tasting on the air: it smells like the alley behind Dot's when she's cooking cinnamon rolls.

"I think I shot his supplies," Banner says, looking the direction Ghostface went.

"Did—did you see her too?" I ask, because I can't not know. It's the difference in the world going mad, or just me.

Banner looks back, interrogates me with his eyes.

"Thought it was a dude," he finally says. "The shoulders."

"I mean—"

I stop myself because I realize that his answer here is that he *didn't* see the Angel of Indian Lake. He didn't see Sally Chalumbert.

It's just me and the high schoolers. Again. Or? It's just me, finally losing it.

"Look," I tell him.

It's the Halligan, knocked loose and left behind.

He nods for me to pick it up and it's heavier than I thought, but has a good balance, like it *wants* to break a door open.

"Come on, we need to—" Banner says about the chainsaw brigade, his stance still wide, his body sideways, one hand held back like I've got a baton to hand off to him.

I'm just standing in place, though, messing everything up. Banner wants to rush up, save the living, but I've still got the dead in my head.

"Bub," I say.

"He's going to get help," Banner hisses, his whole face urgent.

"He's—" I say, or start to, blinking tears away. "And Chin Treadaway. And Walter Mason."

Banner gets what I'm saying, kind of sags in place.

"Even *Walter*?"

I nod.

"But he's been fire chief since . . . I don't even know," Banner says. "Since fire was invented?"

"And Chin."

"And us too if we don't keep moving," Banner says, eyes intense, lips thin, hand still waiting for me.

"Phil Lambert . . ." I add.

"He's over here?" Banner asks, incredulous.

He's in his oven, I don't say, and a nervous giggle threatens to burble up, escape.

This really is starting again, isn't it?

No, it's already *going*, slasher girl. And it's sweeping you right along with it. You and this whole damned valley, right to that chrome drain cover under Marion Crane's bare feet.

I look behind to Terra Nova, still in the light. And then to us, here, the darkness creeping in like particles of nothing.

Every third shadow, it's Jason looming large as a tree himself, it's Michael turning his blank white face ever so slightly, to track me, it's Freddy stepping forward to push me back into another nightmare.

"Wait up," I hiss ahead to Banner, and take his hand.

BAKER SOLUTIONS

Report of Investigation
24 August 2023
#29a27
re: Eyewitness testimony

In her third session with Dr. Sharona Watts [3a for the recording / 3a-tr for the transcription], Jennifer Elaine "Jade" Daniels can clearly be heard thanking Dr. Watts for procuring a "package" for her. The nature of this package [see shipping manifest at 14t-22] is a bootleg VHS copy of *When Animals Attack XIV* (2018), specifically the episode dramatizing the bear attack that resulted in the death of Deacon Samuels in 2015. This episode has been illegally transferred from DVD, and as such is explicitly *not* in keeping with the Code of Ethics for licensed psychotherapists in the state of Idaho; at your request, an anonymous notice can be delivered through the proper channels. As documented in that third session, the reason for this request for contraband was that, in the activity room of Idaho Falls Community Reentry Center, Ms. Daniels claims to have caught the final minutes of said episode, and wanted to see it *in toto*. This is of note to Ms. Daniels's vandalism in that this third session with Dr. Watts, and presumedly her immediate viewing of this episode of *When Animals Attack*, precedes the first instance of destruction of property on Deacon Point by only eight days.

For a complete synopsis of this "Summer of Love" episode of *When Animals Attack XIV*, see Errata 3253-g. In short, the theory being pursued if not proven over the forty-four (44) minutes of the episode is that the bear that attacked and killed Deacon Samuels was lured in with bear bait. The central interview is with Idaho game warden Seth Mullins, wherein he expounds on both typical and atypical bear behavior, documents the presence and conditioned inclinations of a "trash bear" (his term) known to be in the area in 2015, and refers to the sheriff's report of a smell in the air "like donuts," which Mr. Mullins localized to Mr. Samuels's golf bag, and, "probably, that yellow rag with his initials on it?" For more on the context of this animal attack, see eyewitness testimony below.

This is pertinent to Ms. Daniels's vandalism in that one of her many defense strategies for claiming innocence concerning the murder of her father was that there was another killer or killers operating that summer of 2015. Thus, "preserving the crime scene" of one of those killings (Deacon Point) could, for her purposes, eventually establish the veracity of her claims.

As for what evidence could still remain of that animal attack eight years later, efforts are currently underway to discover what, if anything, persists. Whatever the case, the possibility of this motivation undercuts Ms. Daniels's claim of Deacon Point being a historic site. Rather, she could still be compulsively organizing her defense for a crime she's already been cleared of committing.

As for the testimony, it comes from Cinnamon Baker, sole remaining child of Mars Baker and Macy Todd, the only surviving sibling (her twin Ginger Baker fell victim to the 2019 slayings), and the non-active owner of Baker Solutions Investigative Firm. Ms. Baker was reached by videoconference on 26 July 2023, and wishes her location to not be divulged unless necessary for legal proceedings. In addition, she requests that her testimony be prefaced with *forgive me if it goes astray*:

> We were just kids then, right? And at this point I hadn't seen any of Jennifer Daniels's papers or whatever online. I started to read one a couple of months ago, but . . . horror? Why? Not exactly my thing. It's always girls with legs running from the baddies, never those of us with wheels rolling away, living to fight another day. They're kind of ableist, aren't they? But yeah, when the hospital delivered Ginge's stuff from her room,

there were all these masks, like from horror movies I guess, hand-made and everything. I don't even want to imagine Jade putting on one after the other for my sister that day, trying to . . . I don't know. Why do you scare a girl who's already pulling her own hair out? But you're asking about when my parents were still—you know. *Before*. First, and I said this in a deposition already so it's in some record somewhere, Jennifer Daniels, "Jade," "JD," "Jenny," I guess "*Ms.* Daniels" now, history teacher if you can believe that, I guess a school board can be bought after all, she was definitely and for sure *on* the yacht the night everything happened. This is what you're wanting, right? But, as for the yacht, yes, my sister and I confronted her in the hall. She pretended to be there with Letha, and I know Letha covers for her now, out of pity I guess, or maybe they bonded about losing their dads, I don't know, not like they're the only ones, but she was creeping around in her clunky combat boots, wasn't *in* Letha's room. Ginge and I were like these little detectives back then, had to figure everything out, but only in secret, you know how it is at that age, the only things worth knowing are the things you're not supposed to know. Anyway, the mystery that night, it was Who is this intruder, and What does she want? Of course we never got to crack that particular case, because . . . you know. But I know she was there on the yacht and she never had been before, and also none of us had ever been, y'know, *killed* before? Do the math, history teacher. And, if you ask me— yeah, I saw online what she did yesterday, all those mannequins she dolled up like they'd been killed and then threw in the water by that dock. Real cute. But it did get that movie Mrs. Singleton was trying to do canceled, so, score one for the local girl, rah rah rah. What was the movie, the Town That Was Afraid of the Sun? Some Bigfoot trash? But I get where she's coming from with it all. Could be triggering for people who were there that

night. Including yours truly, fine. Not that I'm even in the same
hemisphere to *be* triggered. I only bring the mannequin stuff
up because it comes off like all this social activism, like she's still
fighting the big bad Terra Novans, like she's protecting her cute
little town, some Native American She-Ra. What did that article
call her? "A latterday Naru"? What does that even *mean*? But
isn't it sort of a confession, too? That she had more of a hand
in the Independence Day Massacre than she's let on? Isn't she
just re-creating it with dummies, *for* dummies? Um, don't quote
me on that? Oh, okay, Mr. Samuels, that's what this is about?
Cool, cool. That's probably what I can help with the least. This
is pretty great private-investigating. How did my dad always
win his cases, even, with support like this? Okay, yeah, sure,
whatever. Like I was saying, Ginge and I were snooping around
all that summer, setting up cameras to catch a ghost on shore,
and Ginge was really into butterflies and mushrooms, don't ask,
but we didn't care about Mr. Samuels hitting golf balls, he did
that all the time whenever there was five minutes, just lit them
up like little meteors and *whack whack whack*, except pretty
somehow, because of how he hit, and we for sure never had a
bear show up on film, that would have been everything to us,
I'd probably be a wildlife biologist or something now. We did get
Jennifer Daniels once, though. Yeah, surprise. It's daytime, not
night, but here she comes into frame, slouching right along the
shore like she owns it, like it was *her* dad who sliced it out of
the national forest, not ours, and the way this camera worked
was it took another shot every other step or so, 2015 tech,
she's walking like kabuki played backwards, and for every one of
those thunderous big frozen footsteps, she's carrying a package
to her chest like a clutch of schoolbooks. The package could be
anything, could even *be* books, it wouldn't be fair of me to say
it was greasy on one side or smelled like warm cinnamon rolls,

or that there's a fleck on it that could be an interested fly. But I will say that Mr. Samuels kept his golf stuff under a little lean-to plastic shed thing by the dock, where there were towels and snorkels and floaties for Lemmy, all that kind of stuff. I've still got the picture of Jennifer carrying that package if you want. We thought we lost it all when Ginge went, you know, Swiss Family Robertson in the forest, but—here. I don't think there's a good date on the file, though, sorry. Copy of a copy. That's what happens when your world explodes, and all you can do is walk around and pick through the wreckage of what used to be your life. I mean, *roll* around, which is another thing I should blame her for, since it would have gone different if little miss hero hadn't butted in, but my therapist tells me I can pick and choose which memory I want to play, and which I want to mute the hell out of, and you can probably guess that this isn't exactly helping me do that. Please don't get in contact with me again. I can say that because I own you, can't I? Cease and desist? Lose my number? Zoom me nevermore? I'm still grieving all the people Jade Daniels took away from me. Which I doubt she'll be building any lesson plans on for her history class.

THE NIGHT HAS 1000 SCREAMS

If going *toward* the sound of chainsaw-wielding maniacs is the key to survival, then I guess this is where Jade Daniels starts to live forever.

I wish.

"Can't believe Bub's . . . you know," Banner says.

"You really thought I was Jo Ellen?" I ask back.

We don't exactly cut the same silhouette, I mean. Jo Ellen can shop the teen section.

"You've got—" Banner says, flinging his hand in the most general possible direction at my chest—"and you're wearing this," the hat, "so, yeah. Why?"

He's talking loud because there's multiple chainsaws ahead of us.

Slowly, a tall tree starts to sway.

Banner stops and I stop with him, and we both watch this ancient tree tilt, tilt, try to hold on, and finally . . . *crash* the other direction.

"That's the one tree that's saving Terra Nova?" I have to say, just to have it out there.

"We should never have come here," Banner hisses, moving ahead again.

It's the same realization Letha came to years ago.

"Even in a Casey Jones shirt," he adds.

I stop, look down at the TMNT hockey-mask guy I'm wearing.

"What?" Banner has to say.

"You were into Turtles?" I ask.

"Me and the whole world," he says with a shrug.

"Minus this girl," I mumble, immediately trying to reel it back in since it sounds like an imperative, like an invitation. If everyone's religious in a fox hole, then everyone in the dark woods of a slasher, we're superstitious as hell. Times two. "So Jo Ellen's still out there?" I ask louder.

"She left right after the boats," Banner says, not just super interested.

I'm not sure which question to ask first, so: "Boats?"

"Didn't you see?"

"Would I be asking if I had?"

"Somebody kicked the bottom out of everything that floats," Banner says, stopping again now that we can see this fire mitigation crew, this chainsaw brigade, these clutchers-after-money.

" 'Somebody'?" I ask.

"Either that or they sunk," Banner goes on.

"It was her, wasn't it?"

"Jo Ellen?"

"*Her* her."

"Angel of Indian Lake . . ." Banner figures out with a sigh of resignation. "You're really stuck on her, aren't you? But at least that means she's not you, I guess."

"You thought I was . . . that this was a Scooby-Doo cartoon?" I ask back, more than a little insulted. "That I spent the summer dressing up to spook lookyloos away? What, so all this real estate could be mine? So the lost mine I found can stay secret until I've staked my claim?"

"If people are scared, they stay home," Banner says, studying the flannel backs of probably eight first-time chainsaw wielders. "And if they stay home, they stay alive."

"Is this you thinking this, or Leeth?"

"It's not you, that's what matters."

"Okay, okay," I say, mentally backpedaling. "Jo Ellen . . . *left*?"

"She said she can swim it," Banner says, settling on a flannel back I think belongs to Balty, the only sort-of Russian in Proofrock, as far as I know. My dad used to always watch him walk past, and the way he would slit his eyes to track Balty, I could one hundred percent tell that my dad thought Balty was a spy, and my dad was the only true American standing between Russia and *Red Dawn*.

"But she—she can't take her pistol, if she's swimming," I tell Banner.

"Cell reception's what we need," he says back. "She wrapped hers in a Ziploc baggie. Smelled like peanut butter."

This causes something to stir in the back of my mind, but whatever dim memory it is, it doesn't raise its shaggy head, quite, probably because I'm picturing Jo Ellen getting churned up in the *English Rose*'s bank of propellors like Clate, or getting kicked under by a whole herd of elk, struggling across to the safety of Proofrock.

Well, the relative safety. For the moment.

"So then who did the boats in?" I ask.

"Yeah," Banner says, meaning that's his question as well.

"And who killed all those dead people?"

This stops him, gets him studying me for what I'm saying next. I just shrug.

"There's more to this, isn't there?" he says, breaking a dead branch off a tree to announce our presence, because people with chainsaws need space to turn around.

Balty swings around leading with that whirring blade, just like Banner figured. He's wearing what I presume are *American* goggles, not Russian ones, and his whole frontside is speckled with that fine kind of sawdust that forest fires probably salivate over.

He ups his chin to Banner, considers me, then nods to the tree he's wedging a chunk out of one long bite at a time, beaver-style.

Banner swipes his open hand side to side about the chainsaw and Balty reluctantly turns it off.

"We need to go!" Banner yells, enunciating super clearly because Balty isn't wearing hearing protection, is probably mostly deaf at the moment.

"But I've almost got her down," Balty says in his weird-emphasis accent, which is drawing on a stockpile of Cyrillic letters, I guess.

"Now!" Banner says, and nods to the crew of three gangsawing a particularly big pine. After lingering on me a bit more—I have a spider crawling out of a pimple, dude, what?—Balty hauls himself over to see who Banner's meaning, here.

Which is right when two of those three chainsaws touch in the middle of the trunk. Whoever that is in a welder's helmet opens their hands wide and steps back all at once, like tapping out, but the other hungry-hungry hippo, a man of course, must be telling himself he's almost there, he's almost there.

Until the chain of his saw makes the other chainsaw shoot out. It's turned off, so who cares, but when this first guy yanks his out, he's careful to keep it high and wide. This is well and fine until the third person, Alex from class, I can see now, catches that whirring violence high on the point of his right shoulder. I lunge forward like to stop this even though it's already too late. Banner clamps his hand on my shoulder, pulling me back.

The chainsaw chugs down, carving down into Alex, spewing blood onto the sawdust coating everything, and the one who tapped out tackles the first guy away, hard enough that it dislodges his welding mask.

I'm not looking at their big dramatic sprawling fall, though.

Just Alex.

He's on his knees now, and isn't even screaming, is still trying to process that this is a thing that's really happening. And to *him*.

He brings his left hand up and over to hold his blood in, but the readjustment causes his right arm to start to fall away, taking the shoulder with it, and I swear the ripped-open blood vessels in there are whipping around exactly like *The Thing*.

I jerk away from Banner and rush to Alex, slide in on my knees to pull him to me, trying to hold him together. Pushing his arm and shoulder back into place, I see for a slice of an instant some shiny whiteness in there, and know it for the ball-joint, and I have to suck air in through my nose. The intake of air's supposed to scrub that image from my head—the longest of longshots—but it's too late. Seeing this has pulled me back four years, to Melanie's bench, when Hardy and me both saw a spherical whiteness like that in the ripped-open neck stump of a white elk.

A spherical whiteness that finally raised its head so we could see Melanie's ice-blue eyes.

"It's okay, it's okay . . ." I say, pulling Alex to me. It's a lie, but it's what you say.

Alex is hitching and spasming in my arms, so I pull him tighter to squeeze the pain away, try to take it into me instead, to make this easier for him.

Maybe thirty seconds later, I'm hugging the dead body of a student, and I don't want to cry but I can't help it.

I lower my face into his good shoulder and scream and scream instead, because this *did not* have to happen.

Alex, I won't forget, bud. You were the one up front in the classroom who was always grossed out by Manifest Destiny, by the Oregon Trail, by the Indian massacres, by how the West wasn't paved with asphalt, it was paved with the bodies of the Lakota and the Pueblo and the Nez

Perce and the Shoshone and the Navajo and the Hopi and the Zuni and the Apache and the Comanche and the Pima and the Paiute and the Kiowa and the Flathead and the Crow and the Coeur d'Alene.

And the Blackfeet.

But not this one.

I pull Alex tighter for one long last hug, just in case there's some flicker of him still awake in there, and then I breathe in a musty rich smell I know.

Once again, I came to Terra Nova, wound up coated in gore.

Shit I never thought I'd have to live through again for five hundred, Alex, I say, promising myself to go back to using his name now, to honor him.

At least this time I'm not in a burial chamber made from dead elk, I tell myself. This time all those elk are running, swimming, trying to keep their noses above the water.

Aren't we all.

Banner touches my shoulder and I finally let Alex go.

He slumps to the side but stays mostly upright, and I can't help but think of whoever comes across to collect him. Except I really hope the fire sweeps through, sends him on his journey.

I hitch my right foot forward to try to stand, but stop there, my heart still too heavy to lift.

"He was—he was—" I try to explain to Banner. "We have to tell his par—" but Banner directs my eyes to the side.

Alex's dad, I forget his name, was the tackler, his face the only part of him clean, since the welding mask was taking all the sawdust and chainsaw exhaust. Both him and whoever he was tackling are speared through the chests by the leftover, upright splinter from a tree that already fell.

I give up on trying to stand, fall back onto my knees.

Banner catches me, is holding me to him like I'm nothing. Every pound I have, it's grief and regret. How many are going to die for Terra Nova?

Banner guides me away, maybe thinking I'm too delicate to be seeing things like this, but I shake my head no, no, am hitting him over and over in the chest and shoulders with the sides of my fists. Not all crying involves tears.

He pulls me in tighter, his hand to the back of my head to push my face into his chest for . . . I don't even know how long. Long enough for the rest of the chainsaw brigade to gather round, witness their fallen comrades.

Comrades, ha: I'm thinking like my dad.

And, not "ha." More like "unacceptable."

I breathe in, my air filtered by Banner's khaki shirt, and then nod to myself, push back. Not everybody's dead here yet, are they? If I just wallow like this, they will be, and that's not a thing I can carry, I don't think. Younger me, maybe. Teacher me, no way.

I used to be all about the final girl standing on top of a pile of the dead at the end of the movie, her face dripping blood, her chest heaving, her eyes fierce. Now I'm all about holding the door of the slasher-proof shelter open, so everybody can duck in, ride this out.

"Do they know?" I ask Banner, using my just-for-him voice, and holding his eyes so he can really hear me. Balty's still standing there, trying to make what just happened make sense, and there's other boots shuffling around, but I can't process them yet.

"They know about the boats," Banner says. "But not . . . not—"

Ghostface back there. The Angel of Indian Lake. Chin Tread-away, Walter Mason. Bub.

"*Bodies Bodies Bodies*," I say, in just as much wonder as Balty.

"I know," Banner says, stepping back, his big pistol dragging over my shoulder, his eyes on the body of Alex, the body of Alex's dad, the body of whoever that third Proofrocker was, a counter clicking in his head.

"No, the movie," I tell him. "There wasn't even a slasher. It's like—it's like *Tucker and Dale*? A lot of dead people, no real killer."

"Yeah, this is the time for movie trivia," Banner tells me.

He's not wrong. I'm still hiding in the video store. Only, now, I'm keenly aware of the shadowy figure hulking silently past, a row or two over. His name is Death, and the handle on his scythe telescopes out, so he can reach all of us.

I finally look up from the shuffling boots to the dirty faces of the chainsaw brigade. They're in a rough half-moon around the scene of this crime.

"So they don't know we're not alone out here," I say back to Banner, but *for* everyone. "But you can tell them," I tag on.

"Tell them what?" Banner says.

"That you shot him, and he ran away."

Banner doesn't *yes* or *no* this.

Everybody's looking at him.

There's . . . maybe sixteen people here? Nine of them have chainsaws, seven are axed up and twitchy. Men, women, two more high schoolers. I recognize the faces more or less, but resist the urge to give those faces names I've known since forever, or since the school year started. I can't take another Alex, I mean.

"Shit," Beardo says, seemingly impressed with the terribleness of this.

The woman beside him, Tall Boots, looks to me specifically, says, "Jade *Daniels*?"

As if there's another Jade doppelganging around over here, yes. Unless of course she's slyly suggesting this is the end of *Happy Birthday to Me*, when Ann's Virginia mask finally comes off.

I'm just me, though, promise. For better or, as it usually goes, a whole lot of worse.

I nod once to Tall Boots.

"Why is she here?" Hardhat asks Banner.

"Why are any of us here," Banner answers. "Because we don't *need* to be. Got it?"

It makes about zero sense, but they get the sense all the same, I think.

"*Who'd* you shoot?" Rankin Dobbs asks—shit, don't give them names.

"That's not the important part," Jocelyn Cates says, evidently here the whole time. She's still holding that axe crossbody. And not looking at me, or Banner. She's watching the trees, the shadows. "What's important is that he ran away. Right?"

I nod once.

Jocelyn fucking Cates.

My guess is she fell back in with the rest of the brigade, playacting like she was still in it for the money, for the license to wreak some havoc in the national forest at last. But the moment danger steps in, she's going to cut its head off and spit down the neck.

Plans are great. I have them all the time.

"We're going to have to walk," Banner informs them all, using his sheriff voice.

"We still get paid?" Hardhat asks.

"Yeah," Beardo chimes in, like they're already lining up for their checks.

"You might get to *live*," I tell him, them, everybody. "How's that work for you?"

Which is when, trying to stare them all down at once, I realize that one of these sixteen has his head down, is keeping his face hidden with the wide brim of his county-brown cowboy hat.

And he doesn't have either an axe or chainsaw.

"What the hell?" I whisper, mumble, trying to reel it back in the moment I sort of say it.

What he's holding is—

The golden pickaxe. It's fitted over a new-looking axe handle.

I clamp onto Banner's wrist, and him and the rest of the chainsaw brigade see where I'm looking, and like that the whole world pretty much stops spinning, and the only thing moving anymore in it, it's whoever this is, their hat just starting to come up to level.

"What?" Camo Suspenders asks, his hand to the ripcord of his chainsaw.

The brown cowboy hat tilts up, up, and I'm shaking my head no, no, that this isn't someone I want to see, this is a face I can go my whole life never seeing.

The chin is first, and it's the same dark my skin is, no beard, no stubble.

No, not the *same* dark. It's twice as dark, I can tell. Because I'm exactly, by blood, *half* as dark as that.

Ten minutes ago I was afraid Freddy was going to push me back into a nightmare.

I must have nodded off since then, though. Let my defenses down.

I breathe in to scream, and not only has the world stopped turning, but time itself has stopped clicking forward. It's giving my brain time to dwell on that no-beard, no-stubble aspect of this dark face: it's an Indian thing. A lot of Indian dudes don't have facial hair, can't grow it. It's not a thing I ever knew, since I wasn't exactly a mustache prospect, and my dad was the only Indian in my orbit, but Yazzie told me. Something about her brothers saving on razor money, and how that was the one get-back Indians had going for them.

It isn't exactly helpful right now, though. Or, it isn't stopping this hat from coming up.

Right before it levels out, this mouth grins a grin I think I know, a grin that makes me shake my head no, no, please. My blood thickens and goes cold in my body, my chest hollows out even more than it already was, and like that I'm falling into a hole inside myself. It's—it's that chasm that opens in the wall in *Hellraiser*, and it's sucking me in.

And I'd far rather be in the hell dimension at the other end of that passage than here in the woods.

With my dad.

Tab Daniels isn't in the lake anymore.

What Christy Christy didn't say in her presentation about the golden pickaxe was that, evidently, it grants life to whoever nudges into it down in Ezekiel's Cold Box.

Of all the people to drift into contact with it, though.

This is Jason in *VI*, resurrected from that long iron rod Tommy Jarvis ripped from the cemetery fence, juiced with lightning: it doesn't make sense, except . . . there he is, doing his thing again.

Just like my dad.

"*No!*" I lean forward to scream.

To make it worse, my dad's face-raising-so-slowly thing, which has to be intentional, for dramatic effect—that's the way he is—it has enough momentum that his chin *keeps* coming up, just slightly, like he's seeing an unspoken-for beer across the room. The new weight of the cowboy hat, though, it tilts his head back enough that . . . he's a human Pez dispenser?

That machete I swung into his neck, that didn't go all the way through, it did go *some* of the way through. A ragged rip yawns open on his throat and neck, and his whole head threatens to keep rocking back until the back brim of his hat touches his rotting spine, and, I don't know—and some hand from *Demons* thrusts up from his neck.

Sensing the same possibility, I guess, my dad frees one of his own hands from the pickaxe at the last moment, palms the crown of that deputy hat he must have collected on the shore, and guides his head back down to level, and like that I know that this is his weakness, this is the way to take him down: plant my knees in his back, grab him by the face, and pull back with every last bit of weight I've got, ripping his head off.

And he's just staring at me with his flat, dead eyes. They're one thing that hasn't changed, from his years in the lake.

"Who the—" Hardhat says.

Two chainsaws rip alive.

My dad shrugs his shoulders once like he understands this next part. He understands it oh so well. It's the same thing he did on shore a half hour ago, when he walked up from the lake with the rest of the lost and dead, and decided there could be only one.

He's still in that *Highlander* mode.

He skates his eyes away from mine, lands on Camo Suspenders holding his chainsaw high and loose for his big charge. Before he can get there, an axe thunks into my dad's chest dead center, hard enough that he has to step back to take this impact.

Camo Suspenders stops. Beardo, two steps away from all this already, his chainsaw whirring as well, also stops.

I follow this axe's handle across to Jocelyn Cates, her chest heaving, her lips peeled back from her teeth, her eyes pretty much spitting flame out the side.

"That's for my son," she says through her teeth, and rips this axe out and hauls it behind her, to drive one home for her husband, now.

You can't get your loved ones back, no. But you *can* kill yourself trying.

My dad looks down to this field version of open-heart surgery. It's leaking something black and clumpy, but thin like lake water.

Nothing he needs, evidently.

Without looking, he one-arms the axe Jocelyn is swinging at him, stops it mid-arc, and flicks its butt into the bridge of Jocelyn's nose, spurting blood up all around it.

Jocelyn falls like a ragdoll, and instead of slinging this axe away, my dad chokes up on it to get the balance right, latches on right where he wants, and spins it away from him.

It catches Red Flannel right in the throat, nearly decapitates her.

Next, like this was all choreographed, has been rehearsed over and over for a week, he comes around with that golden pickaxe, drives it through Tall Boots's midsection, lifting her up onto her toes.

She folds over holding onto the axe handle but my dad pulls it back to him, Tall Boots's intestines unspooling like a long meaty tapeworm she's been keeping secret since second grade.

"No, no, *run!*" I scream all around.

Can't they tell that there's no taking my dad on toe-to-toe? Yeah, they're geared up, probably looked bad-ass enough in their mirrors before the trip across the lake, but this is the real deal.

They don't know the rules, that's it. They don't know that this is *my* personal boogeyman. Meaning? Meaning I'm the only one who can take him down in a way that sticks.

Hopefully. If I remember to cross my fingers.

And of course nobody can even hear me.

Welcome to every other day of your life, Jade.

Hardhat's chainsaw comes down hard for my dad but he reaches up with his non-pickaxe hand for the non-chewy part of it, stops it mid-air, his eyes staring into Hardhat's soul. Hardhat's crotch darkens, he starts to lean back, but—

My dad's shiny golden pickaxe is jamming into one side of Hardhat's chest slowly, nosing in under the armpit, then *streeetching* the flannel out the other side until the threads start to tear, showing the sharp gold under it, that's just been cleaned.

"*Nooo!*" I scream again, even though I know full well how useless this is.

Banner's the one with training here, though.

And his pistol's already out.

He shoulders me to the side, widens his stance, and pulls his trigger once, twice, *bam bam bam*, so fast, so out of nowhere.

It deafens me, splits the forest in two.

In the new silence is my dad, looking down to these new holes in his already opened chest. They're each leaking that same thin blackness that makes me remember when Stacey Graves pulled me close, and I could see the dark veins under her pale skin.

Bullets didn't stop her, though.

They don't stop my dad, either.

Banner's bullets just poked daylight right through him, plugs of his rancid meat flying out behind him, probably, to hump and crawl their way back to his leg T-1000-style, nudge into his soggy boot, become part of him again.

"*Run!*" I plead again, with all the volume I've got left.

My dad smiles one side of his face like he does when he's got the upper hand. It's the same smile he used to crack when one of his Westerns would be on the channel he just landed on and Rexall would groan, lean back in his chair in defeat, because he knew my dad wasn't checking out any other channels, that he'd found where he belonged, and everybody else in the room could suck it.

I used to watch from the kitchen, because standing any closer would mean I was hanging out with them.

The gunslingers in my dad's movies, though—I can see this now—they're like he is, here: bulletproof. If Crazy Horse could shake off gunfire because he'd painted hailstones all over himself like his vision told him to, then my dad can shake it off because . . . because he was killed, dumped in the lake like the trash he is.

This is the recipe for a slasher, though, isn't it? It's the unfairness he needs to rise again. It's the lack of justice that makes what he does righteous. Never mind who he was. Freddy rose too, didn't he? Nobody champions his child-raping and child-killing and bad quips and just general evilness, but neither can anyone deny that getting burned alive after the court cleared him was breaking the law.

Shit.

Why now, though, slasher girl?

Halloween, I say back.

Then why *this* Halloween?

Because . . . it's the eighth anniversary of his death? No, who cares about the number eight. Because this is the year he would have turned forty-three—how old Jason was going to be in *A New Beginning*? Fat chance. Because . . . oh, oh: it's been thirty years since Melanie Hardy drowned? Since my mom and dad and Rexall and Clate and Lonnie and Misty Christy all treaded water while she drowned?

Or maybe this is just how long the lake took to put him back together?

He probably doesn't even know why. He just knows *who*: me. He haunted me in life, and now, dead, he's still standing over me, is still winning, still getting away with it. Never mind that it's him against the twelve remaining members of the chainsaw brigade, one sheriff, and the daughter who killed him.

I don't like our odds, here. Not one little bit.

I grab Banner's sheriff belt, yank him back, sending the shot he's squeezing off high, like he's trying to shoot a hole in the fire still a few hundred yards from us. He swings his hand back to free himself but just thunks into my wrist, because my hand's got a deathgrip here.

Our eyes meet and mine are hotter.

"Run," I tell him.

He looks around at the rest of the chainsaw brigade, peeling away just the same, scampering off into the trees.

"But—" he says, which is when he suddenly thrusts his tongue out, and it's sharp, it's pointed, it's . . . it's *golden*.

I track up from this to my dad, still holding the handle of that pickaxe, and I know that the hole in the base of Banner's skull, it's square like the trapdoor in the back of Bub's head, and probably flecked with gold at the edges just the same.

Something too big to scream out wells up in my throat, and, this close to Banner's face, I can see the hazel-flecked brown pupil of his right eye, blown large, ragged at the edges, and I want that to be a well of memory and life and living he can dive down, where Letha and Adie are waiting to catch him, to hold him in their laps, guide his bangs away from his forehead and laugh at whatever stupid joke he tries, and then the stadium lights will fizzle on over all of them, and there'll be some stupid football spiraling so perfect up through it all, and, and—

My dad plants his boot into Banner's back, pushes him off, and raises the pickaxe again, his grin sharp, and all I can think of, Mr. Holmes, it's how you used to tell us about the dreamers over on this side of the valley, chipping into rock over and over, trying to find their future, and how they would swing and swing until hours after dark, so the people back in Henderson-Golding could see their distant sparks, and know their loved ones were okay.

So long as the sparks kept sparking.

I kick at my dad's legs with both heels, which splays me out on the ground, I know, but there's no time to think of anything better, my best friend's husband just died in front of me, *because* of me, and now he'll never airplane Adie around and around again, he'll never saunter into Dot's again for his free cup of coffee, he'll never kick his legs up on Hardy's desk, he'll never surprise Letha with the stupid selfies he takes whenever he's in some pretty place around town, chronicling his day for her.

They were all pretty to him.

He'd found his life, he'd made a home, he has a daughter who knows he's not the actual Incredible Hulk, but she still giggles and hugs him and thinks he's pretty incredible all the same.

He was. He was.

And now he isn't.

I scream up at the pickaxe my dad is swinging down at me with both hands, I scream my whole *life* out at him, and—

BAKER SOLUTIONS

Report of Investigation
3 September 2023
#32d43
re: Treasure Island vandalization

At 2:12am, 21 June 2023, Jennifer Elaine "Jade" Daniels's voice-activated the listening device posted near the headstone of Grady "Bear" Holmes in Glen Ridge Cemetery. Note that Idaho law doesn't preclude the positioning of recording equipment in public spaces. Ms. Daniels was out of breath. Also present at the cemetery was Bethany Manx (25), surviving daughter of former principal of Henderson High Roger Manx (perished during the Independence Day Massacre of 2015), surviving sister of Toby Manx (perished in the Dark Mill South slayings of 2019), and current degree candidate at Brigham Young University. After affirming who each party was, Ms. Daniels asked Ms. Manx if it was okay if she "lit up." Apparently they shared a cigarette (no cameras are installed at the cemetery), during which Ms. Manx asked Ms. Daniels if that had been her at Founders Park in the Halloween mask. Ms. Daniels declined to answer. She also didn't answer Ms. Manx's question about who that was on the swing set with her. Ms. Daniels offered that Ms. Manx's brother had been a promising basketball player. Ms. Manx proffered that Grady "Bear" Holmes had elected to accept a paper from her on the Oregon Trail that took the creative liberty of incorporating the "disappearing hitchhiker" urban legend (see *The Vanishing Hitchhiker: American Urban Legends and Their Meanings*, Jan Harold Brunvand, Norton, 1981). Ms. Daniels suggested that this disappearing hitchhiker was in Pleasant Valley lately, in the form of "The Angel of Indian Lake" [report in-process]. Of import from this clandestine conversation is that, at 2:17:32am, in response to Ms. Manx's question about why Ms. Daniels isn't wearing shoes,

Ms. Daniels says, "If anybody asks you about any, um, certain *items* dropped into the lake tonight, or any splashing you did or didn't hear, then you never saw me, right?" [29a for the recording / 29a-tr for the transcription].

On its own, this doesn't qualify as an admission of guilt regarding the significant vandalism that occurred to Temporary Research Islet H-G ("Treasure Island") the night of 21 June 2023. Taken in tandem with the video footage recently attained from the computer of Regini "Rexall" Bridger, however (timestamp: 1687330927), Ms. Daniels's statement is much more incriminating.

The video footage (1080p, 8:54) is recorded at a depth of 102' with a Chasing Innovations M2 Underwater ROV on a 656' tether on an EZ-Reel, with the ancillary illumination provided by aftermarket dive lights (1200 lumen flood/500 lumen spot) mounted on the top rails of the ROV.

Location: Henderson-Golding (submerged), Indian Lake, Idaho.

0:00–1:42:   ROV navigates the main thoroughfare of Henderson-Golding, continually pausing both to illuminate and record the dilapidated buildings to either side and to allow the silt its eight thrusters have stirred up to dissipate. Note that, due to the proximity of the onboard lights of the ROV (twin 2000-lumen LEDs), the lower part of the image is often washed out due to backscatter.

1:43–2:17:   ROV is directed between two buildings in sluggish pursuit of what appears to be a heterocercal caudal fin measuring between three and eight feet in height—most likely a discarded tarp or other detritus.

2:18-2:58:   Open water as the operator of the ROV attempts
               to steer it back into Henderson-Golding.

2:59-3:26:   ROV is back on the main thoroughfare, now
               slowing to take photographs-while-record-
               ing (Sony CMOS @ 30fps) of a 1910 Diamond T
               parked alongside a colorless building.

3:27-4:08:   ROV approaches a dim steeple.

4:09-5:51:   ROV struggles to move forward, but appar-
               ently its tether has snagged on the main
               thoroughfare, impeding forward movement.

5:52-5:53:   ROV jerks sideways from impact.

5:54-6:13:   Particulate matter occludes the recording.

6:14-6:56:   ROV's field of view is now partially impeded
               by the sensor head of a Leica Chiroptera-5
               (Bathymetric LiDAR) [see insurance claim
               form 1842749].

6:57-7:17:   Particulate matter occludes the recording
               as the ROV struggles against the tether
               (operator error).

7:18-7:42:   ROV, unable to disentangle its tether, rises
               above the derelict sensor head, clearing
               its field of view and presenting again the
               steeple of the church from a level angle
               with the sagging roof.

7:43-7:52:   A 28" plastic wood D-handle shovel, an 11.6"
              Mayouko Portable Tool Box with Shockproof
              Sponge (closed), and three Lyumo Multi Speed
              Flashlights plummet down from the surface
              of Indian Lake, coming to rest in the silt
              of the main thoroughfare. Their contrails
              are streams of bubbles, while their multi-
              ple impacts stir up more particulate mat-
              ter. Two of the flashlights are turned on.

7:53-8:49:   Particulate matter occludes the recording.

8:50-8:54:   ROV is steered away from this barrage of
              debris from "Treasure Island," but as it
              turns to retreat down the main thorough-
              fare, one last item descends from the sur-
              face: a Rayovac 926 12 Volt Lantern Battery
              (5.37" x 2.86" / 2.60lbs / $18.95 MSRP).
              In the last 30 frames/the last second of
              the recording, this lantern battery plunges
              through the roof of the church.

While the damage to Henderson-Golding is negligible, the
replacement cost of the destroyed scientific mapping equipment
is in excess of $80,000.

BLOODBATH

In *Zombi 2*, a woman's face is pulled closer and closer to a crashed-in door, so we can feel every grain of the splinter that slowly penetrates her right eye—Fulci, one-upping some French eyeball-plus-razor scene I've only ever seen in gif-form.

It's what I'm thinking of, with my dad's shiny golden pickaxe slinging down for me: that I wish I had some of that slowness for real, not just in the way my head's dialing everything down to a crawl, like, since there's only half a second left, it wants to savor every hundredth part of it. And then cut those hundredths into hundredths themselves, giving me time to conjure up the poster for *Candyman*: he's a silhouette right there in the pupil, just like Ghostface would be for the Fonz four years later.

I should be thinking of Harry Warden, though, I know: death-by-pickaxe is what he's all about.

If I hold my thoughts just right, maybe I can put myself in *My Bloody Valentine*, even, and relish the honor of checking out like this. It makes me part of something, it plugs me into a tradition older than me, it knocks me into that videotape slot in my old player, so I can get spooled up in that iridescent tape and just loop around those heads forever, always screaming and running, trying to wait to smile until I'm past the edge of the screen.

But . . . why am I sticking on that *Candyman* poster?

I either furrow my brow or start to, once again thinking of the completely unhelpful thing at the perfectly wrong time, and then I squint to see better, can just make out Candyman's hook hand, and some part of me sort of nods: of course. Dark Mill South, right? The killer I killed when he hadn't actually been doing that much killing, was mostly just mutilating, and trying to stay off the world's radar.

It should have been Cinnamon Baker holding a hay hook—no, holding that blood hook from *I Know What You Did Last Summer*. That's the way she would want it: she knows all the slashers, has the inside of her head plastered with their posters, so everywhere she turns it's another killer, another victim.

I understand, I mean. Having all that in your head, it's what you do, it's the only real way to be. How does everybody *not* choose to live like that? It's safer, it's more fun, and everything's heightened, and fair.

Unlike Cinnamon, though, I never stepped into those posters, looked out Harry Warden's goggles.

I did used to want justice to be served on Proofrock, but that was the old me.

The new me just wants to live, justice be damned.

And, why am I even thinking of her? *You're not*, I tell myself. You're still feeling guilty for Dark Mill South, because you should have seen through how Cinnamon was setting him up to take the fall for her sister, her classmates, the whole town—including very much me, who Cinnamon blamed for her parents' deaths.

Bad thing is, though? I don't completely disagree with her.

Used to, I'd plod toward sleep at three in whatever morning by reciting longer and longer giallo titles—the only sheep horror fans need are rabid—but, never mind what Sharona says, what I say *now*, just so I don't ever forget, are names: Jensen Jones, Abby Grandlin, Gwen

Stapleton, Toby Manx, Mark Costins, Philip Cates, Kristen Ames, the rest . . . all the Proofrockers who went down for good, four years ago.

When that's enough, I dial back to the summer of 2015, where Christy's mom died, where Lee Scanlon died, where you died, Mr. Holmes.

I tend to stop there, and just hug my pillow so tight to my face that I can't breathe, and don't care if I ever do, and if oxygen deprivation isn't a cure for insomnia, then I don't know what is.

It was me who called the horror down on Proofrock, though, I can never deny that. Meaning my job now, much as I hate it, is to put down each one that rises, so long as I can still breathe and kick and fight and scream.

Or go down trying. Like's happening right now.

But this isn't actually *My Bloody Valentine*, I tell myself. This isn't Harry Warden, venting his fury on me. This is my loser of a dad, re-animated not with some green juice from Herbert West, not with Tri-oxin, but with a stupid golden pickaxe left over from the frontier days.

Worse, though I try and try to push it from my head, I can't shake that the golden head of this stupid pickaxe is going to *penetrate* me.

John Carpenter says that Laurie and Michael are just two sexually repressed people trying to get it on the only way they can, with stab after stab. I never bought it, really—why does Michael stab her in the back of the *arm*, then, Mr. Carpenter?—but I get the connotation, thank you very little.

And no way do I let this happen again, Dad.

No fucking way.

What I want is for my body to have always had armadillo armor built-in, so it can roll over me, shunt that pickaxe away. What I want are Wonder Woman's magic bracelets, and maybe an armoring-up montage like in *Nightmare 4*, so I can cross those bracelets in front of me, ward off all attacks.

No, what I want is for this to be a nightmare I'm in *control* of,

Freddy, so I can nod that pickaxe into a double handful of fluttering moths, leaving my dad to stumble forward, fall on his face.

Leaving me time to push up with my elbows, run like hell.

Except that's not how it works.

How it works is that nothing stops that golden pickaxe. It weighs too much, it's swung too hard, has been swinging for me my whole life.

All I can do is jerk to the side maybe four desperate inches.

Four inches the right way: the eye my dad was aiming for was my right one, just like Fulci, like that poster from *Candyman*, which is one more way horror can save your life if you let it.

It saves mine. But not my ear on that side. The pickaxe snags in it and tears through, and to get there it drags a furrow in the side of my head.

Almost as bad, my dad's follow through brings his face down even closer to mine, and I'm not Ripley, but my killer is right there nose to nose just like that giant alien was for her.

I haven't even had time to breathe in, but I scream out anyway, and not just with my mouth, but the heels of my hands, my knees, with my hips trying to buck up, away from this. It dislodges my dad's stance so he falls forward, which is about the last thing I want. At least until the butt of the pickaxe handle, its head now planted deep in the spongy loam just over my shoulder, catches him in the gut and pushes through, splashes out at his beltline, hanging him there like the fallen-down scarecrow he is.

His arms are still going, though, his hands are still clawing. One of them hooks into the belly of my thin, expensive shirt but I'm already rolling.

The belly of the shirt tears away like the nothing it is and I keep rolling until I bang into a tree. My face is low enough that there's pine needles stabbing up through my vision. Through them, I see my dad trying to grab onto the handle of the pickaxe. But it's slick with his own oily insides.

His mouth is moving too, but with his throat mostly gone, he can't even whisper.

Damn straight. I don't want to hear one single thing he says, ever.

I pull myself up with the tree's rough bark, and only realize when it moves under my palm that this is the tree Jensen and his dad were chainsawing.

It's falling, now.

"Hey," I say to my dad, upping my chin at him.

Some part of him hears, cranks his head around to me. And then up, up, at the tree slow-motion timbering down, down, down.

It slams onto him with all its weight and all its centuries, driving that pickaxe handle down under it, my dad lost in that destruction.

Eight years ago, I held a broken pole against his back, and wished so bad I had what it took to push it on through. For my mom, for the girl I'd used to be. But I hadn't been able to.

That girl's all grown up now, though, Dad.

And then *all* the trees start to shake, like the whole forest is about to bow down in honor of this. Needles are arrowing down, shit's dancing around my feet, and the air pressure's somehow thrumming, full, about to burst.

I fall to my knees, can't even imagine what might be about to happen—it's Halloween in Proofrock, isn't it?—and when I look up, it's to a wall of powdery red tidal-waving through at what feels like the speed of sound.

It hits me, isn't sharp and granular like salt but powdery and almost billowy, and it's moving fast enough that it lifts me, throws me back, and while I'm mid-air I see the angels that threw this at me blasting past, just over the treeline: three of the fire planes at once, all dropping their loads in concerted effort and then pulling up hard to bank away, the smoke at the end of their wingtips curling into furious little whirlpools.

Their fire retardant is packed into my mouth, my eyes, my nose, and if I don't slam into another tree, one that *doesn't* fall, one that makes me stay awake, then I can't roll over coughing, digging in my mouth to breathe, puke coming up through my nose, two dark red fireproof plugs shooting out.

I'm on my hands and knees for two minutes, maybe.

And then I finally look up.

The smoke is thicker now, but it's slower too, less angry. Like when you've doused a campfire and the last of the smoke's trailing up, up, away.

I sit, hug my knees to me.

All around me, for as far as I can see, everything's powdery red. Like I'm the first Indian on Mars.

This has to be over, now, I tell myself. Sally can check back into her facility, get the help she needs, Chucky can scrabble back into his Good Guys box, Seth Mullins can mourn his wife in a healthy, *non*-destructive way. Me, I'll knock on Alex's front door and try to explain some of this to his mom. How she lost her son and her husband, and we'll end up just hugging, because what else is there?

What else is there.

And then I'll go to Chin's apartment or house or trailer. And Walter Mason's stone house way out on Evergreen.

And and and.

What I'll do is the part you never see in the slashers: hold people's hands as they try to pick their way through this new, empty world. Some of them will knee me in the gut, bring their fists down onto the back of my head, but if it makes them feel better, so be it. I can take the damage, Alex's mom, Walter's wife, Chin's Pekingese.

Well, okay, I probably won't let a dog come at me like that.

Girl's got to have limits.

And then I'll slouch out to see you again, Mr. Holmes.

We'll smoke so many cigarettes together, and, somewhere way out in front of us, Gale Weathers will be staring the camera down with her survivor face, her eyes so piercing and blue. She'll guide some bangs out of her eyes—bangs she'll be losing a couple of installments later—she'll breathe in to be sure to get this right, to do it justice, and she'll start in telling about this last eruption of violence in the most cursed little mountain town in America, and my spirit will be swooping up into the coming dawn like I'm cradled in an ultralight, and when I look over, you'll be right there beside me in your own little plane, sir, and this is how all good stories end, isn't it?

I deserve one of those endings, I think.

But first I have to get back to the other side of the lake. I think there's even still time for some trick-or-treaters, maybe. Or a movie in my living room, more like.

The Legend of Boggy Creek would feel pretty good right now, I mean. Lana Singleton at least had that right.

But, now that I'm thinking about it: *how?* How did she land on *that* movie? She doesn't know horror. Lemmy does, but if even *Scream* is old to him, then 1972 must be *ancient*. Shouldn't he be more into . . . what? All the *Purges?* The *Unfriended* stuff? That whole *Conjuring* thing? Maybe swamp monster Bigfoots go with some drone-stunt he's got planned, though, who knows. Or—Lana's probably got people to do this kind of research, doesn't she? Helper bees who can find about the only G-rated horror out there, as . . . it *might* be tame enough to not trigger a traumatized community?

And I seriously need to wash my mouth out. Fire retardant doesn't taste particularly healthy. It's like pesticide disguised as cotton candy.

Instead of angling over to Terra Nova—I can just see its open space—I feel my way through all the red powder and smoke over to the edge of Sheep's Head Meadow, giving my dad's headstone of a tree a very wide berth.

Fucking Christy Christy, right? I hadn't thought about that golden pickaxe since . . . I don't even know when, really. Had more pressing things, the last few years.

This downslope tip of Sheep's Head on the way to the lake is just one thin wall of young pine. Young because somebody maybe once set a pile of dead elk on fire, and all the mature trees went up like candles.

Shit happens.

I take a knee, use some loose bark as a ladle to guide water up to my mouth, which I'm kind of surprised works. Swish, swish, spit, and then I tilt my head back, pour another ladleful on my face. Inside, I read how the old-time Indians used to make bowls and stuff from bark, but that's such a mystery to me. Grass bowls, bark bowls, spoons carved from bison horn—not me, thanks. Dollar store has all of that, pressed from nice neat plastic.

I'm careful not to *drink* any of the water, though. Not because of beaver fever—is that only in creeks and rivers?—but for the same reason nobody in Proofrock much drinks from Indian Lake anymore, even with those tablets and filters: we know the dead it holds. So, slurping a big mouthful in, a tiny little bit of that's probably somebody you know, right?

Which is of course right when a corpse from a decade or two ago rolls face-up just underneath the surface, below my dipper.

I'd forgotten about them, somehow.

"*No*—" I try to say, but yes: I'm gagging, I'm dry-heaving, I'm scrabbling away from what I have to have just gotten into my mouth.

What does Tom Cruise say in that Jack Torrance–joins–the– Marines movie? *The hits just keep on coming.* Tagline on the movie poster of my life, right there.

I toss my bark out onto the water and the water holds it, starts to move it out over the deep, to suck it down. In elementary, I used to have the fantasy that all the trash we dropped in the lake—Christmas trees, washing machines, spools of wire, so many bottles—that the residents down in Drown Town would go out every morning and pick it all up from their muddy street and incorporate it into their homes, their buildings. Some of the bottles would get cleaned up and sold in the thrift store. Any books that made their way down would have hymns traced over their waterlogged pages, for Ezekiel's unholy choir.

I also thought that Christmas down there must be a couple weeks late, since they had to wait for us to drop all our trees down.

The lake's Proofrock's big trashcan, and we use the hell out of it.

I glare across to the Pier like pissed at it for being so far away, and then look higher, to Main, coming down from the highway.

It's all headlights.

People are coming back.

I turn around to try to see flickering flame over the treetops deeper in the woods, but there's still only thinner and thinner wisps of smoke.

We won, shit. For once. Third time's the charm, right?

I salute all these returning evacuees, step back onto shore, but then turn back, because something's not right.

The *English Rose*.

Instead of where it usually sleeps, out toward Treasure Island, it's parked or anchored or whatever over by the dam?

"Parked," has to be. Hardy told me once that it's too deep by the dam for most chains to reach bottom.

Lana's taken them past the floating cones. Sure, those floats are sun-bleached down to about the color of the lake, but still, she knows lake rules, doesn't she? She has to.

Hunh.

But then I see one of Lemmy's drones buzzing against the coming dusk, and I maybe get it: he asked to go over there, to swoop one of his toys down off the dam again?

Why not. And: doesn't matter.

I run my fingers back through my hair but catch myself at the last instant, because I'm about to scrape the heel of my hand across this new gouge in my scalp. But . . . shouldn't it be stinging in this cool air, and seeping besides?

Gingerly, I prod and poke, then study the paste crumbling on my finger: the fire retardant. Hm. Who knew it was good for head injuries.

I try to mash any back in that I'd dislodged, and nod thanks to the planes for their sudden triage. Sure, it was triage that could have speared me on a broken limb or broken my pelvis or drowned me on dry land, but . . . guess I'm meant to buy it some different way.

Before I start counting any lucky blessings, though—I wince.

Banner.

It's not that I'm dreading telling Letha. Well, there is that, but it's more just the senselessness of it, right? Then too, until the second most recent *Scream*, I figured Dewey was pretty much unkillable. In the movie sense, I get it, the local sheriff being taken out of the picture. It leaves everyone on their own, no authority to appeal to. Only madness and chaos can ensue, now.

Still, though? Why *him*, slasher gods? He's got a wife, a daughter.

There was someone with no one standing just a few inches away from him, wasn't there?

And he didn't even get to creak anything out for me to pass on to Letha and Adie. Will I make something up for them, about his last words? Something he drew in the dirt with a dying finger? And will I see it in Letha's eyes now, Adie's in a few years, that it was *my* dad who took their husband and father away? That, if it wasn't for me, then maybe they get to all stay together?

I won't need to see it in their eyes, though. It's already in my heart. What's left of it.

And I can't stand here all night. I mean, I can, but how many more die from me checking out?

"None," I say, jaw and fists clenched. Because I'm not checking out. I'm not leaving till you make me, Farmer Vincent. And maybe not even then.

Because I know better than to try to navigate the rocky shore— and because I don't want to be in the camera eye of Lemmy's drone—I slip back into the trees to just walk it back to Terra Nova.

Maybe I'll even climb that chalky bluff again, tightwire across the dam like I'm still seventeen years old.

Yeah.

I know I'm taking the back way, the long way. I know I'm showing up back in Proofrock about midnight, scratched and muddy, these gimme clothes—what's left of them—stained fireproof red, my ear scabbed over, this numb cut in the side of my head pulsing.

Through the trees on and off, I can see Terra Nova's plastic dock, and because my head's a traitor, it keeps hanging Tiara Mondragon up in the air again, just to slam her down. When I can stop that from happening, then it's Lewellyn Singleton in the water, his jaw torn off, his head mushy on the inside. And there's Mars Baker, pretty much torn in half.

And—why not—one of these New Founders who swam the lake, he's stomping the accelerator of his car, not braking before that wall of concrete. And his friend, his bud, his investment partner and neighbor, he's dragged someone up onto a conference table, is throttling them.

The Founders we had eight years ago maybe weren't ideal, didn't fit into town, but these new ones, man, they're a different breed, seems.

I shake my head to think something different, please, but when I look ahead through the trees again, I'm still filling the world with boogeymen.

This time it's Theo Mondragon, just a silhouette.

"No," I tell him, because I'm not letting him mess this up.

Except, then, he lowers his head so his left hand can snug a cowboy hat down and on.

Which is when I see the dull glint of that golden pickaxe.

My father's white smile splits his face.

I step back without meaning to, catch my heel on a root, and splat down, both arms out beside me to break my fall, and I flinch from the metal clap in my ear before I even feel the hot electricity spiking up my right arm, branching into my shoulders, my neck, behind my eyes.

I roll hard, away from this sudden pain, this sound, this wrongness, trying to keep my eyes on my dad but I dropped down too far, have already lost where he is.

"What the—?" I say, jerking my right arm out of whatever it's caught in, and the pain doesn't just double, it turns up to eleven.

Which is when I finally have to see.

A bear trap. One of the ones the original Founders put out, when Seth Mullins announced to surrounding communities that there was a trash bear on the prowl.

The metal teeth are gouged into my forearm. Blood's bubbling up, smearing down. I shake my head no, start to pull but—the *pain*.

I rotate around on my ass, desperate to get enough leverage to crank these jaws open, but, even with the heels of Bub's cowboy boots, it's hopeless.

And my dad's got to be coming this way.

I scream through my teeth, straining to get this trap open just enough, even if I have to lose some skin, but . . .

Finally I pull on the chain, follow it to its rusty stake.

It comes up easy enough when I pull straight up, which I guess animals never think to do.

I gather the stake and the chain in my good arm, lift the trap with that hand and huddle over it all, try to convince myself this can work. If I can make the lake, if I can just get there, maybe it's dark enough nobody can see, maybe I can—

My dad's pickaxe spins by me, an angry golden blur, and plants deep in the tree I'm leaning against.

I jerk away from this, losing maybe fifteen strands of hair that went into the tree with that golden point. I take a stumbling step away from this, then another stumbling step, and I'm more falling than running, I know.

But I've got to do something, have to get some distance.

Until, standing between the shore and me is someone else.

A woman.

To brake, I fall to my knees, slide maybe two feet, which is really my knees sliding up into the thighs of these sweats, the waistband tugging down and down, one of my hands out of commission, the other holding a bear trap.

Not my most dignified moment. In a lifetime of undignified moments.

The way this silhouette is standing there in the dying light, though—it's not her against the world, it's her against whatever's coming, whoever wants a shot at the title.

"Letha?" I say, not really loud enough for her to hear.

She's already looking at the rustling panting commotion I am, but when she shifts the axe in her hands, the blade catching the setting sun behind us, my heart both sinks and swells.

Jocelyn Cates.

"Where is he?" she says not so much to me as at me.

I fall to the side, looking behind me, sure my dad's almost on top of me.

And . . . there's a new possibility wriggling way back in my mind? One I don't want, have no time for, but it's a wriggling I have to scratch, too.

When that pickaxe twirled by me, on some instinctual level I'd known that the reason that fallen tree didn't keep my dad down was that I'd been stupid enough to bury him in contact with this haunted gold. You don't bury Jason with his mask, you don't throw Freddy's glove into the hole after him, and you don't keep Michael's mask in the trunk when you're going to see him in the asylum.

But, my dad just *threw* that pickaxe away from himself, didn't he?

Exactly as if he . . . didn't need it?

"It's not the pickaxe?" I mutter to myself instead of answering Jocelyn, who's still waiting.

This isn't tracking, I want to tell her. Was it not the axe that brought my dad back? Then, *what*? Why? I mean, "revenge," sure, he hates me for what I did to him, and just for existing, but what I did to him, first, wasn't exactly on purpose—I thought he was Jason, Jason was what I wanted, what I deserved—and second, way more important, what I did to him should be the justice that puts a temporary cap on the cycle of violence. You don't get to get revenge on people just for getting revenge on you. Do you? If . . . if that's the case, then the whole world's going to bloodfeud its way right to the grave, isn't it? Well, not really, there won't be anybody left to bury people, but the whole world will be a grave at that point, so I guess that won't matter so much anymore.

No, Dad, you don't get to get revenge on me. But? What the hell are you doing here, then? *How* are you here?

Moving wary like Laurie Strode would, never giving her back to whatever tree's the most likely to be hiding danger, Jocelyn works her way to me, gets close enough I can see that her nose is as shattered as I've seen a nose get, so that there's even flecks of red in the whites of her eyes.

She resituates her grip on the axe, says, "What the hell, Jade?"

Aside from her shattered nose, which puts me in mind of some *SpongeBob* character, her face is blood-spattered, mud-streaked. For someone like her, though, that's make-up. She just looks more fierce, more dangerous, more killer. She's Erin from *You're Next*, she's that Grace from *Ready or Not*, she's Juno in the second *Descent*.

"Wish I knew," I tell her. Then, about my predicament, "Can you?"

Jocelyn considers the bear trap I'm holding out, considers our surroundings and the likelihood of this being the thing that gets us killed, then finally, with a huff of disappointment—in her herself, I'm pretty sure—she drops to her knees beside me, stands her axe beside us for me to hold at the ready, and works her fingers between the wide metal teeth of the bear trap.

"This from those hunters who found that old cabin?" she asks.

The ones who supposedly also might have been the first ones to see the white Bronco.

"It's from 2015," I hiss, words being tricky with what her efforts to open the trap's jaws are doing to the meat of my forearm.

Last time I was caught in one of these, it was Letha with the muscles to crank it open. Now it's Jocelyn.

Never me.

"They should—have these—in *gyms*," I tell her, rolling away the first moment I can, my left hand clamping over the magma boiling up from my arm.

Jocelyn manages to let the trap clap shut *and*, in the same action, catch her falling axe. If she's not a born final girl? Then I don't even know what one is.

She steps over me instantly, holding that axe low and ready.

"That's your dad out there?" she says, her cheeks cupping her eyes in disbelief.

I nod, the pain still clamping my teeth against each other.

"So the jury was right," Jocelyn says. "You *should* have gotten off. He's just been living over here?"

"Did you—see his throat?" I ask. "What you did to his—chest?"

It's like those steel teeth are still biting me. But I can't stop applying pressure to my arm, either. I need my blood on the inside, the *inside*.

Jocelyn purses her lips, studies the darkness. My guess is she was hoping I'd have an explanation that could wipe away my dad's throat, and how her axe should have dropped him.

"Night's here," she says, moving past the stuff that's too hard to talk about. "We've got to—" She finishes by hooking her head toward Proofrock, heating her eyes up at me.

"Here," I say, lifting my left hand. She hauls me up. I haven't told her I stripped her dead son's snowmobile gear off to wear, four years ago, and I also haven't told her how small and pale he looked, dead on the concrete floor of the parking garage under the nursing home. But it's there behind my eyes every time I have to look at her concerned face.

She works her shoulder under my good arm, hikes us both forward. And the weird thing is, I let her, never mind that my legs are good this time. It's just my arm that got chewed up, just my ear that got sliced ragged, just my head that very nearly got people calling me Chop-Top.

Still, it feels good to be helped along. To be cared for.

"Good?" Jocelyn says to me without looking.

I nod, am close enough under her arm that I'm pretty sure she feels it.

"You've done this before, haven't you?" she says, straining with half my weight.

"Not like this," I manage, about to cry, I think, just for someone to casually acknowledge all the shit I've been through.

"Why isn't he here already?" she asks, limping us along faster, to . . .

The *shore*?

I was so thrilled to be getting some distance between my dad and us that I didn't even think where we might be going.

Not the lake, though.

I stop hard enough that we stumble.

"*What?*" Jocelyn asks, instantly watching behind us. "I know you swim."

She knows because she's the one who taught *all* the Proofrock kids to swim, year after year. In her even svelter twenties, she made the

Olympic trials for the 200 and the relay—the only world-class athlete Pleasant Valley ever produced. When Theo Mondragon shot you out of the sky, Mr. Holmes, I was doing twenty other things, including escaping from jail, but I got told way, way later that Jocelyn Cates had been smoking another last cigarette at Melanie's bench, saw it all go down—saw *you* go down—and that she didn't even hesitate, was running down the Pier, peeling out of her shirt and slacks on the way, her shoes still at the bench, and her dive into the lake didn't even make a splash, and it was thirty yards before she surfaced, freestyling stroke after stroke to get out there to you.

I also heard that Hardy finally had to pull her from the water himself. She was in her bra and panties, and her lips were blue, her eyes desperate, and Hardy outweighed her by at least a hundred pounds, but he still had to fight to get her in over the side of his airboat, wrap her in his silver emergency blanket, and hug her warm.

Which goes to show you how unfair the world can be. After nearly sacrificing herself like that, after proving herself the hero of heroes, the baddest-ass person in all of Idaho, still, her husband dies almost immediately after that. And, like that's not enough, four years later her son's taken from her.

Just like Alex.

But I can't let myself start dwelling on the dead. There aren't enough pills, Sharona, there aren't enough guided breathing exercises.

"I just, I can't—" I say to Jocelyn, about this terrifying prospect of the lake.

"You want to stay over *here?*" she asks, incredulous. "With him?"

I shake my head no to that as well.

"The boats," I try.

"Sunk."

"Walk," I say, weaker.

"*He* can walk too," Jocelyn says. "But he can't swim, not with a pickaxe."

She's right, of course. Diving in, paddling across like the elk, it's the rational thing to do, the sensible solution, the clearest way out of this, we'll deal with the hypothermia later.

I shake my head no all the same, pull back, away from her.

"*You* don't even swim in there anymore, do you?" I more hear myself saying than really mean to say.

It's common knowledge, though: since the New Founders swam the lake, Jocelyn's given up her daily laps. Which I get. She doesn't want anyone, even one person, thinking she's doing this because they showed that the lake could be freestyled across. Sure, she'd been doing it for years and years before them, just, never for cameras and crowds, never for the front page of all the newspapers. Just for herself.

Since I've been back, though, I haven't seen her white swim cap out in the chop even once.

"It's different now," Jocelyn says back to me, about her not swimming anymore.

"For me too," I tell her.

"I won't let you drown, Jade," Jocelyn says, dialing her tone down to less confrontational. Which is still pretty damn confrontational, nerves and situation being what they are.

I can't explain why I won't do it, though, just keep shaking my head.

"You go," I tell her, flinging my right hand ahead, droplets of blood flicking off.

Jocelyn stares me down about this, not a single ounce of understanding in her whole body.

I look away, breathe in through my nose and hold it.

If it was just me? If I was the only one here, and it was full dark, no stars, then . . . maybe I step out there, yeah.

Maybe.

But there's cameras over at Camp Blood now. I've seen them. And on Treasure Island too, now—*also* because of vandalism. And Rexall's always got his submersibles fluttering around down there somewhere, probably to play some creeper version of Marco Polo with the bowlegged women Quint toasts with his shot of whiskey. And there's Lemmy's eyes in the sky, droning around.

It's getting harder and harder to move unobserved around here anymore. Used to it was only the locker rooms and bathroom stalls around here you had to be careful about. Now the only privacy I have is the cemetery, I guess.

Nobody cares about me talking to you, Mr. Holmes.

"The yacht," I say, pointing with my lips.

"And we get their attention how?" Jocelyn asks. "Start a—a *fire?*"

She's right again, goddamn her.

"There's . . . the others," I finally come up with. "We can't leave them, can we?"

Jocelyn sucks air in through her teeth, hates this.

"Which way did they go?" I ask, getting into this properly, now that it's finding some random traction.

If I were a real final girl, then the remnants of the chainsaw brigade are the first ones I think of, not just something to prop my weak-ass argument up with.

Jocelyn flings her hand loosely out at the forest, meaning the survivors scattered like grouse—it's hopeless already.

"How many?" I push.

Jocelyn narrows her eyes, mentally counting, finally settles on, "Ten?"

I had eleven, but neither of us specified if we were counting ourselves or each other, so: close enough.

"But they've got their chainsaws," she says, like still angling for the big swim.

"That better or worse?" I have to ask.

Jocelyn just hisses air through her teeth, in reply. We're both watching the shadows under the trees behind us, just waiting for my dad to take shape, make all our decisions for us.

But he's hanging back. I can't figure why.

"Why did you come over here?" I ask Jocelyn. "You don't—I mean, I don't think it's for the money."

I've seen her SUV, I mean. It costs more than my house, I'm pretty sure.

Jocelyn doesn't seem to register this, just keeps glaring at the darkness settling in for real and for good.

It's Halloween, all right.

I turn to the yacht with the idea I can wave my good hand, get luckier than hell, but that's when Jocelyn finally answers, quietly: "Because I wasn't coming back, that's why."

This stops my hand from coming up. Probably right when Lemmy was actually looking right at me, yeah.

"Say what?" I ask, trying to make my voice soft, not hard.

"You heard me."

I did, yeah. Just, suicide-by-fire isn't exactly final girl behavior. And, stupidly enough, it's weird for my swim-teacher to be speaking on even terms with me. Baring her soul instead of telling me to cup my hands, kick my feet, *breathe*.

But?

I'm also the girl who drifted out over Drown Town on the town canoe and opened her wrists to let the night in. To let my life out.

I know I told Shooting Glasses it was the price of admission to be part of the movies I love, *permanently*, but . . . I wasn't lying to him, I wouldn't have lied to him. But I've had a lot of counseling and therapy since then, too.

The way Sharona explains it to me is that—and I don't know where she gets this, since I'm pretty sure she grew up in an apartment in the city, or whatever a "brownstone" or "walkup" is—when a deer gets wrapped up in a fence it's trying to crawl through or jump over, it'll struggle some at first, but at a certain point, it just sort of sags in place, accepting its fate.

I don't know about Jocelyn, everybody's got a different story, different reasons, but I sort of think that's maybe what I was doing? The trajectory of my life had only ever been aiming out to the middle of the lake, I mean. I can rationalize it all I want, make it big and romantic, tragic and adolescent, but the truth is that I was that deer tangled so thoroughly in that killer fence that there was no hope.

So, I shoved off the Pier in the town canoe.

And if Shooting Glasses hadn't called Hardy that night, then . . . none of this. Specifically, I'm not embattled here with Jocelyn Cates, a final girl from a previous generation who never got to prove her mettle against some big bad, so just kept it balled up, waiting for the day.

Except then her husband got taken from her. And her son.

Walking away from those two funerals, she had to have felt that same fence tangling her up more and more.

"But, my dad, you didn't—you didn't let him," I say to her, not having to actually give voice to *kill you*, because it's already very much in the air.

"Yeah, well," she says, eyes sharp and hard, her grip on that axe handle both loose and tight, so she can swing any direction. "It wasn't a solo event, was it?"

It takes me a moment to crack this, but: relay. Standing there with fourteen or fifteen other Proofrockers had been a team thing, to her. She wasn't trying to save her own life, she was trying to save *theirs*. And, since I'm now the only one left, this is still a team-event, the way she thinks.

It doesn't mean she doesn't have some sort of grief-driven death wish, but it does sort of suggest, to me anyway, that there's going to come a moment in this night when she pushes me ahead, then turns to face this predator all on her own, Billy Sole-style.

It sucks when the white woman's more Indian than you'll ever be.

"The trap," I say then.

Jocelyn flashes her eyes back to me, then down to the bear trap between us, still slammed shut, then she's back to clocking all the darkness my dad can step in from.

"We recock it," I explain to her. "I'm bait, and on the way to getting to me"—I clamp my left hand shut.

I don't tell her that I'm not being original here, am only proposing this because it sort of worked last time.

"He's not a bear," she says, finally.

Which isn't a no.

Between the two us—three hands and an axe—we crank the trap open by slow degrees.

We probably should have cocked it open closer to where we wanted to put it, not at the shore, but . . . neither of us are exactly trappers.

We carry it between us across the Martian landscape of Sheep's Head, lower it at the part of the meadow that's closest to Terra Nova. It's not quite a bottleneck—you can walk through the trees at any point—but if you're in a hurry, then you want to walk out in the open as much as you can, not have to fight through branches with a pickaxe.

I sift pine needles and leaves down over the trap, turned half away because I know I'm about to spring it. Playing *Operation* on that goofy white guy in fourth-grade free time, I would always have to suck air in through my nose each time my roach clip was about to touch bare metal again, in spite of how careful I was being, how hard I was trying. This is like that, except *Operation* can't chew into your arm, or peel the skin from your face.

Jocelyn stands guard. I get the distinct feeling she's always on guard, these days.

And, yeah, here I am messing with a longshot trap instead of, I don't know, luring my dad out onto the dock and pushing him into the lake, or staging dry branches and fronds over the open mouth of some sinkhole of a cave, for him to crash down into like . . . like Greyson Brust.

Except Greyson Brust was dragged up from there different.

My dad's already different enough, thanks.

What I could also be doing is, you know, denying my dad his main weapon? His pickaxe, I mean. I should definitely specify.

Except . . . there's so many reasons not to try to wrench it from that tree on the other side of the meadow, isn't there? Does it turn its holder evil? Stupider shit's happened than that, hasn't it? And, is my dad hunkered down, waiting for us to do exactly that? And, what if we get there and don't have enough muscle or weight to break it free? It's in there deep, I bet. It must have twirled across forty or fifty feet.

If we did have it, though? Then . . . then Jocelyn could hammer-throw it back out into the lake. Until the dead hand of one of those soggy corpses breaks the surface of the water to catch it, yeah.

Scratch that.

What we could do, though, would be to lean it against a tree, and have the bear trap hidden right there where my dad would have to stand to collect it back. Except then we're touching it. Then it's probably whispering to us in Glen Henderson's corrupt voice, telling us *kill, kill, kill.*

The part I still don't like the most, though, it's that my dad doesn't *need* this cursed pickaxe. It makes me feel like I'm missing something obvious, with all this. Maybe the trick is considering it without my dad. Taking into account its story purpose, like. Kevin Williamson taught us that knowing the genre can be your eject lever, your escape hatch, your magic way through the twisted maze, so . . .

Mr. Holmes, you used to tell us about Henderson-Golding's killers over here hiding their dead in all the nooks and crannies the mountain had to offer, didn't you? This is where Letch Graves, Stacey's dad, hid her mom, Josie . . . Josie *Seck.* But the *non*-killers were over here just the same, chipping up sparks, trying to luck onto a distant vein of that motherlode with no claim already staked around it.

Covered in gold, this axe is the property of the killer from back then, and's maybe emblematic of all the killers from back then. Or close enough for these purposes—close enough that, like Thor's hammer, my dad can now wield that pickaxe? But, what if we hold it to some of the embers still smoldering over here and drip that gold off, let it ball up and hiss in the flames that spurt up? Then this pickaxe is just a tool, not a weapon. Then it belongs to the dreamers, again.

Which is what Jocelyn and me are hoping against hope: that this trap works on a dad who should be eight years dead, and who still hasn't shown his face since trying to pin me to that tree.

And, really? I don't tell Jocelyn this, but if we want my dad stumbling ahead heedlessly, not caring where he puts his next foot, then it's not me *or* a pickaxe that's going to get him that single-minded. It's a six of beer, with big fat drops sweating down the sides of the cans. She grew up with him, though. How could she not know this about him.

"Okay," she says, the trap camo'd enough.

"Okay, yeah," I say, which is me stalling my ass off.

In theory, this was an all right enough plan. Standing in the middle of it, though, there's so many variables. What if he comes in from the side? What if that pickaxe comes twirling in at me? What if—what if that gas-mask Ghostface skulks in, messes everything up? What if Seth Mullins steps out of some tree blind with a duck-call, playing *New York Ripper* out here in the serious sticks?

And, if we're going there, then what if the Chucky-who-isn't runs across the water from Proofrock? What if Sally Chalumbert in her Angel of Indian Lake get-up drifts in? And then there's always the prospect of Stacey Graves. And who knows, maybe Dark Mill South's metal hook the insurance agents dropped out of our helicopter last time I got arrested is down there in the lake like the pickaxe was, just waiting for Clate Rodgers to come together enough to walk up from the shallows wearing it.

Maybe we should have let the fire incinerate the whole valley. Hard to think of a place that needs it worse.

But then I don't have a job. A house. A best friend. A niece.

There aren't any good fixes, I don't think. There's just trying to make it through the next moment, and the next.

For me, that next moment is playing Fay Wray on Halloween night, to lure the monster in. It's understood none of us in Proofrock are supposed to play dress-up, but this is life and death.

"Okay," I tell Jocelyn.

After holding my eyes for a moment to be sure I'm up for this, she nods once and steps back into the shadows between the trap and me. The idea is, once my dad's hobbled with the trap, maybe still lunging for me, she comes at him with the axe over and over, until there's not enough left of him to be any concern.

Still, if we get that far, I plan on using strips of bark or something to deliver those chunks of rancid meat back to the embers crawling along the forest floor. Just to be sure.

Well, also because I hate him.

Jocelyn, reduced to just the whites of her eyes now, nods once to me, that we can do this, and then she's part of the darkness.

I take four long steps back, trying to stay in the moonlight enough, my left arm holding my right—it won't stop throbbing—and say, my voice breaking, "Hey! I'm right here!"

What can happen here, of course, is that that golden pickaxe slams into my mouth, shattering my teeth and cramming down the back of my throat, digging out my chest, its flat top continuing on to crack the bones of my face in.

"Hey!" I say again, possibly not quite as insistent.

The response is the trees starting to thrum all around me.

What the hell?

I lower myself to what would be my fingertips, if I had any free hands. I'm looking up, waiting, and then—

One of the fire planes glides past, its dripping belly almost scraping the tops of the trees, meaning it picked up another load of just water, is making a final pass to be sure they've won, that the fire's really out.

Behind me, over Terra Nova, it banks to the west, over Caribou-Targhee, but its blinking red lights are higher now. Meaning it's not seeing any flickering orange flames.

Good, good.

I stay kneeling down, tell my eyes to adjust already, and ask myself what's the scariest thing I could see. What I come up with is my dad lumbering in the same as he used to in my sixth grade, his eyes bleary, breath flammable, grin oily and sick. It's not something you can get used to, but it can lose its surprise, and if that doesn't mean the world's broken beyond repair, then I don't know what can.

So, something a click or two less scary, Jade.

Sally Chalumbert, then. Her gliding out would plop me back on my ass, sure, get me protecting my face. When she took Dark Mill South down, she knocked all his teeth out and cut his hand off, right? And she'd only been getting started. Locked in that kill-or-die mode, I don't even know if Jocelyn could fend her off, and I know for damn sure I couldn't.

What I could see that would break my heart in *two*, though? That would reduce me to nothing?

Some ten-year-old pirates, running from this tree to that tree.

One of them would be a future sheriff, and one of them would be you, Mr. Holmes.

This whole side of the valley was your playground back then, wasn't it? Was that why you hated Terra Nova so much? I mean, they gave us a lot of reasons, they were easy to hate, but . . . I bet that's where it started for you, wasn't it?

You and Hardy and whoever the rest of the pirate crew was would be having a running sword fight, probably. Back then you all would have been pretending to be Errol Flynn, I imagine. I know the name, I guess, but not the person, not the movies. Not like your pirate crew must have.

And then, spent, you and Hardy and the rest spark a fire up to dry off, because you've been splashing across the shallows, except, over on this side of the valley, those shallows drop out from under you fast.

But it was all in good fun. And one of you's stolen a cigarette, kept it dry somehow, and it must feel so magical to pass it around the fire, inhale that blissful heat in for the very first time and try to hold it in, because you're tough.

Your eyes watering, your palms held out to that sparking fire, the lights of Proofrock flickering across the lake, it must have felt like you'd never need anything else than this. But . . . did you also see a woman out in the deeper dark, her nightgown dirty and torn, her hair matted, her eyes so hungry?

That wasn't Sally Chalumbert, Mr. Holmes. And it couldn't have been Ginger Baker, either. Josie Seck, then, still looking for her lost daughter? One of the campers soon to die in the forest fire you're about to start? Did you and your pirates rise as one and yell at her to go away, even pluck a burning branch from the fire to brandish at her?

You were kids, I'd understand, I'm not saying anything bad here.

The thing about brandishing a burning branch, though, it's that it drips sparks. And those sparks can start other little fires, that add up to a fire you can't stomp out, and soon the whole forest is burning and you don't know what to do so you just paddle back, watch Idaho burn, and make promises to yourself to always protect this place, after this.

Yeah, *that* would scare me. Not for the wholesomeness, though that is pretty much my kryptonite, but because it would mean that I'm also a permanent resident here, since I almost burned the place down just the same.

What I'd rather see is Mr. Bill from Christine Gillette's story, struggling to drag a huge bull elk to shore, to float across. Or those horseback Shoshone riding single file away from the lake, one of them looking back to consider me, because maybe I should be with them, not over here.

But none of them reach a hand down to pull me up behind them.

With my luck, though, I blink long and open my eyes in a rancid little church of dead elk, one with Mismatched Gloves dead in it, and Cowboy Boots, and, at the bottom of it all, suffocating, drowning, *me*, only Letha doesn't find me this time, so her dad leads her away to some airplane and they blast off, never come to Idaho again.

Meaning Adie never happens. Banner never puts the badge on.

But that might not be so bad. Let him go to some four-year college on scholarship, blow his knee out at a homecoming game and end up selling insurance or managing a restaurant, only coming back here to see the folks once or twice a year, his family in tow, their eyes so wide about this place where all his larger-than-life stories are set.

Which is to say, he's alive in this version. He doesn't have to die.

It would be worth it, I think. I can die happily under all those elk, please.

And who knows, maybe, managing that restaurant right after college, before he meets whoever he meets to have that family, a certain princess of a media conglomerate ducks in out of the rain, orders some food just to be polite—she's just here for the shelter—and she sees Banner, remembers him from across a bonfire, and they sit there long after the rain's stopped, and they never mention that girl with all the eyeliner, that girl with the Metal Up Your Ass t-shirts.

But I'm there, sir.

Part of me's sitting in a far booth of that restaurant, so I can watch this moment happen. So I can see this manager walk this princess to the door, and then hold it open while she gets into the car she's called. I'm there when this manager turns around and looks down into his hand, at the piece of paper she wrote her number on, and how she drew a single heart above it.

Through the dead elk I'm buried under, I can just see through the tangled limbs and rotting hide and festering bones and blind maggots, and—

"*Jade!*" Jocelyn screams, from the parking lot of the restaurant, I think.

But then we're still in the woods on the wrong side of the valley, and my dad is a distinct silhouette standing right at the edge of Sheep's Head.

I swallow, that gulp loud in my ears.

Well then.

I was worried what I was going to have to do to draw him in, get him to step on that trigger plate between the open jaws of the trap.

Not anymore.

And I'm not even sure he knew Jocelyn or me were here—this is just the logical place to cross, headed over to Terra Nova, which in turn is the logical place for anybody stranded over here to retreat.

But *now* he knows we're here.

"I'm right here, Dad," I say to him, just normal-voice, because it's so quiet that even normal-voice travels.

He turns his head directly at me, then takes a step my direction, and . . . shit, that's why he didn't jump us at the shore: he *couldn't*. That tree broke his pelvis or his leg or his back or something—he's using that golden pickaxe as a cane, as a walker, as a crutch, and probably had to crawl inch by inch to it after he threw it away—pretty typically great thinking from him.

I step forward, wishing so hard I had a lighter I could flick or a silver can I could flash, to draw him directly to me. But we hid that trap in the most clear space between two trees, too.

It's right where my dad's going.

"*Now!*" I scream to Jocelyn, because we don't even need the trap, do we? With him slowed down like this?

Like this, he's just another tree to be cut down.

Jocelyn must want him to be seriously planted, though. She's waiting for him to step into the trap. No: she's waiting for him to be looking down at whatever's clamped over his foot. Meaning he won't be looking directly ahead, for any axes moving at the speed of fury.

To make sure my dad's keeping his attention on me, I reach up for a branch and shake it.

He sees, seethes about me being so close and also so far away, and accelerates as much as he can, poling ahead with hands on the butt of that pickaxe.

"C'mon, c'mon . . ." I'm telling him, no longer that worried about how or why he's back.

All I want is for that trap to spring. All I need is Jocelyn's axe flashing in to finish the cut I started on his neck, his throat, send his head rolling back into the meadow. Inside, a woman Yazzie knew would tell us stories she had from her lying uncles, and one of them was about a head rolling around the woods, chasing this dude, and it never made sense to me. But now it can. Except I'll stomp on that head until the skull collapses and the bad thoughts seep out, and I'll keep stomping, just to be sure.

And it all starts with—

Clap!

I hear the trap more than see it, and now my dad's just standing there. Exactly like we wanted.

Sometimes things *do* work out. He's even looking down like I'm pretty sure Jocelyn wanted.

She comes out of the darkness like she's been running for fifty feet, her right thigh ahead, the axe held so far behind her, for more weight when it strikes home, and she's screaming to get this right, all or nothing, it's the only way final girls like her know to do it, and—

My dad brings the pickaxe up, only it's so much more than a pickaxe now.

He didn't step into the bear trap, his *cane* did.

The stake we buried so carefully and so perfectly, to be there forever, comes up out of the loamy ground as easy as anything.

Jocelyn's axe handle catches my dad's bear-trap pickaxe head, and she's swinging hard enough that her six- or eight-pound axe head keeps going into the open space over my dad's left shoulder, the wooden handle splintering.

Jocelyn should be falling over from how much she's committed here—the axe breaking is like pulling a rug out from under her—but . . . my dad's freed a hand up from his pickaxe–bear trap–*mace*, freed it up enough to snatch the bear trap's twelve-inch stake from the air, gouge it into Jocelyn's right side, under the ribs, so it comes out high on the left side.

Meaning: both lungs, and that red shininess on the point of the stake nosing out from Jocelyn's side is from her heart.

Final girls *can* die.

I fall to my knees, my face cold, my mouth open, eyes heating up.

"*Noooooo!*" I scream.

Jocelyn looks back to me, blood already burbling down her chin.

"Run," she manages to get out, her back arching away from the violence being done to her. Once when Letha and me were drinking our coffee at Dot's, Jocelyn had come in, placed her order, and then stood there waiting, her lips neatly together, sunglasses still on, and she'd nodded once to us and we'd nodded back, and she wasn't just a magazine cover model standing there, glamorous as hell, you could also tell she was coiled-up fury and grief.

"She's like Macy," Letha whispered to me, when we were alone again.

"Cinnamon Baker . . ." I added on, because I'd never really known Macy Todd, the one-time killer. I hadn't known Cinnamon in any real way either, but I had stood close to her, could feel that same killer coldness from her, that she hid with style and control. But some women, you can tell that in another time, a different age, they would have been leading armies. Or they would have *been* that army.

Letha, Macy Todd, Cinnamon Baker. Jocelyn Cates.

Two of them dead now, one in a wheelchair of her own doing, one recovering from surgery. Leaving me alone to face the father-monster dredged up from my worst nightmare. From my *continuing* nightmare.

I can't even make words, just scream my insides out at my dad. That it's not fair that he's back. That he shouldn't have been able to kill someone like Jocelyn Cates. It's how I should have screamed at him in sixth grade, instead of just crying like it had been me that had done something wrong.

And then I turn, holding my hurt arm to my stomach, and, just like Jocelyn told me to, I *run*.

There's supposed to be light at the end of all the dark tunnels, isn't there? Some brightness to finally step out into.

For me, it always seems to be Terra Nova I crash out into. It's the end of all my tunnels, except it's not some meadow I fall out into, but a killing field. One I left Banner in.

Him and Alex and the rest, all coated in that powdery red, their arms up at bad angles, eyes open—please, nobody take any photographs of them, when you get there? Just wrap them up, cradle them home.

When Letha finds out, I'm going to be there beside her, I know, and her face isn't going to change. Just, everything behind it. Will this finally be what it takes to break her, the unbreakable woman? She had her whole future mapped out. Her and Banner were going to grow old together. They were going to watch Adie become her even *more* amazing self year by year—let her make the mistakes she'd have to make, and be there for her when she needed them.

But I think, for Adie, Letha will keep that mask on, won't she? She'll be strong, she'll take this hit like she's taken the rest, but inside, where it counts, there'll be a shell around her heart, I think. Because she can't take even one more hit.

I'll be there for you every step, though, Letha. I'll sit with you out on Banner's dad's dock and we'll watch the sun set night after night, and then I'll be there with you when it's coming back up, and when Adie shows up in my history classroom, she won't need extra credit, I know, she'll be like you, but if she does, I'll trade in all my sleep to read those papers, whatever they're on, and when she graduates, I'll be there too, handing her her diploma, and I'll have tucked a note in there with it—my hand-written transcription of all the voice memos you trusted me with, that I carry so close, that I've got my own shell around, to keep them safe.

Standing out in the open among the mostly done houses of Terra Nova, I realize all at once that this is where my plan ends: I'm ahead of my dad, but . . . so?

I can already hear him poling through the trees.

I don't even have a *weapon*. Just my heart. My mouth. My hands balled into fists my dad won't care are hitting him.

No, I've got my head too, don't I? Most final girls use their muscles to fight their boogeymen off, but some, like Ginny in the second *Friday*, Nancy in the first *Nightmare*, Sandy in the only *Humongous*, they *think* their way through, don't they?

You can too, I tell myself.

The first thing that comes to me is that Halligan was going to be my key to unlock my dad's head from his body. But . . . I can't even remember when I dropped it, much less where. I'm Laurie, letting that knife go after she finally got it, I know, and can't help. It's easy to backseat drive from out in the audience, but sitting here behind the wheel, everything's coming a lot faster.

But what about the tools the construction crew's surely left around? Give me just one concrete saw, please. Gas-powered, if that's an option. I'll go *High Tension* on my dad. I don't care what your pick-axe is coated with, my buzzsaw's better.

If there are any tools, though, they're in the houses, not out here where it could rain. Meaning I'd have to run into living room after living room for which is the storeroom. And probably look in the closets, too. And I don't have that long.

Push him into the wishing well?

If it had any actual *depth* to it, sure.

Then, then—

The caves? But they're mostly behind us, in Sheep's Head, aren't they? There's supposed to be one under Letha's old house, but it's kind of covered up right now. And, according to Shooting Glasses, filled with concrete, too.

Where's a grizzly when you need it.

Maybe I can catch my dad on fire such that the spotters see him, dump five hundred pounds of red powder on him at two or three hundred miles per hour? Except that doesn't last either. It knocks you down, it pisses you off, but you get back up.

If there actually were justice, then Mismatched Gloves and Cowboy Boots would rise the same as my dad has and pull him back to where he belongs. But Jocelyn dying like that's proved to me that there isn't any justice, that justice is just another stupid dream. All there is is luck, and mettle. But luck's where it's really at. The grim reaper's always rolling those bones.

That doesn't mean I can just stand here and hope to get lucky, either. Like Sarah Connor knew, you make your own fate.

I stumble forward with the dim idea that I'm hoofing it all the way around the lake, looping up and behind Camp Blood, tightroping the dam, walking that switchback road down to the creek on the dry side of the dam, and feeling my way through Hettie and Paul's woods to . . . to Melanie's bench, yeah.

I'll sit there for a thousand years.

I'll feel November's first sun come up behind me, my shadow blasting out across the water but then feeling its way back to me wave by wave, dip by dip, until I've got it inside me again, until I can paint my eyes up right with it, and finally stand up again.

But first I've got to cross all this open space. And then take the thousands of steps that get me home. And keep from passing out from blood loss, from the negative calories I'm running on, from the pill-shaped ache inside me.

I stop at Bub.

He's just like I left him.

"Sorry," I tell him, and rip his left sleeve off, a trick that's so easy and dramatic in the movies, but's really pretty damn difficult and awkward.

I flatten that khaki sleeve, wrap it around and around my forearm, use my teeth to help tie the knot then tuck the trailing ends up and under, their rawness on my bare meat greying me out a bit.

I promise never to wear a fur hat, a rabbit boa, mink boots, or even wrap my braids in ermine. Not if the animals that had to die to give me that warmth had to feel the crunching jaws of a trap like this.

And no, Sharona, you *don't* have to give up when you're too wrapped up in a fence to escape. What you do is writhe and snap when that big hand comes to collect you. What you do is tear with your sharp teeth at the webbing between that thumb and forefinger, and then bring your hind claws around to peel out on the wrist, because this might be too much to live through, sure, that's life, that's death, but that doesn't mean you can't take anyone with you.

I think that's what I'm going to have to do with and to my dad, finally. I can't outmuscle him, I probably can't outpace him, even factoring his shattered hip in, but—this is me trying to think like Ginny, like Nancy—I can lure him up onto the chalky bluff over Camp Blood, I bet. I can lure him up there, tackle him hard enough that we both go over, sail down into the big empty.

Once upon a forever ago, I expected to die in one of those cabins, where I was conceived. Now I can come crashing down through the rotted ceiling of that same cabin, and I promise you this, I'm going to be screaming and biting the whole way down, and I'm landing with my knee firmly in his balls, hard enough to turn his broken pelvis into gravel, so he never gets up again. And if I'm still alive, then I dig my hacksaw up from the floorboards of that cabin and I go to *work* on him: head, hands, feet, arms, legs, and then I saw him from crotch to neck just to be sure—Jason would approve, Art the Clown would approve, those clay Indians in *Bone Tomahawk* would approve.

Oh but to be Tina from *The New Blood*, yeah? To have those Carrie-powers in my head, in my heart, and just lower my forehead at my dad, crumple his bones, lift him up and slam him down again and again.

But you do what you can with what you've got.

If my only weapon is myself, my hundred-whatever pounds of pissed-offness, then that's what I'll use to crash us down onto Camp Blood once and for all.

For you, Jocelyn.

And Mom.

But for the girl I used to be, too.

"*C'mon already!*" I yell to the darkness, to my dad.

I don't have all night, here. I don't have that much blood left in me, I mean.

On cue, my dad steps out into the open, still using that pickaxe-as-cane, its head clamped by that bear trap. If he actually *were* Matthew Buckner instead of just playing him on television, he'd use that trap as a flail, but I think the way it's working with him is that his waterlogged brain can't figure out how to undo those jaws. And their extra weight, and that dragging chain, must not matter to him.

Extra weight's mattering to me, though.

I reach down to the buckle of Bub's now-useless gunbelt, let it fall at my feet. I Frisbee his hat away too, shake my hair out just so my dad can be sure to clock who I am, which'll tell him where he needs to be.

This also ends my cowboy days, I guess.

One Indian, reporting for duty.

"I'm right here," I say across to him.

There's maybe sixty yards between us.

This is the showdown that should have happened in the hallway of my house fourteen years ago, my mom tucking me behind her leg and glaring my dad down, telling him he's not needed here now, or ever again.

Some kids dream of their parents being kings and queens, secretly. Some of us dream it different.

My mom never graduated high school, she worked at the dollar store, she lived with a drug dealer, evidently, but screw all that, that's just life. All I ever wanted from her was for her to guide me behind her leg, and stand in place no matter what.

But I can do that for myself, too, Mom.

Well, I can stand in place until I'm sure my dad's coming, and then I can lead him up to the bluff, finish this at last, where it all started.

I was trying to suss out the story purpose of that pickaxe, but this story I'm in with my dad's bigger than that, isn't it?

And all stories end where they begin.

At least the good ones do.

"Bring it, Dad," I say, not really loud enough for him. But I bet he can see it on my face. In my posture.

He pulls forward on his dangerous cane, slings it ahead of him again—that's how he's using that extra weight—and pulls forward again.

I hope each step is grinding his shattered bones against each other.

I hope he's got the DTs from how little beer he's lucking onto. I hope when he was down there, that the slurry Clate was coiled around him. I hope he knows that his precious mustard moldered in the fridge while I was locked up, and probably got thrown against a wall during some rager.

I'm that rager now, Dad.

Let's party.

I let him get to the far corner of the house Bub's dead against before starting to walk backwards, trying my best to keep his eyes locked on mine.

About thirty seconds later, I trip backwards on—

That secret basketball goal. Meaning I'm almost to the helicopter pad.

I stand, still holding my dad's eyes, and that's when he stands up straighter and slings his pickaxe out to the side like shooting his cuffs, getting ready.

The bear trap rattles, the chain and stake arcing out and coming back.

My dad catches the stake in his other hand and rips hard at it like a chainsaw cord, pulling the bear trap neatly off his pickaxe.

"Shit," I hiss out.

As long as he was encumbered with a way-too-heavy cane, I was pretty sure I could stay one step ahead of him.

Now, though.

He grins his broken grin, and, holding that bear trap by the stake, he starts spinning it like a Cenobite probably would, which is with bad, bad intent.

I dive away the moment he releases it my direction, but he wasn't aiming for my head or even center mass, I don't think.

The chain wraps around my knees when I'm mid-air, and the trap-head and the stake clang together in what I know is more knot than I can manage with one hand.

I'm halfway onto the concrete landing pad, my dad's maybe twenty feet away, I can't walk, can't even *stand*, one of my arms is screaming at me, the sharp tips of my hair are stabbing me in the eyes all at once, and . . . he can't win this way, he can't he can't he *can't*.

Except he is.

I raise my good arm not exactly to fend off the pickaxe coming for me but because that's what your arm does whether you tell it to or not when your killer's suddenly in range to open you up from tip to sternum, however that goes, I don't have time to think—

But then I do.

My hair?

Why am I fighting my own *hair*? Why is my arm-wrapping whipping off, winding away like mummy bandages?

And why hasn't my dad brought that golden pickaxe down on me yet?

I cringe away before I've even realized what I'm doing, and then the world's a blur, it's all *whapping whapping whapping*, but so much faster, and so close.

A big chunk of my dad's beer gut is . . . just erased in a blur, I think? It's instantly gone, like it's been sucked into the ether. And then from what I'm realizing must be God's blender being held upside down from the sky, his chest is torn open, caving him in enough that—

No.

Enough that his golden pickaxe is pulled up, into this blurry whatever, and when it makes contact, it shoots that pickaxe head off in half an instant, driving it back through my dad's face and upper body.

But that metal-on-metal has done its damage to this blender, too.

It goes violently unsteady—a helicopter, a helicopter!—the tips of the breaking *and* unbroken rotors turning my dad to airborne mush, to the finest mist, but those whapping rotors out of control, too, this helicopter jerking forward and tilting down, the blades gouging into the rocky ground, and finally making sparking contact with—

The basketball goal tilted over and hidden in the grass.

This shatters the copter's rotors all at once, shooting them out and away, I can't see where from all the grass and dirt and blood and wind, but it's everywhere at once, it feels like, an explosion I'm exactly at the heart of.

It dies down moments after.

I'm curled up in the flattened grass, I'm shaking and shivering, just trying to breathe, I'm zipped up in Tina's foggy bodybag again, curled around my panic to keep it from devouring me, and the whole world.

Letha Mondragon steps in, unzips it, her hand on my shoulder, her eyes casing the treeline, then finally settling on me.

"That who I think it was?" she says.

Her jaw isn't even bandaged this time, and if Jocelyn Cates looked fierce, that was just because, in Letha's absence, I'd forgotten what true fierceness looks like. Letha's in leather pants that more than hug her, ankle boots, her white blouse is untucked, tails flapping, and—this isn't some fashion magazine.

This is a slasher, isn't it?

It is.

And the real final girl's finally here.

BAKER SOLUTIONS

Report of Investigation
22 September 2023
#66b12
re: Vandalistic tendencies

Through the service JPay, Ms. Daniels has been in intermittent electronic contact with the aforementioned Isabel Yazzie [RoI 04a49], incarcerated at South Idaho Correctional Institution with a parole hearing set for 2029. Ms. Daniels queried Ms. Yazzie for four months / fourteen (4/14) attempts at an average cost-per-message of $2.14 before receiving an answer on 19 June 2023. The following missive confirms that, in keeping with her trajectory of vandalism—various "prank"-related incidents at Henderson High [see directory 3g]; the more severe vandalism of Glen Dam in 2015; the damage done to State snow-removal equipment in 2019; the "minor" demolition of the women's restroom at Henderson High [RoI 01c22]; the documented vandalism of Deacon Point [RoI 01c26]; and the costly damage done to Temporary Research Islet H-G [RoI 32d43]—Ms. Daniels's impulse to facilitate the willful destruction of property would seem to have both extended well beyond Fremont County and "come home" to where it all started: Henderson High, and associated personnel thereof.

The following communication was copied by Ms. Daniels from JPay's text-entry dialogue into an unaddressed email with no subject line that she keeps in the Drafts folder of her web-based mail provider (demonchild_69@yahoo.com). Of note: Ms. Daniels returns to this email regularly when awake after midnight, whereupon she corrects the grammar and spelling, though the message has long been transmitted, and any repairs or rewording are for naught. The following is the uncorrected version she

initially pasted in on 19 June 2023, at 3:28am (superscript added
for coordination):

Yazz—

Where have you been? I mean, stupid question. I know were you ARE.
Where I shouldn't have l4ft you. bc I had a choise, yes. but thank you
thank THANK YOU for finally hitting reply. U&nless I guess your pre-
vliges and access to read this has been limited, I don' tknow. but believe
me please, I'm counting the days. the minutes. the SECONDS. and I'll
be there in 2029, and the whole time before that I'll be having my fingers
crossed. it'll be like the poster for the second Saw, except that middle
finger is laid over the pointer, for luck.

anyway, not why I'm here. just, it's built up inside, for all these Months
of Silence. what I'm getting at is remember how you told me when I
moved to IDFalls in order 2 become a citizen you told me how I should
talk to Clara the counselor? thank you for that saige advice. I wish I'd
had someone like her, who just sits there and listens and touches the back
of my ahnd with her fingertips and says shes sorry for everyhting, that it
wasn't my fault. that I'm a hero actually.

she was like you, except in the blonde body of someone who grew up
in Minnesota, so talks like that.

anyway, so yeah I took that adivce about talking to her for real and I
applied it to the new Clara, maned Sharona, which is another mispell but it
fits too so I'll leave it, because Sharona has hair even yellower than Clara,
but also with those rich people spiral curls. She doesn't touch the back of
my hnad the same but she does sit on the swingsets with me at dusk and
listen pretty hard, and we're both wearing masks like Billy and Stu, or
Mrs. Loomis and Marty, or, you get it, we're two Ghostfaces in the dying
of the light, jsut quietly raging. well, one of is still raging.

Sharona has exercises where I'm supposed to see the past like a movie
I can edit and control, I can pause and change. Letha, whome I told you

about, put us together, and I've missed a few meetings on the swings,[1] for Reasons, but when I miss them, I MISS them, so that's omething, right?

Guesss what I'm saying is that I'm telling her stuff under the umbrella of attorney and client safety, only, it's more like Fixer and Broken Thing legal immunity.

She knows now about me sneaking over to Shooting Glasses' grave for that afternoon,[2] to line all my cigarette butts up on his tombstone and burn my initials in ash onto the hard stone in goodbye and thanks, and how I was so sure that those other two people across the cemetery in Swan Valley, which sounds like a Disney place just w/o the happy ending, were spying on me li8ke waiting for me to Misbehave in order to get locked up again. But that had to just be guilt and paranoai, because I'm s upposed to ask permission to travel more than 50 miles, which is how long my legal leash is. Sharona knows about the fun I keep having with Rexall's little toy submarines too, also for Reasons. and, he's not to be confused with that other one I told you about, Rex ALLEN, even though they sound the same. One's a dead sheriff, the other's a Known Perv. If you could see them side by side, it would be an obvious and easy distinction, even though in conversation saying their name it wouldn't be so easy. I haven't told Sharona about the dollar store though.[3] when I understand it better then I will. maybe.

but thjis isn't all about me. I get that from Leeth, who gave me the coolest thing,[4] that's COMPLETELY LEGAL, anybody else reading this first. I'll show you when you get here. so, food still 5 star there? as in, someone of questionable hygene has pressed their hand and their 5 fingers into it while you stand there regretting it already? does Ramona still sing that song to make everybody go to sleep? does Wanda still tap her nightstick on the bars when she's holding, needs to make a barter sale? anybody get caught sleeping in the dryer again, ha ha?

I miss it. by which i mean I miss BEING there. I hated it, but it felt right too. which Clara tells me is like a disease you can catch from living like we did, like you still are. so, be careful, please? don't be scared in six years when you walk out under the sky. it does feel like it's going to

swallow you, like you're just going to fall up into it. but dont'believe it.
I'll be holding your hand, girl. I'll keep you here.

well, this is probably already like a 6 dollar email, so better salute my
way out the digital door here. but, I shouldn't say that, "door." this where
I am now, it's a WINDOW, one we can see each other through, at least
in words.

what I\'m saying is lets keep this window open maybe, yeah? time
goes faster when it's not just you in there alone. and Sharona's right, you
CAN look back into your history and stop on a single image, hold it there.

I do it all the time, now.

And I think you know what laundry room I go back to, and try to
hold onto.

JaDe

In order, what Ms. Daniels is referring to above are:

1. Ms. Daniels has, since the start of her fall semester teaching
    duties, missed two (2) of the every-other-Thursday sessions
    scheduled with Dr. Watts, participation in which is a spe-
    cial condition of her parole. Of note is photograph 73u74
    taken on 14 September 2023, in which Ms. Daniels is seen
    standing behind a dumpster as night falls, her hand cupped
    around a cigarette so as to hide it in the darkness. In the
    photograph, she's peering around the southwest corner of
    the dumpster at Dr. Watts, herself sitting on their custom-
    ary swing set, already wearing her mask. For the duration
    of what would have been her counseling session, she in-
    stead surveils Dr. Watts, who also remains for the complete
    duration. See close-up of 73u74 for the mask swaying from
    the left pocket of Ms. Daniels's coveralls, perhaps suggest-
    ing that her hesitation over attending this counseling ses-
    sion persisted as far as her approach to Founders Park.

2. On 28 April 2023, six days after being paroled, Ms. Daniels messaged Letha Mondragon-Tompkins to request the loan of her 2023 Toyota Prius, which Ms. Daniels then drove fifty-plus (50+) miles to Swan Valley, Idaho. As this was before Baker Solutions was contracted, Ms. Daniels's outing is reconstructed from text messages, GPS logs, receipts, and eyewitness testimony [see subdirectory 221u]. After visiting the Snake River Bar & Grill (cash, $22.31), Ms. Daniels drove to the Swan Valley Cemetery 4.7 miles away in Irwin, Idaho, where she remained for 4 hours 32 minutes, as confirmed both by GPS from the aforementioned Prius and testimony from the groundskeeper. That groundskeeper's subsequent inspection of the grave Ms. Daniels attended to ("Grade Paulson") produced: a "mess" of American Spirit cigarette butts and a single pair of Bausch & Lomb Ray-Ban Gold Aviator Sunglasses in Kalichrome Yellow, at 58mm, which the groundskeeper had to retrieve from his personal domicile. As this eyewear is no longer in production from the manufacturer and is considered "vintage" on the collectors market, Ms. Daniels presumably procured them from a secondary seller (avg. price, used: $300).

3. Starting 26 June 2023, Ms. Daniels began frequenting Family Dollar, located at 128 Main Street, Proofrock, Idaho. Her first two visits were standard shopping outings [receipts at 10p-24], but these quickly shaded into Ms. Daniels paying for some items (laundry detergent, plasticware, hosiery, toilet tissue, lemon juice, beef stew, corn chips and salsa) while absconding with others. The items Ms. Daniels habitually takes without paying for [see security footage at 28f] are generally from

the "Hair Care!" side of the Personal Hygiene aisle: Garnier Color Sensation "Where There's Smoke" Hair Color Cream; Dark & Lovely Fade Resist Luminous Blonde Hair Color, Revlon ColorSilk Burgundy Hair Color Kit; Clairol Textures & Tones Blazing Burgundy Hair Color; göt2B Metallics Metallic Silver Permanent Hair Color; Bigen Black Brown Powder Hair Color Kits; Splat Rebellious Colors Color Kits in both Royal Red and Imperial Purple. In addition, Ms. Daniels often spirits away a box of eZn Creamy Hair Bleaching Cream, leaving the box and instructional pamphlet, taking only the tube of cream. Ms. Daniels then proffers these stolen items to students, most regularly Hettie Jansson and Paul Demming, claiming to "not need them anymore." Photographs of Ms. Jansson and Mr. Demming [see 18s44] confirm their use of these hair products. See footage at 29f for Letha Mondragon-Tompkins's now-regular sallies to Family Dollar, to pay the managerial staff (cash) for the products Ms. Daniels liberates. The total, according to the managerial staff, now sits at $72.14. Consultation with this managerial staff also confirms that their "system" doesn't allow for reimbursement. Rather, Ms. Mondragon-Tompkins's reimbursements are considered generous contributions to the "coffee fund."

4. The gift Letha Mondragon presented Ms. Daniels with upon her release and subsequent return to Proofrock, Idaho [see photograph at 002-b04], is a pair of machetes mounted across each other in a shadow box with a depth of two inches (2"). The first (or leftmost) machete is a French Army Indochina Senegalese model, colloquially known as the "Coupe-Coupe" (for "cut-cut"), signed

in black by Richard Dreyfuss with the inscription "Keep kicking!" The second (or rightmost) machete is a Corona ErgoHandle 22" Tempered Steel Machete with a taped handle, with the blade submitted to bluing to become "black" via the oxide involved with that process. This machete is signed in silver by: Ari Lehman; Warrington Gillette; Ted White; Tom Morgan; C.J. Graham; Kane Hodder; Ken Kirzinger; Derek Mears; and Corey Feldman. Included on a series of engraved plates below these two machetes are the signatures of: Richard Brooker; Roy Scheider; and Robert Shaw. In addition, the aluminum backing of this shadowbox has been signed by: Jamie Lee Curtis; Adrienne King; Olivia Hussey; Heather Langenkamp; Jennifer Love Hewitt; and Neve Campbell. Neither of these machetes are simulated or "prop" weapons, and are in fact potentially lethal. This shadowbox is on display in Ms. Daniels's living room, on the east wall [002-b05].

Of note is that after composing and sending the above missive to Ms. Yazzie the night of 19 June 2023, Ms. Daniels walked the streets of Proofrock, Idaho until dawn of 20 June 2023, wearing only tactical boots (black) and a nightgown (white) with four parallel tears of approximately five (5) inches each on the front, diagonally from top-right to lower-left [see 72f62–72f88]. While photographs of the so-called "Angel of Indian Lake" lack focus, sightings of her *do* begin in late June, suggesting that Ms. Daniels's destruction of property doesn't completely encompass her vandalism—if she is indeed this purported "Angel," she's also actively destroying the social fabric and well being of her traumatized community, for reasons beyond the scope of this investigation.

OF DEATH AND LOVE

For what I know is the first time and hope against hope is the last time, Letha collapses in front of me.

She just asked where Banner is, while looking from this tree to that tree like expecting him to walk out to us at any moment, give her that wave/point thing up by his temple that means "hey," "I see you," and "we're on the same wavelength," but's also a sort of jaunty salute, and his way of saying he's almost there, he's almost to her again, just like last time, and the time before that, and the thousands of times ahead.

And, Letha wouldn't be looking for him to *be* over here if she hadn't called ahead, got word from Tiff where to put that helicopter down, so . . . she's expecting him, yes.

I mean, she was.

As far as Tiff knows—as far as anybody in *Proofrock* knows—the chainsaw brigade was successful. Look, the fire's gone, isn't it? Score one for the good guys. The ones with a new wad of cash in their pockets.

Did Jo Ellen not make it back across, though? How long does it take hypothermia to set in? Is she even a swimmer? Did she get plowed under by the *English Rose?* By a thrashing elk? Did Ezekiel grab her by the ankle, stuff her into a pew alongside Stacey Graves?

Doesn't matter.

What does is the way I just shook my head no to Letha, holding her eyes the whole time so she would get it without me having to try to make it fit into words, especially once she registered how tore to hell I am, and how dead I was, if she hadn't landed her helicopter nearly on top of me.

All that plus the way I'm pressing my lips together, my own eyes full to spilling, a lump in my throat like I've never felt? And then mix in Letha's paranoia about Banner going into work each day, after the previous two sheriffs didn't retire the traditional way, and how she made him wear that vest under his shirt most days. What she never knew, though, or never called him on, was that he'd leave the house with that armor, and he'd put it back on before going home, but . . . in between? Unless he was meeting her at Dot's, or swinging home for lunch, he didn't like wrapping himself in ceramic and Kevlar like that.

What we never knew, though, was that he should have had *face* armor. He should have had that fencing mask from *Urban Legends: Final Cut*.

But a pickaxe probably comes in a lot harder than the tip of a bendy sword.

Hockey mask, then, I tell myself, just jumping all the way to the end, but . . . an axe does get through that one in *III*, doesn't it? Hockey masks are made to stop flying hockey pucks, not blades. That Mask of Satan from *Black Sunday*, then. The one that looks like the Greek masks in the third *Scream*. Just, without the nails on the inside.

And, yes, Sharona, obviously I'm hiding behind more and more movie shit because I want more than anything to check out of this moment. What I never say back to you when you accuse me of that, though? I'm sorry, when you "identify" that for me, out loud? *Whatever gets you through the night.*

I'll believe in fairies and unicorns if it lets me be somewhere better, I mean. Please. Sign me the fuck right up, twice. In blood. When you live in slasherland, you're always looking over the fence into the happier genres. The ones where your friends aren't lying dead all around you.

The ones where your best friend hasn't just fallen to her knees like a giant pair of scissors cut the strings holding her up.

I go to my knees beside her, hug her to me the same way I did with Alex. At first she tries to shrug me off, but I hold on through that, until she's heaving sobs.

"I'm sorry I'm sorry I'm sorry . . ." I keep saying.

I honestly can't even imagine words that might make this hurt less. And even if I knew them, it would be mean for me to say them, wouldn't it? This isn't supposed to be easy. Later on, if Letha doesn't cry hard enough now, in this moment, then she'll feel like a traitor.

"Um, hey," the helicopter pilot says, somewhere in the upright world.

When I first saw him inspecting the wreckage of his helicopter— it's tilted over, the rotors all stubs—my knee-jerk thought was *Jeff Fahey*. Those panty-dropper eyes? That flowing mane of silver hair? The stubble? That lecherous smile? It's like *Psycho III* had touched down in Terra Nova, and then pushed its yoke forward just enough to shred my dad, save my life.

But no, not *Psycho III*. If I'm going to mummy myself in videotape in my head, it should be something with a *working* helicopter. *The Thing*? No thanks. I fail that blood test, I know. *Grizzly*, then? Don't they fly around looking for that big bear in a copter?

Like that's something I need to conjure, here. Got enough going on, thanks. With my luck it would turn out to be Pizza Bear from *Prophecy* or that cocaine bear, and then we're all deader than dead.

Letha cries and sputters for probably twenty minutes. Like, uncontrollable, involuntary, racked with sobs. This is what it looks like when your whole world changes. I bet . . . I bet a guilty part of her wishes Jeff Fahey had, instead of setting down on the helicopter pad, just bobbed them back up into the sky, where she could float and float. So long as she stays up there, Banner's alive, isn't he?

If I were her, I'd never come down.

Finally, though, "Who did it?" she asks. "Who killed him?"

I tilt my head over to the smear on the grass that was my dad.

Letha studies it.

"I would have made it hurt more, if I'd known," she says.

"Whoah," Jeff Fahey says, then. He's been keeping about fifteen feet away, giving us room for whatever this is.

We both look to what he means: a window of one of the houses?

"There's someone up there," he says.

Letha stands, ready, eyes flaring because this is something she can maybe fight.

"Think they had their phone light on . . . ?" Jeff Fahey adds, like we're doubting him.

"Phone light," Letha says.

"Phone light," I echo.

What we're saying is that someone on the second floor up there using the light on their phone . . . they're not some monster like my dad. They could be a Billy or Stu—just a regular killer, a revenge-slasher—but that wouldn't really make sense, would be a *de*-escalation, after a corpse walking around with a murder weapon from better than a hundred years ago.

"Where is it?" I ask then, casting around.

"What?" Letha asks.

"This?" Jeff Fahey asks, holding the golden head of the pickaxe up. Evidently he'd stationed himself by it, the same way, when you find a ten-dollar bill blowing across the parking lot, you stand by it for a bit before picking it up, to see if anybody's going to come jogging after it.

The pickaxe head's more like half a pickaxe head now, maybe even just a third or quarter of one—that helicopter rotor was going at the speed of fury, must have launched the rest of that heavy little thing miles back into the forest—but what's left still has that dull, unholy glint.

Along with a blunt tip dipped in gore.

"With that?" Letha asks, and I nod.

She strides forward, snatches the pickaxe head from Jeff Fahey, who backs off, doesn't want any bit of this.

Letha's running hard for the lake now, is going to throw this out there as far as she can, because it killed her life, it took her husband, but—

I tackle her at the shore.

Letha comes around with her elbow, not at me *particularly*, I don't think, but at anything stopping her from doing this. Her elbow catches me in the jaw and I see not stars so much as just flickering tatters of blackness, followed by instant warmth on my neck, pooling in my collarbone, coating me under what's left of this thin shirt. If burst-open nearly formed scabs have a smell, then that must be what I'm smelling.

The hit's such a shock that I can't even say anything, can just suck air. I've been hit before, but never like this, never by someone I love and would do anything for.

It's not over, either.

Letha's not Letha anymore. She's just pain and hurt and anger. She's . . . how a dog that's been hit up on the highway needs someone to pick it up, carry it to the vet, but still snaps and snarls and bites at any hands reaching down for it?

I understand what Letha's feeling, I mean. I get wanting to rip enough holes in the world that it falls down.

And I'm the only one here.

I may not be good for much, I might not know Idaho history as well as you do, Mr. Holmes, but one thing I've learned in my twenty-four years on this wild ride is that I'm a girl who can take some damage.

"C'mon, c'mon," I manage to say to Letha around whatever's going on with my head that's slurring my words, and when she just breathes in, getting control of herself, I step forward push her hard with my good arm and yell behind it that it's *my* fault, that all of this is on me, that Dark Mill South never comes to town if I didn't show back up, that Stacey Graves never skates over to the movie if I don't wish and pray for her, that Cinnamon Baker never has to carve her way through the graduating class if she doesn't think I'm responsible for what happened to her parents, that . . . that Banner's head isn't in the path of that pickaxe if I haven't just tugged him back.

The period I put on this is stepping forward and pushing her hard in the chest, my eyes flaring, snot and tears and blood just streaming.

Letha has to step back to take my push without falling over, but when she processes that last part, she sets her lips, holds my eyes.

"No," she says.

"Yes," I tell her.

An instant later, she's coming for me with everything she has, not holding anything back this time, and instead of covering my face, I lift my chin to take this, to give her my throat, my chest, everything I have.

Letha launches up into me and we both fly back, both land on *my* back, and Letha's screaming and pounding at me with both fists, and I told myself that I would be her punching bag for this, but she's Letha fucking Mondragon, and when she brings it, she *brings* it—my right arm, the hurt one, comes up to try to fend this off. She knocks it to the side like the nothing it is, and the heel of her left hand's coming down for me. I turn to the side to keep my nose from getting shattered up into my brain, but that just means my split ear takes the blow, throwing cracks of thunder through my head that leave little chasms where memories used to be.

I buck to the side—weight's the only thing I have on Letha—but she turns it into a roll that's going to end us in the shallows.

I claw my good hand into the shore, keep us here even though that opens my body up for her to knee in the side.

She's crying and hitting and she can't stop, and I can't stop her, not when she's like this, and—and fuck it.

"*It's my fault!*" I scream right into her face, right into her open mouth, I'm pretty sure, and in response she slams her forehead into my top row of teeth, jolting me to the core.

The tatters of blackness start to knit together into a wide expanse of velvet darkness I can fall back into.

Letha hugs me back with her whole body, arms and legs and everything.

She's crying even harder than she was before.

My right hand is on the surface of Indian Lake, but no deeper. I pat it once, then slowly, delicately, painfully, I bring it to Letha's back, press her into me, and I'm crying too, saying I'm sorry over and over, and eight years ago when this perfect amazing princess-warrior stepped out of a stall of the bathroom down by the boys' gym and I flicked my eyes over to her in the mirror of the skank station, I never imagined she could ever matter this much to me.

I've got a best friend.

We've seen each other at our best, rising from the water to fight Stacey Graves, we've hitched each other across the ice to get back home from here, I've stood back while she came at my dad for me, because I wasn't strong enough to, she's saved me from him with a *helicopter*, I've held her little girl in my arms and spun her around, and I've looked up to her husband through bleary eyeliner, out of the darkness of the band closet, and I've seen him walk into marriage, fatherhood, the badge, and then a pickaxe, and I've shared cup after cup of coffee with her on her porch or mine, or under that great bear at Dot's, and I've told myself like a secret inside that this is what all the years ahead of us are going to be like. I've told myself too that, one weak Sunday, when Letha finally gives in and reaches across with her index and middle fingers for my cigarette, I'm going to scooch away, not let her start.

Even at Banner's funeral, when she'll still be wanting to punish herself, to let some of that exquisite corruption in, I'm going to shake my head no, keep her clean.

And I know that, no matter how long I live, no hug will ever be this hug.

I'm *glad* the Founders came to town and staked Terra Nova out.

There, I said it. If they don't, I never meet this amazing person. I never make this friend.

"I love you, final girl," I say into her hair.

She nods into my neck, can't speak yet, I don't think.

After about two minutes, she rolls off me and sits up.

I sit up beside her. There's no way to hold my head that doesn't hurt.

"I'm sorry," she says.

"Thought you were supposed to be *bad*," I mumble back, letting a grin into my voice.

Her frame shudders with what I hope is a laugh.

"I can't believe he—that he's *gone*," she finally says, sniffling.

"He was the best."

"Where?"

Because I'm not sure if she's asking where his body is or where the pickaxe got him, I just shake my head no.

Letha stands, pulling me up with her and holding me until I'm steady enough to inspect, says, "You look like, like—"

"Like always," I finish for her.

The side of my head's flowing again, my bleeding forearm's finally giving me that red right hand Nick Cave's always going on about, I'm not completely sure I have a right ear anymore, and my tongue's telling me something's up with a front tooth.

"What am I going to tell Adie?" Letha says then, in control of her voice, now. But then she straightens, is suddenly intense-Letha again. Which is a full-on dangerous thing. "Where *is* she?" she asks.

"With Tiff," I say. "Over there, safe."

Letha looks across the lake to the lights of Proofrock, and I follow.

All those cars that were streaming back in from the highway, now that the fire's gone enough? A lot of them are bunching up . . . south of town? Past Founders Park? But, the only thing out that way is the poacher road that leads around to the creek. The road Hettie and Paul and Waynebo were on. Until they weren't.

"She said they were . . . going to watch a movie?" Letha recites about Tiff.

"Probably something Disney, with princesses . . ." I say, glancing up with just my eyes to see how this registers with Letha.

After a moment, she nods that this has to be it, yes.

"Guess I better go hug that neck," she says.

"Me too," I say, which is when we both turn back to Terra Nova. In the moonlight—*So where's the Halloween snow, Idaho?*—we can see the outline of the trashed helicopter.

"Oh," Letha says, when that silver light flickers in the second-story window of the Baker place again.

"Weren't even going to break us up?" I say to Jeff Fahey, about the beatdown he had to have just witnessed. He's standing a few feet off again, that golden pickaxe head tucked against his forearm like a football, which just makes me flash on Banner again, and try to gulp it back down.

"Just here to protect her," he says back to me, about Letha. Translation: Letha was in zero danger from me.

Always with the potshots, world.

"Know who you look like?" I say back to him.

"More like he looks like me," he says with a shrug and grin, twirling that pickaxe head up and catching it so easily.

"Here," Letha says about it.

Jeff Fahey looks up to her just with his killer eyes, then, when she's serious, he holds it out to her obediently.

"This is what—what did it?" she confirms with me, taking the pickaxe head.

I nod once.

"And you don't want it back in the lake?"

"I don't," I tell her.

Letha nods that she can work with this, then walks directly over to the wishing well, drops the pickaxe head in and wipes her hands against each other like we're rid of the evil.

"Go see?" she says to Jeff Fahey, about the light in the Baker place.

"Serious?" he asks back.

"You wrecked my helicopter, dude."

"You told me to."

"Yeah, well, I'll get us a better one," Letha says. Then, looking around, she adds, "A better *all* of this."

"Oh, wow," I say, just seeing what she means: when the rotors shattered, they sent shards slicing through everything in their whip-plane. What I can see in the moonlight are three of these houses with a whole load-bearing wall bashed in. Probably more in the day-light.

It's going to be a while yet before anybody lives over here. Again.

Terra Nova's not just the most gated community in America any-more. It's also the most cursed. And, like you told us, Mr. Holmes, it's *all* a make-do graveyard over here, isn't it? They shouldn't have built their Cuesta Verde here. The land doesn't want them here.

Neither does Proofrock.

Too, when I lead the emergency crews back over here, to the bod-ies, I'm going to try to make sure one of these houses is the temporary morgue. No: a body in *each* of them, maybe? Like a row of mausole-ums. A cluster of tombs. And then somebody can leak photos of all these corpses laid out in living rooms, so Lana Singleton and her crop of New Founders will have no choice but to raze them to the concrete foundations, start all over again.

Or not.

"Got it, got it," Jeff Fahey says, and trots off to the Baker place, stooping on the way to pick up what at first my heart knows is a gui-tar, what his character Duane died by, but . . . it's a rusted pipe with a clump of dirt balled around one end of it, because it used to be buried, probably got dug up from the first Terra Nova, or the second.

It makes me wonder what some later Jeff Fahey might dig up, from this time around.

A golden pickaxe head, I guess.

Unless I sneak back over here in a few nights, hide it better.

"No, not over there," I tell Letha when she's casting around for somewhere for us to sit while Jeff Fahey inspects that light in the Baker place.

With her final girl instincts, she was walking us right over to Bub. But we don't need to see any men dead-in-uniform right now. Or ever again.

Instead, we sit down on the front lip of what was going to be Letha's front porch.

"This too weird?" I ask, patting the wood under us.

"Yeah," she says, but doesn't move.

"Well, I don't want to hide under the kitchen sink again," I say, trying for levity.

"I just want to go home," Letha says back, staring across the lake, probably at the light at the end of the Pier. But maybe at her own porch light. She can pick it out, I bet. I try, you'd think it would be easy-peasy, I've lived here my whole life, but I get a little lost in all the twinkling, and just the unsettling feeling that, from over here, I'm looking at town from the backside.

I can sort of see my seventeen-year-old self running down the Pier in her untied combat boots, I mean, a pair of headlights stabbing out behind her, a certain construction grunt standing beside that car, his right arm reaching for this running-away girl, his mouth open to call her name but he didn't even know it then.

But I can also see deeper back, to all us kids lined up on the Pier, for Hardy to spray with the big fan from his airboat. How we'd scream and thrill. And I can see Jocelyn Cates out there in the shallows, holding her arms up for the first penguin to jump off the ice floe, promising us it was going to be all right, that she'd never drop us, and that Ezekiel wasn't really down here, that's just a story. And, from here, Mr. Holmes, I can see your ultralight sputtering home that afternoon, losing altitude, and I know you had to have had one of your Marlboros clamped tight in your teeth when you finally hit the water. That's the only way to do a thing like that. And I can see further back. There's Cross Bull Joe backing his tow truck down the Pier to haul a little dead girl up by the chin, and there's the twelve-year-old Christine Gillette standing in a gingham skirt at the nose of that truck, half hiding behind her father but watching all the same, soaking all this in so she can relay it to me decades later.

Stacey Stacey Stacey Graves.

Jenny, Jennifer, JD, Jade.

I live here, yes.

This place is in me, and I'm in it. My past is here, and my future is as well. However much of it I've got.

Thirty minutes ago, when I was going to fly out over Camp Blood with my dad, I wasn't even going to see November.

Now, here, I'm not even done with Halloween yet, I guess.

In a house I can hear a scream from if I need to, a gorgeous old helicopter pilot's redshirting it around against his will. His head's probably going to come rolling down to our feet any minute, those pretty eyes open wide.

And—and the night isn't nearly over, is it? I can't remember if I ever put this in any of my papers for you, sir, but the easy thing to think about the slasher is that the Reveal is when the slasher's mask comes off and his identity is known, and everybody's like *of course, yeah, this makes sense.*

That's only half of it, though.

The final girl's mask is ripped off just the same, isn't it? Revealing *her* true self, that *she* never even knew what she had inside. Does she watch herself scrabbling and fighting and screaming and wonder how this can be her doing all this? When she's walking back into the light with blood dripping down from her fingertips, and sprayed across her face, and slathered all up and down what's left of her clothes, does she see a line from who she is now to who she was? And does she want to go back?

Letha's told me that all horror, including the slasher, is pretty much conservative, in that it's always fighting to get back to the status quo, back to when things were good, or at least to when there weren't so many people dead.

But *would* the final girl trade in what she's found in herself just to have the people she cares about back?

I know I would.

Letha too. In a heartbeat. In half a heartbeat.

But you can't go back, of course. Only in your head, your heart. Your wishing. And I'm just trying to come up with something that can bring Banner back, Sharona, yes. You're so brilliant, so *insightful*, I'm so lucky to have your voice always in my head these days, even if it's all throaty now from your flu or cold or whatever.

If I *did* somehow go back to before all the dead people, though, then . . . then I'm still living with my dad, living with my own boogeyman, in my own personal nightmare. I'm still flicking that *shit*rock knife open and shut in my right pocket, knowing there's some artery in my thigh I can nick if I do this just right, or just wrong.

I used to tell myself it was a thrill, keeping myself that close to bleeding out like that, with nobody even knowing.

I don't carry that knife anymore, though, Hardy. Mr. Holmes. Mom. Shooting Glasses.

Now . . . now I'm just trudging forward, I'm wading ahead through the gore. I live where I live, and it can be brutal, it's violent, it's sad, it's scary as hell, but—no, this is where I stay. Here, in Proofrock. With Letha sitting beside me. With Adie growing up. With the three of us bringing action figures and Dot's donuts to a certain grave over all the coming years. I'll even sneak out after dark with Adie when she's old enough and give her a flathead screwdriver to carve *daddy* real small and secret on that headstone, and I'll tell her cleaned-up stories of him in high school, because she's going to need to hear about him, and the hero he most definitely was.

But I'll never tell her or Letha about that scared look in Banner's eyes, when the point of that pickaxe burst up from his mouth. He wasn't scared of the pain, or of dying, I don't think. That was there, it was sudden and jolting, but it was already going over. No, when it's too late to stop any of that, when it's already done, I think what you see are the ones you leave behind. Banner was seeing Adie walking down the driveway for her first date. He was seeing Letha hanging all the stuff on the wall of their living room a different way this week, and then a different way next week, and he knows his mom's not going to approve of what the uppity daughter-in-law's doing to the bowling trophy side of the living room—as opposed to the trophy bull elk side of the living room—but him and Letha are going to laugh about it that night over her wine and his beer while they're sitting on the porch, waiting for Adie to get back so they can grill her, so Dad can glare this boy down, and . . . and he should have had all of that, he should have had every last minute of it.

And? If my dad's pickaxe comes in just a few inches to the side, then he gets all that, and *Aunt Jade* becomes the family story, and that's okay, that's fine. Henderson High can find another history teacher, one without a record. The drugstore can get somebody else hooked on cigarettes, like they need to keep their lights on.

It'd leave the ultralight I'm building for you unfinished, Mr. Holmes, but when I'm a ghost, I can sidle into that seat I bolted in there and fly up with you on the *ghost* version of it.

So long as there's ghost-smokes up there. I'm not coming to hang out if there's no nicotine, I mean. C'mon, let's be serious. But? You don't stay if there's none, I know, so . . . all good.

"So tell me what's going on?" Letha says, scrunching her fingers through her hair. Bits of leaves and dirt fall out. She sweeps it all off her thighs. There's an off-kilter rectangular dent in her forehead from one of my front teeth, with blood pressing out at the edges, but she's got enough high-dollar moisturizer that it'll be gone in no time. I don't think real final girls scar, anyway. Or, they carry their scars on the inside, don't they? Well, obviously. Thus the name changes. The drinking. The house turned into a booby-trapped fortress. And the no-life. The paranoia. The isolation. It's the part of being a final girl that doesn't get the glamorous treatment. Once the limelight's done with you, you're relegated to the shadows, to try to deal with it all however you can, alone.

But I'm talking to someone, here, can't hide in my head. I'm not seventeen anymore. It's something I keep having to remind myself of, never mind that the massacre from then's just been going on and on, it feels like, pulsing through the years, just faking sleep so it can scoop another armful of lives to its chest.

"It's just . . . the usual?" I try for Letha, about what's going on here, this time.

Letha shrugs like yeah, she kind of figured that, and then she winces and closes her eyes fast, and I get it: Banner's gone.

When she can, faking it a hundred percent, she says, "But your dad was, um, *rampaging?*"

"I guess?" I say back. "But I don't—none of it's making sense. There's . . . some dad got his head pulled off at the high school? And Phil Lambert's dead in his kitchen."

"Your dad was over there too?"

I shake my head no, I don't think he was.

"The Angel?" Letha asks, sneaking a look over at me.

"She's not you?"

"Serious?"

"Just . . . I don't know."

"Feeling real good about myself, here."

"She *looks* like you, I mean."

"Thanks for that boost."

Letha elbows me lightly and I wince—everything hurts.

"And somebody killed Hettie Jansson and her boyfriend and that . . . Wayne Sellars?"

"Because?"

"They saw whoever it was dragging Greyson Brust around?"

"Greyson who?"

"From the cemetery," I say, waving the explanation away. "Oh, and the game warden's skulking around—this fire's his doing, I guess."

"Seth Mullins?"

"He's in mourning, and wants everybody to know it."

"For Francie?"

"Her and Rex Allen turned up."

"Dead?"

I nod, hate that I should have thought to specify that.

"How long was I gone?" Letha asks, incredulous.

"I know."

"What was . . ." Letha tilts her face up to hold her tears in, starts over, weaker, because I think this is where she was meaning to get: "What was Ban doing over here, then?"

I breathe in, blow it out like smoke, letting her know that I hear her, here—this is the serious part. So I have to get it right: "Ones who didn't evacuate from the fire, they came over here with chainsaws and axes to—"

"*Chainsaws?*"

"And axes, yeah. Does nobody know where we live? It was Lana Singleton or one of them offering cash to save . . . this."

Terra Nova. The New World. Which we should have just let burn once and for all, I'm thinking. Or, I've *been* thinking. For about eight years, now.

"I think my dad was waiting for them," I tag on, like that explains it. "And that pickaxe—"

"Henderson killed Golding with it," Letha says. "Or the other way around? Thought it was lost, though."

"Past tense lost."

"Very past."

"The *past*-est."

"You ever study gothic stuff, in jail?" Letha asks.

No matter how many times I explain to her the difference between "jail" and "prison," Letha insists on getting it wrong. I guess because she's never been.

Hopefully she gets to keep messing that up forever.

"Like *Gothika?*" I ask back, trying to catch up with her. "*American Gothic*, 'somebody's at the do'r?'"

"Like the 'return of the repressed,' all that," Letha says, waving the academese away like the most bothersome fly. "I've been . . . I mean, is that what the slasher is, you think? The dark secrets surfacing after some pre-ordained amount of years? That pickaxe, I'm saying. And . . . your dad."

"I'm not turning you in for what you did to him," I tell her, for maybe the fiftieth time since 2015. Well, okay, since 2019, anyway.

"Even though I did actually do it?" Letha says back. It's her always-comeback.

"You didn't kill him," I tell her.

"Me, my pilot . . ."

"I mean then. With that Cenobite board."

"More like a Negan bat."

"Who?"

"You didn't kill him either, but you're the one who went away for it," Letha says. "I'm saying he's the dark secret here, unrepressing. It's like . . . it's like if you write something true and terrible on a piece of paper and bury it in the ground? Only, that paper starts to unfold all slowly, and—and finally somebody sees a corner of it, gives it a tug, reads what's there."

"He deserved it."

"So did Freddy," Letha says. "That didn't stop him from coming back, did it?"

I can't argue with that. What I can argue with: "Wouldn't the paper, like, rot away before it could unfold?"

"Yeah, let's split that hair."

I hold up my trashed hair, offering some.

"So there's how many killers, now?" Letha asks, squinting like counting in her head.

"One less," I say, tilting my head to the smear over by the helicopter pad.

"If one of them's over there, though——" she says, about town.

"Adie, you're right. And, forgot to say. I think I saw . . . I don't know. A Chucky?"

"Leprechaun size, you mean? *Puppetmaster*y? That doll Karen Black hated?"

"*The Brood*, *It's Alive*, *Basket Case*, *Bloody Birthday*, Gage," I say, meaning *yes*.

"*Village of the Damned*, here," Letha tags on.

"Not wrong."

"But if this *is* a slasher," I say, thinking out loud. "Who's final girl, this time?"

"Not me," Letha says with a shrug that this should be obvious.

I look my question over to her.

"What have I ever really done?" she says. "I'm like—I'm Scully. I always get put out of commission before the real stuff hits the fan."

"Before the *shit* hits the fan," I tell her.

"See? I still can't even cuss right."

"But you have to be out of commission," I say. "Out of commission is where it's safe."

"I don't *ask* to be safe."

"You *have* to be safe," I tell her. "Adie and——"

I almost said "Banner," there. And I think she felt it coming, has to shake her head to make it go away. At least for this moment, if not all the rest she's got coming.

"It's you, Jade," Letha tells me, quietly, seriously. "It's always been you."

"But I'm not—"

"You are."

"Just now?" I say, opening my hand to the beatdown that just happened. "I just get lucky when the shit's flying. Heaven doesn't want me and Hell's afraid I'll take over, you know the deal with me. But you, Jocelyn—"

"Jocelyn *Cates?*"

"Bad example."

"Why?"

I shrug, tilt my head back into the woods. Meaning, again: *dead*.

Letha sighs defeat. Says, "We worked out together on Tuesdays and Thursdays."

"You and *Jocelyn?*"

"Why do you say it like that?"

"I don't—I mean, I didn't know the two of you . . ."

"Knew each other, in a town of not even three thousand?"

"Not anymore."

"Who was your friend in jail, again?"

Prison.

"Yazzie," I tell her. "She gets out in a few years. You'll like her."

"I will."

"But, it's—look at you, *you're* the final girl, Leeth. Now and always."

"Before I got married, maybe," Letha says. "But—"

"Because you were a *virgin?*" I say, incredulous. "That Adam and Eve bullshit doesn't help anybody, does it? The 'pure' and the 'fallen'? C'mon."

"'We work with what we have,'" Letha cites.

Anyone who brings *The Cabin in the Woods* in, they automatically win, I know, I know.

"That's what I'm saying," I tell her. "Virginity's a stupid holdover, it's Reagan-era propagand—"

"I'm not saying it's important," Letha says. "I'm saying . . . I'm saying that I'm a *mom*, now. Moms are in survival horror, sure, they're in home invasion stuff, they're in haunted houses their cheapskate husbands pick out, they're in rape-revenge, they get trapped in Pintos, but—"

"No slashers," I finish.

"And you're not a mom," Letha says. "Do the math, right?"

"But my boogeyman . . ." I tell her back, flinging my hand Dad-ward. "We've already had our big face-off—which *you* ended, not me."

"Then it's not over yet?" Letha prompts, eyebrows up like you making a point, sir.

Goddamn her.

"So, what?" I have to ask. "My dad found the golden pickaxe, and my mom's the Angel of Indian Lake?"

"Your mom was blond, wasn't she?" Letha asks.

"Maybe she's dyeing it."

"So you two look the same."

"I got my dad's hair, yeah."

"Central casting really phoned it in with you, didn't they?" Letha says with an almost-smile.

"Didn't even find a virgin," I add on.

Letha starts to say something back to this, then cuts it off, is just staring at me, like doing math herself: my time as a student at Henderson High, having no friends, less dates; my time in central holding down in Boise, when I was on trial; my first incarceration; my thirty-six hours or whatever when Dark Mill South came to visit, which didn't leave much room for romance; my *second* bid; my time after that back here, with, again, zero dates and no real prospects.

Math sucks. Especially when you're on the wrong side of that equals sign, and everybody's looking at you.

"But—" Letha finally can't help but say.

She's objecting to my *Didn't even find a virgin*. Kindly, but still.

"You're saying that because I've been in lockup, that I must be a unicorn's best friend?" I ask back, hiding the grin that wants to percolate up, show itself. Because I'm leading her right into this.

"I mean," she says. "It's only *women* in there, isn't it?"

"So . . . use your *imagination*? Pretend this isn't Proofrock, that it isn't Idaho."

Letha does, then has to smile, nudge me back a bit.

"Ow," I tell her, playing it up, mostly with my eyes.

"What about that . . . that construction worker?" Letha says, eliminating possibilities in her logical, thorough way.

"Ever listen to that one metal band?" I say, dragging this next part out for her, so she can put the pieces together. "AC . . . *DC*?"

Letha dips her face, actually *smiles* in spite of everything going on, says, "You're saying . . ."

"I'm *saying*, yeah," I tell her, shrugging. It was going to be good and smooth, but my whole right side hurts, meaning I end up visibly wincing. Maybe out loud, too.

"Here, here," Letha says, guiding me around to face her and ripping her loose right sleeve off. It's practically gauze already after our big fight. She snaps for my right arm, flattens the sleeve as good as she can, and starts to wind my forearm in it, and I can see right off that playing Mom is as good for her as it is for me. It makes me wish I had cuts all *over* me for her to attend to, if it keeps her from thinking about Banner. Too, I can't help but picture a horror movie where the hot chick's ripping off pieces of her clothes to bandage somebody, and that somebody's surreptitiously cutting themself, just so this Good Samaritan of a nurse can strip down more and more, never quite catching on to this wonderful game.

More Troma than prestige horror, but I'd watch it. Might even rewind it a bump or two, until I wore the tape thin.

"You're telling me it was Mary Ellen Moffat who broke your heart?" she says, her words somehow making my *Kolobos* wrist throb.

"Something like that, yeah."

"And I had to beat you up before you thought to let me in on this?"

"Never came up."

"Something this important, to do with my best friend in the whole world, with the girl—the *woman*—I model myself after, and . . . it never comes up?"

I swallow and lick my lips, because there are no words, here. Because if I open my mouth even a crack, she'll see my heart beating in the back of my throat.

She models herself on *me*?

"I'm sorry," Letha goes on, her voice sounding more serious because she's using her teeth as a third hand to get her sleeve tied around my forearm tight. "I shouldn't have . . . *assumed*. It makes an asshole of me. That how you say that?"

"You don't have to be sorry," I tell her back.

"Should I be insulted, then?"

"That—that I never hit on you?"

She shrugs one shoulder, keeps her eyes down like this is all just talk, nothing serious.

"It's not because I'm Black, is it?"

"You want to fight again, don't you? I *will* beat your ass, final girl or not, if you ever say anything like that to me again. I'll be Roddy Piper to your Keith David."

Letha shrugs a had-to-ask shrug, says, "Keith David the Black guy?"

"Lived through *The Thing*."

Letha opens her mouth to make a show of breathing out, so I can see there's no frozen vapor inside her.

"Not to mention you're kind of a married woman," I add on.

"Past tense," she says, quoting me and moving on to my head, which is even more of a mess than my arm, I'm pretty sure. The mirror is not going to be my friend, whenever I get to one. But, not like it's ever been, I guess.

Letha reaches up and rips her other sleeve off, applies it delicately to my head. Pretty soon I'm going to look like that guy in *Timecrimes*.

Bring it.

And? It'll be worth it if it means I get to *Happy Death Day* my way back in time a day, to make things happen like they should. "Jade Daniels is reliving Halloween day in her hometown over and over, until she identifies the real killer and saves the day."

I could go with that, sure.

And yes, Jace, I get the cupcake thing now, thank you. Signed, Jade, four years late.

Letha's arranging my hair around my new bandage, like primping me for a walk on the runway.

"Can you see my brain?" I ask, touching the bandages lightly with the pads of my fingers.

"Just your heart," Letha says, holding my eyes.

It would be a hell of a time for her to hold my face on both sides and kiss me on the lips, but we don't get to pick our genre, Billy.

Because of killers like you.

Letha does take my fingers in her hand, though. To still them.

"You're off your meds, aren't you?" she says.

I pull my hand back, lick my lips too fast, no eye contact, and Letha, being Letha, doesn't push it, just moves her shoulders fighter-style in the tanktop she's just made of her eight-hundred-dollar blouse.

"So I can still be Aunt Jade?" I ask, with all due hesitation. I know the answer, but, at the same time, I need to hear it out loud, I think.

Letha squeezes my thigh right above the knee in reply, and we don't have to talk about this anymore.

"Thank you," I tell her.

"Thank *you*," she says back, somehow holding both my hands in hers now, and then shaking them once, gently, and—isn't this a dream or something I had once, long way back?

But there's no time to hide in the past. There never is, around here.

"What are Randy's rules for the third in a trilogy?" I ask.

Letha sits back, unfocuses her eyes to dial them up: "Killer who's superhuman, check. Anyone can die, fuck that check." I golf-clap for her profanity, which gets my right arm throbbing even more. "And . . ." she goes on, picking through Randy's videotaped exegesis, ". . . is it that the past comes back to bite you in the ass?"

"Check?" I ask, about my dad.

"Big check, yeah," Letha says.

"Then it's over?"

"Except for that it's still Halloween. At the—in the recovery room in Denver, there were, like, decorations everywhere. Bats, pumpkins. My nurse, he was wearing a witch hat. And my doctor had a Michael Myers mask on."

"Oh, to live in the normal world," I singsong.

"You never know the rules, out there," Letha says. "In here, in the slasher, we sort of do, don't we?"

"Never helped Randy."

"Didn't it? He made it to 2. And 3, sort of."

"And his niece and nephew . . ." I tag on. "Which Michael mask?"

"*Revenge.*"

"Man."

"I know, right? And I let this guy *operate* on me?"

"Speaking of . . . ?" I ask, leaning back a smidge like to see some incision on her jaw.

"Orthoscopic," Letha says, rubbing her palm over what must be some small incision under the collar of her shirt.

"But it worked?"

She opens and shuts her mouth, showing how perfect her jaw is.

"'Something that wasn't true from the get-go . . .'" I try out loud then, still citing Randy's posthumous rule-laying-down. "So what is that we're so wrong about?"

"I don't think we get to know yet," Letha says, after thinking it through all she can with what we've got, which isn't much. "All you can do is—is the *immediate* concern."

"Adie," I say.

"Adie," she agrees, standing.

"Right on time," I tell her, pointing ahead of us with my lips.

It's Jeff Fahey, leading five survivors out the front door of one of the houses.

Four of them are still carrying chainsaws.

The speaker for the chainsaw brigade is Walter Mason's twin Grace, who married a Richardson, had four sons, and then a grandson who played football, who I'm pretty sure I saw the insides of, down on Main Street.

Ain't life grand.

The other four are, from right to left, Orange Waders—did he think this was a fishing expedition?—Science Goggles, who I think might have taught you and Hardy biology, Mr. Holmes, maybe even been a pirate with y'all, and then Blue Chainsaw and White Chainsaw, both of them about thirty, meaning they must have been graduating high school right before I was a freshman.

I could dredge all their names up if I wanted, but labels are so much easier. You don't see a label's whole past and all their relations when that label mists into blood with the sunrise.

Grace is carrying that Halligan I dropped. Her brother's fireman tool.

She holds it in both hands across her hips, says to Letha and me, "He says you two know what to do?"

Letha looks at me and I shrug.

"Try to not die?" I finally say.

"We were doing pretty fine up there," Grace says, hooking her head back to the house Jeff Fahey just led them out of.

"Plumbing's not on yet," Blue Chainsaw says with sort of an embarrassed shrug.

"So?" Grace says to us, taking charge again.

"We have to walk it," Letha says.

"*Walk?*" Science Goggles creaks. He's old, but looks limber, like one of those senior citizens who keep a sloshing shot of whiskey on their nightstand to slam each morning. His eyes are all the way pissed off, too. Maybe that's what's keeping him going.

"That way," I say, turning to the side and opening my arm to Camp Blood, the dam, the woods, then Proofrock.

They all live here, though. I don't need to tell them how to get around the lake.

"Without a light, you mean?" White Chainsaw asks, squinting his whole face with reluctance.

"We've got numbers," Jeff Fahey says. He doesn't quite hook his thumbs into his beltloops to hitch his pants up, but his matter-of-fact delivery's got that authority.

"And those," Letha adds, nodding down to the four chainsaws, the Halligan.

"What do *you* have?" Orange Waders asks, and I cringe inside, do recognize him now: *Davis* Duchamp, little brother to the headless dad in the hug-n-go lane.

"We *are* the weapons," I say with a grin—me and Letha.

"Yeah, well," Grace says, shifting her shiny mean Halligan. "Think that if you want."

"I'm in front," Letha announces. "Jeff, you're in back?"

Jeff Fahey raises his hand, taking this duty, and, I guess I've probably been gobsmacked before, I have to have been, the shit I've seen, but—"That's your *name*?" I have to ask him.

He gives me a wink and then pivots away.

"I'm behind you, then?" I whisper to Letha, I think because we're supposed to be fostering the illusion of a united front to keep these people from panicking and running every which way.

Letha nods and I fall in, and she leads us well around the helicopter pad, and before a quarter mile's behind us, we've pulled enough ahead that Letha can sniffle, say after sneaking a look back, "How am I going to tell her?" Her chin's pruning up again, her lips in kind of pre-quiver mode.

I think this is kind of where she's going to be living, the next year, year and a half. At least. Every slack moment between this and that, she's going to be falling back into Banner not being around anymore.

I step in by her, take her by the back of her left arm to make sure she doesn't stumble.

"I'll tell her that . . . that when that bad man came for her Aunt Jade, that her daddy stepped between to save me, that he was—that that's the kind of sheriff he was."

Letha nods thank you, pulls her lips in to keep them steady.

"That's true?" she asks, batting her eyes fast enough that mine start to heat up as well.

"I'll never lie to her, Leeth."

"She's going to need you," Letha says back, sniffing in deep now, like trying to make this go over, like reminding herself we're not here to wallow, we're here to *win*.

"I need her too," I tell her. "And her mom also?"

Letha nods, keeps nodding, and then, impossibly, *stupidly*, from behind us comes "Dear He-nderson High, we will upho-old you, hailll the blue and white . . ."

It's Science Goggles, and his high clear voice is actually pretty damn beautiful.

"Dear He-nderson Hawks, we ado-ore you," Grace lilts back, Blue and White Chainsaw coming in bass and loud with "And wi-ish you a good flight."

It's officially the first time our school song hasn't grossed me out. I even sort of want to fall in, sing along. Except I also have to live with myself. Or, I hope to get to live with myself.

"What is even happening," Letha says back to me, her eyes big and round like the dots on cartoon question marks.

"That," I tell her, tipping my head out to the lake.

It's the *English Rose*, over in illegal waters, right by Glen Dam.

Lemmy's got his fleet of drones synced up, finally, like he never could do for the Fourth.

Any Independence Day that doesn't end with bodies floating in the lake, though—Proofrock still clapped for his sputtering-out show until their hands were raw, and more than a few people standing on shore were freely crying, and lifting their hands higher and higher.

Me too, sure. But I think I'd already been crying, that day.

What Lemmy's got his lit-up drones arranged into now, though, it's—

"A fucking *marquee*?" Letha says.

"For the movie," I intone, my face going ice cold, my feet suddenly dragging.

It's one of those drive-in–style marquees, meant to pull people in off the highway, with its frame becoming a blinking arrow pointing down to *here, here*.

Come one, come all.

This is what all the headlights on the south side of town were: Proofrockers going to the illegal movie at the *Footloose* county line. Proofrockers being the dead in *Dawn*, shuffling back to the only thing they know to be true, to be real, to have given them succor once upon a lifetime.

"They can't, they—" Letha says, her hand clamping hard enough onto my bad wrist that I have to suck air in.

"We've got to stop them," I hiss back to her, and then step ahead, taking the lead, almost running, I think.

"Look, look!" Orange Wader says somewhere behind, like this marquee is the thing that's going to save us all.

If only he knew.

BAKER SOLUTIONS

Report of Investigation
12 October 2023
#41a03
re: Indian Lake "Angel"

Taking into account the various medications and substances Jennifer Elaine "Jade" Daniels regularly ingests and depends on [full list at 81a–113d], her sleep patterns have been the first to suffer [for footage of her restlessness, see 002f; for a log of her repetitive wakings, 002-g32; for a sample of her inarticulate mutterings, 002-g34-tr], with the likely result being that the division between "dreaming" and "not dreaming" has likely fallen victim as well, directly impacting her perceptual reliability. In short, Ms. Daniels could be vandalizing Proofrock and Indian Lake in a dirty nightgown *un*intentionally in her sleep, as a result of pharmaceutically induced somnambulism.

As for the guise she adopts for these nocturnal meanderings and subsequent vandalism, the options, based on available evidence, are:

1. Stacey Graves, that being a child from the early part of the twentieth century who fell victim to a children's game on the shores of Indian Lake, and as a result supposedly lived-without-aging, solely to perpetrate the Indian Lake Massacre, as a sort of "revenge" either for how Proofrock residents from more than a hundred (100) years ago had neglected and possibly abused her or as a result of her "peace" having been "broken" [see *Beowulf*, unknown, 975–1025]. Over the generations, and in the absence of competing narratives, this "Stacey Graves"

became known locally as the "Lake Witch." Ms. Daniels, in her writings on horror [1A], espouses both respect and pity for this Lake Witch, and suggests that Stacey Graves's plight was not dissimilar to the treatment Ms. Daniels herself received from the residents of Proofrock. While Ms. Daniels, in her succession of testimonies and defense strategies [1d], never champions nor tries to absolve this girl she claims was actually responsible for the fatalities, she does posit that Stacey Graves's actions were possibly warranted to some degree. Though Ms. Daniels's legal team for this defense revised their argument such that Ms. Daniels's "theories" were evidence of the trauma she had suffered, it's distinctly possible that Ms. Daniels, by adopting, inculcating, or even subsuming the identity of this "Angel of Indian Lake," is still, in a sense, arguing her case, either in the general sense of "The supernatural, though perpetually blurry, is alive and well around here" or in the specific sense of "The Lake Witch is still alive, and she's matured into an even more dangerous (i.e., *adult*) form." If so, then the willful destruction of "intruding" property would be in keeping with this identity's need for revenge, or "justice."

2. Sally Chalumbert (Shoshone, 28). In Elk Bend, Idaho, July 2015, Ms. Chalumbert, rather than retreating from Dark Mill South's rampage against her husband and his company of smokejumpers, elected to take the offensive, grievously injuring Dark Mill South and in the process granting him his characteristic scarred face and absent right hand. After this episode, Ms. Chalumbert, unable to retreat from her own all-encompassing fight or flight response, had to be institutionalized for her

own safety, and the safety of others [see 384-f for a record of Ms. Chalumbert's multiple instances of destruction of property at Greenpoint Residential Psychiatric Treatment]. Until 9 June 2023, that is, when she escaped her institution. Note that the first appearance of the "Angel of Indian Lake" is dated 24 June 2023 on social media [see 53e-h]. As it would be arbitrary for Ms. Chalumbert to journey from Greenpoint Residential Psychiatric Treatment in Coeur d'Alene, Idaho, to Proofrock, Idaho—a place there's no record of her ever visiting (485–558 miles, depending on route)—then blurry pictures of someone with her features would suggest someone is impersonating, or "cosplaying," not only her, but her institutionalized *actions* [384-f . . .]. See photographs 72f62–72f88 on 19 June 2023 for what may have been Ms. Daniels's first tentative foray into this identity. Note too that both Ms. Chalumbert and Ms. Daniels are Native American, and that both have had lethal confrontations with the same serial killer, Dark Mill South.

As for Ms. Daniels's continuing fascination with Ms. Chalumbert, as prototypical of the "final girls" Ms. Daniels persistently valorizes, consider this excerpt from the most recent session [full transcript at FP13a-tr] with Dr. Sharona Watts (5 October 2023, Founders Park):

JADE DANIELS: Here, I'll sit on this side, that way the
                smoke--

DR. SHARONA

  WATTS: No, no, don't worry about it. It reminds
                me of my dad's cigars.

DANIELS: But I thought your dad died of lung--

WATTS: Boating accident. But we're not here to talk
          about little old me. I can't put that on my
          report, can I? "Spoke with patient extensively
          about my father, not hers." Penalty box. Two
          minutes for high-sticking.

DANIELS: "High-sticking"?

WATTS: It goes with those hockey masks you so love
          slashers to wear. Forget it.

DANIELS: You said "slasher," not "serial killer."

WATTS: You're a bad influence, Jade.

DANIELS: And my name, now.

WATTS: Perhaps it's these masks. I'm liking it. Doesn't
          Sid wear one at the end?

DANIELS: Sam too. Twice, now. More important--you WATCHED
          the first one? Thought you were too spooky for
          horror?

WATTS: I've been doing my homework, Jade. But we're
          talking about you. Last week we stopped when
          you--let me check these notes--we stopped when
          you, um . . .

DANIELS: I know, I KNOW. You don't want to hear an alpha-
          betical list of final girls.

WATTS: I do if that's what you see yourself as, Jade.
          I did notice you didn't include yourself on
          that list, or the surviving Baker twin, who I
          understand went toe-to-toe with that large Na-
          tive American man. You did, however, include

Letha Mondragon? No, no, I'm not--I guess what
I'm asking is, how do you distinguish between
cinematic final girls and real-world ones? And
why do you not include yourself?

DANIELS: Cinnamon Baker was no final girl.

WATTS: But . . . I thought "fighting the slasher" in a
death match for all the marbles was a key characteristic?

DANIELS: Letha's for sure one. It's about heart, not
muscles. And, if we're talking real world . . .
do you know about that lady up north who put
Dark Mill South down the first time?

WATTS: I can't say I--

DANIELS: She's the one knocked his teeth out and cut his
hand off.

WATTS: So you're saying she's a . . . a *hero*?

DANIELS: She's a model for us all. A--she's the vessel
we pour all our hope into. Everything good we
could ever be in our best most amazing moments,
she became that for a few minutes.

WATTS: Like Cinnamon Baker, now relegated to a wheelchair.

DANIELS: "Relegated," really?

WATTS: It means--

DANIELS: I know what it means. It's more than she de-
serves, though. And a lot less.

WATTS: You're jealous of her, I take it? Is it her
           youth, or that she's Caucasian? Her privileged
           social position? Her fabulous hair? That she
           waded into battle without a care for herself?

DANIELS: I mean--I hear she makes a killer cupcake.

TRICK OR TREAT

"No answer?" I ask Letha, again.

We've pulled probably twenty yards ahead of what's left of the chainsaw brigade, are plunging into darkness after darkness, struggling uphill. None of them back there are singing anymore. I don't even know if they're still lugging their chainsaws.

In the occasional breaks between the trees, Lemmy's movie marquee drones aren't up anymore. What I refuse to say out loud, about that: because it's already started.

Pronoun antecedent? the Sharona in my head asks, batting her eyes behind her mask.

Early in our sessions, this was her go-to, instead of the *But how does that make you* feel? I'd been expecting, going by other court-mandated therapy I'd sat through.

Okay, Sharona: *it* here refers back to "massacre," which is the understood antecedent where I'm from. Where I *am*.

I'm resigned to that massacre having already begun. Not "without me," but more like *"because* of me."

When I was telling Letha that this was all my fault, she should have kept on whaling on me, because I wasn't just saying that. Jade

Daniels, bringer of maladies, wisher of tragedy, the girl who thought she was hurting enough that calling doom down on the whole valley felt righteous.

I'm sorry, Letha. I'm sorry, Mr. Holmes. And Hardy. And Jocelyn Cates, Chin, Alex—all of you. Even Phil Lambert.

Being sorry doesn't mean I get to hide from it now, though. I mean, the obvious way to make it *through* this night is to step over the wall of that wishing well, isn't it? Curl down there in the darkness with that golden pickaxe then rise with it like it's the boon I've plucked up from all this bloody muck, the thing that can restore Pleasant Valley, get us back on some less terrible path.

Instead, I'm trudging alongside Letha, trying to match my steps with hers, but her legs are so long and athletic.

"Why isn't she answering?" Letha grits out, the right side of her face glowing with her phone.

Pronoun antecedent: Tiff, Adie's babysitter for this ordeal.

Her "going to see a movie" was a lot more innocuous before Lemmy's movie marquee took over the nighttime sky.

I hustle up beside Letha.

"Insta?" I prompt.

Letha considers this, slows to dial the right app up: Tiff might not be taking calls for whatever reason—whatever *fireable* reason—but she's functionally incapable of not checking her feed every fifteen seconds.

Just like we don't need to see, Tiff's posted a set of shots of heads milling around out in some vast darkness—probably the walk out of town, when they started going by foot because cars and trucks couldn't make it any farther. In two of the shots, there's a small head and part of a perfect little shoulder in-frame.

"No," Letha moans, and right as she's lowering her phone, I see—

"What?" I ask, guiding her wrist back up.

It's Sharona's feed.

I palm Letha's phone away—we're still bustling along—click and scroll. Sharona's feed is . . . beaches?

"Where is she?" I ask, this not quite registering. "I just saw her Thursday."

Letha, frustrated, gives an obligatory glance down, says through clenched lips, "The Bahamas? I think that's St. Thomas?"

"But—"

"It's for her dad's funeral, I think? Or, to spread the ashes."

"Her *dad*? What . . . the boating thing?"

"Lungs," Letha says, not that interested, taking her phone back and dialing Tiff harder, like *that's* the thing that'll make her answer.

I follow, squinting, nodding to myself.

"When?" I try.

"When what?"

"Her dad."

"August, I think?"

"When she got sick?"

"Sick?"

"Her—bronchitis, whatever? It's why she sounds like that now."

"Listen, this is neat and all, but—"

She stops because we've just emerged from the trees, are going fast enough Letha has to reach across, stop me short. From stepping off a deep bite crumbled into the bluff above Camp Blood.

"I've got a hacksaw down there," I tell her.

"We've got *chain*saws here," Letha says, hooking her chin to the crunching footsteps in the darkness behind us.

She's right. In the rock/paper/scissors of horror, *chainsaw* always wins. Cops and guns don't work against slashers, trucks and fire are big fat fails, but a chainsaw? If you've got a chainsaw, you're pretty damn golden.

"His email . . ." Letha says then, like she somehow ferreted this possibility up from the caved-in roofs of the cabins of Camp Blood.

"Watch your step here!" I call back to the chainsaw brigade, then get to longstepping it downhill with Letha.

She's swiping and clicking, swiping and clicking.

"Whose email?" I ask, out of breath.

"Ban," she says.

"He lets you—?" I say.

"His phone's always dead by dinner," Letha tells me, about as interested in explaining this as she was Sharona's Caribbean trip. "He logs in on my phone to check work stuff."

"Official stuff," I add.

"It's Proofrock," Letha says, meaning how official can any of these messages be, really?

She's not wrong.

"Tiff send him anything?" I ask, trying to peer into that inbox.

"Just . . . nothing," Letha finally says, and slips the phone into her back pocket like she's in high school.

"Wait, let me—" I say, pulling the phone up, out.

Letha looks back, interrogates me for a moment with her eyes, then presses on.

I enter her PIN—976-EVIL with numbers for the letters, we're such cool girls—find the Instagram app, and . . .

Shit, I don't say out loud.

One of those heads in the crowd Tiff documented, I'm pretty sure it's Rexall. He's taller than everyone else, more lumbery, and, sensitized as he must be to hidden cameras, he's just starting the process of cranking his head back, to clock the source of this lens he's feeling on him.

I'm not sure why I get all dready about him being there, but I can't deny it, either. I think it's just that, since hiring on, I've noticed he schedules his custodial stuff around my hours, so we don't have to have any awkward walks past each other in the hall, afterhours. Our interactions the past few months have pretty much been just the pinhole cameras I crumble down onto his porch.

I want to be able to very primly say someday, about Henderson High and Golding Elementary, that *this house is clean*, but have it be actually true. Cut to Rexall, pushing his console television out onto his porch: victory.

"How far now?" Letha asks.

Her face is sheened in sweat, never mind the chill in the air—Halloween night at eight thousand feet's no joke.

I take a reading, make a guess: "Ten minutes?"

Not to town, but to the creek, which has to be where everybody's being called to for whatever this is going to be.

"Keep up?" she says to me, holding my eyes to be sure, and—what else can I do? Say, *No, no, wait, Adie's not that important?*—I nod, and like that Letha vaults ahead, her run so effortless, so graceful, like the camera crew for a shoe commercial is bounding along beside her in a golf cart.

I clump along behind, my lower lip bitten between my teeth and my thumbs tucked into my fists because maybe that's the secret to going fast. Bub's cowboy boots don't exactly help.

Soon enough—probably ten minutes—we're up to the fork in the sort-of road: cross the dam or take that switchback road down?

Letha looks back, her nostrils flaring, eyes wide.

I nod to the right, the road, not because I'm scared of walking the dam, though I most definitely am—we're not seventeen years old anymore—but . . . okay, it's two reasons, both at the same exact time in my head: the first is that walking the dam probably puts us in rope-throwing distance from the *English Rose*, which is some grief I don't need, thanks, but the *second* reason is the one that hurts: the last time I was up this high, coming down, I was sandwiched between Banner when he was a deputy and Hardy after he was sheriff, and I was uncomfortable and Banner's shifting hand kept touching my knee and him and Hardy were sniping at each other and the drifts were swallowing the treads of our cute little snow machine and, and—what I wouldn't give to be there again, in the warmth of that cab.

But now they're both gone.

Ahead of me, farther ahead than's really great, Letha decides this switching back bullshit is slowing her down too much, so she just jumps right off the road into the darkness on the downhill side, her arms above her like a gymnast, like a superhero. No: like a mother, like a mom who has to get to her precious little girl.

Adie's all she has left, I mean. If Letha needs to, she'll grow wings to get to her.

Even if it means leaving me.

I stop at the crumbling lip she just jumped from, and I've got nerve for a lot of stuff, and I don't care about my own safety just super much, but still, I can't quite get myself to commit to this leap.

I cup my good hand around one side of my mouth and yell down to Letha that I'll catch up, and I hope against hope that I'm not lying.

Back when Banner was churning up here every morning and every night to deliver and then pick Hardy up from the dam, he probably knew there were nine turns in this road, or thirteen, whatever.

Me, I just take them as they come, urging my legs faster, reminding myself to take longer and longer steps, telling myself that gravity's on my side, that I shouldn't be out of breath from this, my lungs know this elevation, this cold.

The thousand and twenty cigarettes still smoking through my system say otherwise.

After either the sixth or eight sharp turn, I have to bend over, suck air, spit the bloody cheese from my lungs. When I look up to try to take my bearings, get a halfway read on how high up I still might be, I'm . . . staring over the hood of a car?

"What the hell?" I mutter.

After checking my six, my ten, my two, I edge forward, finally touch the metal over its headlight hesitantly, like I might be about to nudge Christine awake.

The metal's all brown and pocked with rust, the tires rotted off years

ago, there's no glass in the windows anymore, and the hood, it looks . . .
it looks like the bottom of an upside-down boat, sort of? I guess?

And then I stagger back, my good arm behind me.

I've *seen* this car.

I've seen it in my mom and dad's closet in their bedroom, in a
shoebox of old photographs. This is the Grand Prix my dad wrecked,
his senior year. This is the car that wrecked his face *back*. The one he
should have died in, if the world were actually a fair place. His name,
"Tab," it comes from all the pull tabs he hung from the headliner,
even. All the dead soldiers tinkling and shimmering above him. Until
they fell all at once, driving him off the road.

But . . . not off *this* road.

How the hell does this Grand Prix get up here? Is it here specifically to fuck with me?

"You're dead," I say to my dad, stepping back into what feels like
the car's radius. Its gaze.

The car just sits there, like I guess it's been doing for probably all
of my life.

Waiting for this moment?

"I don't think so," I say to it, and cast around for what I need.
When I find it, I take a running start, slam the dead tree limb I've got
into the car's nose.

The car shudders but takes it, so I keep going, swinging and swinging that branch, which is thicker than my arm and probably too heavy
for me, but fuck it. It's not every day you get to trash out one of your
dad's favorite things.

That fancy hood, which was probably all the rage in the seventies,
dents and buckles, and when the last couple feet of my branch finally
snap off, I climb up, jump up and down right in the center, the hood
really going taco now.

When it gives, it gives all at once, and I fall through, am standing
on the ground again, holding my branch like a balancing pole.

No engine, then. Nothing inside, just a blowing void, a great hollowness.

Feels about right.

I climb out, my right arm bleeding freely through Letha's sleeve, and I make my way up onto the roof that's already crunched in.

Instead of jumping up and down, this time I bring my branch up—now with a splintered point—and drive it down with all the weight I have, and it spikes right through, goes in up to the hilt, and I can feel the whole car groan beneath the soles of my cowboy boots.

I stay there on one knee, holding the butt of that branch, my breaths coming deep, and when I look up, it's to something large and heavy padding down the road, there and gone.

Some elk swim, I guess, and . . . some take the highway?

I leave that branch there, step down, and follow the road, stepping into the dinner-plate-size foot-craters this elk's leaving in the light snow.

"Thank you," I mutter ahead to it, and then I stumble out of the last switchback into the clearing at the creek bottom, have to suck my breath in from what might be the purest shock I've ever had, even more than finding my dad's high school car halfway up the mountain, even more than finding my dad up and walking again.

The creek bottom's always been relatively clear, I guess because the dam's shade keeps the big trees from finding purchase there, or maybe from tailings from all our old mines or maybe it's beavers or something, I don't know—you would, Mr. Holmes—but, for the first time ever, it's packed with Proofrockers with . . . lawn chairs and blankets? Some sitting on four-wheelers. In the back, a few on snorting horses, these riders' arms crossed over their saddlehorns.

The ones who don't have thermoses of coffee lifted to their lips have shiny cans of beer or tippling glasses of wine, and at the periphery of it all, like we didn't just almost lose the town to a fire, there's kids tracing their names in the air with sparklers.

What's worse, they're all facing the same direction: the tall white wall of the dry side of Glen Dam.

I never even considered this possibility.

If you can't get a permit to show your movie, then I guess . . . this is how you do it?

Playing on the whole side of the dam, which is way huger than it needs to be for the fifty or sixty people gathered here, is that pre-show cartoony chatter that used to play before drive-in movies, which I've seen on bootleg stuff online: dancing hot dogs and concessions, warnings against "reefer," and, right when I start to look away, a throwback movie trailer.

I start to turn away, but then a date burns in over the photo of a young couple in the front seat of an old car: *March 3 1946*.

"March 24th," I say, right before the next day lands. "*The Town That Dreaded Sundown*."

I know this trailer. Because, next up, on *April 14 1946*, is Peggy Loomis, which meant a lot to me, once upon a time: she's two years before *Halloween*, is the connective tissue between its Nancy Loomis and *Psycho*'s Sam Loomis, all of them a snowball crashing onto screens nationwide in the form of Billy Loomis in 1996, who's a mental ghost-dad or something now, in 2023.

A minute into the trailer, the crowd transfixed, *Town*'s Phantom Killer's still photo comes on-screen—it's all been still so far—but then he moves, and he's one hundred percent baghead Jason, five years before that sequel.

"What the—?" I say, looking around at all the uninitiated, probably seeing this for the first time.

Right on the tail of this trailer is . . . a "Pamula Pierce Production"?

I cock my head, halfway remember this one too. Not because of Pierce, whoever she is, but because of that *spelling*. Ten seconds later, I don't need to guess anymore: *The Legend of Boggy Creek*, shit. 1972,

Alex, wherever you are. From the same era as my dad's Grand Prix. They maybe even know each other, from some drive-in down the mountain.

This trailer's all about a Bigfoot that "emits one of the most terrifying sounds ever recorded" or something? And it's all kind of . . . almost documentary, like the credits from *Night of the Living Dead* had just kept playing for three or four years, but the Bigfoot in it was camera-shy, just like Spielberg's shark.

More important, this is the movie Lana wanted to show tonight, before my stunt with the mannequins got that shut down.

I track back up that dusty finger of light splashing the *Boggy Creek* trailer up on the side of the dam, and . . . it's coming from about three-quarters of the way up the tallest pine, well behind the crowd, and that projector must have a killer-big bulb and some special, high-dollar lens, with a hidden generator or battery driving it.

It's the height of it that makes me cringe, though: it's too high for me to get to, to stop this. I could pull its cables down, maybe, but they're probably draped across the top of twenty trees to get to that projector. Even in daylight, I could search for hours, only get this movie shut off if I was lucky.

And I know by now that I'm not lucky.

"*Lethaaaaa!*" I scream instead—so much of my life is screaming— and a few heads turn my way, including two horses, but then the trailer's over, stranding us all in some deep darkness for a few breaths.

A few hoots and whoops ring out, and I imagine there's uplifted beers and thermoses and wine glasses, and—yep: a few lighters flicker on out there. And of course the sparklers are still swirling.

Is one of them Adie? Would Tiff let her play with fire like that? She *would* bring her to an illegal horror movie, so I guess that means there's not really any limits to what she will and won't do.

Then the projector flickers its light onto that great concrete screen, and—

It's the elevator from *The Shining*, opening its doors, splashing blood down-valley.

Another time, another me would have stood here and waited for it to wash down over me, absolutely thrilled. Now, here, I'm running ahead, screaming for everyone to leave, to get out of here, to go home!

In the ground beneath the soles of Bub's cowboy boots, too, I feel . . . something heavy? Are the horses rearing and slamming back down, what? Or—no, no—what if this illusion of blood slow-motioning down from those elevator doors is about to become the dam, *actually* cracking open, sweeping us all away?

Then an absolute *roar* bellows out across this open space.

One by one, all the lighters flick off.

It's *Boggy Creek*, it's *Boggy Creek*, I'm praying. The *movie* emits one of the most terrifying sounds ever recorded, which—I hate that I'm falling back on Sharona's *Last House on the Left* advice, that this is only a movie, this is only a movie.

But . . . *please* let it be only a movie? Just this once?

And then the feature presentation lights the side of Glen Dam up all at once, with a scream, baby—even punctuated by a gif of Stu saying exactly that, which . . . *The Town That Dreaded Sundown* doesn't open with him, what?

Neither does *Scream* start there.

Something's clicking in my head, though. I can't quite be sure what, but . . . yeah, yeah: a *student*, right? Asking me about using copyrighted material in her final project, and me telling her that if it's for educational purposes, and if she's not charging any kind of admission, then she should be fine.

"No," I say, and fall to my knees, my hands steepled over my mouth.

On-screen—on *dam*—is all the imagery of the coming documentary reduced to stills, then shuffled through at top-speed, only lingering on one image: Banner on the Pier, holding a chainsaw low and mean, just as a scream erupts to my left. Not from movie-terror, but something deeper, something meaner, more primal.

It's that first scream from that night in the water eight years ago, under *Jaws*.

In the glow sifting down from the opening credits, a body or part of a body goes flying, and all I can think is how paralyzed and entranced Letha must be down in that mix, seeing Banner larger than life up there.

A second scream, then a third, longer and more plaintive, like from someone whose son or daughter was just unzipped, and the title of Hettie's senior project crashes through a wall of glass on-screen, leaves those clear shards flying out at us.

The Savage History of Proofrock, Idaho.

Of course.

I have to convince my legs to run me into . . . into whatever this is.

But? Letha's here, isn't she?

All I have to do is—is zero in on Adie, crying, and then scoop her up, huddle away to hide in the trees, ride this one out. Failing that, I find Adie and somehow flag Letha down so she can become an X-Man, level this whole forest to get to her little girl.

Before Letha was a mom, she was a princess-warrior, the final girl of final girls, always doing the right thing and doing it better than anyone else could have even thought about. Now, though, with Adie in a mess in the making like this—say it, Jade: a *massacre*—now I'm pretty sure we're all going to see another side of Letha Mondragon. And she doesn't need to become some big stupid flaming bird. She just needs to strap a hunting knife to her belt high on her right waist, like a certain unfortunate little boy's mom did once, because she couldn't stop loving her son, and fighting for him even after he was drowned.

Whoever or whatever's doing this, they're at the very end of Letha's tunnel vision, and, tonight, that's a very unhealthy place to be.

Holding my good arm in front of my face because anything can be going on here, I crouch and shuffle into this. It's not how real heroes wade into the fray, but I don't have any illusions about myself. If I were really made of the good stuff? Then I use my slasher Q to anticipate that pickaxe coming for Banner and I push him out of the way, and maybe I duck that sharp point and maybe I don't.

Really, though?

I stood there. I watched it happen. And every time I'm getting coffee with Letha at Dot's for however long she can live in this place that killed her husband, her father, that pickaxe is still going to be a golden blur swinging into my peripheral vision, I know. But when I flinch and look around to it, all I'll see will be . . .

That big bear mounted there, on its pedestal?

Why am I thinking of bears?

It's that sickly sweet scent on the air, isn't it? It's what that cartoon bear in his porkpie hat is always catching, that sends him into that rapturous state. It's what I've been smelling all the way down the mountain, I think. Ever since Banner shot that Ghostface over in Terra Nova.

It's that smell that puts that bear up on twinkle toes, draws him in, and in.

I used to laugh so hard at that, before my mom left. Sometimes she would even playact like she was my dad, catching the scent of dinner on the air and floating to the table in the kitchen, a blissed-out blank look on his—*her*—face.

You can't think about that, though, Jade. It just makes everything after worse, in comparison.

Anyway, I found my own cartoons soon enough, didn't I, Sharona? Violent, operatic ones. And just like what I used to watch in the living room with my mom, these ones always work out in the end.

If only what I was in now was animated. I could erase myself a path through all the bodies rushing past the other way.

Some dude's shoulder catches me in the hip, spins me around, and then a woman with a baby carrier launches me back onto my ass, and she splashes her coffee or wine or whatever down on me when she shoves past, but—

Not coffee. Not wine.

I know what other people's blood tastes like.

"No, no," I say, trying to get my good arm under me to leverage up, not get completely stomped, but that's when the sky above me blots out all at once. My first thought is it's a last roil of smoke from the dying fire, billowing in at the least opportune time, just to up the carnage.

I also know smoke, though.

This isn't that.

In wonder—this is in half a single second, maybe?—I reach the very tipmost of the fingers of my good hand up, to swirl this darkness, and . . . it's soft, it's rough, it's plush and stiff at the same time, and it's got *depth*.

Only once in my life have I felt exactly this. It was the fifth of July, 2015, and I was up on the spine of the dam, on that little flat roof of the control booth where generations of dam keepers had been throwing their beer bottle caps. Some of them chewed deep enough into my knees that I still carry those bite marks.

I scraped them away when that momma bear galloped alongside that booth, though, ushering her cub across, to safety. I scraped that sharpness away so I could lie on my belly, reach down, let the stiff fur of her back course past my fingertips, just to confirm that this was really happening, that I wasn't just making this up in my head.

When it was real, I rolled over onto my back and stared up into the sky and—

It doesn't matter.

What does is what I'm feeling. What I'm feeling *again*: a grizzly. It's surging across me, is in a rage, is going after all the people running away. This isn't *Grizzly* anymore, either, this is *Grizzly II: Revenge*. It was supposed to have been released in 1983, beating *Jaws* to the "Revenge"-punch by four whole years, but didn't actually get all-the-way completed until a few months before I got out the last time. Because I'm kind of compulsive, it was one of the first things I dialed up when I got home, just to lose myself in the horror woods. After you've lived in a cell for four years of your life—eight, really—fast shots of rushing over the treetops are kind of the dream, are exactly what you've been waiting for, even if you're a town girl, a bad Indian.

It's not good, isn't even so bad it's good, but it is this, what's happening here: a trash bear crashes a bad-idea concert in the woods, and rampages through the crowd, bodies flying this way and that.

It's madness. It's a mosh pit with fast cuts of blood and claws.

And—is this what Lana Singleton *wanted*, showing a movie to Proofrock on Halloween? Is this *her* revenge? Just as important: this means Lemmy's footage of Hettie and Paul and Waynebo *wasn't* faked. It was so real, even, that the tape from Hettie's camera was recoverable, *playable*. Meaning . . . meaning their corpses have to be around here somewhere, for the third-reel bodydump the genre requires.

But? The "genre"? Is this even a slasher anymore, or is it a monster movie?

Lying under a bear, my fingers up in the guard hairs of its belly, that bear muzzle dripping gore, its great nostrils sucking all this madness in . . .

If the bear were wearing a hockey mask, then maybe it's a slasher, yeah. Be serious, though, Jade. No: take what you were saying *further*, slasher girl. Past the mask, to the machete. That's all this bear is, isn't it? It's Lana Singleton's machete. And the mask she's wearing, it's respectability, it's widowhood, it's motherhood, it's money.

And she can probably see it from up top of that cliff of water hanging over us all, can't she?

Imagining her up there doesn't mean I'm not still under a bear in the middle of a massacre, though. My fingers still up to feel this graceful monstrousness, my head still blossoming out to try to take this all in, think it through, the sky yawns open above me, the bear gone. It never even knew I was under it, is in enough of a killing frenzy that it's only going after the people acting like prey, not the ones too terrified to even move.

We're easy pickings later.

I sit up as best I can, look the direction the bear went, and then, from the direct opposite direction, there's a very distinct, very long roar.

From *another* bear.

Shit.

Billy just ran past me, but Stu's still over there, rampaging.

A gunshot splits the night over us all, and then another.

I come up to a knee, holding my good arm over my head again because who knows, Lana might be up on the dam Frisbee'ing plates down at us, cackling like Cruella de Vil, and I see the gout of flame when this pistol fires again.

It's Deputy Jo Ellen.

She made it across, probably got caught up in the horde coming to the movie. She's wearing a rain poncho, which kicks something familiar up in the back of my head, and she's shooting . . . up?

Not at the bears?

I look and she's shooting the movie? The *dam*?

I fall back again when I see what she's seeing: a small little form with long hair, spider-crawling through the light of Hettie's documentary, its head moving like an animal's, like an insect's, which sparks another flash of the familiar for me.

This one I can place, though: room 308W, the west wing of Pleasant Valley Assisted Living. It's how Ginger Baker moved, coming across the room to me from her perch in the deep sill of the window— well, it's how *Cinnamon* moved, but she was doing it in mimic of her sister. And it's . . . it's also how Shooting Glasses told me Greyson Brust moved, after he fell into that cave in Terra Nova, got interred in Pleasant Valley Assisted Living.

Jo Ellen's shots spark off the concrete to the left of this small form, and the kid—it *is* a kid, isn't a Chucky—changes direction, then, instead of scuttling down lower, like that senior citizen on the ceiling in *The Exorcist III*, it launches out into open space, holding its arms and legs out like a squirrel, floating down from a tree.

Jo Ellen steps up on top of somebody's cooler to be closer, shoot better, and that's when I get what I almost thought, seeing her in that rain poncho: Ghostface. From the woods. The one Banner shot in the bag it had slung over its shoulder.

Jo Ellen, though?

It can't be. I don't know much about her, but I know there's no tragic backstory. Banner told me and Letha that Jo Ellen had wanted to be a cop ever since some action-figure set her big brother had had when they were kids. And that brother's alive and well, living down in Boise.

There's no reason for her to—

I'm knocked back again, harder. You can't stand still in a storm of bodies like this and hope not to get jostled.

Trying to get up *again*, I have a perfect ground-level view of a massive maw, ripping into the rib meat of . . . is that Judd Tambor's brother? What's his name?

Doesn't matter.

The bear strings meat up from his side and finally the meat snaps. The bear holds its head back to gulp this bite in, stray rib and all, and then it steps over its kill, guarding it from—

Another bear, a *third* bear. Standing, roaring, its lips flapping.

It's maybe the loudest thing I've ever heard, and I can either smell its sweet breath or somebody brought a trash bag of honeybuns, and everybody's been stomping through them.

I roll away from this onslaught of sound and smell, praying Adie's going to just appear, I guess, and then my vision is blotted out again, by a *fourth* bear galumphing past at speed.

What the living hell? How many bears can there be at one movie?

This fourth bear lowers its head without stopping, biting hard into the forearm of an already crying first-grader I think at first is Adie, except she has white-blond hair, which I instantly feel so guilty for being thankful about.

The girl keeps on crying, her feet hitting the ground sideways about every five yards, like a doll being dragged, and in her wake, dropped from her hand that's probably not connected so well anymore, is . . . a powdered white donut?

That is what I've been smelling, the honeybuns I've been tasting on the air, but it can't just be that one donut.

And where that bear's running, it's—

"*No, Letha!*" I scream, reaching.

She's stepped right into the bear's path, is going to come at it with everything she has, never mind that it's a fight not even she can win, never mind that this isn't her daughter. It is *someone's* daughter.

Jo Ellen's still shooting up at this kid squirrel-floating down into our midst, half the world is screaming right in my ear, blood's splashing all around, the ground is thundering from bear paws, there's smoke and honeybuns on the air, and—

And then a chainsaw rips awake, tearing the night in two.

Shit, they're here too. Four chainsaws and a Halligan is exactly what this massacre needs, yes.

I tippy-toe up onto the top of some torn-in-half unfortunate to try to see where Orange Waders and the rest of them are entering this fray, and when I do, Rexall falls past me, carrying Adie with his right arm, his left hand on the ground for a step or two so he can rise, keep moving.

He's lighter on his feet than I would have given him credit for.

Go, I tell him inside, my eyes boring into his back. *Get her the fuck out of here, I'll let it all go, man, I'll forget everything, I don't care, I'll dye my hair dull orange for you for the rest of my life, I'll go topless in the sick eye of all your cameras, just go go go!*

Because Adie doesn't need to see what this bear is about to do to her mom.

What it's going to do unless . . . unless . . .

I stumble ahead with all I've got, grab the first thing my good hand finds, the neck of a spilling wine bottle, and I throw it so hard ahead of me that I bite it from the effort, but for once in my unathletic excuse of a life, either my aim is true or my heart insistent enough to *make* it true.

With my chin in the dirt, I can just see this bottle *thunk* hard into this bear's temple, actually knocking it to the side a bit, and letting the kid it was dragging roll away, her shattered arm flopping and spraying blood. The bear skids to a stop not from the hardness of my throw, though it's everything I've got, but for the annoyance of this fly that evidently needs swatting.

It lumbers up onto its hind feet, and I can see right off that this is the big boar, the undisputed boss of these woods, the silverback of this troop. It roars pure rage at me, at all of this, which is when Blue Chainsaw and White Chainsaw wade in.

White Chainsaw's chainsaw gouges into the bear's hip and it definitely feels *that*. It feels that enough that it comes around with its front paw from the other side, tears White Chainsaw's midsection open from hip to collarbone, his guts unspooling in the air almost beautifully, like slow-motion red ribbons in a clip from an opera on YouTube.

And the bear's not finished.

But Blue Chainsaw is. He drops his chainsaw, turns to run, but the bear's already lunging forward, snagging Blue Chainsaw's right hamstring with its long shiny teeth and shaking hard, like a dog with a stuffed toy, Blue Chainsaw flopping and slapping, somewhere between alive and dead.

Behind them for a frozen instant, there's Science Goggles standing there with his chainsaw. He's just looking up to the majesty of this destruction.

I don't know where Grace or Orange Waders is.

And Letha—this isn't even close to over for her. She's running hard for this now-injured bear, is just going to jump up on it, it looks like, give herself over to this violence, this killing fury, but—

The bear drops down to all fours?

It does.

Letha skids to a stop, hips back to anchor her, eyes fierce but waiting.

Instead of swiping and clawing, roaring and tearing, this big bear is . . . nosing into a bag? A sack?

I push up to see better.

Through all the madness, my eyes lock on Letha's. She shakes her head slowly about this development. It doesn't track.

Monsters don't get bored mid-massacre. Do they?

I track down to what this bear is tenderly biting into, thinking for sure it's another kid, trying to hide in their family's lawn-chair bag, I don't know, but . . . what *is* that whiteness in there? Not quite white, but beige, sort of?

Frosting? Like for a cake?

I suck breath in, sure for a bad moment that this is Cinnamon Baker's revenge, actually—that she's still killing-with-cupcakes. That she's living her name, sort of.

But then, moving exactly like Ghostface, exactly like he was moving in the woods before Banner shot him, that same figure from the Terra

Nova side of things flits past, between Letha and this giant of a bear, and snatches this bag from the bear, keeps moving, his gas mask bobbing behind his neck, now, the mountain-man beard mossed off the bottom of his face only serving to draw attention to his wet, crazed-with-grief eyes.

Seth Mullins.

He's not a ghost anymore, has flitted into this mad world with the rest of us, and the way he's snaking his body to the left so that the bear's swipe barely misses him, I can tell he's reveling in the pure *rush* of being this close to something that can kill you. Turning sideways like that doesn't slow him down for an instant, though—he's dead if he slows. And he's faster now from leaning down to snatch that bag up, keeps slipping past.

The bear looks after him like insulted, like this is some gross breach of etiquette.

Behind him, Letha's taken a knee, is pulling this girl with the nearly torn-off arm up to her, cradling her like she knows to, and the bear's snuffling for more of that frosting, which is when I get a whiff of it too.

It's the same as was hanging in the air when Banner shot Seth, over in Terra Nova. It's the same I caught on the air earlier, when this was all just starting to erupt, spill over. It's that honeybun smell, that white-donut smell.

Sugar. Sweetness.

And then, without even trying—like I have time to *think*—it comes at me all at once, what's happening here: the fire, Seth, the bears, this stupid movie at the county line. Seth Mullins, over in his fire tower, just back from his hundredth swim in the lake, gets word that his wife Francie's body's turned up after all these years, and it sends him to a bad place, where he blames Proofrock for killing her. So, wanting some of that good old-fashioned revenge, he starts the forest burning. Not because he hates the woods, he loves them, actually, they're part of him, but because . . . the *elk*, slasher girl. The elk were all massed up and running away from the flames, weren't they?

And not just them. The bears too. That's the footsteps I was stepping in, coming down here, wasn't it? Because the fire was pushing them, but also because Seth was drawing them in with this bear bait. They *are* a machete, just, he's the one wielding it, not Lana Singleton.

And of course, living out in the trees like he does, talking to the animals or whatever, Seth was the one to stumble onto the prepwork going on for this movie party. The projector, the cables, whatever test-run probably had to happen to get things centered and in focus. Seth knew Proofrock was going to be here tonight, so he whipped up a lot of that frosting and slathered it over everything here, drawing the bears in to visit some serious justice on the people his wife died defending, when she should have been growing old with him.

It's wrong thinking, but, wrong or right, the result's the same: massacre.

And it hasn't stopped yet.

A torn-off foot with about half its pasty white calf rolls up against my shin and stays there. To my right, through the din, a bear is tearing hunks of muscle up from I-don't-know-who and then snarling at another bear padding past, its great paws goofy-loose, a grin pasted on its bloody mouth, its eyes looking for another bite, another kill. Forget cocaine. All these bears need are sugar and blood—it's not just sharks and wolves that go into a feeding frenzy, evidently. With the right scent in the air, you can outdo *Grizzly II* by a fair margin, make its bodycount paltry in comparison.

Including—shit.

Tiff?

She just sat up right in the path of that bear Seth Mullins stole that bag from. And as slight as she is . . .

I wince, look away, but, when I make myself look back, the bear's snuffling the ground like trying to track where its sweets got off to.

"Tiff! Tiff!" I hiss, trying to wave her down, over.

She looks over to me like trying to figure out where she is, and—
I hate this. If she doesn't post her stupid recording, I avoid so much
headache.

But her dying-by-bear now doesn't undo that, does it?

Shaking my head no, I lower to fingertips and toes, scuttle to her
and soft-tackle her back, hold her there, our faces so close.

"J-Jade?" she says, kind of tittering a nervous laugh out.

"Why'd you bring Adie here?" I say down to her.

"Adie," Tiff says, and the way her body stiffens under mine tells
me that this girl who got me sent to jail for my senior trip is worth saving. She's worried about her charge, isn't concerned about the blood
runneling down from her hairline, outlining her sculpted left eyebrow.

"She's with Rexall," I whisper, turning my head to the side to see
if we're getting any unwanted bear attention.

Tiff bucks under me now, wants to get up to, I don't know: fight
Rexall for Adie?

I hug her down with my whole body, and nod to her that it's good
she's at the sheriff's office, she's got the right kind of heart, and I hope
her next boss is as good as the last.

Like she can get any of that. She has to feel the hug, though. From
me, her mortal enemy.

"Stay, stay," I tell her maybe ten seconds later, and push up,
holding her shoulders with my hands until she nods that she will, she
won't move.

"Are you going to get her?" she asks, her eyes welling up. "I told—
I told Ban she'd be okay, that I had her, I—I . . ."

I look back to her about this.

"If anybody can," she says, her chin pruning, "it's you, Jade. It's
always been you."

"I'll find her," I say, and roll off, look around before prairie-
dogging up.

I had the idea I'd been down with Tiff long enough for things to die down some.

Wrong.

Same melee, same killing field, same massacre.

I wheel around for Letha, see instead a small boy wafting down from the sky, the air whooshing up along the dry face of the dam evidently enough that it's taken him this long to get down here. Or maybe he latched onto the concrete, just watched for a while like Spider-Man, I don't know.

This close, too, I can see that it's for sure Jan Jansson. Hettie's missing little brother. He's dirty and there's black veins under the skin all around his mouth and eyes, and his long hair's shaggy and matted, his hands black with blood, probably Phil Lambert's, maybe Carl Duchamp's, and he's got no shirt to speak of, just a rag barely hanging on, and I don't think he's exactly made of meat anymore. Something less substantial.

His eyes, though, they're the thing.

This is what Shooting Glasses meant when he said Greyson Brust wasn't going to be needing his name anymore: Jan's not there. He's dead inside, gone, is only hunger, now.

Where he lands, moving just a fraction too slow, like he's a doll, or a bug, is on the shoulders of that big boar that was just muzzle-deep into the frosting, so its snout is all white and sweet.

The bear swirls up from this unwanted contact. It swipes up and behind it, but Jan's so little, is hanging on so tight. And his face, it's right alongside the bear's, because—

He wants that frosting? Is that a thing? Why would a little dead kid be into sweets? What could turn him onto that? He should be after blood, or brains, or just slaughter and carnage.

But what he wants is . . . something sweet?

To get it, he brings his little arms around, twists this giant bear's head to the side, audibly cracking it over, the bear starting to collapse under him from a broken neck. Jan doesn't stop there, either. With the bear timbering over, Jan keeps pulling, straining, until, right when the bear slumps all the way over, its head pops right off, geysering blood up in huge red gouts.

Jan holds the head, touches that white sweetness with his own nose, then, like stacking blocks, sets the head on the bear's chainsawed hip, moving it this way and that until it balances, stays.

At which point a woman comes stumbling out of the dust and screaming, falls to her knees, screaming herself, but not with terror. With joy.

Mrs. Jansson. Or—divorce, divorce, Jade: *Ms.* Jansson. Or whatever her maiden name is, was, I don't know, and it doesn't matter. What does is that she's opening her arms for her little boy to run into them, she's rushing to him, she's not thinking of anything else but her little treasure, who's been gone so long, he must be so *scared*.

"Navene, no!" Letha screams, holding that hurt little girl to her.

Navene Jansson, then. How does Letha, a transplant, know my town better than I do?

Jan considers Navene Jansson and dismisses her in the same moment, turns to the side to walk past her on his businesslike little legs, but his mom pulls him to her instead, hugging him so tight, all her tears coming out at once.

Jan looks down to her shoulder, to this odd thing happening to him, and, moving very deliberately, like she's not worth the contact, he brings his little left elbow back, to—

"No, no, no!" I scream, rushing for them, but I don't even come close to making it in time.

Jan thrusts his left hand right through her chest, his fist gripped around her glistening spine, its milky fluid spurting out not in heartbeats, but like . . . I saw my dad working on the windshield-wiper sprayer on my mom's car once. When it came loose from its nozzle, it thrashed around, kind of shooting wiper fluid, but kind of just leaking it, too. This is like that. But Navene Jansson's spine's still connected to her skull enough that it pulls her head down into her shoulder some, too, making the skin of her neck bulge out like a frog's, and her tongue shove out from her mouth like a desperate slug, trying to escape this sinking ship.

It's 1968 again all over, and a little kid's killing a mom, and we're all just watching in wonder, Mr. Romero.

Letha screams, I guess I'm still screaming, a horse is lying on its side screaming, everyone else is screaming, and then a *blast* shuts it all up at once.

Jo Ellen.

She pulls her trigger again but her cylinder's empty. The barrel's wisping a curl of smoke up before her, and she can't seem to lower her pistol, and there's practically a dotted line from it to the new hole in the back of Jan Jansson's head. My guess is that, over the top of that pistol, Jo Ellen can see the ragged tunnel she just blasted through this little boy's brains.

Jan wavers on his small legs, extends his arms like to balance, and then Navene falls forward, onto him, and even in death she's still hugging him, because that's how moms are, they just keep forgiving, they just keep believing, and hoping.

Twenty feet past him, Jo Ellen falls to her knees, jolting the pistol loose, and even from this distance I can see she's hyperventilating, that—that she's never shot anybody, has never had to draw her weapon in the line of duty, and now she's . . . she's had to blow a hole in a kid's *head*, because he just killed his own mother with his little hands.

It's too much.

She starts to fall over the rest of the way, but Seth Mullins, in his gas mask and poncho, that sack of frosting slung over his shoulder, steps out, holds her shoulder enough to keep her from tilting forward.

And then he looks up at what he's wrought, here.

For maybe four seconds, he's at the eye of this swirling storm of blood. Finally, he looks away from it, down to this female deputy just like his wife, who probably just cashed in all her coming happiness to keep the community safe.

Like Francie Mullins did.

I can see every step of this on Seth's pained face. His eyes fill, spill down his cheeks into the leaf-matted tangle of his beard, and all at once he sucks air in, like just waking from a death dream, Bob Clark.

That's 1974, Alex, wherever you are.

Seth shakes his head no, then, that this isn't what he wanted, this isn't what he meant. He steps away from Jo Ellen after doing that kind of pat on her shoulder that means he's got this, this isn't on her anymore.

A bear gallops past between the two of them and me, holding a bloody arm in its mouth, the fingers still writhing, and the first step Seth takes is a stumble, because this creek bottom is littered with the dead.

He falls to a knee and fingertips. He lowers his face, shaking his whole head no slowly, and then he's nodding, either with decisiveness or to clear his head, get himself steeled for whatever this is about to be. When he stands again, it's with resolve. He peels the gas mask up and over, lets it trail from his fingers, then he strips the poncho off as well, lets it fall.

He's Billy Sole standing on that fallen-down tree deep in the jungle of life, cutting his own chest and staring his own death down, daring it to come for him.

I nod with him, because this is maybe the one thing I believe in in the whole world: that when it's your time, you don't run from it—you stand against it, you keep your eyes open, and you rip and claw the whole way down, hope you can at least be a worthy trophy.

It's what I fell in love with with final girls, with Laurie and Nancy, Sid and Ripley, all of them from the scream queens up to now, to Sam and Allyson, to Tree and Bee and Millie.

It's what I love about Letha.

And it's happening right now with Seth Mullins. After losing his gas mask, his poncho, he hooks a finger in the neck of his shirt and tears it away easy as anything, baring his narrow, pale chest.

But he needs that skin: watching the dwindling madness for bears, he lowers to his bag, rummages his left hand in, and comes out goopy with frosting, or whatever that shit is.

He smears it across his chest from shoulder to hip, and then he dips again, slathers his shoulders, his arm, his other arm, then the thighs of his game warden pants. Then, for warpaint—he might be a bad guy, but he's a pretty good Indian—his face, which he has to close his eyes for but it doesn't matter. He's all gummed up, the frosting's heated up from contact with him, is melting—

Which is when Science Goggles steps in, leading with his goggles, holding them by their strap. Seth Mullins takes them, clears his eyes, and settles those plastic goggles on, stands a different person.

Science Goggles cases the place for danger, backs off. You don't live to his age by being some idiot, do you?

Then, just like Seth is wanting, a juvenile bear pads in for this amazing *scent*.

The juvenile tastes the air, makes the connection to this meatsack standing in front of him, and huffs its threat out.

Seth Mullins huffs back, knows this language.

When the bear charges, Seth turns, is lighter on his feet than any Ghostface ever was, is already swivelhipping away, somehow keeping ahead of this young bear who's all legs and teeth and hunger.

Two more bears fall in behind the juvenile, and then a third— a big sow I'm seeing for the first time—clomps in, the ground shaking with her heavy run.

Seth Mullins splashes through the creek, the silver spray hanging all around him.

The teen-bear runs through it, making small work of the water, and then the other bears are crossing as well.

Run, brother, I say in my head to Seth, and then someone touches my shoulder lightly, with just her fingertips.

Letha, standing beside me. I hook my good hand into the waist of her jeans, haul myself up alongside. She's holding this little girl whose arm's hardly attached anymore. It's wrapped in some make-do bandage Letha's managed, and the girl's checked out, unconscious or in shock.

I would be. I should be. We *all* should be.

"Ade?" Letha asks, not really wanting the answer.

I have so little idea what I can possibly say, here.

"She's . . ." I start, hoping I figure it out but mostly just squinting my eyes like tracking my answer, disappearing in the distance. "She's okay, not hurt," I finally manage to get out. "Rexall—she's with him."

Letha recoils, her shoulders hunching around her chest, her left hand coming up to cover her mouth.

She clamps onto my forearm, and the way she looks at me, into me . . . no way do I ever have kids. This is a kind of terror I can't even comprehend.

"Where's Tiffany?" she asks, not aware how hard her fingers are gouging into me.

I turn to Tiff, sitting down now, hugging her knees and sobbing. Letha nods, already all business, and passes this half-dead little girl over to me. I take her, work her comfortable, and Letha's running for Tiff, to shake her, interrogate her.

It's not her fault, I sort of want to say.

Letha knows that, though. At some dim level. She's intense enough right now to brain a girl and not even break stride, but she would never unleash like that on someone who didn't deserve it.

I think. Hope.

Instead of watching how it falls out, I drift over to the abandoned bag of bear bait, peer in at all this frosting. It does smell so delicious. I've got my eyes closed to breathe that sweetness in when the speakers crackle, straightening my back.

Like a newborn, I look up to the movie still playing on the side of the dam.

It's Jan Jansson sitting on a swing in the park, his mouth dusted white, his tongue blipping out to dab some of that in—it's obviously confectioner's sugar. I nod, sort of get his sugar jones, I guess, and . . . shit, of course. He was there the night the Angel of Indian Lake wrenched Greyson Brust's head off, wasn't he? After Greyson Brust clawed up from his own grave like all those lake-dead? That's where Jan got his sweet tooth, and the whole decapitation thing.

Nick of time again, I tell myself, because I'm some detective: always solving the case after it doesn't matter anymore.

Panning up from Jan on that swing set, though, up on the tippy-top spine of the dam, maybe forty yards over from the control booth, another mystery's standing there, his silhouette inkier than the black sky behind him.

My first thought, the one I think without thinking, is that this is a Shoshone from the bow and arrow days, like Hardy used to say appeared all at once over on this side of the lake, when it was filling.

One of them coming back now, what would that even mean?

But then this Shoshone's head is . . . wrong.

Not that Indians can't wear cowboy hats—*I* was wearing one, earlier tonight, and I bet Cross Bull Joe did as well, back in Christine Gillette's day—but something about this brim, it doesn't look cowboy, it looks . . . it looks *metal*. As fuck.

"Lemmy?" I say. The *English Rose* is up there somewhere, balancing on that tall cliff of water, and Lemmy was the one throwing that floating marquee up there to get everybody here. Meaning . . . he knew about this? He's part of it?

But, from all the way up there, can he even see this massacre?

I jump, wave my arms, one of them singing with pain, but I'm just an ant down here, I know. Less than that. *"Lemmmmy!"* I scream anyway, because you've got to try, and because I want it not to be him, please. Sure, Billy and Stu were in high school, but this isn't that movie, this is one of my students.

One who was standing right by the house where a drug dealer lost his head.

I slow my waving arms, just watching him, not wanting to have to believe this.

"Lemmy?" I say, mostly to myself, not able to look away from him. Looking all the way up there, it means I'm not paying the right kind of attention to where I am. And it's because I'm already looking—the only one of any of us down here looking, I bet—that I cue into his silhouette getting so much crisper all at once, and limned in blue like he's wearing a jetpack. No, no, wrong genre, Jade. The blue glow swelling up behind him, it's pure *Fire in the Sky*: the aliens are in the trees, on the lake.

Good, part of me wants to say. Not because they'll do better with the Earth than humans, but because, with their technology and off-world viruses and entitlement—they *found* this planet, nobody even knew it *existed*—they'll re-enact on America what America did to *us*, because we don't even count as people, to them. Not when there's riches to be looted.

What does that Klingon say in that space movie I only fast-forwarded through in high school to see the original of Michael Myers's mask? "Cry havoc, and let slip the dogs of war"?

Cry havoc, America.

But then that blue glow isn't the spaceship I sort of want, it's sweeping past him somehow, it's . . . shit.

A giant *shark*? In an instant, I clock the lifeless design—*Jaws 3-D*, anybody would recognize it—but the reason it's lifeless is that, this time, it's made of glowing drones.

This is Lemmy's fleet, finally choreographed like he wanted on the Fourth.

This is his big, unfunny joke on Proofrock. To him it's a gift he worked on so many hours, not the trigger for our collective trauma. But, I have to remind myself, he wasn't in the water that night, only read about it later, when his mom let him.

I scold myself for giving him chance after chance in my head, when he has to be involved with all this somehow—giving second chances is inviting your abuser in for coffee, so you can talk things through—but . . . the way he was protecting me at Phil's? The way he stepped in front of me in seventh period yesterday, protecting me from Harrison and Banner?

It can't be him. I won't let it be him.

Just—the things that are funny and good to him, they're not funny and good to the rest of us, so much.

That's how it is when you're seventeen. Case in point: me. And Holmes and Hardy giving me chance after chance, when no way was I even close to worth it, when all I did each time was take advantage, always counting the days until my next big prank, until I could get my revenge on this place I hated.

I'm sorry, Mr. Holmes. Sheriff.

And, thank you, sirs.

You didn't have to believe in me. You *shouldn't* have. I gave you so many reasons not to. The Girl Impossible to Hug—I know that's who I was.

It didn't mean I didn't need one.

So, no, Lemmy isn't involved. He probably thinks we're all down here awash with wonder, smiling in spite of ourselves that there's this impossible *shark* in the sky.

"Thank you," I mumble, just for him, teacher to student, and then that dotted-outline of this shark passes around him, that blue glow absorbing him for a moment that takes my breath away, because I'm sure he's got some bad-idea plan to ride in that shark like a balloon, like he's being digested by the light.

I fall back, stumble trying to see this moment in all its splendor.

I come up with my left hand and forearm slathered in Seth Mullins's homemade bear bait but who cares, the bears are gone.

By the time I look back up to Lemmy, the shark is plummeting down the face of the dam, the drone fleet probably pre-programmed, and, thankfully, Lemmy's silhouette's still up there, his face under that brim glowing from the phone he's watching this all through.

It looks better from here, though, I know. It has to.

Diving, the drones that make the shark up are shouldering each other for room. It bumps the shark larger by a size or three, and then it completely disappears for a long second, washed out in the dusty finger of light that's *The Savage History of Proofrock, Idaho.*

Or—it doesn't go away. Not quite. The light from the projector's only stripping the blue glow from the fleet. Their tiny robot selves are still hurtling down in that same formation, giving us a glimpse of the cybernetic endoskeleton of this shark, its shadow monstrous and indistinct against Hettie's documentary before the shark sheathes itself in that blue glow again, and turns sharply at the treeline.

It swooshes out over what was supposed to be heads of the audience, rapt on their movie on this Halloween night.

I back up a bit, can't help it—the shark's still stiff, isn't pivoting side to side like a real shark swims—and see, improbably, someone a few feet ahead of me holding her black gloved hand up, so their fingers can feel this magical rush. I can tell she's a her because, reaching up like that, her hip cocks out like dudes can't really pull off so well. Or maybe it's something with how her back curves when her arm lifts?

Instead of watching the shark, I find myself fixed on who here would want to touch this shark enough to reach up for it like this. Who here but me, years and years ago.

It untethers me for a moment, because if I'm over there, reaching up for the grail, then who am I here, watching this? Have the last eight years really been the eight seconds after I opened my wrist out on the town canoe back when? This whole time, has my heart been pumping the last of my life down into the water while my brain tries to hold onto living by dropping me into slasher cycle after slasher cycle? Am I in *Jacob's Ladder* here? The UK version of *The Descent*? Am I Anna Paquin at the end of the director's cut of *Darkness*?

I'm holding my breath, I guess. Waiting for reality to flip this way or that way, like a fish flopping on shore. Drowning in open air, its mouth opening and closing with no sound.

My mouth, I mean.

Whoever this is, she's all in black, like she collected Seth Mullins's castoff rain poncho, against this rain of blood.

Except—there's some sparkle to that poncho?

My face goes cold. My whole body goes cold.

"No," I say, taking an involuntary step back.

But yes.

I know that sparkle. It's from a Father Death robe.

When whoever this is turns around, the long white Ghostface mask matches the robe, which should send me screaming down a tunnel in my head, because this has to be something I made up, a place I've chosen to live in instead of here, because everybody I know keeps dying.

But . . . *What?*

It is Ghostface, but it's the Ghostface with that *Scary Movie* tongue coming down from the mouth. Like . . . no, no please.

It's like the first set of masks Sharona got for us to do our sessions in. I never even asked what she did with them after they were laughably wrong, either. I just assumed that stupid mistakes turn to ash the moment we look away from them, I guess.

Wrong.

"Who?" I say, weakly, not really wanting an answer.

This Ghostface is looking right at me, right into who I really am, and waiting for this all to come together.

It won't, though. It isn't.

I shake my head no, and this Ghostface takes a step closer, like to help me figure this out. She even cocks her head over to study me—Michael, fascinated with this high schooler he just pinned to the wall with that big knife.

And then I see why the curve of her back or the angle of her hips when she was reaching was exaggerated enough for me to clock her even inside that robe: the hand she wasn't holding up, it's gripped onto the top of a *cane?*

Like someone in an old-time dance number, she brings her other hand around to the top of that cane, so it's right in front of her.

"Who are you?" I call across, one hundred percent ready to turn, run for all I'm worth.

In response, this Ghostface shrugs, looks to some commotion to her left—a ratty paint horse, clopping in—then back to me.

"Here," she says, her voice raspy and familiar, but I'm not quite placing it yet. What she's doing is using her left hand to pinch the crown of this mask, and peel it off.

Underneath, like a shampoo commercial, are *yards* of silky smooth platinum blond hair. *Sharona* hair. Instead of looking her in the eye, through the masks we wear, I always spiral down her curls.

She shakes her gorgeous locks like luxuriating to finally have them free, and when they swish past around behind her, to tumble down her shoulders in a way I know so well—

Her face is *painted* like Ghostface. Which is something I've never seen in all my years on the video shelf. When Jason loses his goalie face, he's wicked under there. When Laurie pulls Michael's mask off, he's so much prettier than his actions. When Tina pulls Freddy's face off, he's an animatronic skull.

"You were asking for an episode of *When Animals Attack?*" she says with a grin, holding my eyes, her voice still throaty.

"You're . . . you're not Sharona," I tell her, dialing back through every session we've had at Founders Park. There wasn't any cane then, but . . . she was always sitting in that swing when I got there, wasn't she? And also when I slouched away, the session over. The cane, if there was a cane, could have been buried down in the gravel, couldn't it have been?

That hair, though. All that untouchable blondness.

"*Ginger Baker?*" I say, all the breath leaving my body.

But it can't be. I *felt* the screwdriver jammed into her ear.

Then time slows down so I can realize why this hair's so pretty, so perfect: it's *new*.

She's had four years to grow it.

"Cinnamon," I say, in something a lot like wonder.

She curtsies the most proper curtsy in the history of curtsies, sweeping that Ghostface mask ahead of her.

Cinnamon fucking Baker, goddamn.

When she was *being* Ginger in room 308 back in 2019, she told me that her sister "Cinnamon" was on this big revenge arc against me, for facilitating the deaths of her parents, and had been planning to frame me for all the high schoolers she was killing.

Dark Mill South messed all that up, gave her more heroic options— gave her the chance to play the final girl on the big stage—which sort of seriously backfired, breaking her back, but . . . at her level, I guess you can just order up a new spine? Don't forget that that girl who got hit by the bus in *Mean Girls* is up and walking at prom, in a brace.

Stupider shit happens every day.

And Cinnamon Baker is most definitely the meanest of the mean girls.

No, slasher girl, it wasn't Lana Singleton, it hasn't *been* Lana Singleton. Once again, you've indicted Terra Nova with no real evidence, only suspicions, and what probably boils down to prejudice. No, Lana maybe doesn't love you or this town, but that doesn't mean she's out to destroy it either, does it? Maybe, to her, proposing that movie was actually supposed to have started a healing process? Was supposed to be some "no harm, no foul" thing?

Doesn't matter.

What does is that, standing here with her face painted Ghostface white and black, is a scared little girl I met in the hall of a yacht, eight years ago. This is that same cheerleader who jammed that screwdriver into her sister's ear because she'd become dead weight, then stepped through the broken window of a video rental place to go toe-to-toe with the worst serial killer in America's bloody history.

"Your voice," I say then, putting the pieces together.

Cinnamon shrugs like caught, so what.

Sharona told me that her voice was like that from bronchitis compounded by asthma, all started with her father's icky cigars. But what it's really from, I can tell now, and should have clocked all along, is the butt of a shovel catching her in the throat four years ago.

"Your dad didn't die in a boating accident," I manage to get out.

"An accident on a boat, whatever," Cinnamon says back.

"It's been you this whole time?" I have to say.

Cinnamon shrugs, proud of herself.

"Keep it," she says, about the rags of the TMNT shirt I'm wearing, which is when I re-hear what she said to me once upon a session, about Jason Voorhees: "hockey mask and sticks"—*plural* sticks.

Which Jason never had. But that goalie who was friends with the Turtles always had a few on him, didn't he?

She was telling me all along. While I was baring my soul to her, squeezing the chains of my swing hard so I wouldn't leak tears, melt into the wimp I knew she wanted me to be—the clay she needed me to be, to shape this ending from.

"What did you do with her?" I ask.

"Who?" she says back.

"Dr. Watts."

Cinnamon just pooches her lips out to show how boring all these details are to her.

"This is yours?" I say, opening my arms to all this.

"More than a girl could have hoped for," she says back, lowering her painted face but looking up to me. "Who invited the *bears*, though?"

In answer, she nods down to my hand, coated in bear bait.

"No," I say.

But yes: Cinnamon raises her phone, snaps a guilty picture of me.

"*No!*" I scream at her then, eight fucking *years* welling up in me all at once like lava, and I feel more than see Letha turn around at this. She's still on her knees with Tiff, trying to get whatever information about Adie there is to get.

"'Not *again?*'" Cinnamon, so chipper and bulletproof, says for me about her right hand waggling this new snapshot up by her shoulder. Taunting me with it.

"*It wasn't me!*" I lean forward to scream at her, my hands balled into fists by my legs, and then I'm rushing her without even telling myself to. She's taller than me, younger than me, definitely tougher than me—I'd have never made it from my hospital bed to the chair, much less to my own two feet—but she doesn't know what I'm fighting against, here: jail.

Not again. Never again.

I'm maybe five lunging steps from Cinnamon when she pulls her cane up like to block my approach. But she also . . . leaves it there? How can she both be holding it and it be falling away?

Because what she's done is pull a long, narrow blade up *from* the cane.

Fuck it. I'm so past caring.

I lean in harder, reaching for her with my good arm, to throttle her and not stop throttling her, never mind what that blade's going to be doing inside my chest, the way she's holding it there, waiting for me to spear myself on it.

I make it to her chest, my hand sliding up to her face to claw her eyes out, use her hair like handles to slam her head to mush against the ground, and I'm going to be biting as well, I can tell, who cares about the tip of her knife pricking the hollow of my throat, it doesn't matter if I live, it only matters that she dies, and I'm about to finally get that done when—

Letha's flying tackle slams me to the side, and she's already twisting when she hits me, so my throat twists away from that knife.

"Noooo!" I scream the whole slow-motion way to the ground, my throat stinging from whatever damage it took, my fingers open wide and reaching back but it's useless. Letha's got me.

We roll to a stop and I'm already fighting up to wade back in, but Letha won't let me, and now Cinnamon's standing over us, using her non-knifed-up hand to dab at this bait I left on her, give it an exploratory sniff.

"Smells like a certain golf bag, doesn't it, Leeth?" she says, and actually licks the bait the slightest bit.

"Fuck you," Letha says, letting me go all at once to step into this herself, her eyes even harder than her words.

"She not tell you?" Cinnamon says so innocently around Letha, to me. "It was her daddy dearest who was pissed at Mr. Samuels that day, that whole *week*, really, so . . ." She shrugs, plops her whole finger into her Ghostface mouth, her eyes wide like she's *also* so shocked by Theo Mondragon being a killer.

When Letha looks back to me to see if I'm buying this, I have to look away. It makes me feel like the worst traitor ever.

"It doesn't matter," I hiss. "Long time ago."

"What's done is done, right?" Cinnamon adds, stepping closer. "But he also *really* didn't like that little plane flying over our houses, did he? Almost as much as he didn't like anybody seeing him shoot at that little plane . . ."

"*Shut your mouth!*" Letha screams, actual saliva misting from her mouth, and when she's about to rush Cinnamon just like Cinnamon's wanting—like she's *baiting*—I lunge forward, hug Letha's hips from the back, drag her down with me.

She bucks and pulls, is for sure going to shake me off, which is when Cinnamon steps in, leading with her long skinny blade. She can pin us both like butterflies, here, and call it a night, fade into the trees, never have been at this cute little student film out in the woods.

She doesn't get to win, though. Not like that.

I heave Letha over so I'm on top—my weight's finally good for something—and then I straighten my arms, trying to get enough distance between us that that stupid blade at least won't be able to reach Letha, but—

The burning heat of the stab doesn't come? Even though I'm arching my back in from it, and biting my teeth together so hard, eyes squinted in anticipation of how hot that coldness is going to be, splashing out from my chest?

I peer around, expecting that big needle to run right through my eye.

Instead—it's Tiff!

She's got one arm around Cinnamon's neck. Her other arm's got Cinnamon's blade-hand wrenched around behind her back.

"You can't just *do* this," Tiff's saying, and crying.

"If you know what's good for you, small-town girl, you'll let me—"

The reason she doesn't finish is it was a ruse, a distraction: mid-sentence, she straightens her stronger-than-they-should-be legs hard, all at once. Because she's taller than Tiff, who's not short, it throws both of them up and back.

Letha and me both surge towards this, to, I don't know, to save Tiff I guess, but neither of us makes it in time.

We both stand there, chests heaving, trying to make sense of this: Cinnamon's own cane-dagger is standing up from her open mouth. Because, when Tiff used whatever police training she had to get Cinnamon's arm twisted up behind her, she forgot that one important thing: disarming the perp.

Tiff crabcrawls out from under Cinnamon, is shaking her head no, no, that's not what she wanted, not what she meant, and—

Cinnamon Baker isn't dead.

Both her hands are flaying themselves on that blade, trying to pull it through, push it back.

Over about ten seconds, though, her hands slow, fall to the side.

Her eyes are still open, staring straight up.

"I should have been there for her more," Letha says, "better, I mean," and falls to her knees, palms up in something like supplication. Or, offering her wrists up as payment, for not having shepherded Cinnamon Baker through her grief better.

Never mind her own surgeries, her own grief.

I settle down beside her, pull her to me.

All around us, people are moaning and crying, and I only wish that some of this was new to me.

Up on the side of the dam, it's just Paul's motorcycle now, probably eighty feet tall.

Its long seat's empty. Nobody to ride it anymore.

I close my eyes, swallow, and pull Letha closer. She's racked with sobs, has *become* crying, is beyond hurting.

"Where is she, where is she?" she's sort of saying. "She's not going to be like—she's not going to be like—"

Like Jan.

"We need—" I say, and work Letha's phone up from her pocket, stand to dial 976-EVIL, and am about to do the 911 thing when . . .

Letha's Instagram alerts avalanche down from the top of the screen, are so cheery and hopeful, so completely unaware of where we are right now.

I swipe them away, but one stops me.

Tiff's account?

I sneak a look up to Letha but she's not really here anymore. I look around to Tiff but she's checked out, waiting for the world to make sense.

I tap the "Tiff" in the banner and it drops me to her feed, her wall, whatever it's called. What's playing is the last thing she shot: Rexall, holding Adie to his chest, hunching away like the most guilty human ever.

Behind him, a massive bear is crashing in, leaving pure destruction in its path.

And then, and then—

And then the video goes upside down and every which direction at once. Because Tiff, whom I love and love and will never stop loving for this, she's tossed her phone to Adie.

Adie, either with her mom's final girl reflexes or her dad's tight-end reflexes, or just because she doesn't know she shouldn't be able to do this, she snatches the phone easy as anything with her small hands, and the last thing is her small face so close to the camera, and then that phone's being tucked between her and Rexall, I think, to automatically post its video.

I rise to my knees in absolute worship of this amazing device I'm holding up before me.

"What?" Letha says.

I turn to her, my breath heaving in and out.

"Jo, Jo Ellen," Letha says, surging us both to our feet.

We find Jo Ellen together.

She's blank, gone, hiding inside herself.

Letha shakes her awake.

Jo Ellen swims up through the murky waters she's drowning in, finally sees us.

"Sheriff, sheriff, we need the sheriff," she's saying, sort of. Like what's on repeat in her head is finally finding its way to her lips.

"You all track each other, don't you?" Letha says, holding the phone up as exhibit 1.

"What?" Jo Ellen says.

"Banner told me!" Letha says. "He said you, that you—"

Jo Ellen shrugs like oh yeah, like remembering.

She reaches behind her, works her own phone up—she's just in panties and a bra, under that poncho. Because she swam across, of course.

But her phone's dry. And it smells like peanut butter.

"Code?" Letha demands.

When Jo Ellen just stares blankly at us, at nothing, Letha holds the front camera up to Jo Ellen's face.

Her phone unlocks.

"Find my . . ." Letha mutters, looking for the app. Then, "Please please please."

I get it, finally: Banner and his deputies, they track each other's phones, so they always know where they all are.

It makes sense. But, is the front office in that friends-circle?

"Adie," Letha says then, weakly, blubbering it sort of, crying with gratitude, and holds the phone out for Jo Ellen and me.

"T. Koenig" is a light green blinking cursor out in the woods, moving.

This isn't over, no.

I guess it never really is, around here.

BAKER SOLUTIONS

Report of Investigation
17 October 2023
#39a42
re: Compulsory notice

As Cinnamon Baker, daughter of Mars Baker and Macy Todd (both deceased) and research associate for (and owner of) Baker Solutions, is now boarding indefinitely on the *English Rose*, and has perhaps been working remotely from there since 8 August 2023, we will presume from this date forward that her absence from assigned research, interview, transcription, and fact-checking duties serves as her notice of resignation—thus this intercalaric notification. Ms. Baker has been notified of this as well. We apologize for any inconvenience associated with her presence, and are rescinding any balances associated with work she produced in the continuing investigation of Jennifer Elaine "Jade" Daniels. Be aware that any of Ms. Baker's actions or statements are solely her responsibility, and that she neither speaks for nor acts in the stead of Baker Solutions, Baker Legal, or Baker Enterprises, Inc., including any and all subsidiaries and contractors.

As to the integrity of the reports Ms. Baker had input on before her exit, an internal investigation has confirmed that, until the date of her official departure (14 October 2023), her work was incisive, thorough, and accurate. Her first-hand knowledge of both the Indian Lake Massacre and Dark Mill South's "Reunion Tour" was extremely beneficial, as well as her controlling input on RoIs #04a49, #25a11, #29a27, #32d43, # 66b12, and #41a03. And please note that in no way should Ms. Baker's resignation suggest impropriety or liability on her or Baker Solutions' part. As non-active owner, she can come and go at will. And of course she was vetted and bonded before being granted limited access to any and all investigations and associated documents. In addition, she was processed through the necessary training sessions relating to legal obligations and privacy. She is also, insofar as concerns the product or discovery of any investigation she was involved in or had access to, constrained by Baker Solutions' standard suite of non-disclosure agreements, the drafting of which was initially overseen by her father Mars Baker. In short, your privacy, including but not limited to your identity as a client of Baker Solutions, has not nor will it be compromised by Ms. Baker exploring other avenues of personal and professional interest.

As for Ms. Baker's intended stay in Proofrock (2 August 2023– 7 August 2023) and her subsequent/necessary lodging with you, as Trail's End Motel isn't equipped with ramps and other necessary accoutrements (their limited website clearly states otherwise), the balance for those seven (7) days/nights is being deducted from any future invoices. In addition, negative online reviews and ratings have been submitted en masse (Yelp, Tripadvisor, Disabled Hotel Review, etc.) concerning Trail's End Motel's accessibility issues. Ms. Baker should not have been forced to endure this indignity upon her return, and Baker Solutions is doing everything in our field of capabilities to ensure no one else encounters the same difficulty, up to and including funding the installation of ADA-mandated equipage.

As for any "triggers" or specifics of the assignment that prompted Ms. Baker to transition away from the investigation, that's beyond the scope of this compulsory notice, as would be any photographic evidence establishing Ms. Baker on the *English Rose* or header information confirming the location from which she was submitting her reports and evaluations. As far as Baker Solutions is concerned, Ms. Baker's work was, until the date of her departure, strictly objective, and motivated only by her stated and earnest desire to understand how investigations "worked," an interest she claimed was sparked by various true-crime podcasts of recent years.

As for Ms. Baker's request for our digital forensics unit to secure access to and/or supply the video feed from the Wi-Fi or Bluetooth network supplying support to the various drones (both airborne and submersible) in operation around Proofrock, Indian Lake, Terra Nova, Deacon Point, Temporary Research Islet H-G ("Treasure Island"), and Glen Dam, as this request came in *after* Ms. Baker had failed to return from her temporary duty assignment, this request was declined. Though we would suggest anyone running such drones in Pleasant Valley confirm their network security settings, lest their video feed lose the privacy it presumes and/or requires [see our website's FAQ for recommendations on network settings and/or subscription services].

Again, apologies for the circumstances compelling this singular communication. This is neither common practice at Baker Solutions, nor will our new screening procedures allow its repetition. Please direct Ms. Baker to us if questions arise concerning the cessation of her involvement with this investigation.

THE LAST RITUAL

I t's not even midnight yet.

    Standing in this killing field, my chest heaving, that's what I keep thinking: It's not even midnight, is it? For a lot of these dead, I guess it never will be. It'll always be Halloween, for them. Hettie's documentary will always be flickering on that pale concrete. A horse will always be screaming.

For those of us left, though, there's still so much darkness to get through.

"Leeth!" I call out.

She's bounding away, has to find Adie.

When she doesn't stop, I turn my voice up loud enough that it makes my right ear, or what's left of it, throb. The canyon gouging through my temple and scalp getting *to* my ear is oddly numb, though, even when the fingers of my good hand spider around its ragged edges without me really telling them to, like feeling on a present for where the seam is, so I can unwrap it.

If I do that, though, it's just my grinning skull that rolls out.

"*Leeeetha!*" I scream now, my voice kind of breaking at the end. I fall to one knee from the effort, want to just keep going, lie there on my side in the bloody center of all this, my knees drawn up to my chest so first aid can find me. First aid and antibiotics and my pills and a thousand and one cigarettes.

But first I've got to make it through right now.

Letha's somehow back to me already—her final girl radar heard my shriek, thought I was in danger. She lowers herself, her hand on my left shoulder, the kind of touch that tells me she's here, her eyes probing mine.

"*What*, Jade?" she asks.

The sharpness in her tone is because I'm keeping her from Adie, I know.

"We need something, don't we?" I tell her. "To . . . because he's, he's—"

Because he's Rexall. I remember him slinging Banner and Lonnie through the snow like ragdolls four years ago. How light and nothing they were to him, this linebacker, this mechanic. And this after Letha had peppered him with a shotgun. And in minus-whatever temperature it was.

Letha's bad-ass, no doubt, and her solid gold maternal instinct to never run, only fight fight fight tooth and nail, that pretty much doubles her mass, gives her more muscles, and her grit and love will take her even further than that. But still. What if Rexall just backhands her to the side like nothing, leaving me to try to take him down?

I'm not sure I could. Yeah, I got lucky with Stacey Graves, and with Dark Mill South. I had the lake and Ezekiel for Stacey Graves, though, and the more I think about Dark Mill South, I wonder if what let me kill him was Banner's big black jacket billowing around me like the Black Robes he probably knew when he was a helpless kid, however many generations ago. Rexall, though, does he even have a weakness? Too, he's sort of in my head, isn't he? He'll know the perfect thing to say to get me wrong-footed. Something about playing in the lake with me when I was in elementary, back before I even knew about bras, and like that I stumble, which is all the opening he needs.

"If he hurt her—" Letha says, her eyes harder than I've ever seen them.

"Then we hurt him twice as much," I say right back, coughing what has to be blood up into my throat.

I swallow it back down.

Like always.

Letha stands, pulls me up with her delicately, because there's hardly anywhere to touch that isn't bloody. And of course what I've just told her about coming at Rexall is a lie, I know: no amount of damage done to someone erases what they've done to you. All it does, really, is complicate your life going forward, as now you've got charges to deal with, or a body to hide. But you've still got the same trauma. Just, now you've pulled some more trauma over on top of it.

Is this why slashers get more and more indiscriminate with their killing, as the franchise goes on? They were initially just mad about a prank, so killed those pranksters, but now they can't shake *those* killings out of their head, so have to try to cover them up with more violence, and more violence, until they're standing alone at the top of a truly staggering pile of bodies.

Standing there doesn't mean they're not still that same scared kid, though. That same kid just wanting—*needing*—someone to lower themselves to them, hug them, tell them it's all right, the bad stuff isn't going to happen anymore ever, okay?

I think that's what both Stacey Graves and Dark Mill South probably needed. But the only way we know to deal with them is violence, which is what shaped them in the first place.

Rexall, though.

He's so much more garden-variety. Which I think only serves to make him more dangerous. Maybe he's a hurt kid deep down there somewhere, but there comes a point where you can't give someone a pass, I think.

For me, that's hurting Adie.

I can't lose her, I mean. Really, I don't think I can lose even one more person.

"Here, here," Letha says about all my injuries, and takes a knee by Beardo. I'd almost forgotten about him. He's either had an M80 implanted in his neck and then lit, or . . . a bear tore a big important chunk out of him, and a lot of what he had left spilled out after. Letha strips the flannel sleeve on his less bloody side off, wraps my arm in it for padding, then whips his thick leather belt off as well and makes it into a sling, guiding my arm up at the end so she can hitch the belt one hole higher, to get my hand up a bit more.

"What even did that?" she asks, about the symmetrical tear in my forearm on both sides.

"Doesn't matter," I tell her, ducking what did it because it'll land her back in 2015, when I used maybe that same exact bear trap on her dad, when he was chasing us with a chainsaw.

I stand on my own now and cast around left and right for something we can use against Rexall. And, it's so, so liberating to now have one functioning arm that doesn't have to be holding the other arm.

I settle on Jo Ellen, still on her knees, sort of swaying in place.

"Guns won't work," Letha tells me, getting what I'm thinking.

"I don't even know where she got the one she had," I say back, just now thinking of that.

"I mean, because he's . . . you know," Letha says, using her eyes to get across what she means.

"He's not a slasher," I tell her. "He's just a—a *creep*."

"Maybe he was just keeping her safe?" Letha tries, and I can hear in her voice that she so, so wants me to ratify this, to give her this one, temporary gift.

I love her too much, though. I say instead, "Jo Ellen fired all her rounds anyway, didn't she? At Jan?"

"I already shot him once anyway," she mumbles. "Didn't work."

"You can't kill a bad smell with a gun," I say, obviously.

"That?" Letha says then, about Beardo's chainsaw.

"Too loud," I tell her.

"This isn't," she says, stepping over to haul a machete up. Because there's always a machete in a horror movie, when you need one.

She bonks it on the side of her thigh, though, and it slaps over, the blade rubber.

"Somebody brought a *prop* out here?" I ask.

Letha shrugs, pissed off and hopeless both. She deals with it by baring her teeth and twirling around fast on her heel, flinging that rubber machete up and away from all this.

"Should talk to Sharona about that anger of yours," I say with a halfway grin.

Letha doesn't grin about this, though. Nothing's funny right now.

"You mean Cinn?" she says.

"Who even knew she was back," I mutter, just trying to underline what Letha said.

Her eyes flash up to me in that meaningful way, though.

"No," I say to her, ready to push her in the shoulders. "You *knew*?"

I readjust the belt around my neck, have to bare my teeth from it, hiss a bit of the pain out.

"Lana told me she was staying with her for a while," Letha says, not catching my eye about this. "That she was—that she was going through something."

"'Something,'" I say, casing the devastation we're mired in, here. "It's my fault, really," I add, in case that came out wrong. Letha watches me, waiting for the rest. I shrug it away. No, I probably *shouldn't* have dragged Cinnamon Baker's broken self to Doc Wilson back in 2019. The whole time I was dragging her, even, I knew full well what she'd done. Just, I thought if she was alive, then she could pay for it all.

Like people at her income level ever get perp-walked away. You don't inherit the most storied law firm in the land only to get jammed up with accusations from an ex-con on her second bid. Which is why I didn't even *make* those accusations.

"We can do the analysis later," Letha says. "Right?"

She holds my eyes until I nod, then hooks her head for me to fall in, not waiting to see if I'm going to object. Along the way, not even breaking stride, she stoops to pick something up from the gore: Grace Richardson's Halligan.

She nods to me about it, walks faster, probably because this is the direction, sort of, to "T. Koenig's" blinking cursor. A straight line would be more direct, but about twice as slow—there's less trees and tangle over by the dam, maybe from when the water gets too high and they have to sluice it around like a tidal wave, I don't know. Just, it's better walking, close to the dam.

I'm seeing the blue glow for about twenty paces before it registers that that's *Lemmy* blue, that's *drone*-blue.

"Oh," I say, slowing. Scattered and mostly broken in the scrub are four of the shark-drones. Two are dead, one's flickering blue, and one's glowing steady, its tiny fans buzzing in the snow and grass.

"Flashlight," Letha says, hauling the functioning drone up, hooking her finger into the little plastic fan, stopping it and giving herself a handle.

The light won't work when we need it to, because we're in the genre we're in, but it's comforting to pretend it will, anyway.

Letha palms Jo Ellen's phone but it's locked.

"1239," I tell her.

Inside, you're always looking over guards' shoulders, trying to memorize the pattern on whatever keypad they're punching secrets into. I mean, it's mostly keys and buttons *other* guards are on, behind glass. But every once in a while there's a keypad on this side you're on. And when those digits are being entered, we all stand so, so still, listening with our very pores.

Letha doesn't ask about any of this, just enters the numbers.

"Still moving," she mutters, and starts to step ahead but stops herself, thinking something through. "Here," she says, tossing *her* phone back to me. "In case we get separated?"

"Jo Ellen's in here?" I ask, because I want every *i* dotted, every *t* to have its crossbar.

"Under 'Lemon Squares,'" Letha says back, already moving.

"Lemon squares?" someone asks from so close behind me my back straightens, like it knows sharp claws are coming for it.

I step ahead for room to turn around.

Jo Ellen. Standing there with that paint horse I remember now: it's Wayne Sellars's, from Lemmy's recording.

"Yeehaw," I say, monotone.

"Lemon squares are good," Letha tells Jo Ellen.

Jo Ellen doesn't look to be completely buying this, just keeps on buttoning some oversize mechanic's coveralls on. The poncho she's wearing is just a cape for her now, and she's stepped into some random boots.

"I need my phone," she says ahead to Letha. "I've got to . . . to call in the—everyone."

It's almost a John Connor line.

"Adie's in here," Letha objects, waggling the phone ever so gently.

"You don't even know the code," Jo Ellen tells her.

Letha recites it, her voice even, which isn't the tone to use with a cop, even one this far out of uniform. I step in, say, "Rexall *took* her, Jo Ellen. And—I mean, you know Rexall."

Jo Ellen purses her lips, considering this.

"I just need to call the sheriff," she says, holding her hand out for her phone.

I shake my head no to her the same way I did for Letha. Because we're all trained on movies, no words are needed to get across that Banner's dead.

Jo Ellen winces, her eyes closed for a too-long blink, so she can absorb this.

"You're sheriff now," I tell her, but Jo Ellen looks to Letha for real permission.

Letha nods once, her eyes dead, mouth a grim slash. She's bouncing on the balls of her feet, too, needs to be out there, going after Adie.

"Interim," Jo Ellen says, probably so as to not come off presumptuous. "Where has he taken her?"

Letha holds Jo Ellen's phone face out, showing Caribou-Targhee, and that little blinking dot.

"*Where?*" Jo Ellen asks, and Letha flips the phone around. I'm right there looking with her.

"What the—?" I start, but then that dot's back.

"They're losing signal," Letha says.

"Screencap once a minute," I tell her. "We can stack them up, draw a line through them, figure out a direction."

Letha nods, likes this. The screen of the phone flashes under her fingers, then shuttles this screencap into its camera roll.

"I'll call on the way," Jo Ellen says, stepping across Cinnamon to Letha, handing me the paint's rope or halter or rein or bridle—I'm not one of those Indians who knows horse shit, okay?

"Um, hey?" I say to the horse.

It blows air from its great nostrils, twitches one ear, and cocks its right front foot up, which I guess means it's resting time.

Jo Ellen grabs the phone from Letha without asking again, takes a reading on that cursor, and a few steps into the darkness, the side of her face is glowing with the calls she's placing, to get some flashing lights out here. And animal control. And the state troopers. And every boat that can be scrambled, and helicopters to lift people out.

I'm riding drag on this three-person herd, so I hear it all, and it's not until we're well into the darkness that I look back to the paint horse, falling behind a few paces, its rope pulling me slower.

Letha registers this, looks back to me, her eyes hot with question marks.

"Why are we bringing him?" I ask, about the horse.

"Her," Jo Ellen corrects.

" 'Terry,' right?" I say. "Short for Terrance?"

"Where'd you get Terrance?" Joe Ellen says back, genuinely confused.

Banner, I just manage to swallow.

I shake my head now, that it doesn't matter.

"I can carry Adie back, if that's why we're bringing the . . . horse," Letha says.

I nod, Jo Ellen nods, so I let the rope go, releasing this horse that either is or isn't named "Terry." Which is evidently the stupid, town-girl thing to do. Jo Ellen steps in, moving slow so the horse won't run, and collects the rope, undoes the headgear it's attached to, and *now* the horse is the right kind of free.

It's just standing there, though.

"It hasn't seen people for two weeks," I tell them. "I think it's lonely."

"*Get!*" Jo Ellen barks, whipping the rope against the ground.

The horse dances back, blows again, and I hear Letha and Jo Ellen already striding away. Leaving me to be the asshole who has to turn her back on this lonely, lost horse.

"Sorry," I say to it, reaching up to touch its nose.

The horse leans into my hand, almost nuzzling me with its velvety skin.

"Jade?" Letha calls from ahead enough that I nod, make myself turn around, skip to catch up.

"T. Koenig's" blinking green cursor goes even threadier maybe a mile deeper in—a mile farther away from the closest cell tower. Letha, the tallest of us, holds the phone up high, has to squint to see it, the map spinning to reorient.

For the past few hundred yards I've been trying not to picture Witte Jansson, hearing about Hettie, and Jan, and his ex-wife. How he'll probably be sitting on the edge of a motel bed, his cell to his ear, and one by one all his defenses come down, until nothing makes sense anymore. It was his ancient-old videocamera Hettie was using for the documentary, she told me. Will he want that tape back? My idea of what a normal, not-terrible dad must be like tells me that yes, he'll want the least, last scrap of his daughter's life.

You hold onto what you can, and you hold tight.

I'm sorry, Mr. Jansson. I'm sorry I couldn't save your daughter, your son, your wife. Your whole family.

And he's just the start, I know. Every sixth or seventh house in Proofrock is going to be a house in mourning, isn't it? And if Sharona—the *real* Sharona, the one in St. Thomas or wherever—was right about the stages of grief, then right after all these hurt people stop shaking their heads about how this can't really be happening, then they're going to start lashing out.

I thrilled, thinking of that herd of elk ravaging Main Street.

Elk just pass through, though. These hurting people, they *live* here. If they want to pull Proofrock down altogether, raze it, then who am I to stop them? Who am I to deny them their anger, their raging against the gods? Windows can be replaced, buildings can be rebuilt. But the dead, they don't come back.

Usually.

But I can't blame this on the gods, either—on fate or luck or the brutal demands of the genre. This, tonight, was all because one cheerleader thought she was wronged, and decided to take that out on a whole community. But don't forget the game warden who missed his wife so much that his grief consumed him, came out as bear bait he could paint the world with, so it could hurt as much as he was.

I'm deflecting, though. *I* should be accountable, I know, Sharona. You weren't wrong about that. No, I didn't invite the Founders across the lake to break ground in Terra Nova, waking the horror up, starting this whole bad cycle, but that's just because my prayers were so vague. Did I never watch any of the *Wishmaster*s, what? Beg and pray and long for a slasher to come a-calling, sure, who wouldn't, but also specify the individual *steps* of that, maybe? And also sketch out some boundaries, and maybe an end-date? Doesn't John Connor force some behavioral modifications on the T-800 in *Judgment Day*?

I'm so sorry, Proofrock. But? If I'm the one who started all this, then . . . would my death stop it? Take me and my bad wishing out of the picture, and does Indian Lake fizzle back down? Do all these killers stop rampaging?

More and more I'm thinking *maybe*, yeah.

I mean, what am I really doing here, this time around? It was Letha who killed my dad, not me. It was Jo Ellen who shot whatever Jan had turned into. It was Seth Mullins who Pied Piper'd those bears out after him. It was Tiff who finally put Cinnamon down, when I was failing and failing to do it.

I'm just witnessing it all, this time. I'm in a rattly fiberglass cart being pulled along a set of tracks down the center of the Haunted Tunnel at this nightmare carnival, and I'm watching horror after horror pop up off to the side and then roll behind me, making room for the next jumpscare.

I'm the audience is what I am. I'm an Ancient One, who insists that the twists and turns of the slasher play out exactly like they did the time before, and the time before that, and I won't be satisfied unless, like Randy says, this third time around's a complete gorefest, very much including some of the deck crew buying the farm, not raising their thumb from the stretcher to show they're going to pull through.

"*Whoah*," Jo Ellen says, just loud enough to pull me out of my head.

Letha shifts the Halligan in her hand for whatever's next.

"Leeth?" I whisper ahead.

"I don't—I don't . . ." she's saying, trying to see everything at once.

I clamp my good hand onto Jo Ellen's shoulder to pull ahead, alongside Letha.

She holds that glowing blue drone out like a lantern, and all my breath seeps out, maybe through my pores.

"Holy hell," Jo Ellen intones.

She slaps her waist for that pistol she was using but it's back by the dam, I guess. Not out here *with* the damned.

"No," Letha says, about what the wrong-blue light of her drone's illuminating.

It's Paul Demming, his head nearly disconnected. There's Waynebo, who finally found that damn Bronco. His frontside's been ripped open.

Letha's hand finds my good wrist.

"Hettie Jansson," Jo Ellen says.

Hettie's hair's pink on one side, electric blue on the other, and it's the most beautiful thing I've ever seen. Under it, her head's at the wrong angle, the back of her neck and most of her jaw torn away, and her cheeks are grey and drawn, her eyes dried out and staring, her jaw black with dried blood.

Why didn't you just run away to Boise? I say to her, inside. Or Denver, Phoenix, Tucson, Seattle, LA, it doesn't matter. Not here? Somewhere safe?

"Jade, no—" Letha says then, actually gasping air in and stepping back, which is something from her, who makes herself watch all the gore in all the movies, so none of it will ever surprise her in real life.

I flinch, sure a hatchet is about to come spinning out of the darkness, sure a scythe is swinging our way at neck level, sure that log truck's load isn't secured as well as it could be, sure that metal cable from *Ghost*

Ship is drawing tight all at once, is about to saw right through our stomachs, just leaving our legs standing here in the high timber, our torsos and heads lying back in the leaf litter, staring suddenly up.

"Who's *she*?" Jo Ellen says, looking over to Letha and me.

"Sharo—Dr. Watts," Letha manages.

"My Sharona . . ." I say, quieter.

She's strung up exactly like Gwen Stapleton was, the day Dark Mill South broke out of his convoy. Which is to say this is Casey Becker hanging from that tree. Only, her guts are no longer red—she's been here too long.

"She's . . . your doctor?" Jo Ellen asks Letha, incredulous.

"Therapist," Letha corrects.

"This is it, isn't it?" I say to both of them, in something like wonder, except it's making the floor of my stomach drop out. "The third-reel bodydump."

"Why did the bears not . . . ?" Jo Ellen asks, stepping forward, into this crime scene.

She's right: why haven't these bodies been scavenged by bears, who need to pack on all the fat they can for their big sleep?

Almost immediately, we all realize why: the tree over Paul and Waynebo and Hettie, that Sharona's hanging from, it's got air fresheners hanging from every possible point, like—like pull tabs from a headliner, yes.

Do I never escape you, Dad?

And these air fresheners, just like in *Se7en*, they're all pine trees, their taste on the air so harsh to a bear nose that they didn't come in for a free meal, I guess. Each pine tree has two little pine cones crossed at the base of their trunks, too. Just like the machetes in my living room, that I thought Letha and me could pull down, should the day ever come.

"Who did this?" Jo Ellen asks, getting close to these bodies but being careful not to touch.

Letha catches my eye about this but I shake my head the smallest bit, *no, we don't have time.*

"You know, don't you?" Jo Ellen says to me, trying to see through my eyes, into my thoughts.

Letha's a dim blue light bobbing ahead of us.

I hustle to catch up.

"How far?" I ask Letha, leaning in to see the phone.

Letha just huffs, keeps walking, but I stop all at once, hard enough that Letha and Jo Ellen are on alert.

"What?" Letha asks, casing the darkness.

I shake my head no, that I don't know, I'm not sure.

"Shit," Jo Ellen says, though, when a pair of green eyes open in the darkness, pretty much stopping my heart in my chest. Letha's hand's already clamped on my good wrist, to guide me behind her.

"Oh," she says, though.

It's that paint horse, coming in head down, like embarrassed.

"Go!" Jo Ellen yells at it, rushing it while bat-winging her poncho out.

The horse puts the brakes on, and, instead of backing up—horses not like to do that?—it wheels around, scampers off, tail tucked.

"Idiot," Jo Ellen says.

"It's just lonely," I say.

Letha doesn't care, is already moving, muttering. I tune in enough to get that she's cursing Rexall. Her lips are thin, her eyes hard.

"I can't touch him, either," Letha says, suddenly pulling me into this train of thought she can't let go. When I look my question over to her, she adds, "That settlement for shooting him? There was also a restraining order."

"I think this is special circumstances. Kidnapping is bigger than having to stay a hundred feet away."

"Hundred *yards*."

"In Proofrock?" I have to ask, because . . . in a town of less than three thousand, keeping a whole football field between you and anybody's a real trick.

Letha shrugs, ducks a limb, doesn't lose any speed.

"It's the Stu-rule," I say, more out loud than I really mean to. But now it's out there, I guess.

Letha looks over, telling me to go on, go on.

"It's when," I tell her, trying to get my words lined up right, "it's when the person who's doing all the over-the-top shit that should get them killed, that would *get* them killed in any other movie, they just keep on living."

"Stuff like perv cameras, you mean?"

"Stu was asking and asking for it, wasn't he?"

"So?"

"So when lightning never strikes him like it would anybody else saying all what he says . . . that's the big clue that he's the killer."

"*A* killer."

"You know what I mean."

"So Rexall should have bought it in 2015?" Letha asks. "That's what you're saying?"

I dial back to Rexall and my dad in their mockery of a float, *Jaws* splashed on the inflatable screen behind them. Rexall's duded up in a headdress, and my dad's painted up Indian.

I nod yes, yes, definitely, say, "He was pretty much asking for it."

"Maybe he's just keeping her safe?" Letha tries again, not able to let that chance go.

Because I know she needs to be able to stand up, keep walking forward, I don't shoot this down.

"He's never . . . done anything like this *before*, has he?" she adds, still making her big wish.

"Why *now*, though, right?" I say, not really vetting it beforehand.

"He's been a creep for years, I mean. Everybody knows that. But he's always been a hands-*off* kind of creep, hasn't he?"

Letha pooches her lips out like who cares, says, "Maybe somebody stole all his cameras?"

She's not saying it like that's a serious option, but that doesn't mean it doesn't go right to the center of me: has Rexall metastasized into a *Phantasm* kind of kidsnatcher because "somebody" messed with the viewing habits that have been getting him by all these years?

"Somebody." *Shit.*

"I just . . . I can't stop thinking about her," Letha says, about to cry again. "With—with *him.*"

"We know where she is," I tell her. It's all I can come up with.

"I already lost Ban," Letha blubbers. It makes her walk faster, like to get away from the breath she used to say that. It also makes her stop in her tracks, let her face fall forward into her hands to shut all this out.

I come around, hug her to me with my good arm.

Her whole frame is shuddering against me. Over her shoulder, I see Jo Ellen cueing into this and veering off to the side to wait it out. She stations herself at the edge of the blue light, is just a shape, her back to us to show how much she's not listening.

"If we don't find her—" Letha says, choking it off because you don't even want to allow a thing like that to be out loud, as that's another step toward it getting real and actual.

"Don't even think it," I say. "Aunt Jade's here, right? Will I let anything happen to your little girl? You know what she means to me. And you know what her mom means to me too."

Letha presses her forehead into my shoulder and I hold her to me until she can stand on her own again.

"If anything happens to me—" she says.

"Don't think that either," I tell her. "Just . . . just stop thinking, maybe? This isn't the best time for it."

"Just act," Letha says, getting it.

"Action, not words," I confirm, and I don't think Letha even knows that's a song, which I guess is good. Except then it hits me that that could also sound like me shutting her up, couldn't it?

Bad thing about being an idiot is you second-guess every single thing you do. And also the things you don't.

You can't reel any of it back, though, I know that much.

So, instead, I plod forward behind Letha, Jo Ellen falling in. There's supposed to be caverns or someshit out here, according to a geologist report from sixty years ago we all had to read in class like gospel, but nobody I know's ever stumbled onto them.

After maybe ten minutes of silence, just the three of us breathing, I cue in that I'm trembling deeper than just my fingers—this unsteadiness, it's deeper. Blood loss will do that to you, I suppose. And Idaho at night, in late October. And only having eaten two chicken wings and some gross noodles over the last twelve hours. And being off your meds. And just plain old terror, that'll get you shaking in your boots. But the real reason . . . shit, I'd *rather* be talking, now. It's better than being locked in my head.

I need my pills, please, to pull me away from the drain I'm circling faster and faster. Either that or I need to have a Weedwacker like Jason in *VII*, so I can stay out of Rexall's reach, when we find him. I need— I need that lawnmower from *Brain Dead*, which is what Rexall already is.

I need to save Adie is what I need to do.

"No," Letha says from a few steps ahead of me.

"What?" Jo Ellen asks before I can.

Letha shakes the phone but that never helps. She draws in, holding that glowing screen low, and Jo Ellen steps in, delicately extracts it from Letha, looks at it for only a moment before declaring, "He turned it off, broke it, something."

"Call it," I tell Letha.

"What?"

"Not enough signal for tracking, but maybe it'll ring," I say, urging her on with my eyes.

Jo Ellen shrugs sure.

Letha touches Tiff's face, the phone dials, rings, rings, and—

"Over there!" Letha says.

We're not hearing Tiff's ringtone—the *Friends* theme song, gag—but the face of her phone's lighting up in the darkness.

The call dumps to voicemail before we can get there.

Letha calls, calls again, and on the fourth time, Jo Ellen picks Tiff's phone up from the ground.

"He just left it?" Jo Ellen says to us, and then very quickly and intentionally turns around, like the moonlight's better facing *this* direction.

Letha's staring in the darkness ahead of us, doesn't clock this.

But I can't not wonder.

Jo Ellen drifts after Letha, who's trying to read sign, I think—*track*—which'll go about as good as it would for any city girl at night in the big bad woods, but I hang behind a little, hike Letha's phone out of my left cup and shine that silvery light down to where Tiff's phone was.

It's Adie's shoe. And there's blood on it.

I turn around just as fast as Jo Ellen did, and she sees me doing this, and we hold each other's eyes just a tenth of a second too long.

"What?" Letha says to us both at once.

"That," Jo Ellen lies, upping her chin to something high up on the tree.

Letha falls for it, Jo Ellen shines her light up there, and it's . . . really something, not just a temporary distraction?

"Bike reflector?" I say. With a little thumbtack pushed through its middle?

"Poachers," Jo Ellen hisses, drawing enough attention that I can step on top of that shoe, hiding it from Letha.

"Poachers?" Letha says back, standing taller to see this trail marker better.

"They hunt at night," Jo Ellen explains. "But they need to be able to backtrack their way out with their kill, too."

"Like those two who got lost?" I realize out loud.

Jo Ellen and Letha both study me, waiting.

"Remember what they said all around town?" I ask. "That—"

"That they found Remar Lundy's old *cabin* . . ." Jo Ellen says, nodding it true.

"Why does this—?" Letha asks, looking from Jo Ellen to me.

"Remar Lundy is Rexall Bridger's grandfather," I say, quietly. "Something like that. That's where he's going, isn't it?"

"That's where he's taking Adie?" Letha says, more than a little aghast.

"Shit," Jo Ellen says, and shines her phone light down-trail, all around, until—something bounces that silvery light back red.

"Next one," I say.

Jo Ellen nods, and we move like that for probably two of the worst hours of my life. Not worst because of my arm, my head, what just happened down by the dam, but because we can't go faster. The two times we try, a trail marker slips behind us and we lose twenty minutes backtracking.

It's the worst two hours of my life because it's a hundred and twenty minutes Rexall can be doing whatever to Adie, that she'll never be able to forget, that she'll always be running from, hiding in chemicals and alcohol and sex and, and—

I shake my head, don't want to think about Adie having to run wild just to stay sane.

Letha's feeling it too, though. I can tell by the way her left hand keeps opening and closing, her right gripped tight high up on the handle of that Halligan.

"We're going too slow, we're going too slow," she keeps muttering.

"As fast as we can," I counter, pretty uselessly.

Right after that, in typical horror movie fashion, Jo Ellen catches her wrong-size boot on the side of a root and rolls her ankle, the *pop* of something tearing in there painfully clear.

I can tell Letha wants to go go *go*, but we stop, gingerly slide Jo Ellen's boot off—it smells like a dude—and her ankle's already blue and swelling, like it's pregnant with an alien.

"Can we cut it?" Jo Ellen asks.

"*What?*" I ask.

"This isn't boxing," Letha says, standing. "And we don't have a knife anyway. Just this." The Halligan.

"Yeah, let's not," Jo Ellen says, keeping her eyes on the Halligan, just to be sure.

I guide it back behind Letha's leg.

"Go, go, don't worry about me," Jo Ellen says then, waving us on. "I'm not going to be the reason you don't get to her in time."

"But—" we both try.

"I hereby deputize you both," Jo Ellen says, doing the sign of the cross, I think, which is kind of weird. "So now you have authority, but responsibility too, cool? You detain *only*. Let the courts do the rest."

"Sure?" I say.

Jo Ellen waggles her phone to show how all right she's going to be. But I can see the strain in her face, too. I come down to her level, say, "Listen. This isn't *Red Dawn*. You're not the soldier we leave behind with a hand-grenade, got it? We're not here at all without you. You *live* by staying here."

"I shouldn't have made—the horse go back," Jo Ellen says, trying to shift her whole leg.

I want to help but don't know where to touch.

"*Go!*" Jo Ellen says, waving us away with the back of her hand.

"Scream if you see anything," Letha calls back in what feels like about the most final farewell I've ever heard.

"Because that always works," Jo Ellen says to her back.

"You—you watch these movies too?" I ask.

"Survival training around here," Jo Ellen grunts, repositioning.

Clever girl.

Just two trail markers later, we're there, I'm pretty sure. Or, to the end or beginning of the trail markers, anyway. On this tree there's six of those reflective tacks shaped into a shimmery red X.

Letha's breathing heavier now, getting her muscles oxygenated, her senses dialed in.

Me too, kind of a sympathetic response, I think, or self-defense for whatever's coming, but . . . the air I'm sucking in is fetid, oily, bad.

I cough it out and it doesn't stop there.

I wave my arms just to try to keep standing, then am lurching forward, my puke splashing up and out like there was a kite string in my mouth, diving down my throat, and somebody just yanked it.

When I look up, Letha's got the crook of her elbow hooked over her nose, her eyes glittering over it.

"Done?" she asks.

A little more comes up, strings out, and seeing that makes me cough more, dry-heave harder.

Probably a whole minute later, I'm finally with-it enough to stand on my own, not quite steadily.

"Something died, didn't it?" I say through my tears.

"Whole lot of somethings," Letha says, tilting her head all around us.

There's nowhere to step that isn't a dead animal. This is a pet sematary turned upside down, inside out. But these aren't dogs, they're . . . foxes, I guess? Their ribcages look so delicate. And there's some deer and elk, too, and one black bear—I think that's what it is, or was? And black feathers fluttering in the rot, probably beaks in the mess, if I want to feel down for their sharpness.

"How?" I have to ask.

"Poison?" Letha says with a who-cares shrug, and I nod, can see that: you put out some canned food with the bad stuff in it, that animal dies, and then you poison that dead animal, so the animals who come in to scavenge it get sick and die as well, and you sprinkle white powder on their rotting meat as well, and the whole circle of whatever this is just widens and widens, from a single point of corruption. From Rexall, doing what he does, being the corruption he is, the blight he's always been.

"He *really* doesn't want anybody finding his hidey-hole, does he?" I say.

Letha doesn't have to answer this, but I can see the answer in the heat in her eyes: *You don't need this kind of privacy for* good *things.*

"There, see it?" she says.

After a moment, I can, yeah: Remar Lundy's cabin in the woods, at the center of all this dead and rotting meat. It's so much a part of the trees and the shadows that my eyes have to kind of organize this straight line, that slightly-too-regular edge. Through the years—through a century and more, I guess—it's faded to the same smudged-grey color as the forest, has a thick crown of moss growing on its roof, and there's a big-ass tree angled over it that should have crushed it if its forever trunk hadn't caught in the unlikely fork of another tree, locking in like a Lincoln Log. But, that big-ass tree that didn't quite crush this cabin, it's the reason the cabin's still here: the tree *is* the roof now, more or less. The cabin is kind of under this grand lean-to, is in a sort of hidey-hole out of the rain, the lightning, the *world*. And there's all these saplings shooting up around it to hide it even more, reaching for the few hours of sun a baby tree can get out here among the old, uncaring giants.

There's one small, not-really-square window to the right of the door, exactly as a kid would draw a house in first grade, there's a rusted pipe for a chimney that looks like it's straight from some nightmare version of Seuss, there's so many twists in it, and the hinges on that front door are, I'm thinking, leather?

The real question, though—one of them, anyway—is why did

Remar Lundy go to the trouble to build a lair this secret two or three miles from Proofrock, back in the forties or fifties or whenever? For hunting, sure. But this feels more skeevy than just popping deer and elk out of season. Maybe he just needed somewhere to go all John Doe in the notebooks in his head, without anybody judging him. Maybe he got ran out of town for knocking peepholes into outhouses, like his descendent would do, with technology.

You probably knew, didn't you, Mr. Holmes? Or had a pretty good guess? Except why bring up bad business from fifty years ago, I know. Better to let the past stay back where it is.

Except here it is, unrepressing itself.

And? It doesn't really matter.

We're going in either way.

And, knowing Rexall, it's going to be that underground lair in *Texas Chainsaw Massacre 2*, and all we've got's one Halligan between us.

"Okay," Letha says, catching my eyes one last time because we're about to do this.

I nod, nod again just to be sure I'm committed, and right when I step forward, the front door of the cabin opens hard enough to slap the wall it's on, dislodging a shovel leaned up there.

The shovel scrapes down, down, falls.

The door's hanging crooked and ugly on those ratty hinges, and—

And Rexall's standing right there in the doorway in his work coveralls, his face lifted so he can scent the air.

Does he know the rot well enough that he can taste us in the fester?

He scans, scans, and when we don't give ourselves away by moving, he reaches back in for—

A *crossbow*.

"Shit," I hiss to Letha, not using my lips.

He lumbers out with the crossbow by his left leg, and, after casing the trees again, he angles the crossbow maybe six inches from where it's hanging and pulls the trigger.

That little bolt sucks into the loamy soil up to its orange fletching.

"Now stay *still!*" he barks down to the ground, his voice booming.

Then, like that wasn't enough, he steps around for a different angle, cranks another bolt into place, and fires it into the ground as well.

"Time for little sister to go to *bed* . . ." he says, I'm pretty sure.

"What the hell," Letha says, not moving her lips.

Rexall steps away to consider this patch of earth he evidently has some beef with, his big hands idly cocking another bolt in.

"Rexall Bridger!" a woman calls out then, from maybe fifteen feet to Letha and my's left.

We don't mean to give our location away, but we both look over.

It's Jo Ellen, using a thick branch-as-crutch.

"No," I say, low.

She's holding her badge up like the shield I don't really think it is.

Rexall's looking right at her.

"Where's the girl!" Jo Ellen says, and I can tell she has no idea we're already here—she thinks *she's* the hero here, not Letha.

"Little late, aren' you?" Rexall says with a sort of chuckle.

Jo Ellen holds up Adie's bloody shoe as proof of what she's asking—she *grabbed* that?—and Letha's hands come up to try to cover the sound her heart pushes up, that Halligan falling and falling, finally crunching into what I think must be a wolverine skull, judging by the thick rotting pelt.

It gives us away.

Because Letha isn't thinking, can only think of one thing, I grab her wrists as best I can, yank her towards me just as a crossbow bolt *whirrs* past, thuds deep into a tree right behind where Letha just was, the fletching not even having the decency to vibrate, it's so deadly.

Texas *Crossbow* Massacre, more like. Just, in Idaho.

"Get down!" I yell to Jo Ellen, pulling Letha down with me, which is no easy thing since she's trying to surge ahead, I think to claw Rexall's eyes out, and bite his throat open, and knee him in the stomach until his liver bursts, squelches out the pores of his armpits.

Through the rotted ribs of an elk, which is a view I already know well enough, thanks, I can see Rexall getting another bolt ready, his eyes watching the trees for the rush he knows is coming, for the pistol fire he expects.

I ferret Letha's heavy Halligan up from a crunchy-dead something, pass it back to her, wrap her fingers around it for her.

"I'm recording this!" Jo Ellen announces, which, in today's world, is kind of an announcement that your phone's the only weapon you've got.

"Good luck with that," Rexall huffs, and I have to wince about the point of light Tiff's phone is.

It's a bullseye for Rexall.

He shoulders the crossbow, aims for maybe half a second, and releases.

The light Jo Ellen is goes out, and the sound of her breath leaving her body is so slow, so distinct. She's pinned to a tree, I know. And, I don't want to, but I imagine her tilting forward a month later, a dry rib bone pushing up through her chin, into the corrugated roof of her mouth. Her decomposing knees grinding down onto the sharp knobby points of a line of deer vertebrae.

But no. We can't let it end like that.

"Where's my daughter!" Letha yells then, thinking the same thing, I guess, and, with me dragging back on her arm, she steps forward into the bright moonlight, the Halligan held across her hips like she means it.

Rexall looks up to her, chuckles and leans down to work one of the bolts up from where he shot it into the ground, and I have a seriously bad flashback sort of moment, where he's one of those lumbering backwoods killers from *Just Before Dawn*, except this is the version that was never shot, only scripted, where there's *actually* demonic shit going down, and Rexall's kind of the gatekeeper of it all, a puppet the evil trots out to lure us back into that rancid maw.

And I'm no Connie, no Constance, could never stick my whole arm down Rexall's throat, come up with his life pulsing in my throat.

Letha's about to try, though, I can tell.

"No, Leeth!" I tell her, but she shrugs out of my grip, steps forward.

Rexall's already got that ground-bolt cocked and aimed, waiting for her.

"Where is she?" Letha says low and even, the menace in her voice just dripping. "Where's Adie?"

Her first step is through the spine of some small animal, and her next is around the tall woody rack of a bull elk.

"What? How do you—?" Rexall says, looking down to his feet, to the small grave he's standing on, his foot lifting away like the dirt there just moved the slightest bit.

And then, in a quick snap—rise, release—he lets that bolt fly.

Letha, her final girl reflexes just as good as that dude on the stairs in *Final Exam*, bats the bolt to the side with the Halligan, sending that raspy broadhead slicing across the top of my shoulder.

The blood runs hot down my back, into the waistband of my sweat pants, and I fall to my knees, a rib or something stabbing into the skin by my thigh, and, and—

This isn't working out at all, is it?

Letha quickens her pace, her legs the same size as ever, but they're made of steel now, are pillars crashing forward through bone and rot, and . . . that's not a claw growing up from her left foot. A bone's stabbed up, gone through, and she could care less, is only thinking of Adie.

Rexall, spooked about how she batted his crossbow bolt away maybe, steps back, almost falls himself, having to wheel his arms, the crossbow clattering away.

Instead of collecting it and trying to load it again—there's no time—he scrambles back saying, "Stay away! You don't belong here! *I* live here, not you!"

And now Letha's running, is a fucking terminator if there ever was one, her arms pumping just like that, the weight of the Halligan nothing to her.

Rexall falls back through the door, into the darkness of the cabin, and I'm counting the tenths of a second before Letha dives through it after him, but, but . . .

She's stopped, is standing where Rexall was?

I stand, try to see the new mouth screaming on my shoulder—how deep is it?—but my neck jolts electricity into my spine about being moved, meaning something got nicked. But at least it's on the side my bad arm is, meaning I can clamp my good hand over it, try to keep the air from it.

I weave through the dead animals, the elk rack a turnstile, admitting me to the horror, and I have to say it when I'm finally standing beside Letha, who's just silently crying: "Oh."

It's Adie's other shoe.

There's a crossbow bolt shot through it, down to the plastic feathers.

This is Adie's headstone, isn't it?

I work my bloody hand around Letha, hug her to me.

She's shaking with grief. And a rage so bottomless I'm not sure one body can contain it.

"It's—it's—" she's saying, but can't get it out.

It's not fair, it's not right, this can't be happening: they all work.

"I know, I know," I say, and lick one of my own tears off my top lip.

It's salty and warm and I hate it.

Letha falls to her knees, crams her fingers into the torn-up soil, and is clawing it away faster and faster until I fall onto this small grave, my knees keeping her from opening it.

"You don't want to see," I tell her.

"My baby, my *little girl*," she's saying, I don't know how. "Why—why would he, why—?"

I don't have any answers. Except that he never *does* this, not if I just let him keep his stupid little cameras in all the ceilings.

After this, I know, after all the funerals, I'm walking back into these trees, and I'm never coming out again.

Idaho, you win, you can have me.

Mr. Holmes, I don't want you coming with, either, okay?

You either, Hardy. Mom.

I'm the one who did all the bad here, all the wrong. None of this without me.

So, it should be me who pays, and me alone.

You win, Cinnamon Baker. You win, Terra Nova. You win, Rexall. There's nothing left to take, anymore. I'll never be able to look my best friend in the eye again. There's nothing left for me.

Used to, all the murder victims were buried over here, somewhere.

It's time for me to join them, I think.

That crossbow bolt should have been five inches over, shouldn't it have? Then I'd be pinned to that tree by the head, and everything would be in order, and I never have to know that here a little girl died, and died again and again, when Rexall kept nailing arrows down into her small body.

I don't even want to think about her last moments. About his hands on her. About how he probably told it was all right, that this was good, this was okay.

I've heard it all before, I mean.

"Look," Letha says, her voice a new kind of dead, and without thinking, I do.

This grave is at the head of what looks like ten or twelve more graves, each of them with make-do little crosses coming up from them.

I lower my face.

Wouldn't we have noticed a whole *classroom* of kindergartners going missing? How does a town miss that?

"He must have been ranging out," I decide out loud. Rexall. He must have been snatching kids from all over Idaho, bringing them back here.

For how long, though? Since . . . it was since my dad died, wasn't it? Since I killed him? My dad, terrible person that he was, kept Rexall tethered to something solid. Without that, he floated off into his own twisted head. And needed to populate that fetid space with dummies, with dolls. With kids.

With Linnea Adrienne Tompkins-Mondragon. Because of me. Because I took his best friend away.

This is what hating yourself feels like.

I breathe everything I have in me out, and don't expect to breathe anything back in, ever.

Not Letha.

She surges up, leaves and needles and gore calving off her like she's been buried for a decade out here, not ten or fifteen seconds.

The Halligan drops to the ground right in front of my knees.

Her eyes fixed on the cabin, she kneels, grabs onto that crossbow bolt through Adie's shoe, and stands, bringing a great clump of earth up with her.

She flicks her wrist and that dirt calves off.

"He doesn't get to just do this," she says, and kicks away from me trying to hold her back, and the next I see her, she's walking into that tall square of darkness—into this cabin at the end of the world.

Leaving me on my knees.

I'm cut all over, I don't see how I can have any blood left in me at all. Or any tears.

All I am now is grief and regret.

And rage too.

Always that.

The last time I was in a tomb with Letha, we were in Sheep's Head Meadow over by Terra Nova, and there were maggots wriggling into the corners of my eyes, and whispering their breath into my ears, and nuzzling blindly into my cuticles.

The air coming from Remar Lundy's cabin is drier, wafting past me in the doorway, but I'm pretty sure it's infested with maggots of the soul, to nuzzle into my thoughts, my memories.

I shake my head no, that I shouldn't do this, that there's only death in this place.

Like that's ever stopped me before.

Here I come, Letha.

Related: why can't I hear you already? This place is a glorified outhouse, pretty much, *maybe* the size of my bedroom, which is itself pretty much a closet.

"Leeth?" I call ahead, fully expecting a bolt from the backup crossbow to come whizzing into this mouth I keep on opening.

Nothing.

I step in sideways, I guess with the idea that if a crossbow bolt is arrowing its way to me, tunneling through the air Raimi-style, then sideways presents a narrower target?

I cover my nose with the back of my good hand, but . . . it doesn't smell as rank in here as it does out there, hunh. That doesn't mean it's even partway pleasant, just, it's body odor and beer burps, now. And . . . earth? Turned soil?

I stand there until my eyes adjust to separate an irregular darkness in the corner that's darker than the rest of the darkness.

Letha's phone brightens it right up, making the shadows deeper in the process.

"Great," I mutter.

That darkness is a tunnel, a cave. Remar Lundy's cabin is just the doghouse canted over the stairs down to hell.

Figures.

As for the rest of the living room, there's one sturdy camp chair that maybe used to be blue and an inflatable kayak with a blanket balled in it—I think that's Rexall's bed, maybe? Or, it's where Adie was supposed to sleep if she'd lived, I don't know.

I can't let myself think about Adie like that yet, though. Rexall won't need to shoot me, if I do. My heart will already be full of arrows.

"Here I go," I announce very quietly, and follow my silvery little torch down.

The tunnel's steep and crumbly, but Rexall or maybe Remar's cleared some roots in the ceiling of it for handholds, so it's kind of like a reverse ladder. It takes a few steps of getting used to, but it works— I don't go sliding.

It gets wetter and colder, a few feet down.

"Leeth?" I sort of say.

No answer.

And, I was just joking about *Chainsaw 2*—didn't mean for it to get this real. I should be careful what I say, I guess, even to myself.

Slowly, the floor of the passageway levels out, and . . . and this isn't a bomb shelter, this isn't a secret lair.

It's an altar. Rexall comes here to worship.

Embedded in the wall of this chamber, floor to ceiling, there's—

"Seriously?" I have to say, honestly impressed.

Tupac Shakur's looking back at me every which way I turn. A *damn* fine-looking man, to be sure, with that almost-devious, kind of sparkly-sprite smile, but this is a weird place to make him a saint.

And he won't stop staring at me with those cherubic-hellion eyes.

"Fuck," I say, trying to get away.

If I were clued into the world enough to know lines from any of his songs, I'd toss them up now as a ward, but all I know is Fugazi, and I don't think "Turkish Disco" or "Smallpox Champion" is getting me much mileage, here. *Viva, viva, viva, life and limb* does sound sort of like an incantation, I guess, but—

Shit: there's a shelf dug into the wall, and it's lined with videotapes.

I don't want to, but I draw close, study those labels.

GLM Apr 14. WBR Sep 18, and on and on.

It doesn't mean anything, but then, on the other side of the labels are the names: Jenna, Wynona, Queen Letha, Christy C, and, of course, me.

This is Rexall's greatest hits. "GLM" is the girls' locker room. "WBR" is the west bathroom.

I'm sixteen on the tape with my name.

And, does he have *power* out here to watch these, what?

I run my hand down the spines of these tapes hard enough to dislodge them, get them crooked, some of them spurting out. The first one to fall doesn't crack, but the second third and fourth, landing on their brothers, do, shooting shards of black plastic out.

Letha's right: he doesn't get to just do this.

I run my hand back the other way, pulling the rest of the tapes down, and then I stomp through them, messing up his years of work, breaking his spank bank wide open, and from that glint in Tupac's eyes, I'm pretty sure he approves, that he didn't much like what he was having to be witness to down here.

I thought Rexall was scheduling himself around my work hours?

Wrong.

He's been out here. It's like crawling into the dank interior of his own head, where nobody can see him. Of course he never got his submersible running again. He had something better, didn't he? When you find your happy place, you don't leave unless you have to.

If the world were even a partway fair place, he'd have been sitting in that lawn chair up there one day when the front door burst in. Standing there wouldn't be Seth Mullins and some scrum of bears, or Banner and a posse.

It would be my dad, with that golden pickaxe. That would hurt Rexall worse than anything, I have to think. Instead, he was left alone out here, to wallow in the filth of his *Maniac* lair.

Speaking of, where the hell *is* he? Near as I can tell, this is just a dead-end, not the first chamber of some network or system—

And then Letha's exploding out of the wall, falling in a pile of limbs at my feet.

Behind her, crumbles and clods of dirt spurt out, the dust hanging in the air.

I fall away onto my ass and Letha hits and rolls, sputtering, swinging her crossbow bolt blindly, and pretty damn lethally.

"What the hell!" I say to her, watching all the Tupacs now, sure Rexall's about to juggernaut through them just the same, wrap me up in his big arms, and then carry me into the wall on the other side.

Letha fights her way to her feet, looks to me not like I'm me, but like she's identifying friend and foe.

"Leeth, Leeth, it's Jade, it's me!" I tell her, scrabbling around so I can try to keep her off with my feet if she turns this wildness my way.

She reels it back in, cleans her mouth with the back of her arm.

I look from her to the wall, and, and—she didn't come *through* it, she came *out* of it.

"Fucker dropped the roof on me," she says, the profanity coming so natural, now that she's been buried alive.

I nod of course, of *course* he did: "Drug dealers always have a secret way out, don't you know that?" I say.

I just learned it this morning, but it still counts.

Rexall slithered his not-insignificant bulk into some escape tunnel. One he had rigged to fall, if he wanted it to fall.

Letha considers this about drug dealers, the skin around her eyes wrinkling with thought, and for a moment I can see ahead to her at forty, at fifty, and it sort of takes my breath away.

"Drug dealer?" she asks.

"That's how he got his name," I tell her. Then, "Doesn't matter." Obviously. Old-me goes down every rabbit hole on the way to wherever.

New-me doesn't have that kind of time.

"So you're saying this was his *plan* . . ." Letha's saying, looking back at the tunnel she just crashed out of. Then she looks back to the way I just came. "That means—" she starts, and doesn't finish because she's already blasting off, the same way she did the last time we were here.

Before I can even turn all the way around to track her, she's a pair of feet wriggling back up to the cabin.

I start to scramble after her, then, slowly, by degrees, realize that the escape tunnel wasn't the only place Rexall had rigged.

There's a pole in the center of *this* room, too.

I study it from top to bottom. It's propped on top of a little pyramid of more and more squares of 2x6's, and there's a matching pad of them at the ceiling. Because you can't nail into dirt. But you can wedge stuff against it.

Until you want it to all come crashing down.

I nod to myself, nod again to be sure this can work, and then back up to the wall the videotapes were on.

"Go, go, go," I tell myself, and push off that wall with my right foot, launching me forward to tag that pole with my good-enough shoulder, but I can't stop even for half an instant, am already diving for the tunnel Letha just took.

I get there just as the first big clods of ceiling are raining down onto my heels.

And then a whole big section of the ceiling goes at once, with a deep thump. It blows a cloud of dirty air up this windpipe I'm in, packing all my cuts but pushing me forward just enough to hook my elbows up onto the dirt floor of the cabin.

I have to struggle to get my hips and legs up and out, but that's good. It means the tunnel collapsed behind me. When I stand, the floor shudders under me, falls in about three feet, making me run to the wall.

A sinkhole's trying to open, in here, but doesn't quite. It's just a dry crater, with a camp chair half-buried in it, an inflatable kayak bobbing on top, unharmed.

I can't stop to appreciate all this destruction, though.

Letha's more than a few steps ahead of me, by now.

I crash through the front door—it's swaying in now—see Letha standing there ahead of me. She's looking from the crossbow bolt in her hands to Walter Mason's heavy Halligan and back again, and then she's dropping that bolt into the bone litter, she's dropping it and running ahead, collecting that Halligan along the way, and where she's running, where she's sliding on her knees—

It's to the now-obvious hatch opening out in the dead animals, ten feet past the line of graves.

Rexall's halfway up from it, and Letha's got that Halligan drawn back like a lance, one hand high, one near the head.

"No!" I scream, because this isn't the kind of thing you can take back, but my voice is so small and distant, compared to her need.

That forked end of that Halligan crashes through Rexall's temple, and when it comes out it's followed by a long stringy line of steaming brains, all his most secret passwords dying in the open air, all the souls trapped in there swirling up and out, Indy.

And she's just getting started.

Before I can even get to the line of graves, she's driving that Halligan forward again, into and through Rexall's forehead, and then flipping it around for the axe-end. She hauls it back behind her like a bat, the weight of the bar spinning her on her knees a bit, until she plants harder, brings that blade around with everything she had, right into the zygomatic arch under his right eye, opening his sinus cavities to the world.

He's dead, has been dead since that first shot through the temple, but Letha's rage isn't even near spent.

She drops the Halligan and comes at Rexall with her hands, hooking her fingers under his jaw and the base of his skull. Using every last ounce of the hatred she has for him, the killer who took her precious little girl from her, she pulls and twists and jerks, screaming the whole time, until Rexall's spine audibly gives with a wet snap, loosening his head enough that, when Letha falls back, Rexall's head flops over sideways, just the neck skin holding it.

Letha hunches over, her chest heaving from the effort, her whole body racked with sobs, and she's still not done.

She screams into the ground for so long I think she's going to pass out, there can't be any air left in her whole body, and then she rises again, taking that head between her hands, slamming it again and again into Rexall's chest, and then, when the skin's starting to let go, into the backside of the flapped-open trapdoor, which has a metal frame.

There's blood splashing up and . . . just everywhere. It's up her arms, it's coating her face, her whole frontside, and Rexall's head is just mush now, an empty mask for Lecter to press on, and one of Letha's thumbs is hooked into what used to be his right eye.

His left eye is still intact, though. And open.

I've only ever had one prayer answered, I think—that a slasher comes to Proofrock—but, standing there over this, I make one more request. It's that that eye that's left, it's still connected to the brain enough that Rexall saw some of this happening to him, and knew who was doing it. Really, I want him to have processed every last moment of it, and then take it with him to whatever hell he's headed for. I hope he's caught in that last gasp of pain for eternity, and that he never goes anywhere without feeling watched, seen, exposed.

And then I hope Adie comes to visit him.

But no, no, I wouldn't want her to have to live, or be dead, anywhere Rexall is. He's already the last person she saw. No, what I want for her is for Banner to be waiting for her, to scoop her up, hold her close, the two them spinning around like that forever, Ban pretending to change into the Hulk, Adie grinning with delight, bouncing on her little legs with the purest happiness.

Dad and daughter stories can be good too, I mean.

Some of them have to be, don't they?

Please.

I drop to my knees now that it's over, and I'm right in line with these ten or a dozen kids' graves.

Maybe ten feet in front of me, on her knees as well, wavering back and forth, is my best friend in the world. The one I promised that Adie would be okay. The one whose whole world was just cored out from her, leaving her a kind of hollow I can't even guess at.

We both turn to a bone crunching to our right.

It's Jo Ellen, just standing there, all her weight on one leg, a crossbow bolt buried in her left shoulder up to the plastic fletching, her blue mechanic's coveralls black with blood, her face lit up like there's a spotlight on it.

Detain, she told us. Not . . . not execute.

And, that's not moonlight showing me her expression. It's the phone she's holding. The one she's still looking through.

She wasn't bluffing about having hit record.

I crawl ahead to Letha. She collapses, and it's the way—I remember this from first grade, second grade—it's the way you can skin your knee or bash your finger, but you don't cry until your mom makes those concerned eyes down to you, and you sort of melt, now that you can let go. Now that you don't have to be brave anymore.

I hug Letha for everything I'm worth, trying to control her shaking, and—I would fight ten Dark Mill Souths for this girl, I would pull Stacey Graves down to Drown Town myself every day of the week for Letha. If there were a magic switch Jigsaw'd into both of my wrists I could flip to give her Adie and Banner back, then I chew through that skin right now.

But that's not how the world works. Movies, maybe, but movies are made the fuck up, aren't anything like real. Which I guess is why I used to want to live in them, right? Because I didn't want the reality of my life anymore.

Now, though, now I've got to be here for Letha. Not just for the next couple of hours, not just for tonight, but for fifty years, if we've got that long.

If she'll have me. If I don't remind her too much of all this.

And if I do, then—then I'm gone, I'm out, I never show my face here again. I'll only sneak in at night to leave a burning cigarette on your headstone, Mr. Holmes, Proofrock sleeping all around me, nobody but me remembering those sparks in the darkness on the other side of the valley.

Finally, Letha sags against me, spent. I stand us up as best I can with one working arm, and we make our hitching way over to Jo Ellen.

She *is* pinned to the tree by that crossbow bolt.

"Oh, shit," I say, my eyebrows coming up in worry, some of the dirt evidently caked all over my face sifting down. I turn to the side to blow it off my lips, try to clear the rest with my good hand.

"Here," Letha says, and presses her hand hard to Jo Ellen, that bolt in the crotch of her fingers, and, easy as anything, she snaps it off.

Together, we guide Jo Ellen off the shaft of that bolt.

"I believe this is yours, now," Jo Ellen says, struggling to pass her phone to Letha.

Letha looks down to the phone, up to Jo Ellen, then flicks her eyes over to me as well, so I can clock the uncertainty.

"No, I've got hers, here," I say, holding Letha's phone up like I need to prove this.

Jo Ellen shakes her head no, though, and when Letha gets it like I already am, she breathes in fast, takes a long step back, holding her bloody hands up, away from this phone.

I step forward, take it instead.

"It already on the cloud?" I say to Jo Ellen.

"I don't think so," Jo Ellen says. "Signal's too weak out here to push a recording that big."

What she's doing is giving Letha a chance to never have been out here. To never have done this.

Is Jo Ellen a mom? I don't know. She is a woman, though. And I'm pretty sure she respects what Letha just did to Rexall.

"No," Letha says, shaking her head to make sure we can see her resolve.

"But—" I say.

"But *nothing*," Letha says, reaching for the phone, to palm it away from me. I turn away but her hand clamps on my shoulder, spins me around, and there's not even a hint of the girl I know on her face anymore.

Just the mom. The killer.

Still, I've got to try.

I step to the side, bring my left hand back to my right bicep to Frisbee this phone away, get rid of this evidence.

Letha is who she is, though. She snatches that flying phone midair, before it's even done two whole spins.

And then she glares at me about this.

"Leeth," I say, seriousing my voice down a register or three.

"I *did* it," Letha says right back, holding her arms out to show all the blood.

"But you don't *have* to have," I tell her.

"I'm not my dad," she says to me, just *for* me. She's crying now, again, but it's different, it's softer. "I did it, Jade, and I have to pay."

"No," I say to her, my eyes begging.

"Do you want him," Rexall, "coming back on a technicality?" Letha says to the girl I used to be. "Because the person who killed him *outside the law* was never punished?"

"Like Freddy," I have to say.

"Like Freddy," Letha confirms.

I trained her too well. She's using my logic against me.

"That's just a movie, though," I try. "Listen, if all this . . . if it's taught me anything, it's that the world's got its own rules. And they don't have anything to do with Hollywood."

"Says the girl whose dead father was chasing her across that clearing."

I spin away, hiss air through my teeth.

"This way, he doesn't have any justification to come back," Letha says, quieter. "This is me turning my back on him, taking his power away."

"Turning your back and presenting your wrists," I mumble.

"It's decided," she says to Jo Ellen, handing the phone over. Jo Ellen delicately, hesitantly takes it, flicking her eyes to me to be sure this is okay.

"She can still lose it," I say. "Right, Jo Ellen?"

Letha shakes her head no, and, staring right at Jo Ellen, says, "The sheriff will log it. Because if she doesn't? If we erase this? Then no one ever knows about this godforsaken place. There's other kids here, not just Ade. Other moms, other dads. They need to—to *know*."

She sniffles, tilts her head back.

"Leeth," I say, my good hand to her back.

"What do I have out here in the world anymore?" she says to me, blinking.

"Me," I tell her, and my idiot chin's pruning up, and—and it's not Stacey Graves who was a hurt, lost little kid, it's not Dark Mill South, it's *me*.

I'm losing my best friend, the one I thought I'd never have.

And I fucking deserve it, too, for . . . for Adie. For Linnea Adrienne Tompkins-Mondragon. For not shoving the sharp end of a coat hanger into Rexall's ear while he slept on the couch twelve feet from me, so many nights.

"Then I'll go with," I say to Letha. "We'll sit it out together. I'll—I'll show you how it all works."

"You've done your time, Jade," Letha tells me. Then, to Jo Ellen, "So?"

Jo Ellen nods, drops that phone into the chest pocket of her bloody coveralls.

Her shoulder's bleeding freely, and none of us are even trying to stop it.

"We need to get you back," Letha says, stepping in to take some of Jo Ellen's slight weight.

"Fuck you," I say to Letha, my eyes finally spilling, now.

Letha looks up to me, and it's exactly the way she looked at me on Melanie's bench eight years ago: like she wants to protect me, like she feels sorry for me, like she understands me.

"*Fuck you!*" I say again, and step forward, push her in the shoulders.

Letha takes my wrist without dropping Jo Ellen, pulls me into her, rests her chin on top of my head.

"You're so beautiful," she says to me, running her fingers through my blood-matted hair, and, I guess because I don't really have a stupid ear to slow it down, her words go right to the very center of me.

"I'll be there every weekend, Leeth," I tell her. "Promise. Every weekend. You can't get rid of me this easy."

"Jade," Letha says, pulling me closer.

Into her chest, I say, "I'm so sorry. For Ban, for Adie. I should have—I should have—"

"Picked a different genre?" she says.

I laugh, my whole self shaking with it.

I shake my head no, though, never.

"Me either," Letha says. "Me either, Sid. Laurie. Jess."

"Nancy, Ripley, Sally," I say back about *her*, nodding, finally pushing away, to see her gloriously grimy, war-torn face.

We could do this all night. We can do this for the rest of our lives.

Or, for a few years, on weekends, anyway.

"Um," Jo Ellen says, and when we look up to her, she's directing us to the other side of the pet sematary.

It's that paint horse.

Letha chuckles in spite of everything, squeezes my shoulders once, then turns, takes Jo Ellen—the one arresting her—under her arm, to help her over to the horse so they can get down the mountain, eventually go to, as Letha will probably call it, "jail."

After she's got Jo Ellen propped up on the horse, she stops, looks back to me.

"Bring her home?" she says about the tiny grave.

"Terra Nova?" I ask.

"Proofrock," Letha says, and turns, leading the horse with the deputy on it.

I nod, nod faster and faster, and it's probably two minutes to midnight by the time I can make my way over to Adie's little grave.

All the vomit and pee and worse I've cleaned up in my time as janitor is nothing compared to this.

But I promise to be gentle, Adie. And good on you for having fought hard enough that Rexall thought he had to keep shooting you even after you were down here.

On my knees, holding the Halligan in both hands, messing up any incriminating fingerprints on it, I scrape the dirt away a few grains at a time, it feels like. Until I get to the little girl.

Who's pretty much just a . . . a *skeleton*?

"What?" I say, and look around for somebody to confirm this for me.

It's just me out here, though. Me and Rexall, dead and mostly already buried himself.

"Who?" I say then, about this Adie-size skeleton.

I reach down to touch some of the faded fabric tangled in the bones, and—

The skeleton arm moves!

I push back on my ass, shaking my head no, no, no way.

After a steady hundred count of that skeleton not clambering out on its Harryhausen own, meaning I probably just imagined this, I stand to be farther away, higher anyway, and peer back in.

The skeleton struggles its small skull up maybe an inch.

I want to run screaming.

I swallow, that thrush loud in my ears—how can I even have

anything wet *in* me anymore?—and make myself look a third time, because no way can this be really real.

The skeleton's still again. Until it isn't.

This time it's the jaw, flapping down all at once, a grand total of maybe half an inch.

It's more than enough.

"Adie?" I say, except it can't be.

This little girl's been buried for decades.

"Stay there," I tell her, or him, I guess, and pull the shovel over, dig into the next grave over.

It's another kid, just like I knew it was going to be, but . . . it's also a skeleton? This kid wasn't snatched from a McDonald's playground, or spirited away from a park down the mountain.

This kid's from back before mankind went to the moon.

My heart's beating so hard now.

By the third grave, I know.

This was why Remar Lundy built his cabin up here: he needed privacy for the kids he was stealing away with, using up, and disposing of.

But . . .

I stand over the first grave, trying to make this make some kind of sense. Not the presence of these small bones, but the way, every minute or two, a bony foot writhes into the dirt, or a shoulder joint comes up a bit.

Why does *this* one want to climb back up to the living, and none of the rest?

And then I see what's holding it back: that faded fabric, wending through it.

It's a . . . blanket? Just, not one that was used to swaddle the dead, but one that . . . that's somehow tangled up *inside*.

This is Amy Brockmeir.

It can't be, but it is.

After she ate her blanket down the mountain, in the institution she'd been deposited in once Don Chambers decided it had been her killing kids at Camp Blood, not Stacey Graves, mad about the fire Hardy and Holmes had set, they shipped her home for burial. They shipped her to Remar Lundy. Only, they just snipped off the part of the blanket that was visible, not the part winding down her throat, into her stomach. And Remar Lundy buried her in the little line of graves he already had going, easy as anything.

I take hold of a tattered corner, pull that blanket up and out, and they must have used to make blankets of tougher stuff, because it's still together enough to come out, tug by tug.

Amy tilts her little head back to ease the blanket's long passage. When that last little bit's up and out, her leathery little hands clamp onto my wrist.

I jerk away, stand.

"I'm so sorry, Amy," I tell her, and the same way my dad killed the dead rising with him from the lake, I bring the Halligan down on what's left of Amy's throat, separating her head.

Just like the Angel separated Greyson Brust's head from his body. Just like Jan Jansson did to that bear.

Taking the head off *works*.

But what I said to her right before's still cycling through my thoughts.

"Amy, Amy, Amy . . ." I say to myself, until it becomes "*Adie*."

When Letha asked Rexall where *Adie* was, he must have misheard, thought she meant "Amy," so he looked down, to right where Amy was.

He *wasn't* snatching kids, bringing them up here. Just secret videotapes of them. And me. Well, "just" is the wrong word, but: he wasn't *killing* them, anyway.

Shit.

I let the Halligan fall away, turn to the little bit of Indian Lake I can see so far down there, in the moonlight.

There's red and blue lights everywhere.

"Adie?" I say aloud, my invitation for her to step out from whatever tree she's hiding behind.

Where did Rexall leave her, though? *When* did he leave her? I spin to the cabin, suddenly certain Adie was down in that shrine I collapsed. I close my eyes to see it again, but . . . there were no other doors, no tunnels, no rugs covering any holes.

I look back down the curving and curling path we took to get here, then. Probably two miles of trees, at least. But he must have had her at least until she lost that shoe, yes? Or, was that where she got away, maybe?

I nod yeah, that that must be where it happened.

She slithered out of his arms, and all he was left with of her was one shoe, the other one lost in the darkness.

Meaning Adie's out there now, scared.

I surge forward, into the dried ribs of that bull elk, but then slow, finally stop, just stand there again.

None of this is making the right kind of sense.

I lower my head to think better. To *make* myself think better.

I hate it, but this is what my dad used to do, too. He said it made the blood pool behind his forehead, where the good brain muscles were.

That he's still inside me makes me want to puke, but . . . okay, list it out, slasher girl. Add everything up that's not adding up: Greyson Brust comes back to life years after falling into a hole with Stacey Graves and her mother, Josie . . . Josie *Seck*; Jan Jansson goes missing, then turns back up different, moving like Greyson Brust, like *Ginger Baker*, who somehow lived over here for weeks; my dad and the other lake-dead came back from the lake they were all buried in, and what he rises with is Tobias Golding's haunted old murderous pickaxe—but that pickaxe wasn't the thing that brought him back, he just found it, stuck it on some new handle; and . . . and this Angel of Indian Lake, Sally Chalumbert, is out there somewhere, isn't she? Doing what, and why?

None of the dead animals out here with me have an answer.

Think *better*, Jade.

I duck back into Remar Lundy's serial killer cabin, plunk down in Rexall's tilted over, half-sunk chair.

There's an old iPod on an upturned piece of firewood stabbed into the ground. I hesitantly pull the earbuds up but can't bring myself to stuff their waxiness into my earholes, don't need to commune with Rexall like that, thanks. Even *if* the answer is waiting there in a rap lyric.

I'll just sit here and think.

After maybe thirty whole minutes of this—of getting nowhere, just bogging down at every turn, Adie still out there somewhere, scared and alone—I finally work Letha's phone up from its near-boob-experience, to turn my mind off with a little harmless doomscrolling.

But of course social media's going to be all about the movie at the dam.

I flick Instagram away, don't need to see that.

Instead, Letha's camera roll.

Each snapshot is more of a heartbreaker than the last.

I pull up her voice memos, bounce the last few to my number without listening to them, for whenever I get a phone again. It's too soon to hear Letha's sad, I'm-about-to-die voice like she's always doing—like I know she did before going under the knife this last time, because she always does.

I swipe that app dead, and the only one open now is Banner's email.

The top email is from the state detective he must be in contact with.

Great timing, Idaho.

I consider not opening it, but I also can't *not* open it. It's in official-ese, but it's not hard to decode: authorities in "Bassett," which I think is on 15 to the north, have apprehended someone at "Osgood Grain," whatever that is. It's not the "where" that sits me up straight in Rexall's chair, though. It's the name the fingerprints kicked back, which is why the state dick shot this across to Banner.

Sally Chalumbert.

She never made it to Proofrock. She's not the Angel of Indian Lake.

Then who is?

I feel my way to the doorway, squint out at the darkness, and I one hundred percent expect Pennywise to slowly step out into the moonlight, wearing that Michael Myers mask from my favorite smoking place at school. Just, because he is who he is, when he grins his lecherous grin, the hard plastic cheeks of the mask will come up like Ghostface's, and I'll feel a pressure in my ears, look around at the walls closing in, and finally realize we're in a red balloon together, one blowing up more and more, about to burst.

Why am I thinking *It*, though? It's not a slasher.

"Idiot," I say to myself, looking into the darkness behind me, because giant alien spiders can crawl up from anywhere—I might welcome that, right about now—and when it's still just me, I shut my eyes tight against all this bullshit and try to just ride that silver bike at the end of Pennywise's reign of terror, faster and faster, the world knitting itself together over all the wounds, and—

Is that it, slasher girl?

I open my eyes, squint hard, checking my mental work: that magical bicycle ride at the end of *It* healed things, didn't it?

No, the world doesn't conform to movies, Letha.

Except when it does.

The *English Rose* picks me up at the long plastic dock in front of Terra Nova.

Lemmy's up front holding the rail, waiting for his drone to bob up. It's the one Letha dropped when we found the cabin. He probably thought it was lost forever with the shark stunt, but then, lo and behold, it woke up when him and it got close enough to each other, thanks to yours truly tromping through half the woods of this state.

Also, once that drone started trying to struggle away, its little fan blades so eager for the sky, I turned its camera to my face, hoping this little thing was high-dollar enough to have a mic, and Heather Donahue'd some very specific instructions.

From Hardy's airboat dragging behind the yacht on a bright yellow tow rope, a crew member working on it, I can tell Lemmy heard. That ridiculous little boat is my magic bicycle.

I let the drone go like a butterfly I'd had cupped in my hands and it buzzes up into open air, leans forward for the bow of the *English Rose*, for Lemmy to snatch out of the air.

A ladder unfurls over the side.

When I still only have one arm and not that much blood, Lemmy hops down, and it's not noble, Harrison would hate it, but Lemmy gets me up there in his arms like the damsel I'm not, deposits me on deck.

"You made it," he says, and I have to look away to keep my voice steady.

Yeah, I guess I did.

"We heard about Letha," Lana Singleton says in her severe voice, from behind me.

"Already?" I ask.

"She made that deputy post that damned video on social media," Lana says, her lips tight with disapproval.

Sounds about right. If the footage doesn't start proliferating on its own, then some high-dollar lawyer can get it erased.

I know a thing or two about that.

"She won't be in long," Lemmy says, draping a towel around my shoulders. "She's . . . we'll buy the detention center, won't we, Ma?"

Lana Singleton just shrugs, holding me in her eyes. Cataloging the damage, maybe.

It takes a while.

"She'll outbid you for it," I inform Lemmy, holding his eyes long enough for him to cue in that I'm not joking, here.

Lemmy leads me back to the state room or whatever it is to change into jeans and a black t-shirt. The shirt fits, but when I wear the towel out like a skirt, Lana understands without making a fuss, brings me another pair of the same sweat pants.

The shirt's got a face quartered together on the front: Freddy and Jason and Michael and Leatherface.

"Cinnamon's again?" I say.

Lana shrugs like that doesn't matter, but Lemmy nods.

"She saw that drone footage you showed in class?" I have to ask.

Lemmy shrugs again, not wanting to get anyone in trouble.

She did, though. Had to. It's how she knew to go hide Hettie and Paul and Waynebo, spook the horse off, roll the motorcycle into the lake. All she had to do, probably, was tell Lemmy she wanted to learn to fly one of those drones. While she was steering from her chair, though, she thumbed into the recordings, sent it to herself, erased her backtrail.

"She's . . . over there," I say, pointing with lips to the dam. Last night's movie. The massacre.

"She wanted us to drop her off, yeah," Lemmy says.

"*Butcher, Baker, Nightmare Maker*," I mutter, hitting Cinnamon and Ginger and Mars's last name a bit extra-hard.

"*The Fabulous Baker Girls*," Lemmy adds with a halfway grin.

"You two done with whatever this is?" Lana asks, batting her eyes with impatience.

On the second trip into the state room, my phone's right there where I left it, blinking with Letha's last message—with the voice memos I sent. And there's a cord plugged into the phone, too.

These fuckers. Can't I just hate them and let that be that?

"So?" Lana says when I come back.

She's sitting cross-legged in a chair, is smoking a cigarette. I guess I would have expected her to have a cigarette holder like the evil mastermind in a Disney movie, but she's just using her grubby fingers like the rest of us.

I sit down into the chair evidently waiting for me, and she pushes the pack of cigarettes across to me in a way that makes it feel like the big ante for a poker game.

All right, then.

I pack the smokes for longer than they need—my brand, some-how—work the matchbook up from the cellophane and spark up one-handed, holding that delicious smoke in, letting every last molecule of my body have a proper taste before blowing it back out. There's music coming from the speakers but it's distant, small.

"You knew she could walk?" I finally ask.

Cinnamon. Who else.

Lana doesn't answer that, says instead, "I didn't—*we* didn't . . . she just said she liked being back in Proofrock. That it made her remember her sister. She was just a—a houseguest."

"Boat guest."

"Yacht guest."

"That movie was her revenge," I say. "On all of us."

"She told Lem it was a memorial, a gift to Proofrock. I hope—he's not in trouble for what he did, is he? That drone thing?"

"He didn't know?"

Lana shakes her head no, says, "But how did she get the bears . . . *there*? And the chainsaws?"

"Guess she had . . . four years to plan?" I say. This is something I learned from you, Sheriff: when a killer's in town, then all the killings can just be theirs, can't they? "How many?" I ask—how many died at the movie.

"Still counting," Lana tells me, looking down at her hand, like surprised she's smoking again.

I don't really want to know how many anyway. It's not about the numbers, it's about the names, the people.

"But you finished it?" Lana finally says, staring at me through the smoke. "I mean—*Letha* did, with what she . . . ?"

I shrug my good shoulder, then shake my head no, Letha didn't finish it.

"That's what that airboat is about?" Lana asks, more perceptive than I would have guessed.

"I just want to ride with him one more time," I mumble.

"The sheriff," Lana fills in. "You make it sound so . . . *final*," she adds.

I shrug, don't tell her that I would be going out on the town canoe, but it's not around anymore. And it doesn't really go fast enough, like that silver bike.

Each time the hull touches down, my hand all the way in the throttle, that's going to be another stitch in the open wound this all is.

I hope.

It's stupid and wishful and little-girl, I know.

I guess that's who I still am, though, in secret. Inside.

"What's wrong with it?" I ask—the airboat.

"Throttle-something," Lana says, wagging her cigarette over the details to show how little they matter. "Rodrigo'll get it going, if that's what you want. He says the part was already there, under the steering wheel."

I nod.

That is what I want.

"Thank you," I tell her. "Really."

"My husband," Lana says, working her lips between her teeth like massaging these words before letting go, "he—he said this was the most beautiful spot in the world, did you know that?"

I shake my head no, I didn't. But I don't disagree.

"He also said we never should have come here," Lana adds. "That we—that we were just messing it up."

Again: not wrong.

But it's not all on him, either. Decades before they got here, Glen Henderson was killing his best friend and business partner. Remar Lundy was snatching kids and burying them in a pretty little row in his front yard. And a whole town was making a lost little girl live like a cat in the streets.

And for a few years before Deacon Samuels pulled into Lonnie's to fill up, they were kind of doing the same to me.

They might still, after this night.

This time, though, this time it wasn't me going toe-to-toe with the big bad, so maybe I'm not so much in the spotlight?

That's one thing about the slasher, about the final girl: there's got to be a different way, doesn't there? Can't you win in some way that doesn't involve muscles and blood? This isn't *Rocky*, after all.

Or, at least, it doesn't have to be.

But I do carry the responsibility for a lot of what's gone down in the last day and a half. Well, since Friday the 13th, I guess—since Hettie and Paul went missing.

I can fix it, though. I think.

With Rodrigo's help.

"Can I?" I ask, about the airboat.

Lana shrugs, isn't my boss, so I go to the railing, stand by Lemmy over the airboat.

"How long?" I ask.

"End of the next song, maybe," Lemmy says.

Over here, I can hear the music better.

I turn around, lean back on the rail, study Proofrock across the water, and let the thrashy guitar Lemmy's pushing from his phone wash over me.

And then I pick a word out from it: "Motörhead."

I shake my head, draw deep on my cigarette, blow it out grandly. Say, "They sing their own name in their song? Didn't know metal bands did that."

"What?" Lemmy says, cocking his head up to the song. Then, "Oh—oh, yeah. This isn't them. Or, this is them, *him* anyway, but without the umlaut?"

"Like, an acoustic session? Sounds pretty electric to me."

"No, no," Lemmy says, reaching across for my cigarette and turning his back to his mom to sneak a quick drag. "It's Hawkwind, but it *is* where the name comes from. It's where it all begins, last song he ever wrote before they kicked him out. So he named his new band after it."

I'm following, but not really listening anymore. It's because what he said there, it won't stop circling that *Psycho*-drain in my head: *where it all begins.*

A chill passes over me, from head to what toes I've got left.

I push away from the rail, my eyes staring into the distance so I don't lose this.

"*Where it all begins!*" I say, pushing Lemmy hard in the chest.

I rip the cigarette from his lips, draw deep-deep on it and flick it out onto the lake, past the airboat.

"Hey!" he says.

I'm breathing hard, my face flushed, all my cuts and open meat pulsing in the night air.

"What?" Lemmy says, concerned.

"Where it all *begins* . . ." I say again. "Of course. Of fucking *course*. Listen, I know how to—how to stop all this. How to end it. We have to go back to where it all started!"

"Mom?" Lemmy says, stepping back from me.

Lana looks over, angles her face down like watching me over bifocals.

"I need to go—to go over *there*," I say to both of them.

She turns, studies where I'm pointing. Says, "Treasure Island?"

I nod.

"You sure?" Lana asks.

I'm still nodding.

"Almost done down there?" Lemmy calls down over the rail, his phone held flat before his mouth like a Star Trek communicator, so he can tell the captain or bridge or wheelhouse what we're doing, here.

"Check!" Rodrigo calls back up, and fires the airboat's big fan up.

Lana's standing beside me now, one elbow chocked in the crook of her other arm. It's a posture the old-time smokers can pull off.

"Not the first time you've been over there," she feels compelled to say, I guess. So I can know that *she* knows.

"I'll pay you back," I mumble, my good hand clamped tight on the railing, my fingertips still not touching each other on the underside.

Lana suppresses a smile about me paying her back. Before I can add any more pleas, the airboat turns off, Lemmy says "Go" into his phone, and the *English Rose*, that great nasty girl, starts its big engine. A moment later, the bow swings over, balancing Treasure Island at the tippy-point.

Two minutes later, we're there. Close enough. Indian Lake's practically a bathtub, in a boat this big.

"*This* is where it starts?" Lemmy asks, disbelief in his voice. "It wasn't even here until this summer."

"The lake," I say. "The *lake* didn't used to be here, either."

Lemmy watches me, trying to make this make sense.

"Almost sunup," Lana says, about the horizon glowing orange.

"No," I tell her, standing. "It's just before dawn is what it is."

She doesn't get it, but it doesn't matter. *I* get it.

"You mind?" I ask, lifting the back of my chair a couple inches off the deck.

She shakes her head no, not really sure what she's giving me permission to do. So I show her, taking the chair, dragging it slowly to the railing, and—not easy with one arm—hurling it up and over.

It falls for a long time, goes under immediately.

"Do you have cameras down there?" I ask.

"We do *now*," Lana says.

"Which one?" Lemmy asks, right there with us.

He's swiping through screens on a big tablet.

When he finds the right one, he angles the screen to me.

The chair I threw overboard is right there on Main Street in Drown Town. Sitting upright, even. That's how good I am.

"Okay," I say, and walk back for another chair, drag it to a point a bit farther down the railing.

"Here," Lemmy says, checking with his mom. She nods, so he picks the chair up like it's nothing, tosses it high.

We all watch it slap the water, go under, the lake erasing its entry point fast, like embarrassed by it.

On-screen, it doesn't even show up.

"More," I say, and Lana nods in a way that the whole crew shows up.

Chairs and tables and whatever they can find arc up over the railing, splash in.

"Does this move?" I ask Lemmy, about the camera.

He shows me the control pad, top-right, so I can angle this underwater camera and its big light over to the church.

Just like I knew there would be, there's a hole in the roof, now. Because little sister doesn't miss when she aims her gun—something Yazzie used to say, from a song I don't think I've ever heard.

There's silt everywhere now, from all the stuff we're throwing down there.

"You really hate that old town, don't you?" Lemmy says, impressed.

"Just one of its people," I tell him. Then, "You have mics down there?"

He scrunches his face, not following. "Underwater?" he asks. "In a *lake*?"

"Never mind," I tell him, because I know he *could* throw something together, let us hear.

We shouldn't, though.

That music I heard, sort of, when I was sliding on the plastic dock at Terra Nova, trying to get the yacht to come back, because of Bub? It's the same thing the New Founders heard every day they were training to swim the lake. It's the same thing Seth Mullins was hearing on his icy swims.

Just jumping in for a few minutes isn't long enough to corrupt you, make you go *Berserker* in a board meeting, or make you bait in bears to massacre a town, but spend some regular time in there, and it gets to you, doesn't it? Well, it does if some idiot's poked a hole in the church roof, turning the volume of that choir down there up just loud enough to infect.

And if you happen to be dead down there, and have had some bad contact with the shit this place is known for? Then your eyes pop open, your legs start working again.

Drown Town's church is the battery powering all this bad shit. It has been all along. Indian burial ground my ass—this is a *Christian* burial ground seeping its evil out.

And it's also a prison, for a certain little someone.

"It's not working," I say, just out loud.

"'Working'?" Lana says.

"The chairs and stuff aren't heavy enough," I say, looking around for a convenient safe, a stray car, maybe a pallet of anvils. "We're going to have to ram it," I say with a shrug. It's the obvious next thing.

"The *island*?" Lana says incredulously.

"It's still Halloween," I tell her, nodding to the big orange pumpkin about to bob up over the horizon. "But not for long."

Lana stares at me, stares at me some more.

"I won't tell them she was staying here," I say, not making any eye contact.

"Blackmail doesn't work on me, little miss," Lana says.

I nod, probably knew that.

There's big fat tears rolling down my face now.

Lana's balled fist nudges in under my chin, tilts my face back up so she can look into my eyes.

"Why?" she asks.

"You wouldn't—you wouldn't understand."

"But you're sure?"

"It can all stop," I tell her. "The—*all* this shit. Including what killed your"—about Lemmy—"his dad."

It's another pie-in-the-sky-flying-fuck-at-a-rolling-donut, but maybe if I believe it enough, right?

"I'll pay you back," I mumble, again.

This makes a little chirp of laughter burst out of Lana, that becomes a whole body chuckle.

"*Goddamnit,*" she says, turning around, sparking up another cigarette to help her deal with this. "Lem, when's sunrise?"

Lemmy checks his phone, says, "Eight minutes, Ma."

Lana nods, does some math in her head, I don't know, and then's barking orders.

In maybe three minutes flat, her whole crew are bobbing in two lifeboats, puttering a safe distance away with the airboat.

I go up to the controls with Lana and Lemmy.

"Did you really come at Sheriff Allen with a speargun?" I say on the way.

Lana just shrugs, pulls ahead of me.

There's final girls everywhere, aren't there? I used to think they were the rarest breed, the finest vintage. But everyone who's got something to fight for, they'll fight for it, never mind if it's a fight they should win. *Should* doesn't always matter. What does is that you run screaming into this thing, and don't stop until it's over.

Up top in the open air—evidently there's some way to swap the steering controls there, take them away from the windowed-in control room—with four minutes left till sunrise, Lana brings the yacht around and backs up.

Straight ahead of us, dead in our sights: Treasure Island.

"You're sure?" she says.

I nod, and she shoves that throttle its whole way up.

The yacht doesn't wheelie, but it does dig in enough that I have to grab on. Lemmy's already got my shoulders to keep me from tilting back, one-armed as I am.

"Was the shark cool, at least?" he asks, his voice not booming for once.

"It was amazing," I tell him, and manage to pat the top of one of his huge hands.

"Brace!" Lana orders, and—

We *hit.*

It stops us hard.

Inside, all kind of expensive shit's crashing around.

"Again," I tell Lana.

She backs up, draws a bead, and fires, harder this time. Sliding alongside Treasure Island, we can see it's tilting in the water, something's very broken with it, but it's still not sinking like I need, if this is going to work.

"Two minutes . . ." I say.

Lana nods, accelerates us wide, going farther back, and lines us up again.

"All you," she says, giving me the controls.

My eyes go wide.

"Insurance," she explains. "If I willfully destroy it—"

"Got it," I say, and step in, take a wide stance. "I am pretty good at destroying shit, don't know if you've heard."

Lana smirks, has to look away to keep her composure. She's to one side of me, Lemmy the other.

"Throttle!" I tell Lana, because my right arm's in this sling, and she pushes it ahead, turning this up to eleven.

This time we've got all the speed, coming in. Big waves rolling away from us, our wake probably epic. The emergency boats out on the lake have taken notice, too, are coming our way, flashing their lights, the people standing in the bow waving their arms like we're crazy people.

We are.

"Hold on, hold on . . ." Lana says, a sort of grin to her voice to be doing this, and then we hit hard enough to climb the yacht up *onto* Treasure Island.

For a long moment, we balance there, could tip either way, but then, slowly, by the smallest degrees, our last seconds ticking away, we start to come back down. Kind of sideways, water washing thick over the deck, sloshing everything to hell and back, but, but—

I run to the down side of the top deck we're on, lean as far over as I can.

Treasure Island is sinking, great bubbles roiling to the surface, popping in their oily way.

"Show me, show me!" I tell Lemmy.

"I don't know if the Wi-Fi—" he says, but swipes into the tablet anyway, and the signal's got enough left that, in slow motion, the slowest motion ever, we can watch Treasure Island crash down into the church, crushing its waterlogged self.

Then everything's blotted out by an enormous mushroom cloud of silt.

It blows the camera back, away, but it doesn't matter.

I fall to my knees, turn my back to the railing, and hug my shins with my good arm, sobbing into my knees.

I messed up the diorama, Mr. Holmes.

Hope you don't mind.

History doesn't get to stay in place, though.

The sirens are winding in from what feels like all around, the sun's coming up, and somewhere a bird's chirping, I think.

"One more thing now," I tell them, and stand, conjuring my inner Letha, my Jocelyn Cates, my—say it, say it—my Lana Singleton, hiding in a closet, willing to do anything to save her little boy.

Lemmy lowers the ladder down to the airboat the lifeboats have been holding for me.

"You can drive that thing?" he asks, back on the ladder.

"I grew up here," I say, and moments later I'm you, Sheriff Hardy, I'm you skipping across all the wakes these emergency boats have kicked up, and they're all yelling at me to stop, but, hey, I've only got one arm, right? I can't steer and turn the engine off both at once, can I?

Or something like that.

Just like I learned from watching you, Hardy, I skid way up onto the gravel by the Pier, and then I walk back down, wait there on shore, the water lapping at my toes.

All the emergency boats are attending to the listing *English Rose*, so I've got time. And everyone from Proofrock's bunched up on the south end of town to rubberneck, probably just to say they were there at this massacre.

This is a ghost town, I mean.

In more ways than one.

Ten minutes in, the world absolutely silent, the first head crests up from the water.

Because this side of the valley is gradual, this dead choir member doesn't stand right up, but surfaces by degrees.

And the next one, the next one.

"*Carnival of Souls*," I say in appreciation. Once I went out onto the lake to lose myself in a movie. Now the movie's coming to me.

The choir is waterlogged and rotting, hollow eyed and sharp fingered, their throats sung raw and bloody over the decades, but here they are, still dressed in their finest.

I sit there, let them shuffle past, until—

Ezekiel.

Because the shepherd is always last.

He's tall, I had no idea, maybe six and a half feet, up there with the Tall Man in little Mike Pearson's nightmares, and his shock of white hair is ragged and wild, his eyes overlarge, and his hands are dinner plates, just like the stories say.

He's carrying a soggy bible in one hand. A bible that's steaming, from the sun touching it. Steaming and drying out way too fast. I remember in elementary once, I lost points for not capitalizing "bible," because that's the rule, but even with my second chance, I wouldn't do it, because there were always crosses around when Indians were being killed, weren't there?

Capitalizing that word would make me a traitor.

I stand up to block Ezekiel and he looks down and down to this slight hindrance I am. This annoyance. I'm messing with his holy mission. He's going to convert the world, get them all singing with him.

"Not anymore," I say, and slide what's left of the golden pickaxe head from my sling.

I thought I was just keeping it safe, to dispose of later.

But now, now I know just where to put it.

Ezekiel sneers down at me and my feeble, broken would-be weapon.

"You're not the monster anymore," I tell him, holding that pickaxe by its ragged blunt end, "*I* am."

With that, I jam the point under his sternum, aiming up for his black, black heart and then pushing harder, my legs helping me until I'm up on my toes, until my hand's in his vile body—until that point is a bulge in his throat, coming out to nudge hard against his chin, force his whole big head back, keep him from angling that severe look down at me.

He wavers with it, wavers *from* it, his hands grasping uselessly at the part of this pickaxe his fingers can find, and when he falls to a knee in the shallows, all of Proofrock shakes with the impact, and he's close enough to my level now that I can see it: the point that came out at his throat, it's black again. What's gold now are his rheumy *eyes*. They're filming over with it. And it's leaking from his mouth, his nostrils, his ears, the beds of his fingernails, still scrabbling against this pain.

"Sermon's over," I tell him, and use my right foot to push him back into the water with my foot, out into his own cold box, and it turns out the sharp antlers of Big Daddy, of Rocky—Banner's dad's trophy elk—are waiting right there for him. If they weren't in the shallows, this elk head would just roll away, out from under him. Since they're in two, three of water, though, this mount bottoms out fast, its long wooden tines shoving up through Ezekiel's chest, emerging like a great grasping claw from the hollows under his collarbones, and then his shoulders.

Ezekiel groans, coughs, and that same thin blackness that was in my dad, that was in Jan and Greyson Brust and Ginger Baker, it's pouring out from around the pickaxe.

He jerks, one arm reaching, one heel digging in and pushing back, but his body is failing, failing, from the red right hand of an actual Indian, after all these years.

Well, okay: left hand. But Wes would get it.

When that push Ezekiel started with his heel drifts him far enough out, the top-heavy weight of his body spins him face down all at once, the stumpnecked elk rolling into the open air for the first time in years, and the way the murky water streams away from it, for a snapshot of moment I see that Banner's concern was right—it looks for an instant like this elk head's got a human body, a man's torso and arms and legs.

Maybe even a badge glinting in there.

Over the next eight or ten minutes, Ezekiel and the elk float out into the deeper waters, until Indian Lake slurps them both down. The surface flattens down behind them like a great mother, smoothing the blankets over a sleeping child.

I nod about this, breathing hard, and turn to his black mass, his unholy choir.

They're all corpses now, will all be, as far as the media knows, bodies washed up from the wreckage of Drown Town.

Good.

But it's not over yet.

Standing on top of the water now, head down, long black hair over her face like some vintage J-horror—no, like some *I*-horror, for "Idaho"—is the little girl Ezekiel had trapped in his church. The little girl who was screaming for her mom to come get her—a scream her mom was able to hear, once there was a big enough hole in the roof.

It's the same hole that let Ezekiel's influence leach out, raise my dad, corrupt Seth Mullins and the New Founders, and maybe even get everybody stupid enough to go to the movies.

But? That could just be us, too. That could just be people. At least in this genre. When there's a party in the slasher, you kind of have to go, good idea or not, don't you?

I mean, *I* knew better, but there I was just the same, wasn't I?

Then Stacey Graves looks up sharply, past me.

I turn, my three dead fingers suddenly warm, and the Angel of Indian Lake is standing there in her dirty nightgown, just as rotted and dead as her little girl, but just as alive, too.

Josie Seck.

I step back, out of the way, and Stacey Graves raises her arms in that straight-out joyful way little kids have. She rushes across the top of the water, the soles of her feet making little popping sounds, and when she reaches the gravel shore, she keeps running, *can* run on land like Christine Gillette said. At least she can when her mom's kneeling down to scoop her up after all these years.

Josie Seck stands with her little girl monkeyed onto her, and she breathes a deep breath of mountain air in, to be here again. Not Proofrock, not Pleasant Valley, but in the arms of her precious little girl, and I can see from how delicate she is with Stacey that the stories of her snatching kids to nurse into her lost daughter are just campfire tales. She knows who is and isn't her little girl. How could she not?

Sure, she might have left berries and dead rabbits for Ginger Baker, to keep her alive, and she might have tried to save Jan Jansson from her accidental creation Greyson Brust, and they were both different after being too close to her. But that's not her fault.

All she wanted to do was help. And, in Greyson Brust's case, when he crashed down into that cave, protect her little girl.

With her daughter's face buried in the hollow of her throat, both of them getting less dead moment by moment, touch by touch, Josie Seck turns, walks back into the trees for the last time, her steps so precise and small. So happy.

She's going the wrong way if she wants to get to the national forest, but, when I close my eyes, I can see where she's really headed: up to the highway, to walk alongside the blacktop.

Soon enough, a car with a red handprint pressed on the rear fender, because it's a good pony—well, good enough—is going to see her, clock her long black hair, and pull over ahead, wait for her to catch up. It'll be some Indian family headed up to Montana. Crow, Flathead, Blackfeet, Gros Ventre, it doesn't matter.

What does is that rear door hanging open, so Josie Seck and her little girl can go home.

I nod thank you to the world, for this.

Thank you thank you thank you.

When I open my eyes again, I'm staring down at the gravel between my knees. A dab of wetness lands on a grey fleck and I touch my face, think I must be crying some more without even knowing it.

Wrong.

I turn my face up to the snow we always get by Halloween, coming down on all the living and the dead, and let it kiss my cheeks, my lips, and so ends this savage history of Proofrock, Idaho, Mr. Holmes.

This is my last paper for you, sir.

I hope it's good enough.

BAKER SOLUTIONS

17 November 2023
#76z89
re: Terminal communication

This concludes the investigation concerning Jennifer Elaine "Jade" Daniels's vandalism. Attached, please find one piece of material not included previously, as it has no probative value. It's at your discretion whether to deliver it to its intended recipient. As for its provenance, it was mis-filed in directory 3g (Ms. Daniels's Henderson High records).

The postmark is dated 17 February 2013. The intended recipient is Kimberly Daniels. The subject line of this progress report remarking on Ms. Daniels's classroom efforts is "Slasher 103," in response to the reason for the progress report itself. The course the report is for is "World History":

"Slasher 103"

A copy of this has been filed with the front office, per school regulation.

Having attempted four times to contact you by phone, I thought it prudent to submit this in writing, so we can have a happy little paper trail.

Your daughter's participation in class, while not obstructive, nevertheless leaves something to be desired. Her "pranks," as she calls them, not only take up class time, but could possibly hurt someone if she's allowed to continue. But those disciplinary matters are more the principal's jurisdiction. This classroom is mine. Which brings us to Jennifer's performance on quizzes, tests, and reports. Jennifer is a bright and capable adolescent, I don't need to tell you this. I would even say she's more intelligent than her years suggest, and that she pays closer attention than I usually see in a student her age. You're to be applauded for rewarding this kind of critical thinking in her upbringing. This is exactly the sort of attitude that promotes good citizenship. We need more like Jennifer, I'm saying. However. A mind like hers needs to be <u>directed</u>. Presently, Jennifer's fascination would seem to be the horror film in all its aspects. If she could just apply that same focus to her schoolwork, then I daresay a college scholarship wouldn't be out of reach, especially if she's a first-generation student. Her Native American ancestry could only help on that application. Were Jennifer to improve her course grade by semester's end, then I could be persuaded to write a letter on her behalf, even. What I mean to impart is that I believe in your daughter, Mrs. Daniels. I see in her an aspect of myself at her age, if I can be so bold. She would buck authority, given the chance, and she would push back against the norms of a society that does indeed need to be better, to do more. Who knows, your daughter could someday hold public office and change policy, thus directing the world onto a better course. The sky's the limit with this one. But I fear that this fascination she has with these horror movies might end up siphoning energy better directed elsewhere. As example, I append a Xerox of her most recent attempt at extra credit, titled "Slasher 101," as if <u>she</u> were the teacher, not me, and suggesting that I can only now expect a "Slasher 102," and on and on. While your daughter may indeed someday replace me and my generation, as it should be, I warrant that adopting this pose at her age might result in more resistance than we would want for her. I should comment on the content of that extra-credit paper, as well. In it, as you can read, she's on a dock which I take to be our local pier, and she's watching a boy drowning out in the lake, and everyone from town is there with her, and we're all just watching, Ms. Daniels. But your daughter, in this extra-credit paper that was supposed to be on Greek Drama & Thought (as masks were worn in ancient drama, Jennifer uses that as a stepping stone to get to her movies), she's the only one of all of us to dive in and swim out to this boy, and bring him back to land. While I honor the heroic effort and the self-sacrifice, what concerns me is the indictment your daughter is making about Proofrock, ma'am. Why, of all the adults and law enforcement officers and teachers, and she even places some counselors from Camp Winnemucca over there, is she the only to recognize this child in distress? Of note too is the tourist she places as part of that crowd, whom I take to be an actual tourist she encountered on the pier, or in town. She says he's the "Brad Wesley" type, if that happens to be a friend or relation. This tourist has a bag of golf clubs hooked over his shoulder, the way your daughter writes him, and an expensive camera dangles around his neck, and Lonnie from the gas station would seem to be chaperoning him. I mention him only to draw attention to the fact that you might want to better monitor your daughter's perambulations around town, as she might encounter strangers who are here today, gone tomorrow. I see bright things for her, I mean. The world is hers, if she wants it. She's smart, she's curious, and if she would only apply herself as much to schoolwork as she does to her other hobbies and interests, then the sky's not even the limit for her. Having seen a lot of children pass through my classroom, including you and your former husband, I can say without hesitation (no insult intended) that Jennifer Daniels has just about the most potential of any of them. Had I ever had children of my own, I would be lucky were one of them even half as curious and intelligent and feisty as Jennifer.

If you wish to discuss your daughter's performance in World History any further, I'm at your disposal.

Grady Holmes

THE NEW BLOOD

Two days into November, the last girl standing sits on the bench by the lake for lunch. She's smoking a cigarette, ashing into the palm of her hand, and thinking hard on everything. Her right arm is a Frankenstein arm, but the stitches will heal, and the bone was only bruised, and it's not like she cares about scars.

Scars prove you lived.

That's what her girlfriend in prison used to always say, and will again in six years, when she gets out.

The girl no longer shaking from missed meds can wait.

She breathes her smoke in deep and holds it, holds it, and tracks one of the folded paper boats bobbing in the surf.

Behind her, Main Street is pretty much trashed. The elk who swam the lake to get away from the fire came up by the Pier snorting and scared. Instead of running up the mountain, they gored and kicked, stomped and screamed, venting their anger for how these two-leggeds keep messing the valley up.

Run on, the girl with the temporary pink streaks in her long black hair says every time she passes one of the broken windows, the cars with their hoods stomped in, the former sheriff's tall brown truck, parked where he left it when he crossed the lake for the last time.

The reason no one's fixing Main Street yet is that they're all in the woods under the dam. There's a little girl lost out there, and a media empire's put up a cash reward staggering enough to draw treasure hunters in from all over the world. How they know she's out there is that the girl who smokes cigarettes on this bench finally checked the social media feed on her best friend's phone, and saw a blurry recording of the moment the lost girl's abductor encountered a blurry woman in white in the woods, and dropped the girl, scuttled away.

Because of the reward, Proofrock's a tourist destination again. The forest is clogged with people night and day. Once again, the side of the mountain at night is flickering with sudden pinpoints of light. The paper boats bobbing under the Pier used to be for the boy lost in the lake, but now they're for this little girl who's also lost.

So far, all that's been found out in the trees are the remains of a game warden—his pale foot in a hiking boot by a long-dead white Bronco, anyway—and a dehydrated, grateful helicopter pilot with the bluest eyes, but no little girl.

What they haven't found is a rotted, sagging cabin in the woods, under a lean-to formed by a giant tree that fell years ago. But there were pockets of fire all over the valley on Halloween, weren't there? There were, there definitely were. Maybe one of those floating embers landed on that cabin, burned it to the ground, its charcoaled timbers falling into the crater that opened up under it.

In the trashcan in the faculty lounge of the high school are sixteen thumbtacks with big reflective heads, and because this is a school, nobody will ever question arts and crafts getting thrown away.

The girl with the loose front tooth that's starting to tighten up bumps the player on her phone back a voice memo, listens again through her earbuds.

Her best friend's trial won't start for months, she knows. But that best friend can make it through whatever, now that she knows her little girl's not in the ground.

What this girl with the blackest lungs also knows is that, since there's no body proving what's on that recording actually happened . . . well. With the right lawyers, with the right storied firm, maybe this best friend gets to come home before her daughter goes back to school?

Stranger things have most definitely happened.

The girl who made a promise to that best friend earlier this morning through the bars of a cell blows her smoke out, lets it dissipate, then stands, squinting across the bright water.

What she's looking at are the empty houses over there.

They're full of ghosts, will never be lived in now, and in ten years, after the children's camp has finally crumbled to the ground, that stand of homes over there will be the new place to drink beer around a bonfire, and lead someone by the hand into this or that house, and this is how people move into the future: holding hands, smiling not because everything's going to be perfect, but because now is, anyway.

That's all you can ask for, really.

The reason this girl who used to cry in the band closet of her high school is sitting on the bench and smoking cigarette after cigarette down to the filter instead of walking the woods for the lost girl is the package that was waiting on her porch the morning after it all happened. She hadn't opened it until about three hours ago.

Another videotape.

She stalked from room to room of her house almost until lunch, telling herself not to watch it and telling herself she had to.

Finally, she did.

The opening frames took her breath away: a lake that could be her lake, the camera just drifting along shore.

The movie is by an Italian director at the height of his power, straddling the giallo and the slasher. Once upon a childhood, the girl whose life needed saving found this exact tape in the bargain bin of a gas station, and she's held it close to her heart ever since, and that it's found its way back to her is staggering, is a fairy tale.

But then the tape fizzed, lost tracking—a different speed engaging—and the girl who knows this movie by heart almost stood in anger, that somebody could have done this. What if this was a recording of the lost girl, though?

The girl who could recite that recorded-over movie by heart sat back down, perched on the very front edge of her couch, her hands holding each other between her knees, the fingers worrying, tight.

It wasn't the lost girl, on the tape. What it was was a bit of footage recovered from 2015. Years ago, a disturbed girl in a hospital room had told her about this, but also suggested it was gone forever, sunk along with everything else.

What's lost can be found, though.

It's black and white, and steady enough that it has to be a trail camera, or something rigged to act like one.

At first it's just shoreline at night, but then, for eight exquisite seconds, a ragged little girl with long black hair runs up to the edge of the water *from the lake* and delicately picks something shiny up—a piece of tinsel?—and runs back out, her feet making small little splashes in the surface.

This is the proof the girl who's never had proof needs to make all her lies true.

The return address on the padded envelope the tape was in isn't an address at all, is just the letters *C* and *B*, the second letter nested in the first, like it's being consumed.

The girl whose hair wasn't bright pink yet then knelt down in front of her VCR like worship, closed her eyes, and found the eject button without looking.

She stood with the tape, flipped the cover back, and slowly at first but then fast like ripping off a bandaid, she unwound this perfect movie that had saved her life, the iridescent videotape spooling around her feet, and her breath was hitching and her eyes were hot but this was right, she knew. This was the way it had to be.

After that she went to the dollar store, its plate glass windows plywood now.

The girl with the DVD scar above her right eye stood at the register for three minutes before the only worker not out in the woods sashayed down the aisle.

In the pockets of his red apron was Christmas, already. He was stocking it.

"How's your grandpa doing?" the girl whose name is one letter from this clerk's asked.

"Días buenos y días malos," the clerk said with a shrug that meant *thanks for asking.*

In a small town, you know everyone.

"That too," the girl without a mom said about the little red nutcracker the worker had been about to hang up, because it reminded her of a Christmas movie she likes. One with arrows and axes and hammers. She paid for it and the double-clearance, spray-on hair coloring from the Halloween aisle.

The nutcracker is sitting on the bench now, beside this girl who barely made it through Halloween.

"Keep guard?" she says down to him, but he's unperturbable, can't be bothered to respond, just stares straight ahead with his painted eyes.

She leaves him there, scratches her head because this spray-on stuff is itchy, and pretty much sucks. Double clearance was about twice too much.

For a moment, the girl who has an emergency-room undercut on the right side now, for the monster line of stitches she thinks might make a good centipede tat someday, considers the stand of trees behind her, but instead of forging into them for the lost girl, she nods to them like *later* and hikes the long way up to the nursing home, to finally keep the promise she made all those years ago, to come see someone. Her hope is that if she can keep this promise, then maybe she can keep all her promises.

In the old woman's room, the girl who never had a grandmother sits and listens, wraps the old woman's afghan better around her shoulders, and offers her water but the old woman says that's still not the girl's job.

When the girl with the powdery pink hair scratches her scalp one too many times, the old woman directs her to the sink in the kitchenette.

The girl who's not supposed to get her stitches wet leans over it— the faucet is high and arching like a swan neck, or the ghost of a swan boat—lets the old woman wash the pink from her hair, massaging her scalp with her ancient fingers.

"She can walk on land, you were right," the girl who saw it says, but it's lost in the sound of the spray, and the suds. After, the girl who's never had her hair washed like this before is sitting in the windowsill with a towel wrapped around her head when the old woman wheels back into the room with what she said was going to be a surprise.

It's hair dye. The good kind.

"What color?" the girl with her head in a towel asks.

"We'll see," the old woman says, shaking the bottle.

"I'll come see you again," the girl who means it promises afterward, kneeling in front of the old woman's wheelchair, holding those two tissue-paper hands in her own.

"Is it over, finally?" the old woman asks.

The girl who can't lie about this lowers her head.

"Almost," she says. "It's almost over."

It's what leads her back to the parking lot at the end of Main Street, to the gravel that's the shore of the lake she grew up on. The great brown truck her friend the sheriff used to drive is still there, parked across the yellow lines.

It's mid-afternoon now, already. Somehow.

The little girl lost in the woods has been two days without food. And the game warden's pasty-white foot in that boot isn't giving anyone hope.

But the reward doesn't specify dead or alive.

The girl who's an aunt now shakes her pack for one last smoke, but she's out.

This is funny to her.

She peels the pull tab all the way off now that this pack's empty, and threads that strand of foil into her hair, runs it behind her ear, where it feels right. Then she tucks the empty pack into the back pocket of her torn jeans, dials up one of the voice memos again. This one's about her, but it's *to* the little girl. The mom's voice in it is hitching, sort of crying but not really. She's standing against the outside wall of a big house in the most *beautiful* snowstorm, she's telling her daughter. And she doesn't have long, here, but she wants the little girl to know about her Aunt Jade, that she's supposed to go to her if she ever needs anything, that Aunt Jade will always be there for her, that—does the little girl know about jade, the pretty, green, precious stone? That the only way to test it is to hit it with a hammer? If it shatters, then it's real. What the mom tells her daughter in the voice memo is that that's how her Aunt Jade is. That life has tested her over and over with its big hammer, that it's shattered her time and again, proving her real. But Aunt Jade pulls herself back together each time, that's the thing about her. You can hit her over and over and she'll just look up at that hammer coming down, she'll look up, take a drag on her cigarette and sneer her lip up, and that's why the little girl should always run to Aunt Jade. Run to her, run to her, she's the mom's sister in her heart, she's her best friend for forever, the mom's gladder than anything that she moved to this town on this mountain, because if she hadn't, she never would have made this friend.

"Run to me," the girl who never knew that about jade says, and rubs the stitches in her shoulder, leaves her fingers there because it feels like she's holding herself together.

When the old woman saw one of her ears mostly gone under the new stubble, she'd just tsk-tsk'd, then arranged the girl with these voice memos' hair over it. The girl with the hair that had been pink, though, she shook that hair off, daring the world to stare, because fuck them.

The old woman had nodded about this, and tried to take a drink from her empty mug.

"I don't—I don't have any spit," she said, like that was a funny thing.

It's a line from one of the girl with the bright blue hair's favorite movies of all time, and she walked away listening to it over and over.

Run to me, the girl who sunk an island says in her head, now.

She's saying it because she remembers the lost girl running out to her dad's truck when he'd honk, so he could sweep her up in his arms, swing her around and around.

The little girl knows the sound of that horn.

That's what the girl who never got a driver's license is thinking when she climbs in behind the wheel. Maybe if she drives all around the lake honking the horn, the lost girl finds *her*, right?

It's not like anything else is working so far.

This girl with a record as long as her arm reaches around the steering wheel to start this big truck, figure out how to drive it *while* driving it, but . . . no key?

Figures.

She checks the console, the glove compartment, the little cubby in the dash, and then, because this worked once for a robot from the future, she pops the visor down, opens her hand for the keys to fall into her palm.

They don't.

What does flutter down, though, is a piece of construction paper.

With the lost girl's drawing on it, of the sheriff and his wife and the girl—their family.

The girl who never had that presses her lips together to keep her eyes from spilling, holds that drawing hard to her chest, her breaths coming deep now. Putting that picture back, then—it's not hers—she sits up straighter in the seat.

This drawing might not be hers. But another one is.

Two minutes later, the girl who's only ever wriggled out the bathroom window of the sheriff's office is climbing *in* through that window.

The drawing is still in the ceiling, right where she left it.

The girl who made the promise falls hard to her knees.

Moments later, she's rushing through the front office, not answering the questions the girl behind the desk is calling out.

The drawing is of the lost girl in a cove just off the lake. With a funny tree behind it.

The old sheriff, years ago, giving the girl who didn't even know horror then's third-grade class a tour, had pointed a tree out for them that looked like the one in this drawing, and said that in the old days, the cowboy days, Indians used to tie a tree into a funny shape when it was young, so it would grow up crooked like that, be a good landmark they could use for years and years.

This is that tree.

And, this was just a school day, and the whole class wouldn't fit in the old sheriff's airboat, so . . .

The girl who remembers everything, even the stuff she doesn't want to, rushes to shore out of breath. No one's there with her. They're all out looking for the lost little girl.

But that little girl's not over in the woods behind the dam, where everyone's looking. That's just where she got *lost*. The confused mother who ran her abductor off and knew not to hold this girl, she led or herded or somehow got the little girl back over here, didn't she?

To keep her safe? That has to be why that mother was over here by the Pier the very next morning.

It has to be.

The girl who's seen all the movies and knows all the rules nods yes about this. Definitely. For sure.

Cut to that little girl, playing at the water's edge by a funny-shaped tree. She's guiding a forked branch back and forth on the surface, and making boat sounds with her mouth. When the branch gets away from her, she balances out on a rotting log to get it, but when she looks behind that log, she sees an even better toy: a paper boat!

And there's more coming in, and more, and more, a whole little fleet of them!

The little girl doesn't know it, but if your boat makes it all the way across to the other side, your wish is supposed to come true.

The girl might have wished for someone to play with, please.

It comes true anyway.

When the second and third paper boats drift into the branches of the fallen-down tree she's balancing on, she squats down to try to reach them, keep them safe, then jerks back. Bobbing there right by the log is a very dead *grown-up* girl, her skin rotting away, a small brown bird sitting on her forehead, shoving its tiny beak deep into her eye socket.

This young alive girl watches the dead older girl and watches her some more, waiting for her to do something. The bird keeps eating, doesn't want to give up its find.

"I'm going to go over *here*," the girl finally tells the dead girl, and then she waits to see if the dead yellow-haired girl's going to nod or shake her head no. When the dead girl doesn't do anything, the alive girl wades away, only looking back once, to be sure the dead girl hasn't sat up.

On shore again, the alive girl steers the two paper boats she has through the tall grass and then pushes one of them out into open water again but doesn't follow, doesn't want to get wet, because wet is cold at night, and it'll be dark again before too long.

She does track the little boat, though. It drifts into a pair of legs clad in thrashed-out denim. The younger girl looks up those legs, finds a girl with electric-blue hair, with tattoos up and down her arm, with a silver stud through her eyebrow, and eyes that won't stop staring back at her, lips that are pressed tight together.

She squats down too, to inspect this boat.

"What do we want to call this one?" she asks.

"Credible Hulk!" the girl says, because of course, and then she realizes that this girl with the chainsaw heart isn't standing in the water, she's standing *on* it. It's from the way her fingers got bitten into, once. It infected her blood with the lake, and made her like this, which she only figured out when she stepped out into some frozen cold water once, to try to save an old sheriff from sinking down, and found the water wouldn't take her anymore.

"It's wet now," the girl standing on the water says about the boat, and shrugs, reaches back into her pocket for another sheet of white paper. She folds it into a perfect boat, just like all the rest.

The little girl presses her lips together, doesn't want to smile about this but can't help it.

Her eyes dart over to the dead girl in the water.

"I think she's from the Netherlands," the girl who doesn't fear the reaper anymore says. "She came here with her boyfriend, when I was in high school."

"Is she okay?" the little girl asks.

"We'll tell someone about her," the girl trying not to smile too much says. "So she can finally go home, be with her parents."

This makes the little's girl's lip tremble, her chin prune up.

"It's gonna be okay, you know?" the girl who's an aunt says. "It probably doesn't seem like it, but it really will be."

The little girl nods, not really following, just watching.

The rest of the paper boats are turning sideways with wetness now, foundering, going down to the little boy who needs them.

"Do you want to try?" the girl with trembling fingers asks, holding a sheet of paper out.

The little girl considers this, then nods twice, fast.

"A really old sheriff taught me how to do this," the girl who knows all the history says, making the first fold. "This is the shark fin at top."

"I can't see!" the little girl says, tippy-toeing.

The girl who's actually a woman now, a history teacher, even, holds her hand out, sideways the way adults do.

"I know a place over there we can sit and make all of these we want," she says, tilting her head across the lake, to the meadow shaped like the head of a sheep. "It's where your mom and me watched our first movie together."

The younger girl presses her lips together and nods twice, then nods faster, and steps in up to her knees, splashes out as fast as she can, arms held high to be caught. The woman who remembers being that young and that trusting takes her by the hand then swings her around, up onto her waist, onto the surface of the water with her, and then the real Angel of Indian Lake walks out into the glittering brightness, she walks on top of the water until she can't wait anymore, which is when she starts running.

~~Fade Away~~

Burn Out

MY HEART IS A CHAINSAW

DON'T FEAR THE REAPER

THE ANGEL OF INDIAN LAKE

ACKNOWLEDGMENTS

A few years back, doing a book festival back in my hometown of Midland, Texas, I ended up with the night to myself. All I had to do was take the back way around the lobby, slip out to my rental car, and roll away with my headlights off. Where I was going: the drive-in west of town, that had always been closed when I was growing up. This could even be where my aunt and uncle saw *Halloween*, like I talked about here a time or two ago. That's what I was here for this night. There's something about watching it through your windshield, isn't there? Like back in 1978? It had been a long day of shaking hands and signing books and trying to sound halfway smart and being worried who was and wasn't going to walk through the door, though—I was spent. And it was just me in that rental car, so . . . I sort of drifted off, was in and out pretty much after they find that dog Michael snacks on, that no one ever speaks about. But gently waking every few minutes to Laurie and Michael and Loomis, man. I'm not even sure I've *ever* woken up. I might still be there in that rental car, I mean, only now I'm dreaming about a girl who changes her hair color every week, a girl whose heart's too big for her body, a girl who fights monsters and then forgets how to walk if too many people are looking at her at once.

I didn't get to just write one book with Jade, I mean, I got to write *three*. If that's not the dream, then I don't know what is. It's taught me so much about character, about friendship, about world-building, about *maps*, about this long narrative undulation we call "plot" but that's really maybe "life," I think. It also showed me, once again, what my few strengths and many weaknesses are, kind of writ large across these three books. It doesn't mean I'll play to those strengths from here on out—I hope it means I'll run at those weaknesses, because that's what you do if you want to get better. I also learned that the cool thing about trilogies is you get to use every last part of the buffalo. And what I learned about the *third* installment in a trilogy is that your orders—the orders I heard, anyway—are to mash that pedal to the floor until it gets stuck, and then hold on the best you can, dude.

That's one hundred percent what writing this one was like. I had no idea where it was going or how it was going to get there, but I knew it had to be shriekier and gorier than the two that came before, which had already been pretty over-the-top. I knew I couldn't protect the deck crew, either, which . . . wasn't going to feel good. But? What you do to your characters, it's not supposed to *feel* good, it's how you get *to* the good.

Except, of course, for the first time in years, concerning a novel project, I was *scared*. So, I did what you do: with five months to write this novel, which is pretty gracious, I sat down and wrote another novel: *I Was a Teenage Slasher*. It was my way of clearing my head, of making sure the tank was absolutely empty before starting this one, so I'd have to come up with some other nightmare fuel. *Teenage Slasher* took two of those allotted five months, though. Meaning, when I finished it on a Tuesday, I had to open a new blank document Wednesday morning, get started on this book—still with no premise, no voice, no real idea what to do. I'd done this once before, sort of, and ended up with *Growing Up Dead in Texas*, and I guess this is kind of how *Mongrels* happened, and *The Long Trial of Nolan Dugatti*, and *Mapping the Interior*, so I knew if I held my lips just right, if I counted taps onto everything within reach in just the right order, I could maybe get lucky, pull some acceptable rabbit out of the hat. But, too, there's always the chance that hat chews my arm off, this time. Novels are like that, aren't they? Writing them, I mean. The long road to the reader's heart is lined with the husks of writers novels have left behind—"the skeleton frames of burned-out Chevrolets," indeed.

Speaking of: thanks again to Yerba Mate energy drinks. The pineapple coconut ones. Without you, I have to invent you, in order to write these three books that are my beating heart.

And special thanks to my agent, BJ Robbins, who realized I wasn't going to just be having to burn the candle at both ends to make this deadline, I was going to have to light sticks of dynamite to see my way to the last page. She called my editor at Saga, Joe Monti, and got that deadline moved. This is early June. Both BJ and Joe knew I could make the deadline as it had been, because I don't miss my deadlines, but, Joe said, he wanted to be sure this third book in the trilogy could wrap everything up right, so he wanted to be sure I had world enough and time to get that done. Which means, of course, "*Expectations*, Steve." But that kind of pressure's fun.

So, suddenly, thanks to the kindness and trust of BJ and Joe, I had until September. Talking *six extra weeks*, here. What I promptly did then, as you do, was take three weeks completely off, just to goof around on the trails, galavant around the world, read a lot of books and comics. This after I'd already started the prologue, too, which is a dangerous game to play, turning your back on a novel, because sometimes it never lets you back in. But this third book, man, that's all it was at every stage: the most dangerous game. And I think what I was most scared of was—I'm going to say it: Was I still a horror writer, even?

Every time out, the novel teaches you a lot about yourself, I knew that. But I wasn't sure I wanted to have to question my *identity*. Why I was? It was that *Savage History* prologue, which was the single hardest section of this whole trilogy to write. The reason: I was two or five pages into it when the Uvalde shooting happened. Remember how, right after Columbine, a lot of the horror movies got dialed back, violence-wise? I never understood that until now, even though one of my brothers had been put into a coma in the cafeteria at Columbine, well before the shooting. I mean, after seeing Uvalde on the news like that, I was just walking around with my hands in my hair, because the world didn't make sense, nothing would make sense, how can stuff like this even *be*? All of us were there for a while, weren't we? How can you not be. This is not a thing that should happen. Fiction's always been my retreat from the mad and maddening world, though, the place I can hide, the place where, if I can get all these spinning plates balanced just right, things can make sense for a few pages. So I came back to Hettie and Paul, sitting in that entryway of the library. But? They're the couple at lovers' lane up front in a slasher, aren't they? If that's not a death sentence, I don't know what is. I was genre-bound to kill them, so their blood could grease the gears of the story, establish the mortal stakes, show that anybody and everybody's in the victim pool, all that.

But?

It was turning out to be *so* hard to do, now. And it never had been before. This is why "Here Comes the Boogeyman" is the longest prologue of this trilogy: these kids, these students, they *weren't* disposable. *I* couldn't dispose of them, anyway. Way later in the book, when Jade, the teacher, is hugging her student Alex to her so hard, so desperately, and her world's just crumbling all around her? That's this whole book, to me. A lot of characters have died in the course of this trilogy, and in this book specifically, but I'm not sure any of them hurt as much to write as Paul and Hettie that last week of May.

And even then, even after the prologue was over, I still couldn't let Hettie and Paul go. I never planned for Hettie's documentary to play up on the side of the dam, I mean. I didn't even know there was going to *be* a movie—how could there be, after *Jaws*-on-the-water?—but when playing it meant a dream of hers could sort of come true, in spite of everything? That meant I had to come up with someone to steal that bulky videocamera, which meant that had to be someone with *reasons* to do that, and . . . Cinnamon Baker, in the Quint-spot at the back of the room, upped her chin "sure" about this. Before I could even call on her to ask what she had planned, she'd already left to do it—she's not the kind to, as Mike Birbiglia says, wait for the second half of sentences. I didn't even know she was under that Father Death hood on the swings until way late in the game, I mean, and I was equally surprised to find her contributing to those reports, and it turned out to be so completely lucky that her throat had taken some damage, last time around. Otherwise, why doesn't Jade just clock who she is right away?

But this is how novels happen, for me: I plan, I strategize, I anticipate, and the story does what it's going to do anyway, never mind the dude here at the keyboard.

It's not *all* just stumbling in the darkness, though. Or, okay, it is, it always is, I don't know how else to do it. But I'm lucky to have people standing out in that—as Richard Kadrey might phrase it—"grand dark," to lead me from point to point. This time, Jesse Lawrence and Matt Serafini and Adam Cesare were there to help with some chapter titles when I was about halfway through, and thinking this naming convention was flaming out. Thanks as well to Mackenzie Kiera, for burning through this one, and asking some very hard questions, that made this one different, on rewrite. Thanks to a talk I had with Josh Viola, a version of which showed up here—without permission, I guess. Josh: this okay? -ish? Mark it out if not? Anyway, Josh, as thanks for that talk, as thanks for trusting me, I put Casey Jones in here. I'm guessing you've got that tat of him, by the time this is out. Thanks to Don Henley, for his line *You call some place paradise, kiss it goodbye,* though I've never been able to tell if Henley's line applies to Native America or to the invaders—I think it's to them, maybe, as we only ever called this place "home." It only became paradise in the rearview. But Don Henley also says that "If you find somebody to love in this world, you better hang on tooth and nail," which is Jade in sixteen words, pretty much. Thanks also to Paul Tremblay, for coming up with our main character in this YA novel we did together a few years back. I think the Jade who's in this book shares a thing or two with her. Or, I don't think she'd be who she is, here, without me getting to co-write a girl named Mary. So, in thanks, and with permission, there's a Paul-title in the story. Thanks again to Theo Van Alst, for letting me use your name in these books. To show my gratitude, I may have put a few umlaut-associated things in this book specifically for you. It was supposed to be this big surprise, but then I needed help getting them right. Which you were there for, last-minute. Your help let this whole thing come together. Thanks so much. And, talking music, thanks again and still to Adam Bradley, for answers to my random Tupac questions. Hope I did Him justice. Or at least didn't mess anything up. And thanks to that old animated song or music video or whatever it is, "Ultimate Showdown of Ultimate Destiny." It was my polestar for the last third of this book. Thanks to a Louise Erdrich story from *The New Yorker*, about that head rolling around—I think it was *The New Yorker?*—and thanks even more to her for Nanapush, I think in *Tracks*, who straps moose meat all over himself. That's such an indelible image that I had to snake it. And even more thanks to Louise Erdrich, for starting *Love Medicine* in third-person, for June, whom I've dedicated at least one book to, maybe more, but then shifting into first so easily, so naturally. You doing that gave me permission to do that here. Thanks as ever to Joe R. Lansdale, too, first for everything, for being the writer and person I try to model myself on, second, for always talking Neanderthals with me at any time of day or night, but, talking this novel, thanks for a nervous breakdown you gave Hap, a few books ago. That really hit me, and stayed with me, and told me that the first time we see Jade, here, maybe she's dealing with some stuff like that as well. Also, for the longest time this novel had a big mess-up in it, that I only figured out by asking myself, "What would Joe do, here?" Answer: he wouldn't cheat. So I had to be honest, find a real way to get through to the end, not a fake way I hoped nobody would catch. Thanks to that "Run, brothers" buffalo poem with the long title that I cannot cannot *cannot* find anymore. Does anybody know it? If so, tell me, so I can put it in the acknowledgments of the paperback of this? As well as you, whoever tells me. Thanks to Mike Bockoven for *FantasticLand*, the horror novel I've read the most times, the last decade. To show my true and abiding love for that perfect book, I smuggled a line from it into this book. Thanks to Anurag Andra, for talking *Good Will Hunting* with me enough that my favorite part of it found its way onto the pages, here. Thanks to Devon Broyles, for that "birds in the hair" thing. And thanks to Danny Broyles, for always talking horror—for knowing so much of it, and always having it on instant Rolodex. And thanks also for saving my life so many times. I don't write any of these books if I'm not around, right? Thanks also to Bret Easton Ellis, for that last lyrical blast-off at the end of *Lunar Park*. I knew I couldn't do that same thing here, but, with some different tricks, I could maybe pull something halfway similar off. And thanks, again, I think, to Nelson Taylor, for that "Do Not Eat Fish from These Waters" bit. Remember that line you wrote in grad school, Nelson? "Kicking like Clydesdales up the limestone steppes of Kansas City." That's burned on my soul, man. I can never forget it. We had no idea what to do with that line—still don't—but it's one of the most beautiful things I've ever heard.

Thanks to my mom as well, for forever haunting dams up for me and my brothers. Remember how you would close your eyes and scream the whole way across all the dams we found ourselves on, with us all leaning over the seat, yelling "left, left, *right?*" That feeling of knowing we were about to fly off the side, into a few seconds of silence . . . it's definitely in here. There's a deer in a fence in this book, too, which I owe to William J. Cobb, even though you've told me you don't remember that story, Bill. If you ever do, man would I love to read it again. There's a broke-down old cabin in here that I'm pretty sure I sort of stole from James Welch's *Winter in the Blood*, too. Or, this cabin comes into the story at about the same place yours does, sir. Thanks too to Joe Hill, for giving his fireman in *The Fireman* a Halligan. Been waiting for the chance to use that tool. Thanks also to Bruce Springsteen. I stole a line from your latest Broadway stint, man. Sorry? It was too good not to. Thanks also to *Monk*, for Sharona. I like Natalie, don't get me wrong, she's great. But, for Jade and Letha, Sharona was a better fit. Thanks to one of my brothers, Sky, for teaching me about JPay, even though neither of us really wanted to have to learn it. Thanks to Candace, Phineas and Ferb's big sister, for a certain emphasis in here. Thanks to a used-up Kona Hei Hei and a shiny new Ibis Ripmo AF—the two bikes I rode the wheels off of, writing this.

That's what my days were, the summer of *The Angel of Indian Lake*: a few hours at the keyboard, then twenty or thirty miles up and down the trail, to figure out what comes next. Without these two bikes, I don't know if I get this book done, as it takes too long to reset without all those miles, all those pedal strokes. Thanks to the poetry anthology *Vital Signs*, edited by Ronald Wallace: you were the first book of poetry I ever read. I was nineteen. My favorite poems in there are all still marked, and each of them is such a huge part of my writer-DNA, now. First among them is a poem by John Ciardi. It's about emeralds, but I've been remembering it differently for thirty years, now, and it's sort of too late to change a certain character's name. "Emerald Daniels" just doesn't sound right. And of course I think I really owe Doug Crowell, my first writing teacher, for assigning that book of poems, and talking about them like they were so full of meaning, of heart, of the *world*. They were, Doug. They were, and they still are. I honestly don't know if I ever take writing seriously without you talking about these poems with us like that. Teachers, man, they can be the butterfly who flaps its wings, starts the hurricane, can't they? I've been so lucky to have been in the wash of so many of those butterflies, I think. I'm so lucky for this storm I'm standing in, I mean. But I'm not standing in it alone. Joe Monti, my editor at Saga, is there with me. Without him . . . man. Without Joe's steady pencil in *Chainsaw*, there's no trilogy, and without his input here on *Angel*, I think I finally maybe take the easy way out, and let myself cheat. Joe keeps me honest, though. Without him, none of this. And without Christine Calella, Savannah Breckenridge, and Bianca Ducasse getting *Angel* in so many write-ups and lists and magazines and newspapers and sites and more, *Angel* could have been a drop in the ocean no one heard. Thank y'all so much. Also, thanks for running my life and scheduling me; I sure couldn't do that. Thanks also to Steve Breslin and the whole copyediting and production teams for keeping this all going. Thanks as well to the recent *Baywatch* movie. You taught me something about backstory that I used in this book. But, please nobody ask me what that is? Not because it's secret or embarrassing, but because I don't remember. Writing novels, just because I'm paranoid about not thanking someone, I keep a little scratchpad of who and where I'm stealing from—this is how *Demon Theory* got nearly five hundred footnotes—and really early on in the list I'm consulting right now is just that: "*Baywatch*, for how to do backstory." I don't know. I really don't. I do watch that movie a lot, though, because it's perfect. I do remember what I stole from *Mission Impossible: Dead Reckoning* at the last possible moment, though. So happy I took a couple hours away from revisions to go see a Tom Cruise movie. Thanks to the *Books in the Freezer* podcast, too. After guesting there, Stephanie Gagnon let me add one song (Aretha, of course) to the BITF final girls playlist. When I was writing the first Jade-chapter of this, I found that the playlist I'd used for *Chainsaw* and *Reaper* no longer worked—I think because this was first-person, now? Or maybe playlists just get used up, I don't know. Anyway, I dialed up this BITF final girls playlist, used it for a few pages, but then ended up stealing some of its tracks and progression, deleting this and that song, adding a few more, and in a day or two I had the playlist that burned me through this novel, and kept it from going stale—I think by playing songs I would never have thought to include. But, then, for the last two chapters, when I was needing to bring everything home? It was that old playlist that got me there. Well, that old playlist and great heaping handfuls of Sixlets, mixed with pecans. I always come up with big reasons "Why I Write," but sometimes I wonder if it's not just to eat Sixlets with pecans, and then ride my bike really hard.

But, as for why pecans? Growing up, my grandparents, who always lived in the same place, unlike us, had pecan trees around their house. On Saturday mornings I'd watch cartoons and eat pecans until I was throwing-up sick, and, man, what I wouldn't give to go back, do that again, just one more time. So, pecans get me there, a little bit. Look up the cover of *Growing Up Dead in Texas*, maybe? That's my brother and me—the two kids from *Mapping the Interior*—standing out in those pecan trees, just trying, as Jamey Johnson says, to save each other. To survive.

A big part of me's still there, I think.

And, I said it was scary having no ideas for this third installment but having to write it anyway, but, I mean, I did have Indian Lake and Proofrock and Terra Nova and Camp Blood and Drown Town already, and of course I had Jade, and, instead of speaking in Courier this time, she was getting to tell the main parts. Can't say that was all my idea, though. Across the eight years it took for *My Heart Is a Chainsaw* to come together, all my early readers kept telling me the novel was sort of all right so long as that Jade-girl was narrating, but when Hardy and Letha take over? It kind of sucks then, dude. That told me that, this time out, Jade was taking the mic, that she was the only one who could bring it home.

So, Jade, thank you for fighting through. Thank you for letting me write about you. After this, though? After this, I'm looking away from you, I'm letting you go on without me, into the world, into the life you deserve. Don't let go of Holmes and Hardy and that idiot footballer player from history class, they're part of you, but also cling tight to Letha, and your little niece. Raise her into the fiercest final girl Proofrock's ever seen— which is saying something. And be at that bus stop when Yazzie gets off. She'll be nervous in all this open space, but you can lead her into it bit by bit, I think. Take her out to the Pier, maybe. To Melanie's bench. And just be there with her.

That's what we need the most, I think.

Who I sit on that bench with is my wife, Nancy. Nan, remember that preacher who married us when we were, what, twenty-three, after we'd already been together four years? Before he did the ceremony, he pulled me aside like a test, to ask me one thing about you that made me know you were the one for me. It was a weird out-loud quiz to get last-minute, but I had an answer right off, too. What I told him that day, Nan, was that if you ever see someone in an aisle at a grocery store grabbing their kid's arm too hard, then, no matter the size or scariness of this person, or what the fallout might be for you personally, no matter if the whole world comes crashing down because of this, you'll be right in that person's face about them grabbing their kid like that, and you *won't* be backing down.

I write about final girls a lot, yes.

I think that might be because I live with one. Can't think of any other person I'd rather be in this fight with.

Now, here, let's just watch the lake together, if you will.

I think I see someone out there on the water.

Stephen Graham Jones
Boulder, CO
17 September 2022